IN THE

"*In the Light of the Sun* is a hauntingly beautiful WWII novel that shines a light on wartime in the Philippines and Italy, places rarely depicted in historical fiction. Based on meticulous research and inspired by the author's own family, two sisters are torn apart by war in a story about the unbreakable bonds between family members. This novel balances tension and tenderness, while paying tribute to one family's bravery, hope, resilience, and the stirring power of music to help and heal the soul. *In the Light of the Sun* is a riveting, unforgettable must-read novel that will live in my heart and mind for years to come."

—SHARON KURTZMAN, author of
The Lost Baker of Vienna

"This book is a powerful exploration of the courage of ordinary people, the unbreakable ties of sisterhood, and the abiding bond between music and hope. Inspired by her own family's history, Angela Shupe transports readers across the harrowing years of WWII in a journey both sweeping and intimate. Fans of Kristy Cambron and Mario Escobar will want to put this novel at the top of their reading list. A magnificent debut!"

—AMANDA BARRATT, Christy Award–winning
author of *The Warsaw Sisters*

"At once timeless and of the moment, *In the Light of the Sun* is a luminous and lyrical debut. In this gripping story of two sisters doing their best to follow their hearts during periods of immense turmoil, Angela Shupe has shown that she's a truly gifted writer with a bright future in fiction."

—CAMILLE PAGÁN, bestselling author of *Good for You*

"At the heart of this riveting and compellingly researched novel, two sisters bound by blood and music experience acts of individual resistance and courage in the far-reaching theatres of the Second World War. Resilience and unexpected grace underpin Shupe's careful excavation of a unique history tethered in real-life events. Readers of Kristina McMorris, Susan Meissner, and Yvette Manessis Corporon will be clamoring for more."

—RACHEL McMILLAN, bestselling author of
The London Restoration and *The Mozart Code*

"Heartrending and gripping, a novel of bravery, sisterhood, and the Resistance in a fresh and vividly painted setting, Shupe's debut is sure to capture the hearts and imagination of readers everywhere."

—HEATHER WEBB, *USA Today*
bestselling author of *Queens of London*

in the

LIGHT

of the SUN

in the LIGHT of the SUN

A Novel

ANGELA SHUPE

WATERBROOK

WaterBrook

An imprint of the Penguin Random House Christian Publishing
Group, a division of Penguin Random House LLC

1745 Broadway, New York, NY 10019

waterbrookmultnomah.com
penguinrandomhouse.com

All Scripture quotations and paraphrases are taken
from the King James Version.

A WaterBrook Trade Paperback Original

Library of Congress Cataloging-in-Publication Data
Names: Shupe, Angela, author
Title: In the light of the sun : a novel / Angela Shupe.
Description: Colorado Springs : WaterBrook, 2025.
Identifiers: LCCN 2024061925 | ISBN 9780593601938 trade paperback |
ISBN 9780593601945 ebook
Subjects: LCSH: Sisters—Fiction | Philippines—History—1898-1946—Fiction
| Italy—History—1922-1945—Fiction | World War, 1939-1945—Fiction |
LCGFT: Fiction | Domestic fiction | Historical fiction
Classification: LCC PS3619.H86725 I58 2025 |
DDC 813.6—dc23/eng/20250401
LC record available at https://lccn.loc.gov/2024061925

Printed in the United States of America on acid-free paper

1st Printing

The authorized representative in the EU for product safety and compliance
is Penguin Random House Ireland, Morrison Chambers, 32 Nassau Street,
Dublin D02 YH68, Ireland. https://eu-contact.penguin.ie

BOOK TEAM: Editor: Jamie Lapeyrolerie • Production editor: Laura K. Wright •
Managing editor: Julia Wallace • Production manager: Kevin Garcia •
Copy editor: Rose Decaen • Proofreaders: Rachael Clements and Carrie Krause

Book design by Jo Anne Metsch

For my mother:
her bravery, love, and compassion,
and the beautiful voice with
which she sang into my life each day.

Music gives a soul to the universe, wings to the mind,
flight to the imagination and life to everything.

—ATTRIBUTED TO PLATO

Where there is life, there is hope.

—FILIPINO PROVERB

in the
LIGHT
of the SUN

1

Rosa

The room crackles with energy.

Dots of silver glimmer along the princess's gown, luminescent stars against the midnight dark of the stage curtains. I listen to the mysterious prince's declarations. Finally, the princess's heart of ice melts, no match for his love. At the dazzling spectacle of music, drama, and costumes, the crowd erupts into applause.

My ears ring as I applaud, adding to the ovation following the closing notes of Puccini's *Turandot*. The tenor's performance of the "Nessun dorma" captivated every soul in the audience. Hearts, including my own, are bolstered by this rallying cry offering hope to the most unfortunate in love.

"Stunning, yes?" Nonna's smile is as wide as the stage. I wonder if she is remembering her own past triumphs. She was a prima donna and still is.

She's right. I've never seen anything like this, and I am speechless. This—this is why I came here. Why I left the Philippines and the family I love. To one day perform upon such a great stage and,

I hope, to leave listeners enthralled. Exhilaration from hearing the powerful notes sung with such emotion buzzes through me, head to toe.

"*Andiamo*, come." She leads me from the box and down the sweeping marble staircase to the lobby where people have gathered for an after-party gala. My grandmother's sophistication hasn't faded with age. How many times has she descended these stairs after her own triumphant performance?

"Serafina!" Conductor Signor Gastani greets Nonna like the oldest of friends.

Nonna smiles warmly. "Rocco! *Perfezione*, as always!"

"*Grazie mille!* You are too kind. But now, I haven't yet had the pleasure of meeting this one. Your granddaughter? Rosa, isn't it?"

"*Sì*, she is finishing up at conservatory."

"Your duet at last year's festival was exceptional. You have your nonna's gift. I see good things ahead for you, Rosa."

My cheeks flush. Having a tenth of Nonna's vocal abilities would be more than enough. In the presence of the illustrious conductor, my nerves twinge, and I'm grateful for the champagne, which, fortunately, stills the butterflies fluttering in my stomach. "*Grazie*, Signor Gastani!"

A woman in an emerald gown beckons to him. "Ah, I must go. But I look forward to hearing you sing again, Rosa Grassi!" He takes my hand and shakes it gently before ducking into the crowd and pursuing a flash of green.

This is more than I could have hoped for—Signor Gastani's kindness. My head buzzes, and I can't tell if it's from the champagne or the excitement. It has been the most extraordinary evening.

Nonna circles the room, greeting friends old and new, and she introduces me to those I haven't yet met. As the crowd dwindles, we take our leave. I wrap myself in my shawl against the winter chill till all that is seen of my ruby satin gown is the hem. The dress was a bold choice, but its rich hue exudes confidence.

Outside, on the steps of the theater, we wait for Nonna's car. She continues her goodbyes to a longtime friend, a former violinist. Though I've been here three years, it still amazes me. Rarely is there a time we're out that someone doesn't offer Nonna a hello and their good wishes.

"*Per favore, Signorina.* Can you help us?" Someone taps my shoulder, and I turn to find myself face-to-face with a woman who can't be more than five years my senior. Clutching at her skirts is a young boy, maybe five or six years old. Her son, I presume. Both wear tattered coats. Meager protection against the cold. From the haggard look on their faces, I know they are hungry.

"I . . . I'm sorry, I don't have any," I say, wishing I'd brought money. Anything to give to this mother and her child.

"Here," Nonna's voice comes from behind me. "This should be of some help." She hands the woman a few banknotes.

Tears well up in the woman's eyes as she steps away thanking Nonna profusely for the lira. "*Grazie! Grazie!* May God bless you for your kindness," she says, then leads her son across the street.

As our car pulls away, my gaze lingers on the two. Thank goodness Nonna had money to give. No one should live in such distress, especially not a child.

"What did you think, Rosa?" Nonna's voice breaks me away from my thoughts. She dips her head to the libretto in her hand. I share my thoughts, and she quizzes me about particulars as we break down each singer's performance. All part of my training. But I love it! I know what a gift it is to be mentored by someone as esteemed as my grandmother.

When we return home, it's nearly ten o'clock. But sitting in the living room is my Uncle Lorenzo. Nonna is as surprised as I am to find him here at such a late hour.

"Lorenzo," Nonna greets him.

"Mama," he says, not moving from where he sits. He says nothing to me.

"Why don't you give us a minute, Rosa."

"I'll go change." I'm relieved to get away from the tension hanging in the air like a suffocating blanket, and I take my time before heading back downstairs twenty minutes later.

"The Duce can make things difficult for you, Mama. There is only so much I can do!" As I enter the living room, Uncle Lorenzo nearly knocks me over. Frustration oozes from him. He pushes past me muttering, "*Mezzosangue.*"

I inhale sharply as if slapped.

"Lorenzo!" Nonna snaps.

"Bah!" He ignores her, then turns to leave. Heavy footsteps are followed by the thud of the front door slamming.

Half-breed. Mixed race. My stomach curdles in anger. Aside from those insults, my uncle has barely spoken a word to me since I arrived in Italy years ago.

The silence in the room is deafening. Nonna, her face etched with sadness, stands. "Come, Rosa. He is ignorant." She ushers me into the kitchen.

That Lorenzo could be Nonna's son is a mystery. He is nothing like her. Nothing like my father, the younger of her two sons.

Nonna makes tea, and we sip oolong before the fire.

"I have something for you." She makes her way to the cabinet and pulls something from the top drawer. Her eyes brighten as she hands me a bundle in pearlescent paper tied with a navy velvet ribbon. "An early Christmas gift."

"Nonna, you didn't need to!"

"Shame on me if I can't spoil my granddaughter! Open it, darling."

My breath hitches when I pull the gift from its wrapping. Enveloped in marbleized Florentine paper is a journal covered in peacock swirls in the richest hues of rose and gold.

"It's gorgeous!"

"You like it? I saw you eyeing it at the stationer's and thought you might."

"*Grazie!* Thank you!" I embrace her. Though she is in her late sixties, I can feel her strength as she holds me tight.

"I know you miss your family. And the post is nearly impossible. I thought, with this, you could write and share your thoughts. And maybe one day, if you choose, you can share it with them."

I hug her again. To be so loved warms my heart, especially when regular bouts of homesickness arise. "*Grazie,* Nonna."

She stands to take our cups, and I stop her. Nonna smiles warmly. "Thank you, Rosa."

"*Buona notte,*" I say as she retires for the night. After taking the empty cups to the kitchen, I pluck the journal from the table and head to my room. Excitement pulses through me. I lie back on my bed, reflecting on the night, on Signor Gastani's words. But I can't sleep. I carry the journal to my desk, then begin writing.

I want to capture the wonder of the evening in words, knowing Caramina, my youngest sister back home, would have loved the performance. She'll want to hear every detail. Like me, Cara longs to follow in Nonna's footsteps. Her plan to voice train in Florence can't come soon enough for me. But she isn't old enough yet.

I recount the night's splendid performances. Crystal flutes with sparkling bubbly. Antipasti served on expertly balanced trays by handsome waiters circling the room. Influential people in opera, even some from the ranks of the Ministry of Popular Culture, attended. Men in their best suits. Ladies in the most exquisite gowns. All lit by the warm glow of chandeliers. Delightful.

But I know, this is such a contrast to life outside the theater. With rationing increasing, the city's mood is grayer than the cobblestones lining its streets. People are struggling. They have been for some time. I can still see the faces of the woman and her young son etched with hunger and exhaustion, and my heart aches. I'm grateful Nonna offers help when she can. I feel guilty to have such comfortable arrangements.

Yet Lorenzo's words haunt me. Nonna is no fan of the regime. Just last week, she told me how Nonno Vittorio died. Arrested and beaten after voicing displeasure with the rampant corruption in the government—and that was decades before Mussolini. Bribes and bullying. But things have only gotten worse under Duce. Uncle Lorenzo's support of monsters like those responsible for his father's death is reprehensible. I think he, like so many, is drunk on power and its accompanying privileges. He lives well in Rome. Perhaps he sees supporting Duce as a way to look out for himself and Nonna. But his words worry me. Is she in danger?

There are two Italys now. The one my father spoke of—*Bella Italia,* the land of light, passion, artistry, heavenly music, and ambrosial flavors—is waning. A darkness is falling as Mussolini and his Blackshirts tighten their grip. I'm relieved Papa isn't here to see his beloved Italy under Duce's shadow.

Memories of home come to mind. Thank goodness for President Quezon and our government. They'd never allow Filipinos to fall to such oppression, especially when our country is only a few years from full independence.

My hand cramps from writing, and I rub my palm. Can anyone really change things for the better?

I place my journal in the desk drawer, then climb into bed. I toss and turn. Finally, haziness overtakes me and tiredness descends. I give way to an unsettled sleep.

In the morning, I find Nonna staring at old photographs of Lorenzo and Papa from when they were boys. Sadness fills her eyes. I know she misses my father. I'm certain she must, even more after Lorenzo's shameful behavior.

"Lorenzo had a meeting with the rector of the University of Florence," Nonna says.

"To make sure they're meeting 'state requirements'?" The words slip from my mouth before I can stop them. Nonna gives a pinched look, brows arched.

We move on to more comfortable topics of conversation. After a quick breakfast of espresso and toast, I make my way to the conservatory. I enter the Piazza delle Belle Arti, thoughts swirling over my uncle's words. As I pass through the dark wooden doors of the school, a thought stops me in my tracks. Have I placed Nonna in danger? What I've already written in my journal is enough to cause concern. My breath catches as I realize I must hide it.

Many share my thoughts about the government, but penning them is a dangerous matter. Certainly, Nonna didn't intend her gift to be used this way. Men have been thrown in jail for less. A professor at conservatory recently complained about the ban on foreign music. He was arrested and taken to the Villa Triste.

I don't want to think about what might happen if the journal is discovered. I want to race back to the apartment. But I know I'm being overanxious. Surely it will be safe for the next hour and a half. I go to class, then rush home the moment it ends. At the apartment, I race up the stairs. Relief courses through me when I open the drawer and see the journal untouched.

In the corner of the room is a loose floorboard that lies hidden by a rug. As I pry the board free, my pulse thumps in my ears. Carefully, I set the journal in the small space before replacing the board and rug on top.

I exhale, relieved. But still, a question nags. Is Lorenzo right? Is Nonna in danger? I vow to do whatever I can to keep my grandmother safe.

2

Caramina

Papa always says the light on this island is a true light. A lustrous gold that accentuates beauty and lifts truth to the surface in the most ordinary of lives.

This is a golden time. Tomorrow I turn fourteen. Tomorrow, I will cross the threshold into the rest of my life and become a young woman. I don't know how one day can change a person, but my hands tingle with excitement.

Blush-pink silk organza falls in waves around me, pooling at the floor. Light radiates through the delicate material and shimmers. I haven't found a single dark spot in all of today's preparations. Tiny holiday lights strung from the ceiling are iridescent against the jacquard walls of the dressing room. Garnet roses on an ebony table lend a pinkish hue, like sunsets over Manila Bay. I stand illumined before a mirror.

"Turn, turn, Caramina. See how it lifts so lightly on a breeze," says Florenza, the dressmaker, as she stands back admiring her handiwork. "Perfect for a young lady's birthday party. Ah, and the dancing." She winks at my older sister Isabella. Isabella smirks, and I blush.

"I'll leave you two to talk." Florenza snatches her pincushion and ambles out of the fitting room.

"It's just like yours," I say, peering at the dress.

"It's what you wanted?"

"It's perfect!" I step off the stool and sashay back and forth, arms held out toward an invisible partner. "What do you think?"

"Handsome. Yes, definitely, handsome. But a bit heavy on his feet."

I hum a waltz and laugh as Isabella twirls me. Steadying myself, I step back to gaze at my dress. "Is it really okay, Isa?"

My sister's beauty and style is admired by all the ladies in our neighborhood. She spends hours poring over stacks of *Vogue* and *Harper's Bazaar,* studying designs, and crafting her own. When Isa barraged Florenza with questions during fittings for her own debut gown two years ago, the seamstress, recognizing a budding talent, happily gave her copies of her favorite magazines and has been sending her old issues ever since. Isa even convinced Papa to bring our mother's old sewing machine to her room after promising to do all the mending. It serves as good practice, since she hopes one day to design elaborate gowns like the one I'm wearing. If Isa approves, I'll know the dress is right.

Isa surveys the gown. "You look like a lady. Almost fourteen, and you're all grown-up. The dress is perfect, Cara. Mama would have loved to be here."

That's when the tears come. Isabella stepped into the role of mothering when Mama passed away after our youngest brother Enzo was born, and even more after our sister, Rosa, left for Italy. The reality of Mama's absence today, of all days, simmers just below the surface. My heart pricks as the pain bubbles over.

How can remembering someone so loved create such pain? It isn't the memory of Mama but the reality she isn't here to enjoy days like today that hurts the most. It's like enjoying the vibrant bougainvillea that grows in waves alongside our home, then getting pricked by a thorn. I will myself to remember Mama today—her laughter, beauty, and love—and wipe away a rogue tear.

I gaze into the mirror, its dark mahogany frame carved in exotic vines with oleander blossoms. The young woman in the reflection looks like me, but at the same time someone altogether different. Someone far more sophisticated. Mature. Where's the girl who climbs trees and chases down her brothers?

"No sadness, Caramina. Mama would have wanted you smiling and laughing for your birthday." Isabella stands behind me.

"Sadness? What sadness? No. No. There is no sadness for my little lady today. Come, let me see." It's Papa. His deep Italian accent echoes through the room.

I walk to the entryway of the fitting room. "Oh my!" he gasps. "*Bellissima!* Beautiful! Ah, but you look beautiful splattered with mud after running through the mango grove with Enzo!" Papa bows and holds out his hand. "May I?"

I take his hand, and he waltzes us through the shop as he hums Strauss's "Blue Danube." His smile beams as we move back and forth, faster and faster, until laughter threatens to topple me.

At last Papa stops. He catches his breath and peeks at his wristwatch. "We must go. Esther will have my head if we're late for dinner." He gives a mischievous wink.

Florenza emerges from the back room. "Ah, Signor Grassi."

Papa holds my hands out as if I'm on display. "She's beautiful! Yes?"

The attention is unnerving. "Papa!"

He chuckles. Though my father is a quiet man, laughter comes easily to him. There's no question he loves me and my siblings, all five of us.

"All right, Little Bird. Change now."

I close the door and slip out of the dress. As I pull on my simple cotton skirt and blouse, Isabella folds the gown. She sighs wistfully before placing it in its box and leaving the room.

"It was a challenge for me, but not one I wasn't up to." Florenza's voice drifts into the room. "These Italian styles are so beautiful. It really is perfect on her."

When I open the door, Papa and Isabella are standing in the shop's entrance. Papa holds a newspaper stretched open before him, brow furrowed. I glimpse the cover with its bold headlines telling of war taking place far away.

"Papa?"

He rustles the paper, quickly folding it, then tucking it under his arm. My heart aches seeing him worry about such things. Perhaps he's concerned for Rosa and Nonna. If only I were older, I'd be there now, taking in the beauty of Florence and singing at a prestigious school. Oh, how it stung to watch Rosa leave with Nonna the last time she'd visited. I had bit my lip to stop tears from falling.

When Italy joined Germany in the war over a year ago, there was talk of Rosa returning home, but Nonna felt strongly that she, herself, needed to remain in Florence. Since there is no fighting in Italy, Rosa opted to stay, much to Papa's dismay. In Rosa's last letters to me, she hadn't mentioned anything other than food being rationed. Everything else seemed fine. Surely Papa needn't worry. Rosa and Nonna are safe.

"Look, girls!" Papa points to the lights twinkling overhead in Florenza's window display. White paper stars, lit from within, hang from a silk ribbon and float midair. The *parols* cast a warm light on the chiffon and silk dresses in the window.

"*Maligayang Pasko!* Merry Christmas!" We bid her goodbye as we walk out into the sunlight.

My eyes are immediately drawn to the baubles adorning the trees along the sidewalk. "I love Manila, especially in December. It sparkles . . . like a woman in her finest jewels."

"Your imagination, Caramina." Papa laughs. "But it is beautiful."

Compared to where we live on the northern outskirts of Floridablanca, Manila is a grand city. Our town is small and set deep in a valley of fertile soil rich with crops of sugar and rice. Swaying trees and fragrant blooms make our neighborhood all the more dramatic, set against the backdrop of Mount Arayat. A beautiful place to live, though quiet.

"Can't you feel it? The excitement?" I ask. The city pulses with energy along its busy avenues of tall buildings. When Nonna last visited two years ago, even after touring all of Europe, she was convinced Manila was the Paris of the East, the Pearl of the Orient. Its bay opens to the deep blue waters of the Pacific, welcoming the world to its shore.

Papa stops and stands still. "Yes, I think I can," he says, humoring me. "I'd say this was a successful trip. *Sì?*"

"Yes!" Isabella and I chime in. She's enjoyed it as much as I have. We rarely go to the city. Not just because it's a few hours from our home. Trips are reserved for special occasions, like our visit to the dress shop. Rosa and Isabella have only one or two dresses like the one Florenza made. They're costly, but Papa insists we have them.

As Floridablanca's official town gardener, Papa provides a comfortable lifestyle for us. He loves gardening and reaps the rewards of excelling at his work. Mama's parents, who died long before I and any of my siblings were born, had owned a sugar plantation and were part owners of the biggest mill in the province. When they passed away, Mama's inheritance helped purchase our family home. We rarely want for anything. Even so, gowns like the one we bought today are an extravagance. One day, I hope, I'll wear it for my debut performance as an opera singer.

Papa drives us past the Manila Grand Opera House as we begin our long trip home. My gaze lingers on the honey-colored building. I can picture the stage, balconies, and rows of seats behind its unassuming exterior. Years ago, Nonna described it for me in great detail. Often, I imagine being on that stage.

"One day, Cara, it will be you performing there." Papa glances at me as if reading my mind. "Your 'Ave Maria' last week was superb. *Bellisimo!*"

A week ago, I sang at St. Joseph's, our church. Notes floated from my lips to the listening ears of the congregants. Joy blossomed within me as I sang the sacred aria, hoping it was flowing straight into the hearts of those perched on the dark wooden pews. With the last note sung, I opened my eyes to a hushed, candlelit church. The scent of frangipani wafted on a warm breeze. I brimmed with life. Singing had that effect on me.

"Father was moved by your song, and he wasn't the only one," Papa says.

He'd watched as one of the neighborhood grandmothers tapped me on the shoulder afterward and presented me with an orchid of the palest of pinks. "*Magandá.* Beautiful," the lola said, her eyes glistening.

Now in the car, driving away from the city, I picture myself in my new gown singing in the Opera House, enraptured by music. Maybe Papa is right. Maybe one day, my voice will rise from that stage, meeting the ears of those in the highest balconies. My heart thumps wildly at the thought.

Rays of morning sun pour through the crack between the curtains and onto my bed. Today is my birthday! I'd begged Papa for months for a big party and couldn't wait for the festivities. But my hopes went beyond celebrating. My party, I'd hoped, would help people see me for who I am and accept me. Singing is like that, too. A way for me to prove myself.

But now, my head is pounding, adding to the scratchiness I felt last night in my throat. I massage my temples, willing the pain away. An unfamiliar noise hums faintly. Not the usual sounds of church bells or noise from the occasional passersby. This is different. A distant thrumming. My skin prickles warm, and perspiration dampens my nightgown. It must be an exceptionally hot day or maybe I've struck a fever.

My father comes into my room to see why I'm not up yet. Papa frowns, then walks over and puts his hand on my forehead. "You're sick, Caramina. You must stay in bed and rest. What kind of father would I be to let you go to church today?" he says. "Rest. Just rest. I promise, when we return, we'll celebrate."

"But the party?" I spent weeks helping to plan and prepare, and I relished every moment. Seeing all of my hard work wasted is devastating.

"Caramina, if you are sick, we'll postpone the party. But not to worry, we'll still celebrate." Papa pauses and holds out a small box, wrapped carefully in light-blue paper with a white satin ribbon. "It's from your grandmother. I was going to give it to you later, but I think now is just right."

"*Grazie,* Papa." Nonna had to have planned months in advance for it to arrive in time for today. I prop myself up and slowly unwrap the box. Perched on a small robin's-egg-blue velvet pillow is a gold necklace with a locket.

Seeing the sunflower etched on the front, I smile, remembering Nonna's words from when she last visited years ago as she comforted me after I'd had a grueling day at school. "Look at the sunflowers, Cara. See how they keep their faces to the sun. '*Buongiorno,*' they say. See how happy they are. We must do the same and keep looking for the good. It's all around us if we just look."

"It's beautiful!" I say, then gently push the tiny lever. The locket springs open, revealing a picture of Mama, and I gasp. Mama's eyes are filled with the warmth of love.

Papa bends close to see the photo. "Thank goodness your nonna loved singing here! Or I wouldn't have met your mother. I still remember the first time I saw her. The picture of pure elegance as she listened to Nonna's aria. I couldn't take my eyes off her. Afterward, I followed her into the lobby. She looked angelic in the glow of the chandeliers. When she turned and spoke to me . . . Oh *mio!* I was smitten. We were inseparable during the after-party." He smiles at this precious memory. "We fell in love, and I never left."

"Here, Cara. Let me." He secures the necklace around my neck.

As I lean forward, my dark, wavy curls tumble down, the locket falling against me.

"*Perfetto!*" Papa smiles. "Ah, there is a letter, too." He riffles in his pocket and hands me an envelope with my name penned in Nonna's sweeping script. I pry it open and pull out the two-page letter. Papa kisses the top of my head and then leaves.

My hopes for my big day have crumbled. But this—a present from Nonna—fills me with happiness. From my bedroom window, I watch as Papa, Matteo, and Enzo greet neighbors on their way to church. Only Isabella stays, promising to look in on me. Carefully, I unfold the letter and breathe in the familiar, subtle scent of orange blossoms from Nonna's perfume. It's as if she's right here in the room. I can't help but smile.

October 5, 1941

My Darling Caramina,

How is it you are already fourteen? Your father sent me the photograph of you singing at church. He told me you sang the "Panis Angelicus." So beautiful! He is so proud of you, as am I. Your mother would have been so proud to see you. You remind me so much of her, Caramina.

I know it is your desire to sing. You must continue to practice, as I taught you. I told you, when I come again, I will bring you to Florence for voice training. Singing for a living is a dream come true. But it is also the result of much hard work, which I know you will do well.

Most of all, you must sing because it is in you. It makes your soul come alive. This is a gift from God, who has entrusted it to you. Sing for joy, and those around you will be blessed, too.

I hope you will enjoy my present. Remember the sunflowers and always look for the good.

You are in my heart, mia bambina.

All my love, Nonna

I peer up at the framed poster from Nonna's performance at the Manila Grand from long before I was born. One of my most treasured possessions, it makes me smile again, thinking of her beautiful singing. Carefully, I fold the letter, yawning as drowsiness sweeps over me. I drift off to a fitful sleep. When I again awaken, my throat pinches, dry and achy. Thirsty, I grab the glass at my bedside. The warm water does little to refresh. Despite the heat engulfing the room, I shiver.

There is that noise again, only it seems much closer. A relentless thrumming vibrating through my body. I stand. Unsteady, I reach for the bed. The sound pulses into my toes pressing into the dark bamboo floor. As the noise gets louder, I feel my way along the hallway. Even the walls tremble. I'm desperate for something to cool this fever and stop the pounding in my head.

The savory scents of *pancit, lumpia,* and Papa's special pasta fill the hall. Despite feeling ill, my stomach grumbles. I've not eaten at all this morning. I step into the kitchen, grateful for its cool dimness. Then, I see it. I stop, stunned by the marvel before me.

One of the most ornately decorated cakes I've ever seen rests in the center of the table. Esther created such a perfect confection. I circle the cake, studying its ornamented layers. Various shades of lustrous pink blossoms over silky white frosting. I fight the urge to swipe my finger for a taste. I'd have to answer to Esther. But this is my cake. I may not have my party but, surely, I can have a small taste. Gently, I pry off one of the tiniest sugared flowers skirting the base and pop it in my mouth. The heavenly sweet melts on my tongue as I stand admiring the shimmering blooms. It is all so lovely I almost forget the thrumming.

Then, I hear a scream. Isabella is racing down the hallway toward me. I stare at her, guilt now souring the sweet's taste.

"It was just a tiny flower. You can't even tell. What's wrong?" It isn't like Isabella to be upset over something so small.

"Caramina!" Isabella yells. "We have to take cover!"

What is she talking about?

The walls begin to shake, and the crushing sound of an explosion deafens me temporarily. For a few seconds, I can hear nothing but a whooshing sound. I stand frozen on the kitchen tile. Another explosion splits the air, and the icebox next to me shakes.

Isabella screams, her words piercing through the chaos. "We have to get out of here!"

Noise explodes into the room. The icebox lurches, then violently rocks back and forth. My chest tightens, and my pulse pounds in my ears. I squeeze my eyes shut, willing it all to stop. Then something hits me, throwing me hard across the floor. I feel myself smack against the tile, and then there is a crash.

"Caramina! Caramina, answer me!" Isabella is shaking me by my shoulders.

I pry open my eyes, terrified of what I might see. On the floor next to me, the table lies in splintered pieces, crushed by the icebox. In the dim light of the kitchen, I look up at my sister, who stares back with terror in her eyes. Isa brushes my hair from my face.

"Isa." I attempt to speak, but my voice is a strained whisper.

When she pulls away, I see her hands. They are scarlet, covered in blood.

3

Rosa

"*The Clark, Nichols, and Del Carmen U.S. air bases have been hit. We'll report as we learn more from the Philippines.*" The Radio Londra announcer's voice breaks off. Static sounds over the radio, and I can't breathe.

Japan has bombed Luzon's air bases after bombing Pearl Harbor in Hawaii. My family is now right in the middle of a war. Nonna's expression is calm, but her face is ashen. She refuses to show fear as she puts her arm around me.

"We must trust they are okay, Rosa. The air bases may have been hit. But that doesn't mean your family has been affected." Neither of us speak what we know to be true. With any attack on the Del Carmen air base, my family would likely feel the reverberations.

"Your father will keep them safe. You must have faith, *mia cara.*"

I inhale slowly to steady myself against the dizziness I feel. Images of my siblings, of Isabella, Matteo, Caramina, and Enzo, flash through my mind. Oh God, please let them be okay. Papa is the smartest, bravest man I know. Perhaps what Nonna says is true.

Right now, I'm grateful Nonna is willing to risk listening to the news despite Mussolini's ban on foreign broadcasts. It's dangerous, but I'd go out of my mind not hearing anything besides what's allowed in the newspapers. I want to stay by the radio, but I know it's futile. The next broadcast won't be till this evening.

I force myself to go to the conservatory. The last thing I want is to be there, but Nonna insists it's better to keep busy. My fruitless pacing will do nothing but wear a hole in the living room rug, so I splash water on my face, wash away my tears, and leave the house.

The early-morning streets are filled with an eerie silence. I find myself wandering aimlessly by the river. Before I realize it, I'm standing before the Basilica di Santa Croce. My footfalls pad quietly over the ancient tiles, and I light candles while whispering a prayer for my father and each of my siblings. How many have done the same for their loved ones over the centuries? May God be merciful.

After arriving in class, it quickly becomes clear I cannot concentrate, so Maestro sends me home. Later, Nonna hands me a tureen of soup to bring to Maestro's apartment. "Fresh air will help. You need to get out of the apartment, Rosa."

I know she's providing a distraction. But what can distract me from this?

Reluctantly, I head out the door to bring Nonna's minestrone to Maestro. I've never been to his home before. When I arrive, the apartment door is open. I enter and find him talking to the most adorable little girl who peeks up at me.

"I'm Eliana."

"Well!" I'm taken aback by her precociousness. "Hello, Eliana. I'm Rosa."

"How old are you?"

"I'm nineteen. How old are you? You must be at least seven," I say. Maestro smiles at me, tousling her hair.

"I'm four. I live there." She points to the apartment across the hall.

Maestro insists I bring the tureen to her parents, Betta and Giuseppe. Betta is so grateful—the look in her eyes when I hand her the soup breaks my heart.

Maestro thanks me after I return. "Giuseppe taught at conservatory."

"I've not seen him before."

Maestro's face darkens, and he leans in to speak quietly. "He lost his professorship when Mussolini passed his 'racial' laws. He lost his job because he is Jewish, Rosa. Mussolini's hateful rule has affected so many good people."

"I . . . I didn't realize." My words stumble out. I've heard of such things happening but thought them hearsay. "This is abhorrent!" I'm shocked. Since I arrived, Nonna has made it her mission to shield me from such things, fearing for my safety. But now I wonder if I should have realized the truth of Mussolini's cruelty.

"This is Luca," Eliana says, interrupting my thoughts. "He says hi." She lifts her stuffed bunny's arms out as if to embrace me.

I hide my disgust from Eliana. "Hello, Luca. How lovely to meet you!" I hug the bunny. For a moment, hearing Eliana giggle, I'm back home with my little brother, Enzo. My stomach twists in knots, knowing I've no idea how he or any of my family are doing.

Eliana tugs at my sleeve. "Luca wants to play."

"Is that so?"

"Ah, sì. Luca is an expert at jacks. Isn't that right, Eliana?" Maestro winks.

Eliana plops onto the floor, motioning for me to join her and Luca.

"It's been some time. But maybe he can remind me how to play," I say.

"Oh yes!" Eliana says, a smile blooming across her face.

Eliana, like Luca, is quite the expert at jacks. She beats me three times. Afterward, Maestro brings out a plate of almond biscotti. I read to Eliana, and then we sing with Maestro looking on, no doubt restraining his critique. It's funny to see him like this, like a kindly grandfather rather than the staunch taskmaster I know him to be at conservatory.

I stay at Maestro's just over two hours. Eliana's laughter has lifted my spirits. I think she has the same effect on Maestro. On my way home, I stop at the Duomo to pray once again for my family, for the Philippines, and for Italy. The whole world has gone mad. Surely this will all stop. Someone will do something, won't they?

My last note lingers, a wisp of sound drifting on the slight breeze wafting through the auditorium. I inhale deeply, then bow to an audience of my peers and the professors scattered around the hall, a few of whom will judge my performance as worthy or lacking. The acoustics in the Sala del Buonumore are superb. This hall at the conservatory has stood for over a century and a half and is remarkable. Applause flows through the room. I spot Maestro. He nods his affirmation with an enormous grin. I know I've done well, and relief floods through me. He waves, motioning for me to follow him to his office.

Today is the day of vocal quarterlies at the Conservatorio di Musica di Firenze Luigi Cherubini. Every vocalist performs the work they've been preparing for months. Performances to test how we're progressing.

I wasn't sure I could even sing for my exams, but Nonna has been such a comfort. She believes my family is safe and tells me I mustn't worry. From the news reports days ago, it does sound like it was only the bases that were affected. Though I wish with everything in me I could hear the voices of my father or my siblings. It would calm my unease. But I must hope for the best. I've plodded along by continuing to rehearse for my exams. And now, *è finito*.

Once we've reached his office, Maestro bursts out, "*Bravissima!* Your nonna was right. *Sì?* Your breathing work paid off. It was one of the best performances, Rosa. And now, we start getting you ready for a large stage. The Fiorentino, eh?" His hands move this way and that in time with the excitement in his voice. He pours me a glass of water, then hands it to me.

"Wait here. I'll be right back. And breathe! You did well." His footfalls fade as he disappears down the hallway.

I do as he advises and breathe. It's not just nerves but the excitement of it all. Performing is electrifying. I think about Caramina. Blessed with a rich tone, her stunningly beautiful voice reminds me so much of Nonna's. The thought of Cara makes my heart ache. I wish she were here. Safe.

Minutes pass, and Maestro hasn't yet returned. I know not to panic. There is always that one professor agonizing over the minutiae of all that goes into our performances. Then footsteps sound in the hall, and Maestro appears in the doorway. Red-faced. My heart plummets into my stomach.

"What's happened?"

He sets three score sheets on his desk. "This"—he points to the top sheet—"is not a reflection of your performance." He speaks slowly as if to do so any faster would unleash the fury scrawled across his face.

I look at him, not understanding. He turns the sheet so I can see the marks. The scores are low, and suddenly it's as if the floor beneath me has caved in.

"This man . . . è pazzo!" Maestro's voice quivers with anger. "There is more at play here than skill and talent."

I've never seen Maestro so furious. He hands me the other score sheets. "This is evidence of that! Read them. Go on, read them. This is what I want you to remember!"

I lift the two sheets and read the comments. Though there is some helpful critique, these two professors are exceedingly complimentary, even offering their best wishes and declaring they will be proud to see me begin my career professionally.

I glance down at the third sheet. Maestro places his hand over it, preventing me from reading the harsh, angular script. "Rosa, this man's opinion means nothing. He is a fool. Do you understand? I will only let you see this if you tell me you do."

"I understand," I say, though I don't.

He releases the sheet. I read the comments that appear to have been penned in an angry flurry. "All Italians must follow Duce's example to let true Italians shine in the arts. Though Signorina Grassi displays some degree of talent, she should be grateful to attend this prestigious conservatory and leave the opportunity for advancement to those who are of true Italian blood. In the interest of our country, and this conservatory with its long history of forming exceptional talent in the musical arts, I am marking Signorina Grassi as I believe her standing deserves."

"My standing . . ." My cheeks grow hot and flush with anger.

"Pay it no heed, Rosa. We will continue working. You will continue singing. Do not let this man deter you from what you've worked so hard to accomplish." His voice has softened, and he reminds me of my papa. I'm grateful for his wisdom. For his belief in me.

Having a professor knock points off my performance because I am part Filipina and not fully Italian is reprehensible. It has nothing to do with my singing.

Maestro tells me he confronted the professor. Clearly, the encounter has left him fuming. Maestro won't tell me which teacher or what he said. But I have my suspicions.

The policy of teachers marking score sheets anonymously was put in place years ago. But not to protect a man such as this. I leave Maestro's office with my hands clenched tight. I know I should heed Maestro's advice, but my blood boils as I make my way to the rehearsal room to pack my things. When I step out onto the street, the burst of frigid air shocks me. My fury gives way to a steady pulse of anger.

I'm fortunate my other scores are high. But this professor's marks will lower my grade, which may affect my placement at next year's music festival. Top performers garner a much wider audience, including theater owners who keep an eye out for future talent.

Maestro is urging me not to be dismayed. He believes once I finish conservatory, I'll be able to perform where I'd like. He's a bit overzealous. He truly is, other than Nonna, my most ardent supporter. I am indebted to him and determined to keep singing. I will tell him so when I see him next. The image of his smile after my performance, stretched wide like the Arno around the city, bolsters my spirits. Not everyone is ignorant. There are still good people in this world.

4

Caramina

Dirt rains down, as we huddle in the makeshift shelter, after an explosion splits the air. I don't know how long the bombs fall, but when the pounding finally subsides, I hear screaming and soon realize it's coming from me. Papa puts his arm around me and pulls me close. "We're all right, Cara," he says. I take a steadying deep breath. After the first blasts, Papa hurried Isa and me from the kitchen to the ravine behind our house.

"They're bombing the airfields," Papa says. After days spent in the ditch, the sounds have confirmed his suspicions. Catching my eye, he smiles, then stands and walks to the end of the shelter where he peers out at the sky. I watch as he mouths the words "Father, protect them."

"Surely they're nearing the end of this." Esther shakes dirt from her hair.

War was on the other side of the world. Not here. Not on our island. My head is pounding, and I feel the sting of the cut on my cheek. I reach to touch it and wince.

"No, Cara, don't." Isabella leans close, then wipes the cut gently with the hem of her blouse.

More hours pass, and it seems Papa's right. The Japanese aren't bombing our home, but the noise and reverberations from the explosions at Clark Air Base sound as if the bombs are aimed right next door. With every hit, the ground quakes. We and our neighbors, Martin and Evie, watch our homes helplessly. Windows shatter, raining down glass shards. The buildings shake as if made of sticks, but both houses remain standing.

Everyone is huddled, waiting. Helpless. Martin and Evie's youngest, Emma, hasn't moved from Evie's lap. She's clutching Evie, whimpering, and my heart breaks. She's inconsolable. Instinctively, I begin to hum. My throat aches, but it's the only thing I can do.

"Please sing, Caramina," Evie says.

The others nod in agreement. Emma creeps off her mother's lap and makes her way to mine. As she rests her head, I feel Nonna's locket press against me. Just holding on to someone steadies me. I begin to sing quietly and feel Emma relax.

I sing for Emma, for myself, and for the others. It's a small thing. Insignificant, really. But if this is what I can do, it's what I have to— to fight the fear gnawing at our hearts.

Hours pass before the silver light of night turns coral as the sun peeks over the horizon. I open my eyes to see Papa approaching with Martin and Stefano, their arms filled with supplies—food, blankets, and a bucket of water.

"Here," Papa says, as he and Martin hand around a bowl half filled with *pancit*. Everyone is ravenous and digs in to eat the noodles with savory bits of chicken, carrots, onion, and cabbage.

"Can we go back in, Papa?" Isabella asks.

"Both houses have fared well. But the bombing may not be over. For now, we'll stay here." Papa hands me the bowl.

At the scent of the noodles, hunger pangs radiate through me. I take one bite and stop, realizing this is my birthday meal.

My birthday was over before it even began. This war stole it. My family, my country, has never done anything to the Japanese. Why would they bomb us? Why declare war on us? My throat tightens, and I gulp to force down the bite in my mouth. Thinking of Nonna's reminder, I grasp my locket. How can any of this be good?

"Cara?" Papa drops down next to me. We sit quietly for a long time, neither saying a word.

Moments creep by. The shelter feels like an oven in the afternoon sun. I lose track of time. Has it been one day or two? The earth has stopped shaking. The cacophony of explosions has finally stopped. Still, we sit hunched together. Papa passes water around.

In the silence, there is a loud crack. With it, Martin and Evie's house crumples, and Evie screams. One moment it was standing. Now it's a heap of broken wood and stone.

There is no smoke, no fire, just a cloud of debris. Emma and her brother, Ricard, begin to cry. Martin reaches for his wife and children and holds them close. As he does, I see his eyes racked with pain and I glance away.

This war has now stolen one of our homes. What else will it take? I fix my eyes on the dirt beneath me. The ground quickly grows blurry. One by one my tears fall, mixing with the dark soil.

Though we're all on edge anticipating another explosion, it doesn't come. Papa declares it's safe to return home. He's adamant that Martin and Evie stay with us. Our two-story house is one of the larger homes in the neighborhood and has more than enough room. Martin agrees, but only until he can get word to his parents in San Jose. He hopes to bring his family there, once it's safe.

After the cacophony of the last few days, the silence is deafening.

"Not so bad," Papa says, surveying our living room. "Here, Cara." He hands me a dustpan, and everyone begins cleaning.

Built long ago by the Spaniards who'd settled in Pampanga, the house has fared well. Shards of broken glass and furniture lie splintered on the floor. Some odds and ends have fallen.

Matteo sets Papa's wireless radio upright. He switches it on, and static fills the room as everyone stoops to clear the debris. Then the sound of a voice flickers. "It works!" Matteo says. As he twists the dial, a man's voice emerges clearly. A news broadcast. Everyone listens as the announcer describes the devastation from the Japanese attack on Pearl Harbor.

"In other news, Filipino President Manuel Quezon has issued a statement. It reads, 'The zero hour has arrived. I expect every Filipino—man and woman—to do his duty. We have pledged our honor to stand to the last by the United States and we shall not fail her, happen what may.' May God be with us all during these times."

"Stand to the last?" I look to Papa for clarification, but he says nothing. At the broken look in his eyes, my heart aches. He turns down the volume. Music fills the space, floating quietly through the room. Papa walks back to the pile of debris and continues shoveling it into a wheelbarrow. No one speaks.

"Esther?" I enter the kitchen. The table lies in pieces on the floor with my once beautiful cake splayed across it. With food splattered across one side of the room, the kitchen is a canvas. My birthday dinner is now a piece of art, colors haphazardly slung in streaks and dots.

Broken glass litters the floor. There is a scratch on one of the tiles. A few dark red spots speckle one area. Blood. My blood. I skim my finger along the scab etched across my left cheek.

The west side of the kitchen is unscathed. Bowls filled with food sit untouched. The dining room opposite the west kitchen wall is laid with Nonna's china, brought many years before, a wedding gift for my parents. The crystal goblets and china sit unaffected as if the intended celebrants have been magically swept away. It's like I'm in a dream. I've walked in on what was supposed to be my party, but no one is in sight. Only an eerie stillness fills the space.

5

Caramina

"Cara, catch!" Enzo tosses me the ball.

Weeks have passed, and still no Japanese have arrived. But a cloud of fear hangs over the town. Papa's been like a flint trying to keep some sense of normalcy for us, so he sent us outside for a late-afternoon game of catch. The bombing is still fresh in my mind, and I wonder at my little brother's ability to be so carefree.

I spin quickly to catch the ball, then toss it back. It hits Enzo's glove and bounces away. He chases after it down the street. But before he reaches it, I spot them.

"Enzo, wait!" I say. Two boys, a few grades older than my brother, round the corner, and I know they're up to no good. Enzo stoops to get the ball as one of the boys kicks it, sending dirt into his face.

"Hey!" I yell.

When they see me, they scoff. Before strutting away, they sneer, then yell, *"Bangus!"*

"Don't pay them any attention." I stifle my anger and dust off the ball. I don't want Enzo to give them a moment's thought. They're not worth it. "Come on, let's play!"

Some people treat me differently because I'm *mestiza,* a half-blood. They call me ugly names, like *bangus* (whitefish) and *asong kalye* (mongrel). I try not to pay attention, but the sting of their words burns. Each of my siblings has experienced the unfortunate taunts of narrow-minded bullies. But the fact that Enzo now has to hear these words breaks my heart.

Papa has always told us to be proud of who we are. The fact I'm half Italian is something I love. Being in a family that speaks not only Tagalog and English, but Italian as well, has been a connection to the world far from the shores of my country. Now, with the war, that connection seems frayed.

I push the thought from my mind, then throw the ball again. We play till Esther calls us inside for dinner.

Candlelight glows in the dining room, along with light from the *parol* star lanterns.

"Cara." Isa hands me a plate of *pandesal,* pulling me from my thoughts of the encounter with those two boys.

Papa determined we'd have an early Christmas celebration today despite our precarious position. Normally, we'd never consider celebrating until after the midnight service on Christmas Eve. But under the circumstances it seemed best to do so before Martin and Evie leave for his parents' home.

"Let's focus on the good things we have," Papa says, seeing the look on my face. "We have each other and this beautiful meal. *Delizioso, sì? Grazie,* Esther! *Grazie!*"

Everyone heartily agrees, digging into the feast. Having food to celebrate is something to be grateful for. Esther carries in the ham, and the savory aromas blend. No one seems to miss the roast pig or other traditional Christmas dishes, except for Enzo, whose favorite is *lechon.*

"Pasta?" Papa holds out a plate of his pasta, smothered in rich tomato sauce, to Enzo. Papa cooked it himself as he always does. At the sight, Enzo perks up.

My mouth waters as I peer up and down the table. We've not eaten so well since that first night back in the house. A breeze sweeps in, blowing out the candles. For a few moments, we sit in near darkness but for the pinpoint lights from the *parols*. Stefano relights the candles, and we finish our meal.

"Time for carols!" Papa stands and leads us into the living room where we gather around the piano and sing. "*Silent night. Holy night. All is calm. All is bright.*" Our voices blend with Papa's rich baritone booming beneath.

"Caramina, would you sing the 'Panis Angelicus'?" he asks.

The last time I sang the aria feels so long ago.

Papa plays the chords quietly and glances at me. How can I refuse? I close my eyes and take a deep breath. The beginning strains ring out from the old piano.

The words spill from my lips like wine from a carafe. I pause to take a breath, letting the music bubble forth from deep inside. "Music is alive," Papa once told me. "You breathe it out in song, and it lives outside of you for all to enjoy."

I finish the last verse, and the piano fades. The room is silent and still.

"We wish you a Merry Christmas, Papa!" Enzo says, and the moment slips away. We all sing again until Emma stops abruptly and wishes us "*Maligayang Pato!*" She'd meant "*Maligayang Pasko!*" At her declaration of "Happy Duck!" rather than "Happy Christmas!" Enzo and Ricard break into fits of laughter, and Emma wrinkles her nose in disgust.

We almost finish the song, when a loud noise startles us. Someone is at the front door banging wildly and yelling.

Papa slowly rises from the piano. An ominous feeling descends. My heart sinks, and my hands tremble. Emma starts to cry. Evie immediately scoops her up, then grabs Ricard.

"Let me, Arturo." Stefano steps between Papa and the door, holding a long, curved bolo knife that he grabbed from the hall closet. Papa stands with his hand on his belt. There's a slight impression on his hip, just under his shirt. He moves his hand, and I gasp. It's a gun.

"Everyone to the kitchen," Papa commands.

"I can stay," Matteo says.

"Everyone!" Papa directs Matteo to go with us. "Do you have what I gave you?"

Matteo nods, lifting a knife from his belt. He hurries everyone into the kitchen. I stand close behind him, determined to see who is at the door.

Stefano throws the door open, brandishing the bolo. "What do you want?"

"Sirs, I mean you no harm!"

I recognize the man's voice. It's Mr. Dalisay, Anna's father. Anna is Matteo's sweetheart. They live a few streets away.

"We got word a Japanese garrison landed earlier and is moving toward town. They're rounding up the men and have killed many. They've also taken some of the women—young women. It is unspeakable." He shakes his head, disgusted. "The mayor caught me in the street as I was getting my family ready to leave and asked me to let others know. Please, you must leave now!"

Papa thanks him and closes the door. Everyone stands in the hallway, faces pale.

"Go upstairs now. Pack what you can. Only the essentials," he says.

After quick but painful goodbyes to Martin, Evie, and the kids in the dark of night, we squeeze into Papa's Packard for the long journey to my aunt and uncle's. Enzo sits on my lap. It will be a tight ride until we drop Stefano and Esther off by the foothills. The two are heading to Esther's sister's house. The idea of saying goodbye to her is unbearable.

As we pull into the street, I look back at the only home I've ever known. My entire life has existed here. Now, no warm light illuminates the windows. There's no sign of life or the celebration that filled it just hours before. I wipe away my tears and force myself to look ahead.

The main street in town resembles a market hit by a typhoon. A throng of men, women, and children move slowly along. Others trudge the only road out of town, pushing their way through the masses. Families ride in *carretelas,* perched high in carriages pulled by horses with luggage, food, and other goods spilling onto the ground. A few cars attempt to bypass the chaos. With the crush of people fleeing, they don't get far.

Children hold hands with parents or siblings, crying as they walk. A woman with an infant strapped to her chest balances a screaming toddler on her hip. She struggles to keep up with her husband, who is forcing his way through the crowd.

"We need to go faster!" Matteo says, but there is no way around the horde.

Papa's calm demeanor is a striking contrast to the chaos.

A man is grasping in every direction for chickens toppling from his rickety cart. He screams at the birds in a futile attempt to corral them. Paying him no heed, they shuffle this way and that, their clucking rising along with the hysteria of the crowd. One chicken breaks free and darts next to our car.

The man races after it, yelling. He leaps at the car, landing on the outer step. In a flash, he grabs through the open window to hold himself secure, demanding Papa pull over to let him load his crates on top of our vehicle. Then he loses his grip. He flails his arms in a desperate attempt to grab hold again. I lean back as far from the window as I can, my pulse racing. But then he grabs my arm, digging his fingers into my flesh, and I scream. Enzo begins to cry. Matteo lunges forward and shoves the man off our vehicle. I rub my arm, which is now streaked red.

The man appears again, this time at Papa's window, yelling words I've never before heard. When he grabs the side of the vehicle, Papa hits the brakes. The car lurches to a stop, and the man stumbles forward.

Papa opens his door, steps out calmly, and walks right up to the man.

"Papa!" I yell. Matteo motions for me to be quiet.

Papa says something only the two men can hear. The man's head spins around toward his chicken crates. He races back to them, yelling at the birds and a group of young men pillaging his belongings. One old woman tucks a chicken under her arm and scurries off into the crowd.

Papa walks back to the car and resumes the slow drive out of town.

"What did you say?" Isabella asks.

Papa is quiet before speaking. "I told him, 'Your chickens are flying the coop. You'd better tend to them.'"

Stefano laughs. Matteo frowns and says, "He got what he deserved."

Papa catches my eye in the rearview mirror, offering up a momentary sympathetic glance. When I look outside, feathers are flying everywhere, and the madman is moving in circles, screaming. My peaceful town is in turmoil. I lean deeper into the seat, desperate to hide from the chaos erupting all around.

When we finally turn onto the road heading from town into the mountains, the usual fifteen-minute trip has taken over an hour. Wide-open fields stand in sharp contrast to the buildings clustered at the town's edge.

The drive drags on mile after mile as the foothills grow closer, their lush foliage reminding me of an emerald velvet dress, billowing in the wind. I feel myself calm at the sight.

Few people are walking on the road now, most having fallen far behind any vehicles. In the distance, an elderly man walks alone. He limps, pausing before taking his next step, and Papa slows the Packard to a stop.

"Sir?" Papa's voice is gentle.

The man is breathing heavily. Thrown over his shoulder is a bag that couldn't possibly fit more than two coconuts' worth of goods.

"Can we give you a ride? We're going into the foothills," Papa says.

The man pauses, leans back, and huffs a few breaths. He surveys the car. "Too full . . . I can walk."

"We have room. It's not a bother." Papa opens his door.

"Yes," Esther says, scooting onto Stefano's lap. Papa leads the man to the car, and he slides in next to Stefano.

"We're heading east," Papa says.

"I'm going to my son's home in Rizal," the man says.

Rizal is just south of where Esther's sister lives. "My wife and I are heading that way," Stefano says. "We'll be happy to have your company."

"*Salamat po.* Thank you," the man says.

"Is your son expecting you?" Papa asks.

"I tried to send word. Times are not good, are they? These men, the Japanese. No good. I've heard of their deeds in China. What they did in Nanking . . ." His voice falls away.

Papa shakes his head in disgust, his brow furrowed deep. "We must do what we can," he says.

I've no idea what they're talking about and don't want to know given the look on Papa's face. I survey the man. He's older than Nonna. Deep creases line his face, darkened from years in the sun.

Esther offers him an empanada. He's reluctant to eat what we've brought for ourselves. But Esther is the most convincing person I know and soon persuades him there's plenty to share. He takes one and savors each bite. I wonder when he last ate—he is so thin.

We drive in silence until we reach San Jose, where everyone gets out. Stefano and Esther collect their things.

Saying goodbye to Martin, Evie, and the kids was painful, but this is excruciating. I fight back tears when Esther grabs me in a tight embrace. I've never known life without her—none of my siblings have.

"You are Lola to me," I tell her.

"Oh, Cara. You are a young woman now. It will be okay. I'll see you again." Esther kisses my cheek. "We will see each other again. Yes? Take care of your brother." She glances at Enzo, who is kicking pebbles into grooves at the side of the road.

"I will."

Papa hands money to Stefano. "You and the children need this." Stefano refuses Papa's offer.

"I insist," Papa says.

Reluctantly, Stefano accepts. Papa gives him a little more while saying something out of my earshot. They shake hands. Then we watch as Stefano, Esther, and the old man disappear into the trees.

Everyone is quiet as our vehicle lumbers down the road once more.

"Will they be okay?" I ask.

"I believe so," Papa says.

"How can you be sure?"

"We must have hope, Cara. Without hope, we have nothing."

"And the old man . . . How will he make it?" He'd struggled so much on the flat, dusty road. I can't imagine how he'd fare on the rocky terrain deep in the hills.

"He's strong. He made it from town halfway to the hills. Stefano will arrange transport to his son's home once they get to the outskirts of the town."

That's what the extra money was for, I realize. I lean back, sticky from the heat, grateful Papa cares so much. He knows how to take care of people. He knows how to take care of us. Everything will be all right.

6

Rosa

DECEMBER 23, 1941

Florence, Italy

"No, no! Again, Rosa. Again!" Maestro taps his heel emphatically from the first row of Teatro Fiorentino. I don't know what's gotten into me. Today is my first time singing on such a grand stage. But that isn't what unsettles me. The professor's low marks at quarterlies grate in my mind. I shake my head as if to toss my muddied thoughts to the tawny wood-planked floor.

My gaze falls on the sweeping burgundy stage curtains. The rich color brings to mind one of Papa's prized rosebushes. I close my eyes and will myself to think of our garden back home in Floridablanca. I can almost smell a hint of the blooms. Hear the rustling palm trees swaying in the gentle, warm breeze. It calms my nerves.

I inhale deeply, then sing the refrain again. This time my breathing flows more naturally, falling at the right intervals. Maestro instructs me to sing the entire piece again. Halfway through, light spills in from the back door of the theater. With the brightness of the stage lights, I can't see who has entered. Ignoring it, I reach the final note of "Il Dolce Suono" from *Lucia di Lammermoor*.

"*Molto bene,* Rosa! Very good! We'll start again after the holiday," Maestro says, smiling warmly.

"Thank you, Maestro." I descend the stage, relieved to have finally gotten the timing of my breathing right.

My eyes adjust to the darkness as I gather my things and make my way down the center aisle. The theater is elegant with its plush seats and gilded adornments.

As I walk, I hear a clap, followed by another, and another. My gaze searches the empty seats until I spot the applauder. In the back row near the wall is Ciro.

"*Perfezione,* Rosa Grassi." His words drip with charm.

I raise my eyebrows and smirk. "Enjoying the dark, are you?"

"Enjoying the performance—and the view. The soprano is a friend of mine. We are quite close. And she is beautiful. *Bellissima!*" He winks, and I shake my head at his antics.

"I finished my shift at conservatory and came looking for you. I'm starving, Rosa. *Ho fame!* Let's eat!" He jumps up and helps me into my coat.

"Only if you promise not to speak of *il governo* again."

"I make no promises." He gives a rakish grin and bends his elbow for me to link my arm through.

I last saw him days ago at Nonna's apartment to celebrate his twentieth birthday. A philosophy student at the University of Florence, Ciro is passionate about how Italy should be—an empire for its people. His regular criticism of Duce and the government is risky, and I worry about his recklessness.

"You know, the Philippines has had considerable success in its efforts toward democracy and independence," I had told him after listening to his latest thoughts on the regime the last time we met. He scoffed in response, saying, "Not just a prima donna of opera but of ideas." I presume he said that because I'm a woman. Now, to keep the peace, I leave the politicking to him.

I take his arm, and we saunter to a small café to tame our midday hunger. We share panini with prosciutto and a small amount of pecorino cheese.

"*Mamma mia*, to have another piece of that cake," Ciro says, downing his espresso.

My mouth waters at the thought of the *pan di Spagna*—a sponge cake doused with rum and filled with vanilla pastry cream. The owner of the *pasticceria* where Nonna purchased Ciro's birthday cake is a friend, and he made it especially at her request. "You need to have another birthday so we can have more cake," I say.

He laughs, and his dimpled cheeks make him look younger than his twenty years. A lone ray of sunshine peeks through the window lighting our table.

When we first met, I thought Ciro brash. But his charm and confidence are something to behold. The girls at conservatory follow him with longing gazes, and he savors every moment. He's hard to resist with his mop of honeyed curls and strong Roman features. No doubt he is handsome, charming, and—trouble.

But he's a close friend of Nonna's, and he's my only friend in Florence. Training hasn't left much time for friendship.

Yet his invitation to have lunch at the café is a surprise. We've only spent time together with Nonna at her apartment and villa. Never just the two of us. "I thought you came to speak with Maestro," I say.

"Maestro? No, I came to see you, *amore mio*." His tone is suave. I laugh, grinning at his look of mock hurt. He pulls a book from his worn canvas bag. "Have you read *Il Principe*?"

I shake my head, readying myself for his thoughts. His insatiable appetite for reading makes for interesting conversation.

"You should, Rosa. Machiavelli is a master of governance. I would give you my copy, but I need it for class."

"My Papa read Machiavelli."

"He is a learned gentleman."

"I didn't say he liked it."

"A man who doesn't like Machiavelli is no man. Of course he liked it."

I stifle my laughter at his bold assumption. But the mention of my father brings to mind the crouching fear that my family may be in danger.

Without pause, Ciro's bravado softens into concern. "Nonna said you have family in the mountains?"

"*Sì*, Tia and Tio."

"I'm sure your father would have sought refuge if he thought it was necessary. Yes?"

I nod, knowing Papa would do whatever is needed to protect our family. And Tia and Tio's farm is the most likely place for them to go. The news announcer did say people were fleeing the larger towns and Manila. I put on a brave face, knowing full well there is no way to know if my family has fled Floridablanca and, even if they have, if they're okay.

"You never speak of your family, Ciro." In all the time Ciro and I have known each other, not once has he mentioned his parents. He spends a lot of time with Nonna and Maestro. Nonna treats him like a son. A most mischievous one, to be sure. But her door is always open to him, and he often joins us for meals.

His eyes darken, and I immediately regret bringing up his family.

Fidgeting with his spoon, he glances out the window. "There's not much to say. I'm an only child. My mother died when I was eleven. A weak heart, they said. And my papa . . . He died when I was sixteen."

"Oh, Ciro, I'm so sorry." Instinctively, I reach for his hand. An attempt to offer some semblance of comfort.

At the gesture, a glint of charm flickers in his eyes, and I know he's covering his grief. I've done the same.

"They said it was an explosion that killed him."

I gasp, horrified.

"It was because of his views on this. On all of this." His gaze rakes over the people at the surrounding tables. There are a few Blackshirts and some everyday folks out for a quick bite. He's speaking quietly, but I find myself squeezing his hand and hoping he'll not do something rash with the Blackshirts just a few tables away.

"My uncle took me in. Supported me until I got the job at the conservatory a few years ago."

From Ciro's tone, I assume he and his uncle aren't close. It makes sense now. When Ciro started doing odd jobs at the music school, he met Nonna and Maestro. I'm glad he's found family with them. The idea of not being close to my family is foreign to me.

"My mother would have liked you. A true Italian girl. Traditional."

At his words, I don't even try to stop my unladylike cackle. The thought makes me grin. I question how my voice training halfway around the world qualifies as traditional. Duce's highest calling for women is to be homemakers and mothers, not opera singers.

A couple at a table nearby stand up. As they make their way to the door, I realize I've no idea how long we've been here and glance at my watch. "Oh *mio*! I have to go." If I don't leave now, I'll be late for my music theory class. I reach into my purse to pay.

"Absolutely not." Ciro pulls some banknotes from his pocket.

"I have money!"

"No! This is not for you to do." He stands and pays the bill, and I wonder at the absurdity. Why is it so off-putting for a woman to have money of her own? I don't have much. But I can pay my way.

He holds the door open for me as we exit the café. "Tell Nonna I'll be by later to fix the stove."

"*Grazie!* I will."

He flashes me a dimpled smile. We part ways as I head to conservatory and Ciro turns toward the university.

7

Caramina

Golden sunshine streaks across the bed. I glance from side to side, my pulse quickening in confusion. The unfamiliar room comes into focus. Then I remember. I'm not at home.

Early this morning, after a long and arduous drive overnight, we arrived at my aunt and uncle's farm deep in the jungle. I was so exhausted that I nearly wept at the sight of Tia and Tio's house.

Framed by the lush foliage of a hill and set apart by a meandering stream covered with a wooden bridge, their home still takes my breath away. As a child, I considered it the perfect castle.

More modern than the nipa huts native to the jungle villages, the bungalow is built of hardwoods, *ipil* and *narra,* with a large veranda in front and an enclosed porch overlooking the backyard. A generator provides electricity for lighting, small appliances (including an icebox), and the pump system designed by Tio that allows for indoor plumbing. Tia has worked hard to make their home inviting, sewing curtains and the throw pillows that are scattered on the sofa and chairs, and filling the house with the mouth-watering scents of her delicious cooking. Set in the back of a meadow, the house is hidden by a surrounding canopy of trees. Beside it, Tio's rice fields fall away in graduated steps in a small valley. Green terraced plots built into limestone stand proudly meeting the sun.

Papa said we'd be safer here. After pulling up to the house, we found Tia in back hanging wet clothes to dry. She threw down the shirt she was holding and ran over to hug each of us tight.

"Isabella. You're a grown woman! And you, Caramina. My goodness, you're a young lady now! Beautiful, both of you!" she'd said.

Her lips had crinkled into a smirk as she peeked around me to see Enzo. "But oh *mio*. Who is this boy? Where is Enzo, the little one?"

Enzo appeared thrilled to think he'd grown beyond recognition. "Tia! It's me!"

"What? You are Enzo?"

"Yes! I'm grown, too. See!" Enzo stood tall, stretching his arms and puffing out his chest to impress.

"The eyes are the same. The hair is curly like Enzo's. The voice . . . a little lower. Come give me a hug and I'll know it's you."

Enzo had run into Tia's arms and squeezed her tight. I laughed, knowing Enzo would've picked up Tia to prove his strength if he could.

"Enzo! It is you! My, how you've grown. It's been too many years. How old are you now?"

"I'm eight!" Enzo said triumphantly. His attempt to mimic Papa's voice made me smile.

Afterward, Tia took us to the kitchen and I was thrilled to see her produce a plate piled with the banana-leaf-wrapped treat *suman*. We nearly finished off the entire stack of sticky, sweet coconut rice bars as famished as we all were.

Now, after napping well into the afternoon, I draw back my bedsheet. It doesn't seem possible so much has happened over such a short time. The mirror atop the small curio won't let me forget the ruby crescent-shaped scab on my cheek. I'm tempted to leave my hair down to hide the blemish. But instead, I brush my hair and secure it with a mother-of-pearl barrette. A birthday gift from Esther. Then I head to the kitchen.

"Hello there, sleepyhead," Isabella says.

I throw a smirk her way and perch myself on a chair. "What can I do, Tia?"

"I'm glad you were able to rest, Cara. I'm just about to roll these. If you want, you can help." Tia points to a savory meat mixture, the filling for the egg rolls.

I bring the bowl to the table where thin *lumpia* wrappers rest on a plate. Isabella joins me, setting down a large platter.

Carefully, I pry a wrapper from the stack. I manage to loosen one without tearing it, then place it in front of me. I lay a spoonful of the mixture in the center of the *lumpia*. Tia places a small bowl of water on the table. I dip my fingers and run them along the edge of the wrapper before rolling it into a perfect, tiny egg roll. Tia sits opposite me, and the three of us roll together, chatting as if no time has passed since our last visit.

I tell Tia about one of Isabella's admirers, much to my sister's dismay. Diego was a regular visitor to our home. Isabella waves her hand, shushing me.

"No reason to be embarrassed," says Tia. "If he isn't the one, he isn't the one. But you can't blame the young man for falling for such a beautiful young woman."

I smile seeing Isabella blush at Tia's words. My sister is beautiful. But whenever a compliment is given to her, she looks as if she wants to run and hide.

"One time he sang to her. She hid in her room till evening, refusing to come out."

Tia chuckles.

"Why couldn't he just listen? I said I wasn't interested," says Isabella.

"Ah men! They say we're a mystery. Bah! It's they who are a puzzle. When you meet the right one, you will know. Like I did with your tio." Tia's face softens, as it always does when she talks about my uncle.

Tio is the love of her life. And it seems their twenty-five years together have only made them sweeter on each other. It isn't that way with some of the couples I know from our neighborhood. Mama and Papa were the exception. They'd been married for many years when Mama had Enzo, and they always seemed in love. Maybe Tia is right, when you meet the right one, you know. And perhaps, love grows even stronger through the years.

"When I met Tio, we were so young. But the moment I saw him, I knew he was the one. We were at Victoria Ramos's debut. Your mother was there. I knew her from school, but I had never met her older brother. When he asked me to dance, I was so excited I nearly tripped walking onto the dance floor. I kept thinking, *How have I never seen him before?* I was the only one he asked." Tia pauses, happily lost in the memory. "Oh, there were many other girls interested in this mysterious young man. But no, he asked only me.

"After that night, he kept calling on me. My father would see him coming down the street and say, 'Again?' We were married within the year. It was all I ever wanted . . . to fall in love and marry. What Filipina doesn't want to settle down and have a family?"

"Some of us are in love with other things." Isabella tips her head toward me.

I wipe my sticky hands on a towel. "I want to sing. Nonna's promised to take me to Italy. I'm to voice train like Rosa when I turn sixteen. Imagine singing in a place of such beauty."

A puzzled look flashes on Tia's face. Tia has never fully understood why Rosa went to Italy. She never said she disapproved of Rosa's decision, but she'd hoped Rosa would marry and settle down like most Filipinas.

"One day I'll get married, but there's so much I want to do first," I say.

"He'll have to love music as much as you do. Maybe he'll be a singer, and the two of you can spend your nights serenading each other." Isabella throws her arms out wide. She lifts her face high, pretending to sing, eyes squinted in mock emotion.

In response, I grab the towel and throw it her way. Tiny pieces of filling stuck to the towel come loose midair and land on the floor.

"Cara!" Isabella chides me, and Tia laughs.

"This war . . . Well, we don't know how long it will last." Tia sighs as if it depends upon her to settle matters. "You might change your mind, Cara. And there is nothing wrong if you do."

"Even if it takes ten years, I still want to go and sing." I'm adamant. It has never occurred to me that I wouldn't follow in Nonna's footsteps. No matter what, I intend to do so.

Isabella exhales. Tia says nothing but stands to carry an empty plate to the sink. The door swings open abruptly.

"Gabriel!" Tia wipes her hands quickly and embraces the young man now standing in the middle of the kitchen.

"Gabriel, these are my nieces, Isabella and Caramina." He hands a basket brimming with fruit to Tia.

"It's nice to meet you." Isabella shakes his hand.

"Yes, and you as well," he says.

"Hello." I glance up from the *lumpia* I'm rolling. He catches my eye for a moment, but I quickly look away.

"Thank you so much for the fruit, Gabriel," says Tia.

"Of course. There's still quite a bit at the market. Not sure how long that will last."

"Let's hope it continues." Tia pulls a mango from the basket and places it in a bowl. "Gabriel's been helping Tio since he was a boy. Makes the trip all the way out here from Timbales a few times a week, and usually arrives just before dinner." Tia smirks and ruffles Gabriel's hair.

"You know I can't pass up your adobo."

Tia smiles wide. "Gabriel's a jack-of-all-trades. He helps out in town, too. So much, the townsfolk have nicknamed him Mayor." Pride sweeps across Tia's face, and Gabriel's cheeks redden.

"Are you here for a while? I mean with the war and all?" he asks, looking my way.

"We think so. Of course, it's up to our father," says Isabella.

"It'll be nice to have you all here. I just met your brother, Matteo."

"You should stay for dinner. We have plenty," says Tia.

"*Salamat po*, thank you. Maybe another time, I need to get back. But first, I'll go help Matteo. He was chopping wood by the shed." He then looks my way and says, "It was a pleasure to meet you both."

"And you, too." Isabella says.

I can feel Gabriel's gaze on me. His staring is unnerving. My cheeks are on fire, and I keep my eyes glued to the *lumpia*. "Yes," I say quickly, wishing he'd just disappear.

"Stop back in before you leave. I have something for you." Tia places the now full bowl of fruit on the table.

It isn't until I hear the door shut that I dare look up. Both Tia and Isabella are watching me, smiling. Immediately, I turn back to the plate speckled with *lumpia* filling.

"I'm getting Enzo up. Otherwise, he won't sleep tonight," Isabella says, leaving the room. I can hear her chuckling as she runs up the stairs.

Minutes later, I race upstairs and flop onto my bed, face red with embarrassment. After a few moments, I pull myself up and unearth the bundle of letters I brought from home. Reading Rosa's and Nonna's words is always a comfort. Plucking one from the ribbon-tied batch, I unfold the delicate paper. It's from Rosa. She sent it when she first arrived in Italy.

September 30, 1938

My Dearest Caramina,

Buon giorno! For such an old city, Florence is so vibrant. So many people are pursuing their art here. And one day you will, too, Cara.

Yesterday, Nonna and I strolled the Boboli Gardens with its peonies in full bloom. Afterward, we sipped tiny cups of espresso and nibbled sweet pastry at a café. Delizioso!

Maestro Silvieri is not easily impressed. My first day I left in tears. Nonna assured me he has a tender heart. Mostly, my sessions have been filled with practicing technique. Scales and arpeggios without end. From the way Maestro stomps his feet to keep time, I was certain he was disappointed. But the other day he stopped me abruptly and said I was ready to begin the "Dove Sono" from Figaro. Then he presented me with a plate of sweets. Perhaps a kind heart beats behind that marble exterior after all.

The bell tower is chiming. I must hurry and not keep Maestro waiting. Keep singing and give my love to everyone.

Much love,
Rosa

Rosa's words are reassuring. Surely this war will be over soon. I carefully place the letter back in the bundle before heading downstairs again. Enzo and Isabella are already at the table. Papa and Tio are washing their hands, as Tia balances a teetering platter of adobo. My mouth waters at the scent of the salty, tangy pork.

"Caramina, could you get the rice, please?" Tia gingerly sets down the platter, taking care not to spill the rich juices.

I grab the bowl, piled high with white rice, and place it on the table.

"There she is!" Tio says. "The last time I saw you, you were only this tall, Cara." He holds his hand out about chest height. "Look at you! Must be your papa's pasta, yes?"

Papa laughs, and I kiss Tio on the cheek. "I'm fourteen, Tio."

"Ah, I see . . . Well, you look like you are sixteen!"

"Not so soon!" Papa protests, shaking his head. We sit, and Tio holds the rice bowl out as Papa spoons fluffy white kernels onto his plate.

"Okay, okay." Tio laughs. "Well, you certainly are a beautiful young lady."

Tio has always been kind to me. People that don't know my uncle well assume he's a simple farmer. But even in his work clothes, he is distinguished and self-assured. He may have chosen this life, but he lived a very different one when he and Mama were young. My grandparents had seen to it that Mama and her older brother were well educated and cultured. Had he wanted, Tio could have chosen life in a town like Floridablanca or in the metropolis of Manila. Instead, he chose a simpler life and never looked back.

Matteo joins us, and Tio says grace. Conversation flows easily even after too much time apart. We chat about friends and family. Papa, Tio, and Tia reminisce about their lives before I or any of my siblings was born. Talk of Mama is sprinkled throughout the meal. Remembering her through the eyes of those who loved her, especially Tio, is like cool rain on my heart. He tells stories of Mama's antics growing up and from when she first met Papa.

"I can still see her face when you dropped those eggs," Tio says.

Papa sighs. "What can I say, I wanted to impress her." He chuckles, a sheepish grin on his face.

"We tried to warn you, Arturo, but you wouldn't listen." Tia faces me. "He was sure he could juggle those eggs. Reached right into that bowl, grabbing how many? Three? Four? I don't remember. I do remember them falling . . . Splat! Splat! All over the clean floor."

"And Eva didn't say a word." Papa laughs, his eyes lit with happiness.

"She said if you really could juggle, the eggs would be safe." Tio laughs.

"How was I to know they weren't hard-boiled? It was the day before Easter, and they were just resting in that bowl."

"The look on her face, when they hit the floor one by one!" Tia shakes her head, chuckling.

"The look on your face, Arturo! Ah, I'd never seen you so surprised." Tio slaps Papa's shoulder good-naturedly. "It was worth seeing you red-faced."

"I suffered for love." Papa shrugs, grinning.

"Well, clearly she didn't fall for your juggling skills," says Tia.

"She did ask me to dance after that." Papa gives a satisfied smile. Seeing him this way makes my heart happy.

Papa stands and switches on the radio. "All right, that's enough of tales." We huddle close to listen to KGEI from San Francisco, one of the few stations we can get over the shortwave. We listen intently when the news announcer mentions Italy. I thought Rosa and Nonna were safe in the heart of Italy. I'd not given much thought to their being in danger. But the concern on Papa's face makes me queasy.

> *"In other news, we turn to the Pacific. Since the Japanese bomb-ings of our air bases, Clark, Nichols, and Del Carmen in the Philippines, the Japanese have landed on Luzon at the Lingayen Gulf in the Northwest, and they are advancing toward Manila."*

The announcer continues, detailing the Japanese attacks in the Philippines.

Papa sits, eyes closed. Lines crinkle his forehead as he takes in the news. No one makes a sound. It's as if we're waiting for instructions. Yet no directions come. The news broadcast ends, and the announcer introduces Glenn Miller's "Chattanooga Choo Choo."

Music crackles, and Enzo spins circles in front of the couch. He grabs my hand for me to join him. But I don't budge. Since the bombs first exploded into our lives, Papa has said little to me about the war. And, frankly, I didn't want to know. But seeing the concern on everyone's faces now, I need to know. I listen for any assurance everything will be all right.

"Roberto got word the Japanese are also fighting hard toward Bataan." Tio opens a cigar box and offers it to Papa. "The United States doesn't run from a fight, and neither do we. We'll run them off soon enough." Tio puffs his cigar, sending little clouds of smoke floating.

"They've been planning this for some time. Their strikes have been well organized. Likely, they've been planning for years. All for a Greater East Asia." Papa spits out his last words and shakes his head in disgust.

Matteo told me Greater East Asia is the name the Japanese have given to their dream and is supposedly the reason for their attack.

"Their idea of a Greater East Asia is to take what isn't theirs. They want to be gods. Men lusting for power." Papa's voice drops off.

Most adults I know are excited about the Philippines becoming independent. Back in 1934 American President Franklin Roosevelt signed a treaty promising it independence on July 4, 1946, after a transitional period. After over three hundred years of Spanish rule and almost fifty years as a U.S. territory, we would finally become an independent nation. Then the Japanese attacked. What will happen now?

Matteo shoots up in his chair. "MacArthur won't let them get away with this."

"MacArthur will do what he can," Papa says, "but he isn't in control."

"We'll stop them. We're strong. We'll fight!" Matteo snaps, and I wince at his boldness.

"You have no idea what they're capable of." Papa's jaw is set tight. "Or what it means to fight."

Matteo shakes his head. I can tell he's about to burst. He wants to counter Papa, but he holds back instead. Not only is there a war to be concerned about, but now Matteo's disagreements with Papa have become more frequent. I don't know if he's directing his angst over having to say goodbye to Anna at Papa or if he's upset over something else. Either way, it's unlike them to be at odds.

The room is silent until Tio speaks. "Your father is right, Matteo. War is the last thing any of us want. Sometimes it's necessary to fight to protect those you love. But it's never something to be taken lightly. I don't think you do. But it's something I wished none of us would ever have to see. And yet, here we are. So, we do what we have to."

The song crackles in the background, the lively brass out of place amid the tensions of war.

8

Rosa

DECEMBER 25, 1941

Fiesole, Italy

"*ttento!* Careful!" Beatrice scolds Ciro. She hugs the Tiffany lamp to her bosom, protecting it from the wayward branches of the tree he's dragging through the front hallway.

Perched high in the hills overlooking Florence is Nonna's Fiesole villa. Despite its warm amber stone exterior, it is slow to heat even with fires blazing in its fireplaces. I tug my cardigan close around my shoulders and shut the door, then follow Ciro into the living room where Nonna waits. The box of glass baubles she's unearthed from the attic rests at her feet.

We hang ornaments by firelight. Now and then, Beatrice joins us after wiping her hands on a kitchen towel. The savory scents of her cooking drift into the room, and my stomach grumbles.

When we arrived a few hours ago, it was colder than Esther's icebox back home. Beatrice was already buzzing about lighting the fires and making up the beds. She reminds me so much of Esther.

"I've known your papa since he was a baby, Rosa," she says, seeing me looking at a family portrait.

"Beatrice started helping me before your father was born, and she has been ever since," Nonna says.

"Your nonna and I have had some good times. *Sì*, Serafina?" Beatrice glances at Nonna. The two smile the warm smile of long-time friends.

Nonna chuckles and stands to hang an aquamarine bulb that glints in the firelight. "Remember how Arturo used to steal your biscotti, Bea?"

Beatrice laughs as she sits on the fading emerald velvet sofa that gives way to her weight. "*Sì!* Especially my *biscotti al cioccolato e mandorle*. I'd barely have pulled them from the oven, and he'd sneak in and grab a handful while I cleaned. He thought I didn't know. Ha! I always knew. But how could I be cross? Such an adorable boy. Big brown eyes like a puppy, and curly hair that could never be tamed— Oh my! I'd better check on the pasta," Beatrice interrupts herself, attempting to jump up but slowed by her girth.

A knock sounds at the door. "That will be Antonino," Nonna says.

"I'll . . ." Beatrice looks torn between answering the door and the thought of her pasta overcooking.

"No, no! I'll get it." Nonna heads to the front hallway, and Beatrice sighs with relief as she hurries to the kitchen to save our dinner.

It's tradition for Maestro to join us at Christmas. Every year since I've been in Florence, Nonna has also invited Ciro. He usually declines since he visits his uncle in Milan at this time of year, so I was surprised to hear he accepted. But I gladly welcome his company.

The four of us sit around Nonna's antique mahogany table to enjoy the meal Beatrice prepared. Once all the dishes have been brought to serve, Beatrice joins us. Her *penne al ragù* is superb. Though there is less beef than usual, Beatrice worked wonders with what little she had. Nowadays, meat is a luxury. Each bite is delectable, and I have to force myself not to finish every last drop of the sauce.

Along with the meal, we share a bottle of Chianti that Nonna has unearthed from the cellar. Afterward, Beatrice joins us in the living room by the crackling fire, and we enjoy her *torta di mandorle*. Her almond cake is one of Nonna's favorites, and I can see why. I indulge myself by having two pieces—as do the others.

Afterward, we hang more ornaments by the persimmon light of the fire. Beatrice heads to the dining room to clean up. But Nonna waves her off and tells her to go home to rest. Though reluctant to leave, she agrees. When Nonna goes in search of the jars of apricot jam she and Beatrice canned last summer that she intends to give as gifts, Maestro follows her into the kitchen.

Ciro and I hear them speaking softly. He refills our glasses and plops down next to me by the fire. "They're in love," he says.

"Don't be ridiculous. They're friends. Good friends."

"Good friends fall in love," Ciro says matter-of-factly. He sets his hand over his heart and smirks. "Oh, Serafina, *la mia bella farfalla*. My beautiful butterfly." His face drips with mock emotion.

"And you, Antonino, the breeze that lifts my heart," I say.

At this, we break into a fit of laughter. When it subsides, Ciro leans in closer. "You know they're working together. Helping the partisans."

"No! I don't believe it," I say, stunned at his words.

"Why do you think they always meet secretly?" He waits for my response, then says, "You know, your father was quite a resistance fighter."

Now he's being ridiculous. What does he know about my father? "Papa?"

"Why do you think he never returned to Italy?"

I take a deep breath and face him directly. "Because he fell in love with a Filipina, had five children, and has to support them all without the help of his beloved wife—on the other side of the

world," I scoff. "You and your theories! Must everything have to do
with politics?"

"Absolutely." He then tells me he is in a resistance group with
Nonna and Maestro fighting to overthrow Duce and his regime. "In
a time like this, we have no choice but to take a side. What will you
do, Rosa?" From the look on his face, I can't tell if he's challenging
me or playing games.

It's absolute nonsense. Nonna and Maestro in the Resistance?
And Papa? Clearly, Ciro has no idea what he's talking about—
though his own involvement with the partisans doesn't seem so far-
fetched.

"Of course, I'm opposed to Duce. But I'm no politician, soldier,
or spy. I'm grateful to those who work to stop such evil. But I came
here to voice train. That's it. And I'd appreciate it if you didn't bring
this up again!"

Fear courses through me as I speak. Doesn't he know what the
regime is capable of? Even a hint of such things is dangerous. If
anyone overheard us . . . I don't want to think what might happen.

A flare sparks in his cool green eyes as they widen in shock, and
a satisfied grin spreads across his face. *Mio Dio,* is he handsome!
How many other girls has he urged to take a side? I wonder. Just
last week, I spotted him with a tall blonde in the conservatory courtyard. A violinist, I believe. Giggling like a schoolgirl, she tossed her
golden locks over her shoulder as the two whispered. I can certainly
understand his appeal. Being in his orbit is like basking in the rays
of the sun.

Gazing at me, his cheeks dimpled, he moves closer. The musky
scent of his aftershave mixes with the fire's smokiness. His stubble
grazes my cheek, then his lips meet mine. A warm flush rises along
my back. At that very moment, a clatter shatters the silence. Nonna
and Maestro rush into the room, and we pull apart.

"Just an ornament," Ciro says, reassuring Nonna as he retrieves
the still spinning bauble from the floor.

I watch as he restores the bulb to its place on the tree. My heart is unsettled by Ciro's behavior, and my mind frazzled at the reality that every day brings something new to fear. I want those I love to be safe. But under the regime, life seems more and more precarious.

The ornament glints in the firelight. At least it survived its fall.

9

Caramina

In the weeks since we arrived, life on the farm has taken on a new sense of normality. News comes regularly from Gabriel. He reports on battles won and lost by the Americans and Filipinos against the Japanese as well as the goings-on in nearby Timbales, a quaint hamlet with just over five hundred residents. The residents, according to Tio, are understandably on edge, wondering when and if the Japanese will descend and occupy town. Despite this, our day-to-day affairs remain mostly unchanged. People go to work and church. Children chase each other throughout the plaza and play kickball. Just like years ago.

"I don't remember it being so quiet here."

"Quiet is good, Cara." Tia smiles and hands me a papaya. My reward for helping her deep clean the kitchen this morning.

I carry it to the front porch and sit down with a bowl teetering on my lap as I slice into the juicy fruit. As I take my first bite, I spy a man emerge from the jungle and cross the bridge. Startled, I almost drop the bowl, spilling juice onto my legs.

The man is in military uniform. A rifle at his side swings as he strides toward the house. I don't recognize the uniform. It's not like those worn by the soldiers on the U.S. air bases near home.

"Hello there!" he says, smiling warmly.

I don't know whether to scream and run or say hello. Before I can respond, the front door swings open and Papa appears. "Good to see you, old friend," Papa says, smiling as he shakes his hand. "Caramina, this is Captain Torres."

"Hello," I say, wondering how they know each other.

"Good to meet you." The captain gives Papa news of fighting in the Bataan area, which isn't far from our home in Floridablanca. I listen intently.

"They're fierce fighters," he says about the Americans battling to stop the Japanese. "But they're fighting with limited supplies." He shakes his head. "All the grit in the world won't help against a military better outfitted."

"Let's hope it's not a losing battle," Papa says.

"My men and I are doing whatever we can to help," Torres says, and I wonder what he means.

"Well, I should get back. But it's good to see you, Arturo. Anything you need, just send word."

Papa thanks him and shakes his hand again. Then the captain crosses the bridge and disappears through the trees.

"Isa's ready, Cara. Time for school," Papa tells me, and I stand to go inside and begin my studies for the day.

Papa is insistent we keep a schedule similar to what we had at home and expects all of us to contribute while at the farm and to continue our schooling. My main responsibility is to watch Enzo once our schoolwork is finished. This frees up Isabella to help Tia with housework and meals. Papa and Matteo are helping Tio in the fields. Even Enzo has a job feeding the chickens each morning.

Along with doing schoolwork and minding Enzo, I keep practicing my singing, since Papa has encouraged me to not stop voice training. Without a piano, it's more difficult. But he brought his gramophone, along with records of some of the operas he loves. In his words, music is fortifying for the soul.

Balancing studying, practicing, and watching Enzo is more challenging than I anticipated. He's always impatient to play outside, and he finishes his schoolwork before I do. Earlier this morning, I promised him if he stays in the house while I practice, we'll go swimming or exploring afterward.

After my schoolwork, I practice my scales. When I finally finish, I find Enzo devouring a banana in the kitchen. Before I say a word, he jumps up from the table and races out the back door.

When I catch up to him, he's in the shallows of the stream in front of the house. His eyes are set on the trees in the distance. I squint to see what has captured his attention. The stillness of the branches is broken by an abrupt jutting movement.

"I think it's a boar. Come on!" He tears off down the stream and over the bridge after the mysterious beast into the jungle.

"Enzo! Wait!" I chase after him. When I reach the tree line, I can see him standing knee-deep in the water.

"You can't catch me!" He races farther down the stream, and I follow.

Before I reach him, he freezes. A wild boar stands hunched on the shoreline. The animal is perfectly still. I can hear its labored breathing over the gurgling water. Then it drops its head and gives a snarling grunt so loud I jump. Enzo whimpers but doesn't move.

The boar stomps its hoof, splashing wet dirt in splotches all over its body. The animal glares at me. Then it rears its head, tusks flailing through its coarse, swarthy hair.

"Run, Enzo! Run!" I scream.

For a moment, he doesn't move. Then he races away from the stream. The boar lets out another loud grunt. Its hooves hit the ground, and it gives chase. Enzo darts through the dense foliage, pushing through the breaks where he is small enough to fit.

I race behind, torn between running to the farm for help and staying with Enzo. Anything would be better than facing this wild animal. But I don't dare leave my brother, so I chase after the two.

Through the trees, I can just make out Enzo with the boar not far behind. A thick branch lies in the dirt a few yards ahead. I swoop my arm low and grab it. Something skitters across my hand, and I muffle a scream when I see the long, shiny brown body of a millipede snaking along the stick. I smack it hard against a tree, sending the insect flying. I continue to race after the boar. *Please let it stop,* I beg silently. I've no idea what to do with the branch. But it might help ward off the animal, and it's all I have. My hands tremble as I grip it tight.

The boar continues chase for so long, I'm sure an hour has passed when, all of a sudden, it halts abruptly. With a deep-bellied grunt, it spins around, facing me with a toothy snarl.

My hands shake violently, and I nearly drop the branch. I steady myself and hold the limb out like a sword. The beast rears its head. I squint my eyes, bracing for it to charge. The boar gives one loud snort.

I cringe, peeking one eye open in time to see the animal spin and race off into the trees. I gasp in relief, knees wobbly. I look down at the branch I'm clutching, my knuckles white.

Enzo stands a few yards away, watching. His eyes fall to my makeshift sword, and he giggles. I must be a mud-splotched mess with hair stuck to my face and sticking out all over.

He grins. "You look like a crazy knight."

I shake my head, wanting to scold him for having been so careless and running wild through the jungle. But I know there was nothing he could've done when the animal gave chase. I glance at the stick in my hands and laugh. I'm still holding it out, wielding it like a bolo. I pry my tingling fingers from the crude weapon and throw it to one side.

Then it hits me. I have no idea where we are. The trees around us hang so thick the foliage blocks sunlight from filtering through.

My eyes flit back and forth, searching. There is no path. My heart thumps as it dawns on me: We're lost.

Being lost in the jungle scares me nearly as much as facing the boar. The last thing I want is to alarm Enzo. I breathe slowly to calm myself and steady my voice. "Do you know which way we came?"

Enzo scans the area. "Sure, this way." He points to the trees on his right. He is confident, but I'm not convinced. He pushes his way through the growth.

"Wait! Why don't we listen for the stream?" If we can hear the sound of water, it should lead us back to the farm. Enzo comes close, and we stand listening.

"I don't hear anything. Are we lost?" His voice cracks.

I turn away quickly so he doesn't see the fear in my eyes. I scan the area, desperately hoping that this is the way. But my mind is fuzzy with panic. I fight to keep calm, gripping my fists tight, nails pinching into tender palms.

"This way," I say, pushing through the trees and motioning for him to follow. We walk for some time, neither of us hearing the water. Then there is a noise. I stop to listen with Enzo close behind.

"I want to go back," he whines, digging his heel in the dirt.

"I hear something," I whisper. The sound comes again. "I think it's a voice." Maybe we've made it back to the farm, and it's one of Tio's workers.

"Come on." I push away the foliage. Soon other voices sound from behind a grove of trees. But it's so dense I can't see anything. We make our way in the maze of green, snaking through the heavy growth rising from the jungle floor.

A sliver of light breaks through the wall of leaves. On the other side is a clearing, so hidden no one would ever have guessed it was there. A single hut stands at the far end of the grassy field. There has to be a path somewhere, if I can just find it. We continue pushing our way through the trees to the other side of the clearing near the hut.

We go a small distance, and I draw back a branch. Surely someone here can help us. I grab at another branch twisted heavily in
vines, just as a scream pierces the air.

I freeze, and Enzo smacks into me. I spin to face him. Tears
begin pouring down his cheeks, and he rubs his head. He opens his
mouth to speak, but I thrust my hand over his lips. I pry back the
green leaves blocking our view. Another scream shoots out. A pri-
mal scream.

Through a crack in the foliage, I spot four men standing by a
tree with their arms held up. Their hands are tied to a large branch
directly above them. One of the men looks familiar, like one of the
guerrilla soldiers we passed on the trip to Tia and Tio's farm. In
front of them, another man stands rigid, holding a rifle. He wears a
military uniform of drab brownish green, different from that of the
men tied to the tree.

Two of the men are badly beaten, their faces and hands bloodied. Tears cloud my vision, and I blink to focus. I gasp in horror:
Their hands aren't tied to the branch. Their thumbs have been
nailed to the wood. I swallow a scream. My stomach twists, filling
my mouth with bitterness.

One of the men nailed to the tree is young. A boy, really. He
can't be more than a year or two younger than me. Another man in
uniform stands far back from the group. The soldier by the tree
yells in a language I don't recognize. He draws back his rifle and
brings the stock of the gun down quickly, slamming it on the young
man's head.

The boy's head flops forward. The soldier pulls the rifle back
again, then swings hard, beating the boy in the ribs. He flogs him
relentlessly, yelling as he strikes him. He yells again and again. The
soldier's screaming is amplified by the silence of the boy. Then the
soldier stops. He lifts the rifle and takes aim at the boy's head.

A woman's scream bursts out. I spin my head to see a woman
crouched at the foot of the other soldier, sobbing. She grabs at his
legs, desperately begging for mercy for the boy. The soldier smiles

down at her. For a moment, her eyes widen, full of hope. Then he thrusts her to the ground and yells to the soldier with the gun.

I realize Enzo is watching, and I grab him, pulling him close to cover his eyes. An explosion blasts through the air, and the woman shrieks like a wild animal.

At the sound, my heart stops. I don't dare look. I'm breathing so fast I'm dizzy. We have to get away from this place. Now. I grab Enzo's hand and run as fast as I can.

"My son, my son!" the woman screams.

I run, willing myself and Enzo to go faster, farther and farther from the screams. Flashes of green pulse by on every side. Nothing matters but getting away. Far away. I grip Enzo's hand, dragging him behind me. My mind is a blur as I race through the brush. I'm certain I hear voices and shake violently at the thought of the soldiers closing in.

"Run, Caramina. Run!" Mama's voice whispers in my head, a memory from so long ago when she urged me to keep up with Matteo, Rosa, and Isabella as we chased each other in a game. I shake my head to clear my thoughts. Faster and faster, I run, as fast as my legs will carry me, dragging Enzo along behind. If I could, I'd scoop him up in my arms. But he's too big to carry. How far have we gone? And will we ever outrun those screams?

"Papa . . . Papa," Enzo moans. "I want Papa."

"Shh. Quiet! You must be quiet."

"I want Papa." He sobs, his voice getting louder with each heave.

"Enzo!" I snipe, which only makes him cry harder.

Who could blame him? The only thing I want is to collapse under a mango tree and let my tears flow until they're spent. I'd promised Papa we wouldn't go far. But we did. Now my baby brother is running for his life. And it's all my fault.

An eerie whistling sweeps through the bamboo, and a breeze lifts the ferns sprouting from the jungle floor. I listen for footsteps. Apart from the whistling wind, the only sounds I hear are those of Enzo crying softly next to me and the thudding of my heart.

How far have we gone? I can still hear echoes of the woman's screams in my mind. I scoop Enzo into my arms and hold him tight. His small frame shakes as he whimpers.

The whistling falls silent as the breeze fades. Maybe we've gone far enough for now. I lead Enzo to a tree and collapse against its trunk hidden by the thick overgrowth surrounding it. It's cooler here under the canopy of leaves. Sunshine breaks through in spots dotting my dirt-speckled feet.

"We'll sit, but just a little while," I say.

I put my arm around Enzo and pull him close, humming, hoping to calm him. He lets out a deep sigh as his eyelids bob up and down. Soon his cries fade into little puffs of breath, and he falls asleep. I hold him with my back pressed into the trunk. The rough bark of the tree scratches through my thin cotton dress. Exhausted, I almost drift off, hearing nothing but the song of hornbills in the distance.

Then something moves in the brush, startling me. It's moving quickly. My chest tightens as I think I hear footsteps. I wake Enzo, holding my fingers to my lips, motioning for him to be quiet. The noise grows louder. It's closer now, behind us to the left, coming fast. There's nowhere to go. I hold my breath, hoping whoever it is will pass us by.

Then from behind, someone grabs us, thrusting a hand over each of our mouths. I fight to wriggle free. I scream, but all that comes out is a muffled gasp.

"Quiet! Don't move." The voice is only a gruff whisper, but I recognize it instantly. Relief surges through me. Slowly, I turn my head. Crouched behind the tree, Matteo stares back at me. Somehow, he'd found us.

He takes his hand from my mouth but motions for me to be quiet. Then he nods his head to the left.

I follow his gaze and gasp when I spot two soldiers walking slowly through the brush.

"Japs," he whispers.

My stomach lurches, and I have an intense urge to run. I lean forward, but Matteo grabs my arm, shaking his head.

The soldiers circle the area and now stand facing our direction. Matteo tightens his grip over Enzo's mouth. He locks eyes with me, urging me to be still, as one of the men steps closer. I don't move or breathe. The silence is broken by the snap of a branch breaking under the man's boot, and I wince. He seems to be looking directly at us, his glare menacing.

I hunch lower, trying to disappear deeper into the thick brush at the base of the tree. The soldier lifts his foot to take a step closer but stops midair when the other man barks what sounds like an order. He turns, and the two set off in the opposite direction, moving through the jungle with their bodies crouched down like animals ready to strike.

The three of us wait, breathless. My legs tingle from sitting with them folded under me awkwardly. Matteo's gaze is locked on the trees through which the soldiers disappeared.

"Now! Let's go!" He grabs Enzo and hurries into the brush behind the tree.

I follow without saying a word. Though Matteo moves quickly, his steps fall silent. I attempt to mimic him, muting the noise of my steps. We walk like this for a long time. Eventually, we emerge at the edge of a clearing. Matteo sets Enzo down, and we stand quietly. Then Matteo motions for us to follow as he edges along the perimeter of the field.

I recognize the familiar slopes of rice fields, and relief sweeps over me. We've reached the farm. But Matteo keeps walking. I'm too tired to question him, so I follow silently. We ascend the hill, staying at the edge of the fields.

Matteo points ahead. "It's over that ridge."

When we reach the top, Tio's fields stretch out before us. The house and shed are hidden by the canopy of trees lining the property. I hope with everything inside me it is enough to shield us from the Japanese. Matteo leads us toward the stream, and I spy Papa at the edge of a field. When he sees us, confusion spreads across his face.

"It was Tia who let me know that you both didn't return," Matteo tells us. "She didn't want to alarm Papa."

I break into a run. The look on Papa's face shifts to concern as I race into his arms, and he looks to Matteo for answers.

"It's okay, Caramina," Papa says.

"We saw them, Papa! We saw them. It was . . . They were awful! They . . ." I struggle to explain.

Papa holds me by my shoulders. "What did you see?" His voice is calm. "Tell me." Agony is scrawled across his face.

I inhale deeply, steadying myself. I tell him about the two soldiers and the men nailed to the tree. I recount seeing the young man beaten, the sound of the rifle exploding, and his mother's screams. Papa's eyes are kind, but I watch the sinews in his neck twist tighter.

"It's all my fault. I'm so sorry!" I crumble to my knees, spent. "Enzo was playing in the stream on the other side of the bridge, and I didn't tell him to come back. He wanted to see the boar, and then it started to chase him. He had to run. I ran to help him and got us lost. It's my fault!" I hunch over, my sides shaking as tears spill down my cheeks.

Papa helps me to my feet as my family forms a circle around us. "It's not your fault or Enzo's," he says. He picks Enzo up and holds him tight. "Let's get you cleaned up." He speaks gently, his voice distant.

I know his mind is turning over what I told him. Papa is a born problem solver. He always fixes things. But this? No one, not even Papa, can fix this.

10

Rosa

JANUARY 15, 1942

Florence, Italy

"I won't be long, Rosa. But you'll probably be gone before I return." Nonna shuts the door behind her as she makes her way to the *panetteria*. In the kitchen I find toast with jam and espresso waiting on the table. It's not like Nonna to leave so early. But these days, the lines at the butcher and *panetteria* seem only to be getting longer. Marketing, which used to be a twenty-minute endeavor, now can take over an hour. I swallow my *caffè*, grab an orange from the cerulean-blue bowl on the counter, and hurry toward the door to get to class. I spot Nonna's handbag on the bureau. She must have forgotten it in her haste. I grab my own bag, then hers, intending to bring it to her since the *panetteria* is on my way.

When I reach the shop, I see the long queue but no Nonna. I peek in the window. She's nowhere to be seen. Perhaps she stopped along the way. But where? I don't have time to linger or I'll be late to class, and Professor Armento isn't one to be trifled with. I'll just give it to her later.

When I reach the conservatory, I hurry to class and take my seat.

Of all the professors here, Armento is the most infuriating. He doesn't even hide his look of disgust when he sees me enter.

The man makes my blood boil. Though Maestro still won't tell me which professor marked down my grade at quarterlies, I'm certain it was Armento. He travels to Germany and brags about being in the European Writers' Union headed by Joseph Goebbels. That is nothing to boast about! I hate having to sit under his teaching. Nonna told me Armento's writings on race were part of the impetus for Mussolini's racial laws. Shameful.

Armento's nasally voice intones various melodic flourishes and embellishments to use for improvisational sections of arias. Though the information is helpful, I grit my teeth through his lecture. My mind wanders to my family, and I wonder how they've spent their holiday. Did they even celebrate? I swallow back a pang of homesickness.

With a flick of his wrist Armento dismisses us, and I leave, grateful to get away from the man. The rest of my day is uneventful. Rehearsal with Maestro and a few hours spent in the library looking over scores for possible arias to sing.

When I return to the apartment, bread rests on the cucina table. I set Nonna's purse on the counter, wondering how she paid for the rustic loaf. Perhaps Signor Gaspari at the *panetteria* took pity on her forgetfulness.

Voices flutter in from the terrace where Nonna and Maestro sit speaking softly. I leave them be, not wanting to interrupt.

Nonna has been secretive lately. Perhaps her secrecy has something to do with the two of them. There's no question they are close. Could they really be in love?

Maestro's wife, Giuditta, died many years ago. According to Nonna, she was a beautiful Jewish woman, and, sadly, they never had children. Nonna has been alone for so long. Nothing would make me happier than for her to find love again. Goodness, Nonno Vittorio died when my father was just a child.

Nonna still wears his wedding band next to hers on a gold chain.

Close to her heart, she says. Years ago, Duce declared his Day of Faith. Women were called upon to donate their wedding rings to be melted down for the benefit of the regime. She told me she couldn't part with their rings, so now she keeps them hidden.

Faith in this twisted regime? I'd have done the same and kept my ring. Nonna deserves to find love again. I walk with heavy footsteps so as not to startle them, then join them on the terrace after Nonna calls to me.

11

Caramina

JANUARY 21, 1942

Mountain Province, Philippines

The fan buzzes a circular blur as I lie staring at the ceiling. Its spinning is futile. Rather than provide relief, it simply displaces the oppressive jungle heat lingering in the small room. I inhale the warm, sticky air, and peer over my shoulder at Isabella, asleep on the bed near the window. Since the incident almost two weeks ago, I've struggled to sleep. All night long images of those men strung up and the boy shot by the Japanese soldier play on a reel in my mind. How could anyone do such things to another human being?

I sling my legs off the bed, tiptoe to the bureau, and unearth a pale blue cotton skirt and white blouse. I'm desperate for relief from the heat engulfing the house.

After dressing, I peek into the back porch to see Papa asleep on the rickety rattan couch. He lies perfectly still, his eyes shut. His quiet breathing is methodical. It's good to see him this way. Since we arrived at the farm, lines have taken up residence on his brow. But now, he looks relaxed. Peaceful.

I creep across the room, push open the screen door, and step outside. The yard is bathed in fresh morning light as if the sun is whispering a greeting to early risers with no idea of the horrors occurring elsewhere. Morning is my favorite time of day, and it's so early that the jungle is hushed. Here I feel safe. A few birds sing their morning arpeggios. And even they sing pianissimo. Gently, I close the door behind me.

"Up with the birds, Little Bird?"

I peek inside and see Papa staring back.

"I didn't mean to wake you, Papa. I'm sorry."

"I was resting my eyes. I've been listening to the birds for some time."

He stretches his arms out wide. "Come, let's talk. But first, I must get coffee." He starts for the kitchen, looking over his shoulder to make sure I'm following.

I sit quietly as he makes his coffee. He drinks it black. Although we hear that coffee beans are growing scarce in town, I'm glad Papa can still enjoy his morning cup for now.

Steaming coffee in one hand, he uses his other hand to offer me a guava from the large yellow bowl on the counter. "Let's walk." He holds open the door.

We walk to where the stream curves closest to the house. Papa steps into the cool water and perches himself on a large rock. He pats it, motioning for me to join him. I sit and take a bite of the guava.

"I've been thinking, Caramina." He speaks gently, but his tone is serious. He's been quieter than usual since the incident. I know he's concerned. Since that day, he instructed us to stay within eyeshot of the house. We can go to the stream in the front or back as long as Tia can see us.

"I brought you here—all of you—to keep you safe." He sighs. I'm about to take another bite when he turns to face me. "I promised your mother I would. But now I know it's not safe for you or Enzo." A torn look spreads across his face.

"Papa, you have! You have kept us safe."

"No, Cara. This was a mistake. And now with Matteo fighting, well, it makes things even riskier."

"Matteo fighting?" What is he talking about?

"I've talked to a friend. He's a wonderful man, Father Bautista. He runs a home for children in Timbales, not far from here."

"Papa!"

"Caramina, listen to me. You and Enzo will be much safer there than with us."

"Papa! You mean an orphanage?" He can't be serious. This is crazy. Pain flashes through his eyes, and I know my words have wounded him.

"You are not an orphan. And neither is your brother. I am your father. And you have a family that loves you dearly." He bends his head low, holding it up with both hands as if the weight of it all might crush him.

"You are loved, Caramina."

The thought of being left alone, abandoned, in a strange place makes my heart plummet. My eyes well up, and I fight to stop tears from falling. Everything is out of control. Papa turns and wipes my cheek tenderly. My tears fall, droplets mixing with the water in the stream, driven away by the current. Like me.

"What about Isabella? Is she safe here?"

"Isabella will stay close to me and Tio. We need her help in the fields and house. It's only for a short while, Caramina. It's not forever."

"Papa, I'm sorry for getting Enzo lost! Please don't do this!" I gaze at him in desperation, pleading.

"This isn't a punishment, Cara. What happened wasn't your fault. But this is the only way I know to keep you both safe." Now his are the begging eyes.

I know he would never do anything to hurt me. Papa would give his life to protect us. He loves us more than life itself. But the thought of being separated from him is excruciating.

"I need you to look after your brother. Father Bautista is a good man. He will help you."

I gulp, feeling a lump in my throat. "When, Papa?"

"Tomorrow. Matteo and I will take you." He puts his arm around me, drawing me close.

Nonna's locket shifts as I lean against his shoulder and wish things were different. I grasp it, feeling the lines of the sunflower. Any goodness I've felt here has been swallowed up. We sit in silence. Papa holds me till the mist disappears, and the sun's rays fall harsh upon the ground.

That afternoon, I'm in the living room staring at a record in my hands. I'm determined to eke out any sense of joy I can before I leave, so I place the record on the turntable. As I turn the volume low, Papa's voice filters in through the window. I spot Captain Torres approaching.

"Arturo, my friend."

Papa steps forward and holds out his hand. "Roberto, good to see you."

Torres shakes Papa's hand, then pulls him into a bear hug, slapping him on the shoulder.

"I wish I were here under better circumstances," Torres says.

"Ah yes. But we do not control this chaos, do we? War lives in the hearts of men and dogs us, doesn't it?" Papa motions for Torres to sit.

I hear the clink of glasses and peek closer. Papa pours something from a brown bottle, and they hold their glasses up in unison.

"*Cin cin!*" Papa swallows a gulp of the amber liquid.

"*Cin cin!* To life and goodness, even during these times." Torres takes a swig from his glass.

Papa savors the drink, looking out over the field as Torres sips quietly. Both seem content to enjoy the moment, reluctant to have a necessary conversation.

"You know why I'm here, my friend?"

Papa nods.

"That boy of yours is something. Like his father. You have one brave boy there, Arturo."

Like his father. Papa certainly is brave. He isn't afraid to take a stand. When war broke out, I worried he might join the guerrilla fighters. Though I can't imagine him as a soldier. Losing him would mean the end of my world.

Papa takes another swig of his drink, savoring it before swallowing. "He told me he talked with your men. Did he speak with you?"

"Yes. He ran across a few of my men. He helped them. We spoke when he came into camp afterward."

Papa looks surprised.

"They were a few kilometers from camp loading supplies when they spotted a small contingent of Japs. They had to work quickly before taking cover. Matteo came upon them and helped load the supplies. My men told him to leave before it came to a head. But he refused. Kept right on loading as fast as he could. He's a hard worker. You've done well with him."

"Bah! Stubborn, that one!" Papa shakes his head. "But thank you. He's a good boy. Boy? Phew, he's a man now. He's bent on fighting, no matter what I say. He has no idea . . . this war."

"Yes." Torres takes a slow drink from his glass, then drains it.

Papa motions to the bottle between them.

"No. Thank you. I must get back." Torres glances out at the trees. "I'll keep my eye on him. I take the safety of my men very seriously. And he is your son."

"Thank you, my friend. It's all I could ask."

"He reminds me so much of you. Tenacious. Determined to get the job done. Ready to face whatever comes his way."

Footsteps sound behind me, and I turn to see Matteo. He shakes his head in mock disapproval. "Tsk, tsk. What would Papa say?"

I know I shouldn't be listening, but I need to know what is happening. I move away from the window. "You can't, Matteo!" I don't even try to hide my exasperation.

"Caramina . . ."

"No! You can't leave us!" I stare at him, willing him to change his mind. He sets down the banana in his hand and lowers his gray canvas sack onto the floor.

"Cara, I don't expect you to understand."

"What don't I understand? They're doing evil things, and you want to stop them. I want them stopped, too. I just don't want you to be the one to fight them."

Matteo pulls me into a hug.

"I don't want you to go. I can't lose you, too!" My voice is raw. Losing Mama years ago was hard enough. I don't know how I'd survive another loss like that.

Matteo pulls away and cracks a smile. "Lose me? Where am I going?"

This isn't funny. How can he be so cavalier?

"I've no intention of being lost, Cara. I'll be back. You and Enzo will be having fun. Isa will be toiling away here. And you won't even notice I'm gone. Besides, what kind of man would I be if I didn't do something to stop them?" His chest puffs out, and he pulls his shoulders back.

I can no less stop him than stop the moon shining silver at night.

He kisses the top of my head. Then he grabs his bag, slings it over one shoulder, and tosses the banana in the air as if he hasn't a care in the world. Catching it, he winks and leaves to join Papa and Torres.

Defeated, I watch from the window as Captain Torres rises from his chair. Papa stands, too. "Whatever you and your family need, I'll do whatever I can," Torres says.

"*Grazie*, Roberto. It's good to see you. Thank you for making the visit." Papa looks at Matteo, then back to his friend. "War is war, but having him serve under you gives me a bit of peace. *Grazie*."

The two men shake hands again. Torres turns to Matteo and pats him on the shoulder in a fatherly sort of way. Then he walks down the steps and looks over the meadow, waiting for Matteo.

Papa holds Matteo by the shoulders. "Keep your head down, son. Be safe." He holds him out at arm's length and looks him in the eye, then pulls him into a giant hug.

"I will, Papa."

Matteo and Torres tread across the field and disappear into the trees. I'm about to join Papa on the porch, but stop when I see him lower his head, shaking it back and forth. In one swift movement, he grabs his empty glass and hurls it to the ground. Shards splinter every which way, and I fall back, stunned. Papa never loses his temper. I hug my arms around myself to stop from shaking.

I watch as he stoops and lowers himself to his knees, then scrapes up the shards of glass. He sits silent and still for a moment. I know he's praying, begging for Matteo's safety and ours. When he walks by the window, I glimpse his eyes, wet, like my own. He plods down the steps and heads to the fields.

I creep back to the gramophone and drop into a chair. Matteo is gone. The music plays on softly, but I can't hear it. Our whole family is falling apart, and I can do nothing to stop it.

12

Rosa

Signora Bianca Conti adds another pin to the bodice of my gown, sighing wistfully. *"Il primo amore non sì scorda."*

"Ah yes, you never forget your first love." Nonna nods in agreement.

I'm glad Nonna can enjoy this time with her longtime friend and reminisce. The two have known each other since Nonna's days in the opera.

Perched on the wooden fitting stand, I listen contentedly as precious memories of their past loves are shared. Nonna's love for my Nonno Vittorio. Signora Conti of her love for her late husband.

Signora Conti peeks up at me. "And you, Rosa? Love is on the horizon?"

"Not yet," I say, stifling the memory of Ciro's stolen Christmas Day kiss.

We've not spoken of it. But he never tires of attempting to charm me. I know he's a Casanova, and I let it go for the sake of our friendship. We've continued on as we were before the holiday.

Since that day, I've seen him twice with the blond violinist. And just last week, I came around the corner at conservatory to find him whispering to a young woman who tossed her auburn curls this way and that.

"Such a beautiful signorina as yourself will find love, I have no doubt." Signora Conti stands. She circles me, studying her creation, then snaps her fingers and calls to one of her aides, who immediately hurries toward us. "Help Signorina Grassi out of her gown," she commands.

"Come, Serafina. I must show you something," Signora says, and the two old friends saunter into Conti's office.

This is my third fitting at Signora's atelier for the gown I will wear for my senior finale at festival. The shop on the Via de' Tornabuoni is tiny but elegant. Signora is much sought after for her expertise, and she outfits many of Florence's elite. Italian designers have risen to the challenge in lieu of the Parisian houses since the German occupation, and Signora Conti is one of the best. My sister Isabella would be thrilled to have the opportunity to meet such an esteemed designer. I'm certain Isa's seen Conti's designs featured in *Harper's Bazaar.*

Signora Conti and Nonna emerge from Signora's office. Both women exude sophistication and the confidence that comes from longtime successful careers.

"I'll see you again, Rosa. Next week. We're getting close. Only a few more fittings, I think." Conti smiles warmly, and I thank her. Soon the fittings will be about trimmings and adornments. I can't wait to hear her ideas.

As we leave, Nonna suggests stopping at a nearby café. I'm famished and, frankly, exhausted. We make our way to the small café and stand at the counter to place our orders. It's been a relentlessly busy few weeks with Maestro helping me prepare for festival. He insists this year's performance will set the stage for my future as an operatic professional. Rehearsals have been nonstop.

After the café, I make my way to the conservatory. I'm nearly there when I hear a man yelling. I round the corner and see two Blackshirts glowering at a young man lying on the ground. Fear surges through me.

"You insult Duce?" one of them yells.

"No, no! I wouldn't—" The bull-like thug kicks the young man in the gut. He moans, clutching his side.

"You wouldn't? You did! We got word." The second thug punches the man hard, and he slumps over.

"Think twice before crossing Duce!" The first thug kicks the young man again. The two Blackshirts grab the man's meager bag of food. They leave him balled in pain on the sidewalk as they walk away laughing, and fury rises within me.

A few passersby emerge from doorways, having hidden during the spectacle. They pay the injured man no attention and walk on by. I'm stunned.

"Here, let me help you." I approach him.

"No. You shouldn't."

"Nonsense." I help him up, grab his knapsack, and offer my arm for him to lean on. He accepts, and slowly we make our way to his apartment one street away.

The door opens and a pretty young woman appears. "Oh!" she gasps.

"I'm fine," he says, reassuring her as blood trickles down his cheek. "*Grazie*," he says to me.

As I turn to leave, I spy a scowling face in a window of the building next door. A woman is watching.

"It was our neighbor," I hear him say. "Said I insulted Duce."

"But you didn't!" She helps him limp up the steps and then closes the door behind them.

I continue on my way to the conservatory, incredulous that we're living in such times. More and more, fear simmers below the surface.

I can't stop thinking about the Blackshirts and the young man. They were brutal. I mull over Ciro's words about Nonna and Maestro working with the Resistance. When I saw him a week ago, he hinted at it again. The idea of Nonna taking such risks worries me. Though I wish someone would stop Duce, I put it out of my mind. It's too dangerous.

One week later, Signora Conti eyes my gown with the satisfaction of a job exquisitely done. "*Perfetto!* Next time, we will discuss shoes," she says as we are leaving.

Once again, Nonna and I stop into the café, grateful for its warmth. Nonna has enjoyed this process with Signora Conti. I wonder if she wishes she'd had a daughter to share such things with.

"Oh my!" Nonna looks up from her watch. "I must go."

"I'll go with you," I say, curious what could be so urgent.

"No, no! You stay, Rosa. Enjoy!" Nonna quickly pays for our order. "I'll see you back at the apartment." She kisses my cheek, then rushes out the door. Her behavior is odd. But I stay to enjoy my *caffè*.

In a flurry of motion, the barista sets down my drink along with a *cornetto alla crema* that I didn't order. I'm about to tell him there's been a mistake, as he's rushing back and forth behind the counter, when he sets down another *caffè*.

"You're not thinking of heisting my pastry, are you? That's the last of them, and they are my favorite," a man says from behind me.

The nerve! I spin around to set this man straight, and I find myself looking into the most lively, intense blue eyes I have ever seen, accompanied by a roguish grin. My frustration immediately fizzles.

I eye the pastry, taking it in hand. "Clearly, there's been a mix-up. But I was thinking about it," I tease. My words surprise him, and he's as silent as my little brother, Enzo, when caught sneaking a plate of *lechon*.

He lifts both hands, an act of surrender. And we both laugh. His laugh is deep and musical, and it carries through the small café.

"You enjoy it, Signorina," he insists.

I reach to hand him his pastry. "No, it isn't mine."

"*Grazie,*" he says. He downs his *caffè* and, *cornetto* in hand, turns to leave. At the door, he looks back and flashes me the warmest smile. All the tiredness of the last few weeks and the cold of winter melt clear away.

I watch him disappear through the door, then finish my *caffè*. Funny how such a little thing can brighten your day.

13

Caramina

JANUARY 22, 1942

Mountain Province, Philippines

"Cara, I don't need to know where the Japanese are. I have faith that those who do will help us, when and if we need assistance. And if Papa says it's best for you to go to Santa Maria's, then we have to trust it is. I will miss you both terribly. But you know he'd never do this unless it were absolutely necessary." Isabella finishes folding the last of my blouses and sets it in the open suitcase. "It'll be all right," she says, hugging me before leaving to help Enzo.

I don't understand why she never questions anything and always believes things will somehow turn out okay. I head to the back porch and sit alone, crestfallen. Isabella has always been there for me. Always. How will I manage without her?

The kitchen door swings open. I spin around to peek out the window. Maybe Matteo changed his mind and I won't have to go. I catch a glimpse of Gabriel. It's early for a visit. Usually, he arrives in late afternoon.

Over the past several weeks, we've become friends and I've

started looking forward to his visits. But now I'm leaving for Father Bautista's within the hour. I lean into the couch and spot a bird flitting from tree to tree. Its bright green feathers are tinged fiery red, reminding me of a painter's palette. Colors in the jungle are vivid, alive in their brilliance. The bird stares back from its perch. I watch it closely, envying its freedom. Surely this war can't touch a thing of such beauty.

Gabriel appears in the doorway. "I thought you might be in here," he says. His gaze follows mine to the bird. The couch creaks as he sits next to me. "I think he likes you."

"Maybe he's saying goodbye."

Quiet passes between us before Gabriel says, "It's a tailorbird. They're usually in pairs . . ."

"Enzo and I are leaving," I interrupt. "I guess I won't see you again."

He exhales slowly. "Matteo told me you were going to Father Bautista's. I'm here to accompany you, since he can't."

"You knew!" The skin on my neck prickles warm, and I feel my face flush. I take a deep breath. "I'm sorry. I just don't want to go. I don't see why it's necessary. Surely we're safer here." I lower my eyes, and when I look up again, his calm, kind gaze meets mine.

"Your father thinks the world of you, Caramina." He leans toward me. "And I don't think he'd entrust you with Enzo unless he thought you capable of caring for him."

Embarrassment over my outburst reddens my face.

"As for not seeing me, I certainly hope not. I do come to town now and then, and I thought I might visit you. But only if that's okay."

"Of course!" I laugh at the absurdity. "Why wouldn't it be?" A heavy weight lifts off me, and I feel a newfound lightness. Knowing I'll still see him amid all this change is a great relief.

He smiles his slightly lopsided grin and taps my knee with his, and I can't help but smile.

Enzo's voice floats down the stairs. "But what if Father Bautista won't let me play?" he asks with all the desperation of an eight-year-old.

"It will be like being here only with more friends." Papa appears in the hall. He ruffles Enzo's hair affectionately.

Even with this painful decision, I know deep down Papa would never part with us unless he believed it was unavoidable. He assured me that enemies wouldn't attack an orphanage full of children, even in war. But what does that mean for the rest of my family? How safe will they be staying at the farm?

The trip to Father Bautista's takes nearly the entire afternoon. Papa insisted we stay off the main road and Gabriel agreed, so instead we hiked through the jungle on a narrow, hidden path I've never seen before.

We finally arrive. Floridablanca is a metropolis compared to the small mountain village of Timbales. At the town's center is the Plaza Santa Maria. Catedral de Santa Maria, the town church, borders the plaza, as do the mayor's residence and a few businesses. Beyond the square lie streets and neighborhoods where residents live. Since it is a jungle town, Timbales is surrounded by thick greenery. It all seems much smaller than I remember from my few visits years ago.

The Santa Maria Center for Children lies tucked into an obscure corner of town. The stone building that houses the orphanage looks as though it's been here since the first Spaniards set foot on the island. As we walk through an archway, we emerge into a courtyard with various plants and two large star apple trees. It's eerily quiet until a bell rings and children of all ages spill out into the yard.

"Forgive me, Arturo. The first of our afternoon classes just ended, and I'm playing catch-up." A middle-aged priest strides toward us and shakes Papa's hand warmly.

"Not a problem, my friend. May I introduce my daughter, Caramina, and my youngest son, Enzo. And this is Gabriel, a family friend kind enough to accompany us."

Father Bautista nods at Gabriel and shakes my hand gently. I smile at the gesture. Something about the way he greets me makes me think he understands I'm too old to be here.

"It's good to meet you. Your father has told me so much about you," the priest says kindly, as Enzo squirms—he's spotted three boys kicking a ball back and forth. It's been a long time since he's played, and I know he's eager to join them. Still, it won't do to offend Father Bautista.

Father calls out to one of the boys. "Enrico, this is Enzo. He's a good kicker I understand." I exhale, relieved.

A shaggy-haired boy waves Enzo over, and Papa nods his permission. The grin on Enzo's face is bright enough to light the courtyard. He races over to the boys. Papa sighs, and the lines crinkling his forehead relax. Seeing Enzo happy is an obvious relief.

While Papa and Father Bautista speak, I seek out shade underneath one of the star apple trees. Everything in me wants to bolt and run back to Tia and Tio's. I steady myself, breathing slowly.

Gabriel joins me under the tree. "Plotting your escape?"

"That's for tomorrow, once I get the lay of the land." I try to muffle my fear and sound like John Wayne. I saw him in a cowboy movie I watched with Matteo, Rosa, and Isabella at the theater back home.

Gabriel chuckles. "I'll stop by next time I'm in town. I go to the market every couple days to visit friends."

I wonder who his friends might be. He's always wary about discussing what he does when he isn't at the farm. I've often seen him and Matteo talking near Tio's shed or by the stream, noticeably out of earshot from the rest of the family.

"Caramina?" Papa calls me over. "Father Bautista has agreed to let you help teach the music class. I told him you would love such an opportunity."

I look at him as if he's lost his mind. "Papa, I'm just a student!"

"Not here, Caramina," Father says. "We're fortunate to have you. I understand you're a skilled singer. Sister Faye, who teaches our music class, has been asking for help. Your assistance would be greatly appreciated. I'd love to have you sing at church as well, if you'd like."

"Thank you, Father." I wasn't expecting this. Singing on its own is a comfort to me. But perhaps doing this will make things easier for Enzo. I remember the two boys back home and how they treated us for being *mestizo*. Perhaps if I garner their respect, any naysayers will leave him be. "I don't know how much I'll be able to teach them." I glance around at the children skipping through the court-yard.

"I think you'll find, whatever you share, they'll be most appreciative. Now, the bell will sound soon, so I must go. Will you and Enzo meet me in my office after the bell rings?" He points to a room just inside the doorway. "Then I can show you your rooms."

I nod, and Father Bautista says goodbye to Papa before heading to the shaded walkway.

"I'll be checking on you both, Caramina. I may not be able to come for some time, but I want to make sure you're okay. Gabriel has promised to check on you for me."

I bite my lip. Gabriel had said he'd visit. But now I wonder if it's only because Papa arranged it.

"He offered, Caramina," Papa says, as if reading my mind. "And if he hadn't, I'd have asked him."

My heart skips a beat, and my lips curl into the tiniest of smiles. Gabriel genuinely wants to see me. It makes this awful change somehow a bit less difficult.

Enzo runs over, and Papa hugs him. "I love you both. Listen to Father Bautista. He's a good man. I'll see you again soon." He ruffles Enzo's hair, and Enzo races back to his game. "I will see you again, Cara."

I try to smile. It's all I can do. If I try to speak, emotions will well over.

He pulls me close. "If you need anything, let Gabriel know. He'll tell me." He smiles at me, then joins Gabriel at the entrance.

Gabriel waves. I wave back, forcing a smile, then watch them exit through the stone archway.

As I walk to my spot under the shade of the tree, my locket rustles against me. I hold it out, studying the sunflower. I glance at the tiny sunflowers growing along the edge of the flower bed and remember Nonna's words, "Remember the sunflowers and always look for the good." But how can any of this be good?

14

Caramina

After dropping Enzo off at the boys' dormitory, Father Bautista brings me to my room where he introduces me to my roommate.

"Caramina, this is Clara. I'll leave you two to get to know each other," he says, then disappears down the hallway.

"Hello!" Clara's smile is as wide as the sun. "I'm so excited you're here. There aren't any girls our age," she says, as if sensing a need for an explanation. "I'm twelve. How old are you?"

"Fourteen."

"This is your bed." She points to the bed by the window, and I set down my suitcase. "It's not so bad here. I think you'll like it. The only one you need to watch out for is Sister Faye."

I look up in concern.

"She's got a bad temper. I heard it's because she was an old spinster after her fiancé broke off their engagement and married someone else. I think he's better off, given how sour she can be. I guess she never made peace with it and joined the convent. Too bad for us. She's been taking out her frustrations on us kids ever since.

"You'll be fine. Just stay out of her way. You'll love Sister Hannah and Sister Valencia. They're young and really nice. I overheard them talking once, and Sister Hannah said she grew up poor in San Pablo. She joined the order after she turned eighteen. If anyone can light up a room, it's Sister Hannah. Everyone knows when one of the little ones is upset to bring them to her. She always makes things better.

"Oh, and Sister Valencia—her family was rich. It's like something out of a novel. Her father wanted her to marry a businessman, a really old businessman. And do you know what she did?"

I shake my head.

"She refused! Then she joined the church. Ha! I don't blame her. I wouldn't want to marry someone so old. Would you?"

"Definitely not!"

"Well, Valencia's pretty brave. A few times I've heard her stand up to Sister Faye, and that is something to see."

"Then there's Father Ortiz." A dreamy look mists in Clara's eyes. "He's a lot younger than Father Bautista. But he fills in when Father Bautista helps in town at Catedral de Santa Maria. Sister Valencia told me he's from Manila. He was supposed to be an attorney. But oh, it's so sad! He lost his fiancée to tuberculosis. He was devastated! Apparently, he drowned his sorrows in wine. Then he met Father Bautista, who brought him into the church. I, for one, am glad." Clara pauses to take a breath. "He's got hazel eyes, and his hair is the color of sand. Golden. Sometimes he comes across tough as nails. But he's really kind."

"What about Father Bautista?"

"I don't know much about him other than he became a priest in Manila. He's a good man. He keeps things working here.

"Oh! And you'll love Wednesdays—it's Dessert Day."

I'm relieved to hear about this bright spot to the week as, apparently, every Wednesday with few exceptions, the children are served some kind of sweet treat. A true *merienda*. According to Clara, Father Bautista tries his best to ensure there are sticky sweet rice cakes, *puto,* or the crunchy, sugary fruit-filled fritters, *turon.*

"If we're lucky, it'll be *leche flan* this week. Oh, I can just taste the caramel." Clara's eyes brighten at the thought.

She happily chatters away, telling me about the schedule—our wake-up and mealtimes, as well as school details.

Suddenly, Clara's face darkens. "Make sure to look out for Enrico."

The boy in the courtyard? He didn't appear too menacing. "Enrico?"

"Yes, he has a mean streak! Last week, Sister Faye cornered one of the boys, demanding the name of the student who stole leftovers. Immediately afterward, Enrico's chores tripled. He was so angry, he tied up a cat that boy befriended after it wandered into the courtyard. When the boy got scratched trying to free the cat, Enrico just laughed. No one crosses Enrico. Everyone's afraid of him. Though he does have a soft spot for Rae. But who wouldn't love her? She's one of the younger kids, and she's a sweetie. I think even Sister Faye might sneak her extra dessert on Wednesdays."

When I ask her about herself, Clara tells me she's been at the orphanage since she was three. Her mother never married and simply couldn't take care of her on her own. Clara has never even known her father. Despite the sad story she is sharing, her voice is bubbly and joyful.

I smile, attempting to listen despite the thoughts roiling in my mind. How can Clara find happiness under such circumstances? Perhaps, if living at the orphanage is all she remembers, it's understandable. It isn't a bad place. Not dark or run-down. The children seem genuinely happy. But they also haven't just left the only family they know.

I know I'm being foolish. Most of these children come from desperate circumstances. I feel guilty being so resistant to the idea of living here temporarily. One day I'll go home or, at least, be with my family. These children will never have that chance.

"We have to go! We can't be late." Clara interrupts my thoughts. "Sister Faye doesn't take kindly to latecomers." She moves her hand in a swatting motion, squints, and purses her lips like she's eaten a slice of unripe mango.

I laugh nervously.

"She's not really that bad," she reassures me.

⌒

The chapel windows open onto the square with a view of the trees. The faint scent of honeysuckle breezes through the room. Father Bautista isn't here. There is a young priest at the altar. "That's Father Ortiz," Clara tells me.

Children of all ages squirm in wooden pews, the older ones shushing the younger to be quiet. I recognize Enzo's blond curly mess of hair in the second row. Next to him sits the boy from the ball game, Enrico. I can only say a quick prayer and hope this young boy doesn't turn on Enzo because he is *mestizo*.

Enrico leans over and whispers to the young boy on his other side. The boy's cheeks turn pink, and he laughs. Enrico bolts upright with a look of pure innocence on his face as an old nun spins around. She glares at the unfortunate boy, and from his terrified expression, he knows he's in trouble. This must be the infamous Sister Faye. The old woman marches him to the back of the room, her hand firmly on his shoulder.

Clara glances at me and makes a small swatting motion. I can't imagine the boy being spanked for so small an offense.

I peek over at Enzo and silently pray he doesn't fall for Enrico's shenanigans. If Enrico tries to take advantage of him, I'll set him straight.

We close our time with Father Ortiz with a short song and everyone files out. The quiet of the chapel is quickly broken by the laughter of children playing. I walk to the courtyard and sit under one of the star apple trees. A bird's song floats through the branches. I look up to see a lone tailorbird just like the one at Tia and Tio's.

"Singing your lonely song again?" I whisper.

Just then, another bird chimes in. From a branch higher up, the bird's mate sings in harmony. I savor their duet, relaxing into the trunk of the tree. The bird isn't alone after all.

A week passes, and I've yet to teach any music. Instead, I sit as Sister Faye leads our class through "Faith of Our Fathers." Though not a favorite of mine, I remember singing it at church back home. Rather than being a comfort, Sister Faye's rendition only makes me homesick. Someone must have told her volume was indicative of talent because she sings louder than everyone else. Her choppy, aggressive style hurts my ears. Watching her attempts at conducting, moving her hands abruptly as if she were swatting a fly, I find myself stifling a laugh.

Father Bautista introduced me to Sister Faye my first night here. He told her how fortunate they were to have a skilled vocalist at the center and that she'd now have the help she'd wanted. When Father Bautista walked away, she looked me up and down, pursed her lips, and said nothing. Her look would have frightened the most courageous soldier.

Now I sit facing the dour nun with nothing to do but sing along with the rest of the class. I glance around. It saddens me that this is what these children think music to be. No life. No emotion. No passion. No fun. Even Clara, in the back row, is staring at the floorboards and singing half-heartedly.

Then the singing abruptly stops. I turn my head forward to see Sister Faye glaring at me, and I know I've been caught not participating. The old nun's cheeks are red, and her eyes flare with anger. I brace for the torrent of words I know is coming. But before the woman utters a word, Father Bautista arrives.

"Sister, your assistance is needed in the dining hall. Immediately."

The nun's eyes dart from Father to me and back again. Slowly, she stands to follow him.

"Caramina, would you take over for Sister Faye, please?"

"Me, Father?" My throat tightens with panic when I see the scowl on the nun's face as Father glances around the class.

"Yes, of course. I'm sure you have a repertoire of songs. It would be most helpful, since Sister Faye won't be able to continue today."

He stands in the doorway, motioning me forward, and waits until I make my way to the front of the room.

"Children, Caramina is your teacher today. Please give her the respect you would give Sister Faye." As Father Bautista speaks, the children look from him to me. A collective nod of agreement goes around the room.

"Good!" Father Bautista smiles and walks out the door. He hesitates a moment to make sure Sister Faye is following. His voice echoes down the corridor as he explains the predicament in the dining hall to the flustered nun.

I face the class. With Sister Faye gone, a look of relief moves across their faces. "Perhaps we should start where we left off," I say quietly. Groans and sighs reverberate through the room.

"Let's not!" A boy's voice shoots from the back. "No one wants to sing that stuff anyway." Enrico stands and struts to the front. Nervous laughter makes its way around the room.

It's like a tennis match. Heads spin back and forth between the two of us to see who will score the next point. I focus on the music on the stand in front of me. There's no way I'm letting him get the upper hand.

"We'll finish with the song we were singing; then we'll move on to another. Now, please take your seat. You're holding up the class." I speak with as bold a voice as I can muster.

One boy in the front row gasps. Has no one challenged Enrico before? My hands tremble slightly, and I hold them together on the music stand to still them, hoping no one notices. The room is silent but for a paper rustling from a breeze blowing through the window. Everyone awaits Enrico's next move. I stare at the notes on the music sheet, waiting.

An eternity passes before the silence is broken when he bursts into laughter. "All right, teacher. Please, go on."

The emphasis on *teacher* is not lost on me. Despite his mocking tone, he walks to the back of the room and plops into his seat.

The entire class exhales in relief, as do I. My eyes scan the score as I read it quickly. Then I take a deep breath and raise my hand, directing the class to begin where we'd left off. I sing, picking up the tempo, while looking out at their faces. Listening to me, one by one the students join in.

Slowly, the song takes on life. With their melodious voices, the song swells and rises like a sunset ocean wave, lifting and cresting, and radiant with tangerine-infused light. I can't help but smile. A few of the children smile back. When the song finishes, one little girl even giggles. It's as if I've taught them a delightful game they never knew existed. The room comes alive again with their voices blending into a playful and pleasing mix of exuberant sound as they sing "Magtanim ay 'Di Biro." Clara radiates with joy as she sings, and Enzo's face beams at me with pride. When the bell sounds, the children file out slowly, reluctant to leave.

"Thank you," I say.

One by one, they stroll out the door, smiling. The little girl who giggled comes toward me, shyly. "I'm Rae. You have a pretty voice," she says, before skipping away.

I stand alone in the room. Music is still alive in me, after all. My heart brims with gratitude. I close the songbook and then follow the children into the courtyard, scanning the square for Enzo. I spy Sister Faye staring out through a window in the dining hall. When the old nun sees me, a scowl darkens her face. Why must she be so hateful?

"Never mind that old bat." The voice startles me. It's Enrico. "She's always harder on us *mestizo* kids. And she's jealous she can't sing." Before I can say a word, he runs off.

15

Caramina

I dress quietly and slip out of my room, not wanting to wake Clara this early in the morning. Though I haven't eaten since breakfast yesterday, I've no appetite. I force myself to walk to the small dining hall. Usually there is rice for breakfast, mixed with whatever scant bit of meat or fish is left from the previous night's dinner. But it's just before sunrise, and the morning meal isn't yet prepared.

I grab a banana from the counter and head outside. In a far corner of the courtyard, I drop down and lean against the stone wall. Coolness seeps through my thin cotton blouse. This area is shaded even in the hottest part of day, shielded by tall fronds of fern. A breeze wafts by, freshening the air around me, and the ferns sway gently. After stripping the banana of its peel, I eat the sweet, mellow flesh, one bite at a time.

Papa comes to mind, and I wish more than anything I could be with him now. If he had any idea it would be like this, he'd never have brought us. But he did bring us. "You're not an orphan, Caramina," he'd said. I'm still alone. Gabriel hasn't visited as he promised. Not even once. He isn't one to not keep his word. And I haven't even received any letters from home. I gulp back a dry sob. I know this is wartime. But I can't help but feel abandoned by my closest friend and my family.

My mother would always pray, especially when things were difficult. Mama always seemed to find the good even on the worst days. But now my necklace, with the only picture I have of her, is gone. Nonna's reminder to look for the good is gone. In another act of unnecessary cruelty, Sister Faye saw me looking at it and snatched it away, claiming it was an idol. She wouldn't listen to my pleas. Enzo and Enrico witnessed the whole thing. So humiliating. Maybe it's better this way. If life is void of goodness now, what benefit can come from remembering any goodness from before?

I've tried prayer, but my words fall flat. When Enzo was born and the doctor said Mama needed to rest, Father Cruz had told me I should pray hard that her bleeding would stop. I had just started when a song began playing in my mind. Often, I've wondered if Mama might still be with us if only I'd prayed harder instead of letting music carry away my thoughts.

"Is there any good in this world?" I whisper as I gaze up at the white cotton clouds and sea of blue sky. A tear escapes the corner of my eye and falls to the ground. I reach into my pocket for Rosa's letter that I grabbed on my way out. It's one of many from the ribbon-tied bunch I'd brought to the orphanage. Unfolding the crisp stationery, I see Rosa's beautiful script and hope it will bring some comfort.

August 6, 1939

Dearest Caramina,

What a beautiful surprise Nonna gave me! We saw Verdi's Aida at Terme di Caracalla, the Baths of Caracalla in Rome. Breathtaking! Performed in the middle of Roman ruins. The stage was set between two enormous ancient stone pillars. Beniamino Gigli was Radamès and Iva Pacetti, Aida. Gigli's voice is like honey!

On our way back to the hotel, we stopped into Basilica di Santa Maria Sopra Minerva. Rome's only Gothic church. The facade is simple. But when you step inside . . . the ceiling! It's as if you're looking into the bluest of midnight skies with stars flickering gold.

I'm so grateful to Nonna. I can't imagine living life and never experiencing all of this. I can't wait till you come. Give my love to Papa and the others. I miss you all greatly.

Con affetto,
Rosa

I imagine the Baths of Caracalla, the blue-ceilinged nave of the church, and the honeyed tones of Gigli's voice. It all sounds so wonderful. And yet, so out of place here. So out of reach. How I wish I could be there now. Not having to worry about old nuns and Japanese soldiers. And being alone. I'm glad Rosa doesn't have to endure this war like we do.

I rub my eyes, feeling my strength return. The bell will ring soon, though I'm not ready to leave this cool corner. Resting my head against the wall, I close my eyes. Then I hear movement in one of the star apple trees. For a brief moment, branches flutter, then the familiar birdsong floats through the courtyard. I scan the tree to find the songbird to no avail. Just then, someone enters the courtyard.

It's Gabriel! In his arms is a basket. I jump to my feet, fighting the urge to run to him. He doesn't see me. A momentary pang stabs in my gut. Why hasn't he visited until now? But the sheer joy of seeing him again wins out.

"Gabriel!"

"Caramina!" He turns quickly to face me.

"It's good to see you."

"And you!" he says, sounding relieved. "I've come by a few times, but one of the sisters told me you were in class and couldn't be disturbed."

My shoulders fall.

"You did receive what I brought for you? I left a couple baskets for you and Enzo." His hopeful expression gives way to bewilderment as I shake my head.

Relief floods through me. The fact he kept his promise means more than anything.

"There were letters from your father." His jawline tightens.

Papa didn't forget me.

Anger flashes in Gabriel's eyes but is quickly replaced with concern. He places his hand gently on the small of my back and leads me to the bench under the tree. We sit shoulder to shoulder.

I fidget with my fingers. We've never sat so close before. Flutters drift and bob in my belly like feathers on a spring wind. We sit still, listening to the song of the bird.

After setting down the basket, he relays the latest news from Tia and Tio's. Things are pretty much the same, though quieter. Isabella, Papa, Tia, and Tio are all safe, thankfully. Apparently, most of the men who work for Tio have left. I ask where they've gone, but all Gabriel says is they, like Matteo, felt it was time to do something to help.

"Papa said it would be safer for us here. I just don't understand why."

"With Matteo fighting alongside Torres and his men, I think your father is afraid it could put you at risk. Thinks it's safer this way. I think he's right, Caramina."

"What about you? Why is it safe for you? Don't you help?" When I was back at the farm, I knew Gabriel kept odd hours. Often, he'd show up unexpectedly with information for Papa and Tio, along with the baskets of food. His carpentry work has slowed to nearly nonexistent with the war. So why is his schedule a mystery? He seems to be on the move regularly.

His eyes are fixed on a baby fern sprouting next to the bench, its emerald-green spiral just beginning to unfurl. "I can't talk about it, Caramina. It's better for you that way."

I want to ask why, but a noise startles me.

"Caramina! Go inside!" The unmistakable voice of Sister Faye shoots across the courtyard.

We spin around to see the old nun glowering, lips cracked in a sneer. My face instantly reddens, and I squeeze my hands in frustration. Boys and girls aren't allowed to sit close together at the center, and the rules are strictly upheld. Gabriel stands and faces Sister Faye.

"You may leave, now." The sister dismisses him as if he were one of the children under her tutelage.

"I have business with Father Bautista."

My eyes widen at Gabriel's boldness.

"Then it will have to wait. Father is not here. He'll be back later this afternoon. Perhaps I can give him a message for you." Sister Faye's dark eyes bead.

"Won't be necessary." He turns to face me. "I'll see you again, Cara. And I'll tell your father how you're doing."

The last sentence he says with added emphasis, staring directly at Sister Faye. The woman glares back. She's a tank, immoveable and menacing.

"Thank you for visiting." I smile nervously at him. Then I hurry toward the building, hoping to escape the nun's tirade.

"Wait! You forgot your basket," Gabriel calls out.

I glance at Sister Faye, then walk back to Gabriel.

"Thank you."

"You should be more careful, young man. It's not appropriate for a young woman to sit so close. Mind yourself, or you will not be welcome here." Sister Faye's voice seethes.

"Give my regards to Father Bautista. I'll be sure to speak with him the next time I come." Gabriel speaks firmly before turning to leave and disappearing through the entryway. At that, I sprint to Enzo's room with the basket, heart racing and spirit renewed. I'm not alone or forgotten, after all.

16

Rosa

MARCH 10, 1942

Florence, Italy

I whisk out the door of Signora Conti's atelier after my latest fitting. Humming as I cross the street, I spot the small café Nonna and I visited. I'm ravenous, having not eaten since early morning. I know I should just go back to the apartment. But I stop in instead. The barista recognizes me, nodding as he takes my order. A *caffè* and a *cornetto alla crema.*

The barista sets my order on the counter. *"Grazie,"* I say, contemplating whether I should stand at the bar to enjoy my food or find a table.

"Couldn't resist, could you?"

I recognize the voice immediately and smile to myself. Slowly, I turn. Sitting in the corner of the café is the man from the other week, *cornetto* in hand. He raises it for me to see and smiles.

I laugh, and he tips his head to the empty chair at his table. I probably should leave. But instead, I let him pull the chair out for me, and I join him.

"Tommaso Donati. And you are?"

"Rosa Grassi. Nice to meet you, Signor Donati." I sip my *caffè*.

"Please, call me Tommaso."

"All right, Tommaso."

"Signorina Grassi, what brings you to this small café?"

"I hear these are not to be missed." I take a small bite of the pastry. The flavors blend perfectly. Sweet but not overly so. Buttery-rich. I nibble another bite.

"Clearly, whoever recommended this has impeccable taste. *Sì*, Signorina?" His eyes have a playful glint.

I laugh. "He was quite right. And you can call me Rosa."

"Rosa." He says my name slowly. "Bella, like a rose. Tell me, Rosa, are you a native Florentine?"

This interlude, so warm and inviting, could be snuffed out in a moment's time. Caution simmers under the surface of my thoughts. I study his eyes, wondering what and how much to share, and see nothing but kindness.

"I'm here finishing up voice training at the conservatory. My grandmother lives here—is from here. I'm from the Philippines."

A burst of icy air gusts through the small café as someone pulls open the door.

"The Philippines?"

Slowly, I set the tiny ceramic cup on the table and wait for it. The letdown, the slight of comment about being half Filipina that will prick my heart like a heavy-gauge needle.

"Your family . . . They are there? I am so sorry. Have you had any word of them?" When I meet his gaze, it's warm, his concern palpable.

I'm taken aback and realize I've been holding my breath. I exhale, both surprised and relieved. From his tone, it's clear my heritage is of no matter.

"I haven't. But . . ." I stop myself from saying it appears the air bases have been most affected. The only way I could know is if I've been listening to Radio Londra. "I really believe they are okay. I have to."

Tommaso is silent. Watching me.

"My father is a very brave man. I believe he will keep my family safe."

His eyes soften. "Fathers do that, don't they?" He swallows a bite of *cornetto*, then says, "So, Rosa Grassi, you are a world traveler. And a singer? A soprano?"

"*Sì.*"

"*Bella Italia* is heaven for music lovers."

I smile in agreement.

Another burst of frigid air blasts through the door as a patron enters. Tommaso shivers comically. "Our freezing winters must be a shock for you."

I chuckle. "Three years, and I'm still not used to the cold. But I've learned to be prepared." I point to my heavy coat and scarf.

"It is a beautiful country. The Philippines," he says, then asks about my family. I tell him of my siblings and my father.

Tommaso listens intently. His good nature and genuine interest are a refreshing surprise, like the first blooms of spring breaking through frozen winter soil.

"And you, what about you, and your family?" I ask.

He tells me he is twenty-four. An architect, he travels quite a bit for his job. He comes from a large family in Brindisi and is the oldest of five siblings. Four boys and one girl.

"No doubt your mother was exhausted when you were young," I say.

He chuckles and begins telling me how he and his brothers got themselves in and out of trouble—teasing each other relentlessly by hiding each other's treasures like cards, balls, and spinning tops that led to squabbles for which their mother played referee. He loves football and American baseball. He sounds quite the sportsman. My brother Matteo would love that. Best of all, he loves music! His stories make me laugh. But I sense that like me he, too, is homesick.

We talk for so long before suddenly I realize an hour and a half has passed. "I must go," I say, wishing I didn't have to leave—I've so enjoyed his company.

"Of course. Please let me escort you home."

"That would be lovely," I tell him, and we continue talking as we walk. We reach the apartment in no time, but both of us linger, not ready to part ways.

"I'm leaving in the morning for work. But I'd love to see you when I get back."

"I'd like that very much."

He lifts my hand, kisses it gently. "*Ciao,* Rosa Grassi. *È stato un piacere.*"

"It has been a pleasure," I agree.

"I will see you again," he says matter-of-factly, as I make my way up the porch stairs.

"*Sì, buon viaggio,* Tommaso."

He tips his hat, then turns on his heel to head back the way we came. As I ascend the stairs, I hear him humming a tune as he goes. It makes me smile.

Upstairs in my room, I grab my journal. My day has been eventful, and I savor mulling over my time with Tommaso. Such a lovely surprise. He is genuinely kind and makes me laugh. And there's an intensity about him, as if he's squeezing the most out of life. He's different from Ciro in this way.

Ciro's energy seems to come from simmering frustration and anger over what's happened to him and to Italy. I don't know Tommaso well, but he appears to live with gusto, embracing each day. His good humor is a balm, lightening my heart.

Is it possible to know someone for such a short time, yet feel you've known them for years? There is something so comfortable about him. I can be myself. I can't wait to see him again. Until then, I will focus on preparing for festival.

17

Caramina

Scrubbing furiously, I hold a little boy's shirt over a steamy tub of water as I help Mae, the laundress. It's been three weeks since Gabriel's visit, and Sister Faye's behavior has only worsened. The old nun has wasted no opportunity to make my life difficult. Yesterday morning as I entered the sanctuary, Sister Faye stood guard. She spotted a tiny stain on my sleeve and snapped at me to change. As a result, I was late. She then punished me with making me help with the laundry in lieu of free time.

Father Bautista isn't aware of the woman's conduct. Running a parish in wartime that serves an entire town keeps him inordinately busy. Unfortunately, he isn't at the orphanage often. At least when he's present, things are a bit easier. For such a small town the problems are endless. Goods are growing scarcer, and people are feeling the strain. With less to go around, bad behavior is becoming rampant. There have been reports of stealing and assaults. It saddens me—it's not like my countrymen, who prize hospitality as a virtue.

Mae wipes her forehead with her arm after wringing out a bedsheet. "This is the last, Caramina. Go and hang the rest, and then we're done. You can have some free time." She smiles warmly.

I grab the basket, clothes spilling over its sides. As I walk outside, I remember my encounter with Sister Faye. So different from Mae's nurturing kindness. No melody flits through my mind now. I hang shirts, skirts, underclothes, and pants in silence. Then I walk to the courtyard to enjoy the shade in my fern-covered corner.

I've just rested my head against the stony building when Father Bautista enters the courtyard with a middle-aged man. The man's face is contorted, and he's speaking quickly.

"Father, this is no good. I don't know what we can do. We can't hide them. I'd have warned you earlier, but I just got word from Torres's men about those evil . . ." he sputters, struggling to find a suitable word. "Beasts!"

Father Bautista's face is etched with lines, his eyes sober and grave. "Thank you for telling me. We'll do whatever we can. Jesus, have mercy." He shakes his head. "I don't want to alarm the children. Let's pray conscience wins out. Certainly, they wouldn't . . . These children are so young."

A knot tightens in the pit of my stomach. I lean closer, intent on hearing what the men are saying.

"What kind of men steal young women—girls—away from their homes and do such evil? They're shooting anyone who tries to stop them on the spot. A young boy was shot trying to help his sister!" The man's face reddens, his eyes pulsing with anger.

"Torres's man said the Japs have already taken several girls from the villages south of us, but they're still a distance away. Maybe they'll pass over our town. It is small and quite hidden."

A shiver creeps up my spine. Despite the coolness of the shade, beads of sweat dot my forehead. I swipe them away. Images of those poor men strung like meat from their bloodied thumbs, and the young man shot in the head, race through my mind. My stomach twists. I force down the bitter bile on my tongue, then take a deep breath to slow my racing thoughts.

"Thank you for telling me. I'll make my staff aware," says Father Bautista.

A somber expression darkens both men's faces. The man nods, then lumbers back through the arch and into town. I watch Father Bautista as he shakes his head and walks slowly to his office. His shoulders stoop forward, weighed down from the news.

Only a few hours pass before Father Ortiz gathers all the children in the courtyard, along with Sister Hannah and Sister Valencia for a "drill." "We're going to play a new game," he says. "And it's extremely important you follow instructions exactly. When we say walk, you walk. When we say quiet, you must be as quiet as you can be."

"Like a mouse," Sister Valencia adds.

The three adults divide us into two groups, each with one of the nuns in charge, and with Father Ortiz observing. We march to and fro in the courtyard until lunchtime, then again afterward, until everyone follows on command.

After this, the two sisters send us to our rooms where we are to pack one bag with a change of clothing, only what we'd need for an overnight stay. The nuns stop at each room to ensure everyone is packed.

"We're going on a hike," Sister Valencia tells my group. She says that tonight we'll go to bed early so we can rise before daybreak. Several of the children think this is a great adventure, but I know the adults are only shielding us from the truth. We are fleeing the Japanese. Seeing fear in my eyes, Sister Valencia pulls me aside, a sober look on her face. "You are brave, Caramina. We'll be all right," she says in her usual confident tone, acknowledging the danger without saying another word.

On the way to dinner, I pass Father Bautista's office and overhear him speaking with Father Ortiz. "They're expecting you at San Paulo. They're making room for the children now. Do you have what you need?" Father Bautista asks.

"Yes, this should do," Father Ortiz answers huskily. Peeking into the room, I see him set a handgun on the desk along with a box. The box opens, and several bullets spill out. "I have my bolo as well."

"Take these, too." Father Bautista places an identical box next to the one on the desk.

Father Ortiz shakes his head, his brows knitted in concern. "You may need these."

"No. I will be fine. The children need protection. It's been confirmed. The Japanese were spotted heading north. You should be safe heading east, but you need to leave as early as possible."

"You should come with us," Father Ortiz says.

"It's better if I stay. The townspeople will need me. Especially when the Japanese arrive. Sister Faye is also remaining to help with the parish."

Father Ortiz nods soberly. He gathers up the weapon and boxes of bullets and places them in a rucksack.

"May God be with you," Father Bautista says, shaking the other man's hand and pulling him into a fatherly hug. The young priest chokes up as he speaks. "And you, Father."

I duck through a doorway as Father Ortiz steps into the hall. My stomach twists. I blink back tears thinking of my friends who've become like family and of what I know the Japanese are capable of. Surely Father Ortiz will get us all to safety. He has to.

Then a thought sends chills snaking down my spine. If the Japanese are heading north, they might come upon the farm. Captain Torres must have warned Papa. Will my family flee again? But where will they go? And how will I ever find them? Will they even know we've fled to San Paulo? My heart beats so hard I shake. What if I never see them again?

Enzo and I can't stay here. And we can't go with the others. We have to get back to the farm before it's too late. I won't let this war separate me from my family permanently.

I want to run and get Enzo this very minute. We could run away. Back to Tia and Tio's. But if we leave now, we'll be stopped. I have no way to contact Gabriel for help. I don't even know if he's in town. I force myself to breathe, calming my nerves. It's better to wait. I'll wake extra early before the hubbub of getting all the children in order. Then I'll get Enzo, and we'll leave for the farm. Hopefully, it will be an hour or two before anyone realizes we're gone.

As I walk down the dimly lit hallway, a scream pierces the quiet, and I jump. At the end of the hall, Sister Faye towers over Enrico. Next to him is Enzo.

"You know you're not to be in here!"

Both boys are standing outside Sister Faye's room at the end of the girls' section of the dormitory. I fight the urge to help Enzo. If I try to intervene, it will only make matters worse. And nothing can get in the way of us leaving.

"I'm sorry, Sister. We wanted to tell you we enjoyed your singing the 'Ave Maria' yesterday," Enrico says.

I cringe. Enrico has led Enzo into this. That boy is always getting into trouble. I've warned Enzo to steer clear of him, but he won't listen.

"Get to the dining hall, immediately! You'll be cleaning all the dirty dishes. Go!"

Sister Faye isn't easily fooled. Enrico's appeal to her ego makes no difference. If Enrico's antics get in the way of us leaving, I'll do more than just have words with him.

The boys shuffle toward the dining hall, and I hear Enrico chuckle. I grip my hands tight to stop myself from confronting him. A thud echoes through the hall as the old nun's door slams shut. I shake my head and tiptoe to my room.

When I open the door, I exhale with relief. The room is empty. I can pack my things without anyone being the wiser. Something glimmers in the golden sunlight on the chair next to my bed. It's my necklace! I rush over and scoop it up, coiling the chain around my fingers. The sunflower glints up at me. How in the world did the necklace get here? Surely Sister Faye didn't have a change of heart.

A creaking noise sounds in the hall. I stuff the necklace in my skirt pocket and peek out the door.

Enrico stands just down the hall. "It wasn't hers to keep," he whispers. He flashes a quick grin, then runs toward the dining room. I'm stunned. Enrico stole the necklace back for me. That was why he and Enzo were caught outside Sister Faye's room. The boy makes no sense. Now I could give him an enormous hug.

I shut the door and throw my clothes into my suitcase along with my treasured bundle of letters from Nonna and Rosa. I work as fast as I can, hiding the valise under my bed when I'm done. By the time Clara returns from helping clean up the kitchen, I'm already in bed. Having missed dinner to pack, I feel my stomach growl as Clara opens the door and tiptoes across the room.

"I'm not asleep," I say, sitting up.

Clara smiles, and she props herself against her pillow. My heart breaks knowing I'll be leaving my friend. But she'll be safer with Father Ortiz and the other kids. And what other option do I have? Taking her to the farm wouldn't be fair. The people at the center are her family.

We read a chapter of *The Secret Garden,* and then talk for hours. "It's odd, right? The hike? There must be more going on," Clara says. She's smart enough to know the adults haven't been forthright.

Clara has become a trusted confidante, and I can't not tell her. So I confide what I overheard between Father Bautista and the messenger, as well as the priest's conversation with Father Ortiz. Clara's eyes widen as she hears the news the Japanese are heading this way.

"I'm not going to San Paulo," I say. "I'm taking Enzo, and we're going back to the farm. I can't let my family leave without us if they flee."

Clara nods in understanding, her eyes glistening. "I'll miss you."

"I'll miss you, too," I say. "We'll see each other again. Let's promise."

"Yes, absolutely." Clara wipes her eyes. I give her a hug, then wipe a tear from my cheek.

I unearth the last of Tia's dried mango from the basket Gabriel brought and hand Clara a piece. As we nibble, Clara asks about Gabriel. "Is he your boyfriend? Have you kissed him?" She stifles a giggle, and I laugh.

I mentioned Gabriel briefly before to Clara. I tell her Gabriel is just a good friend, which is true. He really is the closest friend I have, except for Clara. But when I see him, I feel myself warm like when you stand in the rays of the sun. My heart brims with happiness, and watching his eyes light up when he sees me makes me smile. Or maybe it's just the war turning everything upside down. Everything familiar has been toppled. Perhaps friends naturally become closer under these circumstances.

"No, he's just a good friend," I say.

"You said he wasn't afraid to stand up to Sister Faye. And he went all the way to the farm and back, just to bring you news and gifts from your family. He sure sounds like he cares about you a lot. Wish I had a 'friend' like him," Clara says, grinning.

"I'm sure you will one day. Maybe Enrico."

"Enrico?" Clara laughs at the absurdity.

"You never know," I say. "He's got a good heart, I think."

Clara muffles a giggle into her pillow, and it isn't long before I hear her breathing slow as she falls fast asleep. I say a prayer asking for safety for Clara and the others, and for Enzo and me, and our journeys. A tear falls onto my bed as I realize I may never see my friend again. I miss her already.

18

Rosa

MARCH 17, 1942

Florence, Italy

A gentle breeze blows cotton clouds through the spring blue sky as I sit admiring the sunshine from under the shade of an awning. It's early, and no one else is outside the small café except Tommaso and me.

He regales me with tales of his hometown. "I think you'd like it."

"It sounds lovely. Maybe one day I'll get to see it."

"Wow!" he says after checking his watch. "I'd better be going or I'll miss my train." He takes my hand, kisses it gently. "Goodbye, Rosa. I'll see you again soon."

"*Sì,*" I tell him. He smiles warmly, then rushes off.

I sip my *caffè,* contentedly, looking over a score. I enjoyed our brief time together this morning. I smile, thinking of the times we've spent together. He makes me feel like I'm the only one in the room. My attention is drawn away by a young man, a university student, as he emerges from inside, *caffè* in hand, and sits at a table close to the street. He slings his rucksack over his chair and opens a book to read.

A black car creeps along the street, stopping not far from the café, and a man emerges. A Blackshirt. Another man steps out of the car. It's Uncle Lorenzo. The two men stand staring at the café. Uncle Lorenzo says something, nodding curtly toward me—his glare icy and face emotionless. Immediately, he gets back in the car and it speeds away.

The remaining Blackshirt struts toward the café, and my pulse races. What could he possibly want with me? Spotting the Blackshirt, the young man slowly reaches into the open rucksack behind him and pulls out a paper. Holding it low and out of sight of the Blackshirt, he crumbles it into a wad and tosses it.

The paper lands at my feet.

"What do we have here?" The Blackshirt sneers down at the young man. Relief surges through me at the realization I'm not his concern. But I can't breathe wondering what he'll do next.

The man nods to his book, nonchalantly. "My morning *caffè* and a little Dante."

The Blackshirt reaches behind the man and grabs his rucksack. He tosses the contents all over the table. Rummaging through the items and not finding what he's hoping for, he grunts.

Nerves prickle my neck. He must be looking for the paper. The pedestal of the table blocks the view from the street. I take a deep breath; then, without getting up, I slowly set my bag on the ground in front of the wad. Trembling, I lift the paper into my bag.

Sitting up, I drink the last of my *caffè*. Then I place my music in my bag and stand. I force myself to walk slowly to not arouse suspicion as I leave. When I round the corner, I rush home, certain someone is following. But when I ascend the steps and peer around, I realize it's just my nerves.

"Nonna?"

Thankfully, there is no answer. I'm alone. I make my way to my room and unfurl the paper. A partisan newspaper! My breath hitches. Uncle Lorenzo and that Blackshirt were looking for this, ready to punish the young man.

I grab a match, striking it to light the paper, but stop. Eliana comes to mind, and the look on Betta's face when I gave her the soup from Nonna. It's disgusting what Duce and his regime, including Uncle Lorenzo, do. Good people are hungry and unable to work. I think of the young man attacked on the street by those Blackshirt thugs—and of his sneering neighbor. This is what things have come to. People snitching on neighbors out of spite.

I blow out the match and read the paper. It details the plight of the Jewish people who are now struggling even more desperately to find food. And how the regime is giving rewards to those who inform on the Resistance, regardless of whether the claims are true. I think of Ciro's words. In the eyes of the regime, you're guilty by suspicion. I'm infuriated that Uncle Lorenzo is a part of such things. I won't let Nonna know that I saw him. It would only break her heart.

I hear the front door click shut, and my pulse races. I can't be found with this. I strike the match and light the paper over a silver tray. The paper coils into itself until all that is left is gray ash. I throw the ashes in the trash bin, knowing I won't forget what I've read. Nonna can't know my plans—I refuse to put her at risk. I may not be a partisan, but I can help Eliana and her family.

19

Caramina

MARCH 18, 1942

Timbales, Mountain Province, Philippines

My eyes crack open, and I struggle to focus in the muted darkness. Knowing I needed to wake early, sleep eluded me all night. I creep out of bed and slip into my pale-yellow cotton dress, fixing my delicate gold chain around my neck. I grasp the locket for a brief moment, then grab my sandals and valise from under my bed.

Clara is sound asleep. Gently, I set the tattered copy of *The Secret Garden* on the chair next to her bed. It's the least I can do.

I pry open the door and peer into the hallway. All is quiet. Barefoot, I tiptoe to the boys' dormitory. At Enzo's door, I push the latch gently, willing it to be silent.

Asleep beneath his mess of blond curls, Enzo looks angelic. I smile. I know better. I tap him, whispering, "Enzo."

His eyes flutter, and I place a finger to my lips, signaling for him to be quiet. He sits up, rubbing his eyes in sleepy confusion.

"Put these on, quickly," I say in a low voice.

Lazily, he pulls himself out of his pajamas and into the shirt and shorts I hand over. I stuff his remaining clothes into my bag, grab his shoes, and gesture for him to follow, which he does without questioning. We make our way quietly down the hall and safely outside. Now we only need to make it out of the courtyard. My heart beats quickly as I scan the area. Thankfully, no one is around.

"Where are we going?" Enzo's voice is hushed and dreamy.

"Home," I whisper.

"Home?"

"To Tia and Tio's. This way." I point.

After exiting the stone archway, I stop and lean against the outer wall. I scuffle into my sandals. Then stooping, I help Enzo scramble into his shoes.

When I stand, I spy a face peeking from a window in one of the boys' rooms. It's Enrico. My heart flutters in a panic. Is he going to give us up? But he simply smiles. I smile back, relieved, and he waves. Enzo and I wave goodbye. Then we hurry to the alley leading to the outskirts of town.

The shops lining the alley are quiet. An unsettled feeling comes over me. Just then, a man peers out of Miyoshi's Shoe Shop. Before he disappears back into the darkness, I catch his menacing scowl. I grab Enzo by the hand and break into a run.

When we reach the end of the business district, I exhale, relieved. No one followed us. Houses line the alley here. Fortunately, most of the townspeople are asleep. By the time we reach the edge of town, Enzo is fully awake—as is his stomach.

"I'm hungry," he says over and over.

In my haste to leave, I forgot to pack food. Hopefully, we'll come across a tree bulging with fruit.

The last house has a single window. On its sill rests a mango and three bananas. My mouth waters when I see, next to the fruit, a plate piled high with sweet rice cakes.

"I didn't eat dinner last night. I'm hungry!" Enzo groans.

I spin to face him. "You didn't eat dinner?"

His eyes fill with tears. "No! Sister Faye wouldn't let me. She told us no dinner for being in the girls' dormitory." His eyes droopy from sleep, he bites his lower lip, and my heart stings.

I had no idea he's not eaten since lunch yesterday. I glance at the plate of rice cakes on the sill. I've never stolen anything before. The broken look on the face of Mr. Aronzo, the baker back home, when hooligans pilfered and destroyed goods before Christmas comes to mind.

But I must get Enzo to safety, which requires we both make it through the jungle. And to do so, we need food.

My stomach flinches. I know what I have to do. I lead Enzo to the hedge alongside the road and tell him to sit behind a tree.

"Stay here."

He opens his mouth to argue but, seeing the look on my face, keeps silent.

Quickly I peek inside the window, grateful to find the house quiet. I hope God will forgive me for what I'm about to do. I inhale deeply; then with one quick lurch, I swipe two bananas. Gathering the hem of my dress into a makeshift pocket, I place the bananas inside the billowy material. Then I grab three of the small cakes, balancing them in one hand as I hurry back to Enzo.

The faint scent of sweet coconut wafts through the air, evidence of my wrongdoing. A stab of shame lights through me when I see Enzo's eyes large as saucers.

I'm about to explain I had no choice, when I hear mumbling. In the window a woman stares at the plate on the sill. She lifts her gaze and, immediately, spots us. Her puzzled expression quickly gives way to anger.

With almost a single motion, I shove the food in my skirt, grab my suitcase, drag Enzo to his feet. "Run! Run, Enzo! Go!" The two of us shoot down the alleyway, kicking up dust as we go.

"*Mágnanákaw! Mágnanákaw!* Thief! Thief!" The woman's voice rings out.

I don't dare look back. I run until we're swallowed up by the darkness of the jungle, only then slowing our pace. Neither of us speak.

Thief. I am a thief. I should feel ashamed. But I only did what was necessary.

Enzo's footsteps fall heavy behind me. For such a small boy, he walks with force. I'm certain this is the trail we took to the orphanage, but I don't remember it being so wide. Maybe it opens closer to town. I simply can't remember. Weeks have passed since we traipsed through the wild with Papa and Gabriel.

The jungle grows steamier the farther we go. Even the shade of the trees provides no relief. The air hangs thick enough to slice. We've been walking far too long for this to be the right path. It feels like hours have passed since we left town. At least we're far from the orphanage. Surely we're safer here in the jungle.

Then I spot a clearing through the trees and stop as I remember the field where the Japanese tortured those men. Enzo knocks into me, sending me stumbling onto a log lying across the path. He shrugs sheepishly, and I rub my shin to numb the sting.

He plops down next to me. I hand him our one remaining banana. He peels it immediately and breaks it in two. I take a bite as we sit in silence, savoring the mellow sweetness. After finishing, I lean forward to stand and spy a large building through a hole in the dense brush. My stomach plummets.

A dozen or so Japanese soldiers are standing idly in clusters by the hut. Throwing one hand over Enzo's mouth, I point with the other to the soldiers. We have to get away. Now. I whisper for him to move as quietly as possible. He stands and follows me. Every crunch beneath our feet is thunder to my ears.

Between gaps in the brush, I can clearly see the front of the building—a three-sided bamboo structure with the front open to the outside. Steps lead to a raised platform where cots are lined up against the back wall and more soldiers mill around.

A dozen or so young women—some just girls—sit at the base of the building. Next to the building, three young women are hanging clothes from a line strung between two trees. They look about my age. A few of the girls are even younger. I wonder if these are the girls the man told Father Bautista about, the girls that were taken.

We're close enough to see the faces of the women on the steps. One young woman's cheeks are stained with tears. Her right eye is bruised, and a bloodied scratch runs the length of her cheek. The girl turns, and my heart buckles. She looks just like Anna, Matteo's sweetheart from back home. Surely it can't be. Or could it? I want to yell to her. To help her get away. But any attempt, I know, will likely send us to our deaths. I grind my feet in the dirt with frustration and gulp back tears.

Two soldiers step out of the building, half dressed, shirts hanging open. One is buttoning his pants. The back of my neck prickles, and a shiver snakes down my spine. The men plod down the steps. One of them stops next to Anna. He shoves her with his knee, and she crumples to one side.

My cheeks flash hot with fury. I have to do something. But my feet are locked in place. The soldier mutters something to Anna, then the two men stomp down the steps to join the others sitting under a tree.

Momentary relief sweeps through me that they've passed by Anna, and I motion to Enzo to resume walking. But when another soldier appears in the doorway, my chest clenches, and I stop dead still. It's the officer who haunts my dreams. The one who tortured those men, nailing them to a tree. His eyes are dark and piercing. I remember his hateful look when he threw the boy's mother to the ground and shot her son.

The officer walks slowly down the steps to where Anna sits cowering. *Do something, God. Do something,* I plead silently. When the officer reaches her, I'm dizzy with terror. I reach for something to steady myself, grasping at air. *Please, not Anna.*

The officer cups Anna's chin, raising her face to his. She stares back blankly. Every moment watching this is agony. Behind me, Enzo whimpers.

The officer brushes a few strands of hair from her cheek. Seeing the cut, he cocks his head to one side with concern. Anna looks up at him. Hope flickers in her eyes. Then he laughs, twisting his lips into a thin, cruel smile. She crouches low, defeated. The man raises one hand as if to strike her. But instead, he gives a raspy cough, lowers his hand, and shoves her.

Then he turns to a young woman sitting a few steps behind Anna, grunting something I can't hear. The woman doesn't move. He bends low. With his mouth to her ear, he yells for her to get up. Even from where I stand, I can see her trembling. He grabs her by the arm and drags her into the entrance of the building, then stops. The two of them stand half lit by the dusky light of lanterns inside the structure and half obscured by the darkness of shadows.

He shoves her hard, and she falls to the ground. A sickening thud sounds as her head smacks the floor. She scrambles to get away, shuffling along the floorboards, but isn't fast enough. The officer lifts his boot, slamming it into the poor woman's side. Her scream pierces the air as she clutches her rib cage. Then he bends low, grabbing at her blouse and skirt. I turn away, but in my heart I know the terror that's coming for her.

Shaking violently, I grab Enzo and pull him close to shield him. I can feel him trembling. His chest rising and falling rapidly as he breathes in short, quick spurts. I have to protect him. I take his hand, terrified he's going to cry, and glance frantically back and forth, deciding which way to run. When I look back at Enzo, I spy a face peering through the trees.

We've been caught.

20

Caramina

A young Japanese soldier is staring directly at me. My heart is hammering in my chest. The soldier stares back unflinching.

Has he been watching us the whole time? He doesn't move or say a word. A momentary sadness flickers in his eyes and then he nods to one side. I'm afraid to look away. What will he do? I glance quickly. Following his gaze, I spot a path, different from the one we took, a path that forks off from the trail and leads away from the clearing.

Why would he help us? He's one of them. One of the soldiers destroying my country. I look back, and he jerks his head toward the path again. Urgency flares in his eyes.

"Hiroshi!" A voice shoots through the air. The young soldier rises slowly and walks toward the other men.

I grab Enzo's hand, pulling him toward the path. We've gone only a few steps when a shriek pierces the air, and I know. It's the woman in the building.

Tears spill from my eyes as I run, dragging Enzo behind me. I don't stop, even when we're far from the clearing. The constant thud of my heart mixes with the sound of my sobbing. But nothing can drown out the shriek now echoing in my ears.

An hour or so passes when Enzo stomps, refusing to go any farther. A cacophony of birds taking flight sounds overhead. I glance at him. He's stopped crying, but his cheeks are red as a ripe mango. Exhaustion and confusion are scrawled across his face.

The area around us is thick with trees, and I'm certain I hear the faint sound of water gurgling. The path has shrunk to a single-file trail, much narrower than the one we took from town. Chatter filters from the treetops as monkeys fling themselves from limb to limb, oblivious to the terrors of war. The sound of jungle life is a small comfort. Thankfully, no one has followed us. Though I know we won't be safe for long.

"We can stop for a minute," I say, catching my breath.

Enzo slumps on a mossy rock. In my haste to get away, I dropped all but one cake. Now I sit next to him and tear the remaining cake in two. I hand him a piece and watch him bite into the sticky mess.

"What did that man do?" His voice is barely a whisper. "What did he do to her?"

This is the last thing I want to talk about with my little brother. He's far too young to know of such things. *I* barely understand how these things can be.

"He hurt her." It's all I can bring myself to say.

I rest on the rock next to him, my head throbbing, my mind dull and fuzzy. My feet sear with pain, and I lean forward to loosen my sandals. Both heels are red and blistered, the right the worse of the two. One edge of the blister has already rubbed away, exposing raw flesh underneath.

I try to focus. I've no idea where we are. Once again, I've gotten us lost. I don't want to scare Enzo, so I say nothing. We lean against each other, both as spent from what we've witnessed as from running. Again, I hear the faint sound of water gurgling in the distance. But what direction is it coming from?

Enzo perks up. "I hear it."

I stand, motioning for him to follow. "Let's stay on the path. Hopefully, it runs into a stream."

After the incident with the boar, I learned it was always better to stay on the trail. With each step I take, my heels sting. I clench my teeth and try to focus on the sound of the water.

At home, if I ever worried, a song would play in my mind to soothe me. Now there is nothing but silence. The comfort of music has eluded me as I think about Anna and the woman's shrieking.

After a while, the gurgling morphs into a rush of water. Any waterway is a likely spot to come upon wild animals or worse. The path turns sharply past an enormous tree smothered in thick vines. Just beyond the tree, a fast-flowing river is in full view. The trail ends at the water's edge.

I stop. If I can see the water, someone might be able to see us. Enzo waits patiently while I creep forward. I scan the area until I'm certain we're alone. When I reach the water, I realize I've been so intent on finding it I haven't considered how we'll cross it. But there's no going back. Maybe we can walk along the shoreline. But I quickly see it's a muddy maze of moss-covered rock. Too slippery.

A loud splash sounds, and I spin around to scold Enzo. The smallest noise could alert any Japanese soldiers lurking nearby. Before I can say anything, I see him already in the water. He wades in the cool water by the shore. I can't blame him. The heat is excruciating.

There's no telling how deep the river is or how strong the currents flow. "Don't go in too far!" I warn.

I plop onto a rock at the river's edge and dip my feet in, wincing as my heels sting. The coolness of the water soothes them. Looking around, I see a boulder rising from the center of the river, protruding from the water like Mount Arayat. Water flows around it, spinning whirlpools that rush downstream.

I peer up and down the river, deciding which way to go. When I turn back, Enzo is wading out to the rock.

"Enzo!"

It's too late. He's gone too far and, in an instant, is pulled under. I scream and dive into the water after him. My throat tightens in panic as I gag on a mouthful of water. My eyes flit back and forth. There's no sign of him. Then, the top of his head breaks through.

"Cara!" He barely gets my name out before he's dragged under again.

I'm a good swimmer. Papa made a point of teaching each of us. "When surrounded by water, you either learn to swim or you sink," he'd said. Enzo can swim, too. But neither of us is a match for the strong current.

I reach out and feel Enzo's arm brush against mine. I grab and, for a moment, catch his arm. But he slips away. I grab again but feel myself being pulled from behind. Someone is gripping me around the waist and is dragging me to shore.

"No!" I scream. I fight and strain to reach Enzo. I keep thrashing about, fighting to tear free. I have to get to him. I have to save him. But it's no use.

I feel myself being heaved onto the muddy shore. Struggling to catch my breath, I cough and spit out water. A man towers above me, his eyes focused on the river.

"My brother!" I yell.

Another man's head breaks through the water's surface. He sputters as he swims in a jagged motion. The man has one arm around Enzo and is dragging him to the riverbank. Enzo is bobbing back and forth like a limp doll.

When I see his motionless body, everything around me slows. "Enzo!"

The man sets him on shore and begins slapping him hard on the back.

I push myself up to run to Enzo, but my knees buckle and I fall to the ground. Then I hear him gag and cough. It's the most beautiful sound I've ever heard.

The man carries Enzo to me and sets him down. I grab my brother, hugging him close. I thought he was gone, carried away by the water. He wriggles in my arms, and I finally loosen my hold. When I look up, both men are staring down at us.

Then I spot two rifles resting at the base of a tree. Both men wear drab olive uniforms. I look from one to the other, puzzled. If these men meant us harm, surely they wouldn't have risked their lives saving us.

"We'll have to go back." The man who dragged me from the water doesn't hide his frustration.

The other man shakes his head, sending droplets spraying in every direction. He gives a muffled laugh. "Maybe we should leave them." After wringing out his shirt, he grabs one of the rifles and slings it over his shoulder. He tosses the other gun to his friend.

"Come on, you're coming with us," the man who saved me says gruffly.

"Why should we come with you? We don't know you." I try to sound undaunted, but my voice cracks.

The man smirks. "I'm sorry, we've not introduced ourselves. I'm Alfonso, and this is Cesar." Alfonso points to his friend, then holds his hand out to help me up. I don't take it.

"You don't trust us? Good! You should be careful who you trust." He pulls out a brown canvas sack and squats down to my level. "But you can trust us. We saved your hides. Here, take this." He unearths a piece of bread from the sack and tears it in two, giving one piece to me and one to Enzo. "We're with Captain Torres. We'll bring you to him, and he can decide what to do with you."

"We just want to go home."

Alfonso shoots me a wry look. "And where would that be?"

The last thing I want is to tell him where Tia and Tio live. He seems to sense this and snickers.

"I know who you are. You're Arturo Grassi's kids."

I inhale sharply. How does he know?

"Come on, we don't have all day. You're coming with us. I'm not leaving you here to drown again."

Alfonso and Cesar start marching upstream along the slippery mud and rocks. Enzo looks up at me, bewildered.

"Let's go!" Alfonso barks, not turning back to see if we've followed.

Quickly, I squirm into my sandals, wincing as my raw heels scrape against the straps. I scramble to my feet. Holding my suitcase in one hand, I grab Enzo with the other, and we follow the two men who fished us from the river.

21

Rosa

MARCH 18, 1942

Florence, Italy

The tapping of my heels is the only sound in the hallway as I sit waiting for Maestro outside his office. I run through the finale of the piece I've been rehearsing in my mind but my thoughts drift to home.

I wonder how my sister Caramina is faring and if she's continued to sing. I hope the war hasn't stopped her. Isabella comes to mind. I long to tell her about Tommaso and ask if she's met anyone. Countless times we discussed such things strolling through the mango trees back home. Wondering how, when, and if it would ever happen. I now know, when it is time—it simply does. I hope she's still pursuing her design work. Once the war is over, surely there will be opportunities for her to share her designs with the world. I'd love to introduce her to Signora Conti. My thoughts next turn to my little brother, Enzo, and I imagine him racing around playing ball. And Matteo, how has he kept busy? He's not one to sit still. I hope with everything in me he's not doing anything reckless, given the war. And when I think of Papa, I see him in his garden, singing to the roses. Helping them bloom, he'd say. But I don't even know if they are home. I breathe slowly to release the fear that has gripped me over their well-being.

Maestro comes around the corner and hands me a sheet of music. I thank him and leave to go home.

The moment I step outside, I spot him. Tommaso. Waiting across the street. Even with his back turned, I recognize his athletic build and dark, wavy hair. My spirits lift seeing him. As if he senses my presence, he turns. He smiles and waves, then crosses the street.

"*Ciao, bella* Rosa!"

"Tommaso!" I don't even attempt to hide my pleasure.

"You said your class on Wednesdays ends at noon. Thought I'd surprise you. *Il bellissimo uccello canoro!*"

Beautiful songbird, he calls me. And I can't help but smile.

He swings a picnic basket forward for me to see. My stomach grumbles at the sight of the provisions. "Oh, *grazie*! I could kiss you. This songbird is ravenous."

He leans forward for a kiss and says, "No argument here."

I snatch away the basket. He gives a playful, wounded look, placing his hand over his heart, and I laugh.

"*Vieni, mia bella.* Follow me," he says, and we head off to enjoy our lunch.

He asks about my training, and I recount my travails from my breathing work on my latest piece. I ask about his work, and he tells me about a project he was on in a nearby town. We spend the rest of the afternoon enjoying the fresh spring air.

The next day, we walk along the Arno and through the Boboli Gardens. We talk of our days and our dreams. At times, we walk in silence. But even our silence brims with contentment.

This time, I brought a basket with bread and cheese, a little fruit, some wine. And we share a meal in the warm sunshine in between spring's rainy days.

Resting in the shade of a towering elm tree, I share with him the pain of losing Mama. Rather than trying to talk it all away, saying what people do in their futile attempts to help the grieving, he simply pulls me close and holds me. We sit for a long time. His arms around me, his back against the tree. Then, he draws me to himself and kisses me tenderly. Without hesitation, I kiss him back.

It's the most natural of things. Feeling his heart beating against mine is a comfort. He feels like home. I had no idea how strong my feelings could be. Is it right to call this love?

Tommaso is always so considerate. Always making sure I'm all right. He's a gentleman through and through. Draping his jacket over my shoulders when the wind gusts and, effortlessly, placing himself between me and any Blackshirt we pass. They're never the wiser. But nothing escapes Tommaso's notice.

When I've had a particularly grueling rehearsal, he's aware without me saying a word. Once, I voiced doubts about my abilities.

"A nightingale. That's what you are. 'When the nightingale sings . . . Leaf and grass and blossom springs . . . And love has to my heart gone.' You have a beautiful gift, Rosa. No worthwhile pursuit is void of fear. Following your heart requires bravery. You're one of the bravest people I know," he tells me, and I force back the tears that well up at his words. His belief in me spurs me on when my own wavers.

We make plans to see each other that evening. After we part, I go to the conservatory. When I enter the courtyard, I'm thinking of Tommaso when I spot Ciro. I haven't told him about Tommaso. I'm not ready. I haven't even introduced him to Nonna.

Ciro grins like the Cheshire cat. "Rosa!"

I've not seen him in some time and am glad for his company. "You're looking mischievous," I say.

"Me?" He gives a look of mock innocence, and I laugh. Together we walk through the courtyard studded with orange trees.

Ciro leans in, and he lowers his voice. "*La Resistenza* could use someone like you, Rosa. Assuming roles is a specialty of one in the opera, *sì*? It's child's play for you."

Why won't he give this up? It's dangerous. "Now you're an expert in opera? And all this time I thought you hung around conservatory only for *'le belle ragazze.'*"

"Rosa, you wound me! You know there is only you." His smile shows off the dimples that, no doubt, melt hearts throughout the city.

A serious look flashes in his eyes. "You would be an asset to the fight."

Why won't he leave it be? It's maddening. Though he's spoken quietly, there's no telling whose ears are listening. My eyes dart around to make sure we're alone.

"This isn't a game, Ciro. Your charm won't keep you safe. It's dangerous!"

"My charm? Dangerous? Perhaps." He smirks. "Come, let's have lunch, Rosa."

"No. I have class and don't want to be late." I spin on my heel and head to the door, my mind buzzing with frustration at his recklessness.

"Another time then. *Ciao!*"

I wave my hand in response and rush to my next session with Maestro. After this exchange, I know my decision to wait to introduce Tommaso to Ciro is the right one. Ciro's blatant disregard for our safety could cost us our lives. Infuriated, I take a deep breath to calm myself. Regardless, I want Nonna to meet Tommaso first, at the right moment. I think of my father. If I were home, Papa would have already met him. He'd like Tommaso. My whole family would.

22

Caramina

My foot catches on a root, sending me stumbling, arms splayed out, and I teeter before falling to the ground. Despite having saved us from drowning, Alfonso doesn't seem to mind if we die from exhaustion. He's like an animal scrambling over rocks and roots, never once losing his footing. My feet throb, and I massage my battered toes. Enzo's occasional whimpers are a telltale sign he is spent. If the two men weren't with us, I know he'd be crying.

Alfonso finally stops. He gulps water from the canteen dangling from his neck and wipes his mouth with his sleeve. "Come on, we don't have all day!"

I look back at Cesar, who's following from behind. He walks past me and pulls the branches back for us to pass.

Once through the thicket, I see a small clearing. It's a camp. Men are scattered all around. They are Filipino, speaking Tagalog and a spattering of English. Alfonso hurries into a large nipa hut while we follow Cesar.

"Wait here," he says, before ducking into the woody structure.

All around us, men, most of them young, mill about. At the sight, my muscles tighten, and instinctively I clench my fists. Is it safe here? But no one seems to notice us. Rifles and other weapons lie strewn about the camp. A few men sharpen knives on stones as they talk, while others clean their guns, parts scattered on the ground.

"All right, come on." Cesar appears in the doorway, waving us inside.

I grab Enzo's hand and step into the hut. The scene from the Japanese camp—and those terrified girls—plays in my mind. Five men hover at the back of the one-room structure. A single cot is shoved against the wall. Seeing it, I shudder. Everything inside me urges me to run. I clutch Enzo close.

A tall man stands before a long table, his back to the door. "I see you've gotten yourselves lost," he says, turning to face us. It's Captain Torres. With his hair tousled and shirtsleeves rolled up, I didn't recognize him. Though unsettled, I feel relief realizing it's him. He gestures toward two boxes sitting side by side.

"Sit, please," he says. "Cesar, get our young guests some water and food."

Cesar nods, while Alfonso glowers from the back of the room.

"We'll have to see about getting you back to your father. My men can take you. They'll be going that way later today."

"Captain, we've more important things to do than babysit." Alfonso groans but looks respectfully at Torres.

"You and your men will be heading that way, anyway. You shouldn't encounter any problems till you're well past where they need to go."

Captain Torres sits behind the table. Leaning on one elbow, he rests his chin in his hand and rubs his graying stubble. Though he looks tired, a fiery intensity burns in his eyes.

Cesar enters just then, balancing two bowls and two metal mugs. He hands them to Enzo and me. The bowls hold rice flecked with bits of chicken. *Arroz caldo.* Tepid water sloshes onto me as I take the mug.

"Go ahead. You must be hungry," Torres says.

Enzo digs his fingers in, lifting the rice to his mouth and swallowing quickly. Torres chuckles and leans back in his chair.

I take a bite, feeling my stomach squeeze. Now that I have food, I'm ravenous. I force myself to eat slowly.

"Get your men ready." Torres looks at Alfonso, who nods, then marches out of the building. The other men file out after him. Cesar is the last to go. "Alfonso's a bit rough around the edges, but he's one man you want on your side."

Rough is an understatement. Like saying it's warm out while roasting in the blistering jungle heat.

"You're safe here. My men won't hurt you." Torres is staring at me. Does he sense my fear? Does he know what I've seen?

I glance up, unable to speak. His eyes soften, and he has a fatherly look. I wonder if he has any children. My face warms. More than anything, I need to be strong. I pull myself together.

As if he senses the emotions battling within me, he speaks quietly. "War is a savage thing."

I wait, expecting him to ask questions, horrified I might have to recount it all to a man I barely know. Thankfully, he doesn't ask. I rub at a dent in the side of the mug and take a sip of water. My stomach settles.

"Sir," a familiar voice says. Matteo steps inside, presenting himself to Captain Torres. When his eyes fall upon us, he rushes over.

"I'll give you some time." Torres pulls a pipe from his pocket and strides out the door.

I jump up, nearly spilling the bowl in my lap. "Matteo!" I throw my arms around him, and he hugs me. He ruffles Enzo's hair and then faces me.

"What were you thinking, running away?"

"A man came to Father Bautista's. He said the Japanese were coming. Father Bautista was evacuating all the children to San

Paulo. I was afraid you all might flee. I wouldn't know where you were or how to find you, and I might never see you again." My voice shakes. "I had to get Enzo back to the farm." I pause before continuing. "Matteo, the man told Father what they were doing to young women." My voice catches. Tears well up, and I breathe to steady myself. I have to tell him—I have to tell him what I saw.

"Matteo, I saw them. I saw him. The man who tortured those men and shot that boy. It was him. He was there, and he was awful. They had young women there, and they were . . ." I try to continue. "He shoved her, and he—he hurt her."

Panic and anger flash in his eyes. "Caramina?" His fervor scares me. "Did he hurt you?"

"No . . . no!"

He's gripping my arm so tight it hurts. Now he lets go and exhales. The taut muscles on the side of his neck relax.

"Matteo, that's not all."

His eyes squint in alarm.

"I think I saw Anna," I whisper.

He stumbles back as if hit in the chest. He clenches his fists, knuckles white. The last time I saw the two of them together they were laughing under a mango tree at a party. Ages ago. I remember the smile fixed upon his face long after the party ended. He cares about Anna. Deeply. I drop my head into my hands and weep.

He crouches next to me, placing his hand gently on my shoulder. "It will be all right," he says, strangely calm.

I lift my head and meet his gaze. For the first time in a long time, I feel safe.

"Let's go outside." He holds out his hand to help me up. I stand, bowl in one hand, my dress splotched and patchy with river water, grime, and salty tears.

I wish Enzo hadn't heard our exchange. But he'd been there and seen it, too. Now, he raises his empty bowl, cocking his head slightly, and looks at Matteo.

Seeing the forlorn look on Enzo's face, Matteo smiles. "There's more. Follow me." He leads us to a shady spot where a large pot hangs suspended over a pit, a fire smoldering beneath. He spoons *arroz caldo* into Enzo's bowl and then turns to me. I shake my head. I haven't yet finished what Cesar gave me.

"You need to eat, Cara. We've a long walk to Tia and Tio's." Matteo pours half a ladle into my bowl. He refills our mugs with water from a barrel and leads us to the base of a nearby tree.

A young soldier with a guitar plops down next to Matteo.

The young soldier looks over at Enzo, then at me.

"This is Ray." Matteo introduces him.

Ray tips his head in greeting, strumming his guitar softly. I force myself to swallow a few bites of rice. As I eat, Ray plays. He doesn't sing. Just strums notes to what I guess is a folk song.

As I listen, my mind is silent, my heart numb. Matteo is watching me, his brow furrowed. I force a smile. The pained look in his eyes makes my heart sting.

He turns his attention to a small chunk of wood. I watch him fumble it in his hand, turning it around and around. He pulls something from his pocket. It's the knife Papa gave him when the bombs first fell on Floridablanca. He puts blade to wood, and thin shavings fall to the ground. My head pulses in time with the rhythm of the guitar. I rub my temples, trying to stop the throbbing.

Matteo pulls out a shirt and rolls it into a makeshift pillow. "Here, rest, Cara."

I lie back on the meager pillow, grateful to close my eyes. For a moment, the earth spins. But resting in the shade of the trees is a welcome reprieve. A breeze wafts over me as soft chords from Ray's guitar slip in and out of my mind.

I jolt awake unaware of how long I drifted off. My chest tightens in a panic as Matteo rushes past me toward a group of soldiers entering camp.

"Get Doc!" one man shouts. Two men are half carrying, half dragging a soldier. "Jay's been shot!"

Another man runs toward them, dragging a long piece of wood.

The two men help Jay onto the plank, and each man grabs an end. A man playing ball with Enzo rushes over. Together with Matteo, they carry the makeshift stretcher into a hut.

The soldiers who just arrived are covered with dirt. A few have blood streaked across their clothes, faces, and arms. My stomach drops.

"We got 'em, all right." One man stands before Torres and speaks for the group. "We were heading back. Everything was clear. All of a sudden, seven of those Japs came around the bend. One jumped Carlos before we even dropped our supplies." He glances down at the two sacks of rice he'd set at his feet.

A soldier next to him with dark, wavy hair rubs his bloodstained shoulder. This must be the unfortunate Carlos.

"Savages! One tried to get away. Jay went after him. Jap turned right around, slicing the air like a maniac. Got Jay with his bayonet. Jay just kept fighting, until the bastard shot him. Ernesto got there just in time and took him down."

A few men look over to a man with a blood-splattered shirt. The man, presumably Ernesto, shrugs, then grunts. "He'd have warned them, if he got away." By this time, more soldiers have joined the men circled around Torres.

"This was supposed to be a routine supply run," says Torres.

The leader of the disheveled group shakes his head. "Before we even asked, farmers were offering us supplies. They want those Japs out of here as much as we do. One guy got word from his brother down south they are taking all their rice and food. People left nearly starving!" He spits his words out.

Torres stares at the ground. "That's the third scouting party they've sent in the last two weeks. We'll have to move camp. Pack up. We leave tonight." Torres is decisive. He turns to a young soldier at his side. "Get the dispatches ready, and make sure the runners are aware."

The young man runs to Torres's hut. The group splinters off, soldiers heading in every direction.

"Matteo, get them home." Torres glances at me and Enzo. "The Japs are getting too close. It's not safe here. Go now. Take Gabriel with you."

Gabriel? I blink. Gabriel isn't a soldier. He can't be here. It must be another young man. Then I spot him. Like the others in the group, he's covered in dirt. I stare in disbelief. Thankfully, except for a scratch on his brow, he is unharmed. Why didn't he tell me he was helping Captain Torres?

Gabriel catches sight of me, and his eyes widen, locking on mine. His gaze rakes over me, concern etched across his brow.

"Alfonso," Captain Torres puts his hand on the shoulder of the towering man who dragged me from the river. "Our plans have changed. You and your men will go northeast."

An hour later, I'm once again hiking through dense jungle with Enzo tripping alongside. Using a bolo knife, Matteo hacks at the thick vegetation. It's disorienting and impossible to see what lies ahead. I don't ask if there is an easier way. If Matteo is taking this route, no doubt it's the safest.

It's unnerving to see him like this. Rifle strapped to his shoulder, eyes intense, and jaw set tight with the determination of a warrior. He's still my big brother. But now, I'd be hard-pressed to pick him out of a line of soldiers. Has he had to fight like the men who returned to the camp bloodied and dirty? The thought he might have killed a man sends shivers through me. I force myself to think of something else and clutch at my blouse clinging to my back in the hot, sticky air.

A bird caws overhead, along with the occasional screech of monkeys. I take another step, then freeze. A rustling sounds just ahead. I wait, expecting Matteo to signal to crouch and hide. I fight to breathe calmly. My fear has grown with each step on this hike. Gabriel stands so close I can feel his warm breath on my neck. We wait, but still Matteo says nothing.

The vegetation thins as Matteo sweeps through with his bolo. For the first time since leaving camp, I can see him clearly through the maze of greenery. Gabriel pushes back the last of the branches, and I step out into the light. We've come to a trail. A real trail.

For a moment, I worry Matteo will cross it and begin hacking away on the other side. Instead, he turns to the right and leads us to the base of a giant tree. The ancient tree's roots reach through the dirt, like fingers with knuckles worn and gnarled from age.

"Here." Matteo hands his canteen to Enzo, then to me. Gabriel gulps from the bottle dangling from his neck.

I sip the water, feeling myself relax. "How much farther?" I ask.

"A bit longer, but it'll be easier now." Matteo wipes his brow.

As we start down the trail, my thoughts draw back to the woman so brutally attacked. Her screams still echo in my mind. The distinctive call of hornbills floats through the trees but only flits on the edges of my consciousness. With each step, my soles burn, blistered and raw. Pain sears into the ball of my right foot.

Gabriel moves closer. "Lean on me."

Grateful, I shift my weight against him, wincing as I hobble along. "Why were you at the camp?"

He takes a deep breath and exhales slowly. "It's better if you don't know."

"Why? Are you fighting like Matteo?"

"I can't tell you . . . I don't want to put you in danger. You understand, don't you?" He pauses to look me in the eye.

I nod yes. But I don't. If I know Matteo is fighting, why can't I know about Gabriel? I've already seen him with Torres and his men. He doesn't dress like the soldiers. He wears the simple clothing of most young men in the mountain villages. Maybe his being there had something to do with helping the townspeople. He once told me he cared deeply about them and would do anything to help them. Whatever he's doing, it's dangerous. It's bad enough worrying I'll lose Matteo. Now, I worry I'll lose Gabriel, too.

With every step, my limping grows worse. Pain stabs through my foot relentlessly, and I find myself leaning on him even more. The muscles in his forearm are taut and flexed as he helps me, and it has to be exhausting. But he doesn't seem to mind.

Focused on my pain, I almost don't notice the man running toward us far in the distance. Spotting him, I gasp. Matteo ducks, signaling to be quiet. Quickly, he leads us off the path behind a tree. Enzo and I crouch in the brush behind him.

With one swift movement, Gabriel yanks a knife from his belt. He moves as if he's done it many times before, which shocks me. I didn't even notice the knife till that moment.

Matteo lifts his rifle and aims it at the quickly approaching man. I can't see him, but the man's footsteps come faster and faster. My chest clenches tighter. Watching Matteo shoot a man is more than I can bear, so I shut my eyes.

The man is nearly upon us when he slows to a walk.

I shrink back, anticipating the gun's explosion. But there is nothing but silence. Then Matteo chuckles. Confused, I throw open my eyes.

It's Papa! He walks cautiously, one hand resting on the gun at his side. His eyes dart back and forth, scanning the trees. He knows he isn't alone. He moves like one of Torres's soldiers, listening for the faintest sound, ready to strike. I've never seen my father like this.

Matteo calls out softly. Slowly, he stands, showing himself from behind the tree. Papa stops, and his hand falls away from his gun. I stand up.

"Cara!" Papa looks surprised. He embraces me and Enzo. "My God, thank you! *Dio mio, grazie!* You're safe!" He holds us out, looking us over. His eyes narrow when he sees my face. "I had no idea where you were." He shakes his head, his eyes a mix of relief and despair. Then he pulls us close. His heart beats fast against my cheek.

"We're okay, Papa." My voice is muffled against his shirt.

"I got word the Japanese were heading north, and I was about to set out to bring you back. But Torres sent a message the center had already evacuated. The runner didn't know where. I was on my way to ask Torres if he knew where you'd fled."

He shakes his head, pain in his eyes. "I only wanted to keep you safe."

"I know," I whisper, burying my face in his chest. A few rogue tears spill down my cheeks. It wasn't his fault.

When I look up, his eyes are racked with pain. "I should never have sent you away." He pushes a tendril of hair from my face, then looks over at Matteo. "How did you find them?"

"Caramina can tell you. I have to go. Gabriel can go with you," says Matteo, and Gabriel nods.

Papa walks to Matteo and pulls him into a quick embrace. "Go. Be safe, son."

I look at Matteo, willing him to stay with us. I know where he's headed. His eyes glare with an alarming ferocity. He's going to help Anna. He pulls me into a quick hug. "I must go help a friend," he whispers.

I want to tell him to be careful, that those men are savages. I want to thank him and tell him I love him. But the words are swallowed up by fear. He nods to Papa. Then he runs off down the trail until he's just a speck in my eyes.

23

Rosa

"Are you sure it's okay to be here?" I ask, stepping into the empty apartment building designed by Tommaso's firm. Somehow it doesn't feel right to be disturbing its peace.

"Of course, *amore mio*. More than okay," Tommaso reassures me. "Wait here. I'll be right back." He lopes up the stairs with his long strides, taking two at a time.

Moments later, he returns. Together, we head to the second floor where an apartment door is creaked open. He ushers me in. I enter and, once inside, see the newly painted walls of the sitting room as the late-afternoon sun slants through the windows. Not a single piece of furniture is in the room but then I spot it. In the corner sits a gramophone. And next to it rests a stack of records.

Tommaso takes my cardigan and drapes it over a ladder resting by the door. Then he walks to the gramophone. He places a record on the turntable, rests the needle, and switches it on.

Glenn Miller's "Sing, Sing, Sing!" drifts through the room. Not loud. But just right for us to enjoy.

I'm stunned. "You did this?"

"*Sì*, I thought we could dance."

I look at him like he's lost his mind. But glee at hearing the music bubbles up inside me and can't be stifled. This song, like so many, has been banned. He lifts his hand to me. I put my hand in his, and we dance.

Oh, do we dance! Kicking up our heels to this song, then "In the Mood" and "Boogie Woogie Bugle Boy." I don't know if I'm more out of breath from laughing or dancing. He's a surprisingly good dancer.

"Not bad," I say.

"Not bad, yourself! We make a good team."

We swing our way through one song after another. Though he towers over me, somehow, we're perfectly paired. Who knew a boy from Brindisi could cut a rug like this? Slice a gaping hole is more like it. We spin dizzyingly around the room, enjoying ourselves as if it's our last chance.

Gasping for air, we stop. Tommaso pulls two tin cups and a bottle of wine from his knapsack. We sip while catching our breath. When I look at my watch, I realize nearly two hours have passed. Begrudgingly, I tell him I really should be getting home.

He shakes his head. "Can't miss the finale."

The finale? As if dancing to contraband music and having the time of my life isn't enough. This is the most fun I've had in years.

He sets another record on the turntable, takes the wine from my hand, and pulls me close. "A Nightingale Sang in Berkeley Square" begins playing, and I almost cry.

"You remembered," I say. I told him when we first met how I love the song. It's been forever since I've heard it.

"It reminds me of you," he whispers in my ear.

He pulls me closer, his arms around my waist. We dance until the record crackles, and there is nothing else but the sound of our breathing. Then he leans down and kisses me. I taste the sweetness of the wine on his lips. Feeling his heart beating in time with mine, and the softness of his navy wool sweater, I breathe in the woodsy, clean scent of his aftershave. My heart races when we draw apart.

His aquamarine eyes are flecked gold like the waters of Castiglioncello in the fiery setting sun. His fingers grasp through my hair, and he draws me toward him. Another kiss. A kiss that eclipses the first.

I feel alive. Truly alive. The emotion of missing my family, my nonstop work preparing for festival, the heaviness of the war—all of it—vanishes. I want to stay in this moment forever.

As we part, he reaches for my hand, and we stand fingers entwined. I never knew how intense my feelings could be. I know now, without question, this is love.

After hiding the records in a crate, Tommaso walks me home. "I'm going away for work, Rosa."

My heart sinks at his words. But I know there's nothing for it. He has to go. "I'll miss you."

He squeezes my hand in his. "I'll miss you, too."

"Tommaso." I peer around to make sure we're alone. "I loved that. The music. Dancing with you. *Grazie!* But please, don't take such risks!" We both know if we'd been caught with the records, we'd have been arrested.

He nods, then looks at me, seriousness in his eyes. "I'd never put you in danger, Rosa."

"I know. But I've heard stories about what happens at the Villa Triste." The Florentine fascist police have been known to inflict untold misery and pain on their prisoners.

"I worry for you," I say.

"Me? You have nothing to worry about. I'm as boring as an architect can be. Really, don't you worry about me."

"Boring isn't a word I'd use to describe you."

He laughs, and as we approach the apartment, Tommaso tells me he has a friend, Jack, who's stationed in the Philippines. "He might be able to get word to your family, Rosa. At the least, let them know you're okay."

My heart lifts at his words but stings with the sharp edge of fear. "I don't want to put you in danger."

He stops, looks me steady in the eye, and gently holds my hands. "Don't you worry about me, *amore mio*." He kisses me tenderly, his late-day stubble tickling my cheek. "I'll see you soon," he says, then turns to leave.

The last thing I want is to put him at risk. I remember my uncle's words of caution to Nonna months ago. But Tommaso sounds so confident and sure. Maybe there is a way. Not having word of my family saddens me greatly. I long to hear from them and to know how they're doing. I ascend the stairs, hopeful. Effervescent love bubbling deep within.

24

Caramina

MARCH 19, 1942

Mountain Province, Philippines

I squint my eyes open as I hear the door creak. Tia tiptoes across the floor with one of my dresses draped over her arm.

"I didn't mean to wake you. I just wanted to bring this up. It was hanging on the line when you left." Tia sits on the bed next to me.

"What time is it?"

"You slept all night—and much of the day. It's about three."

I yawn, spreading my arms wide in the rays of the afternoon sun. Tia gently brushes loose curls from my face.

"I didn't realize how long I slept. I'm sorry."

"No need to be sorry, Cara. You needed rest." The creases on Tia's face have deepened, revealing a tiredness that wasn't there when we were last together. "You had us worried."

My head throbs, and I rub my temples. "We had to leave. I didn't know what else to do." I twist my fingers into a knot. "We saw things, Tia."

I haven't told anyone but Matteo what we saw the soldiers do to Anna and the other poor woman whose screams still echo in my mind. The moment the farm came into view yesterday, any remaining strength I had seeped out. I nearly collapsed from exhaustion. Papa helped me inside and up the stairs.

Tia had immediately drawn a bath. I'd lain still in the water as she gently washed my hair. When Isabella entered, a fresh towel in hand, deep concern welled in her eyes. As clean water spilled over my head, I watched dirty suds rinse down the drain, wishing my memories could wash away so easily. Though clean, I felt raw. With Tia's aid I had hobbled to the bedroom, where I fell asleep the moment my head hit the pillow.

Now I glance at my aunt perched on the side of my bed. "They did things, Tia."

The door rattles, and Isabella enters. She sits quietly next to me. Tia nods for me to continue.

I don't want to tell them. I swallow, twisting my fingers tighter. "There was a building and so many soldiers." I pause. "They were doing things to young women. Cruel things." My voice cracks, and a flush spreads across my face. "Anna was there . . . At least I think it was Anna." My eyes sting. I hide my face as I begin to weep. Isabella draws me into her arms. I try to speak, but a hoarse rasp comes out instead. A heaviness rests on my chest, and my head sinks low. Despite having slept well into the day, I'm exhausted.

Tia rests her hand on my shoulder, takes a deep breath, then lowers her head. But not before I see deep sadness in her eyes. "They are evil men, Cara," she says. She brushes a few tear-soaked strands of hair from my face. "They will be stopped." She speaks quietly, her voice unwavering, face set in determination. She leans in and embraces me gently. The bed squeaks as she stands. "I'm so glad you and Enzo are back safe. You rest now."

Tia closes the door behind her softly. I know she's going to tell Papa what I said. It's a relief. Maybe this way, I won't have to.

Just then, Clara comes to mind. What about everyone from the orphanage? Were they able to get away safely? And have the Japanese reached Timbales? Had my friends left in time? My throat tightens as panic rises just thinking about Clara and little Rae. And what about Sister Hannah and Sister Valencia? And Enrico? I pray silently Father Ortiz was able to lead them to safety.

For a moment, the image of the young Japanese soldier, Hiroshi, peering through the trees comes to mind. He helped us, pointing out the trail leading away from their camp. Why he risked his life is a mystery. He's one of them. The enemy. It makes no sense.

I feel Isabella's gaze upon me. Her concern is palpable. I scoot to the edge of the bed, pushing myself up. "I'd like to get dressed."

"You don't have to get up, Cara. You should rest."

"I'm okay. I'd rather sit downstairs. I've been gone an eternity." I stand, flinching when my feet touch the floor. Instantly, I fall back against the bed. My right foot is wrapped.

Isabella flits across the room and grabs the dress Tia brought up. She helps me wriggle out of my nightgown and gently pulls the frock over my head. It slips easily over me and fits loosely around my waist.

Both Tia and Isabella are thinner now than when I left, too, their cheekbones more pronounced and hipbones poking through their skirts.

"Is Gabriel here?"

"He left right after you got back," says Isa.

I hadn't expected he'd still be at the farm, but seeing him would have been a comfort.

As we pass Papa and Enzo's room, I spot Enzo running a toy truck along the floor. I hobble down the stairs, stepping gingerly. Isabella holds my arm to steady me. Hushed voices from the kitchen fall silent when we round the corner.

Papa jumps up from his seat. "Caramina! You should be resting." He puts his arms around me, hugging me tight. I rest my head against him and feel his steady heartbeat. I breathe in the faint scent of his aftershave. The familiar hints of bergamot and cedarwood comfort me, and the tension in my body eases. I'm safe.

I sit at the table. No one says a word. All eyes are on me. I know they're concerned but the attention makes my skin prickle. Next to a cutting board before me is a knife. I reach to pick it up. My hand shakes as I cut the sweet potato resting on the board. The *camote*'s flesh is firm. I slice it into the inch-sized pieces I know Tia will boil.

"No, leave that. You must eat." Tia grabs the cutting board and knife and moves them to the counter. She returns with a heaping plate of rice.

I push away the plate. I should be ravenous, but I'm not.

"You need to eat, Cara." Papa speaks softly.

I scoop up a small amount of rice. After a few bites, I set down the fork. I didn't feel hungry, but now my belly comes awake. I take another bite, then another until I'm satiated. I've barely made a dent in the pile of rice but can't eat another morsel. Tia hands me a glass of water. I sip, grateful for the cool liquid on my dry throat.

Tio smiles at me. "Thank God you're okay, Caramina."

"Oh! I didn't want you to lose this." Isabella pulls something from her skirt pocket. It's my necklace. "You left it in the washroom."

I shrug when I see the delicate chain. Last night when I undressed, I unclasped it and set it by the mirror. As I lay in the bath, I'd stared at the golden locket. It was wishful thinking, this looking for the good. I've been searching for it like buried treasure and all I'd found is more darkness and evil. I left the necklace by the mirror, not giving it a second glance.

Isabella walks toward me. I acquiesce and lift my hair for her to latch the chain. Once set, I tug at the locket. The sunflower grazes my fingers.

"MacArthur's arrived in Australia." Tio breaks the silence. "Let's hope he can keep his promise. Things change quickly in this war."

"War is fluid, but MacArthur gave his word. 'I shall return,' he said. He'll return. It's just a matter of time," says Papa.

Papa and Tio rarely talk about the war in my presence, but now they speak freely. According to Papa, the American and Filipino troops are fighting a brutal battle in Bataan. Their supplies are dwindling, and they're struggling against the savagery of the Japanese forces. The head of the American forces, General MacArthur, had been forced to retreat to Australia. Some U.S. troops are still fighting. But to win, MacArthur had to retreat and strategize so he could return full force with the necessary troops and supplies.

I hope Papa is right.

Papa helps me stand. He leads me into the living room and places a record on the gramophone. The two of us sit quietly while the music plays. It might as well be static. I rest my head on his shoulder, and my tears keep falling. We sit still long after the music stops. The room is silent, but for the gramophone clicking, over and over.

25

Caramina

APRIL 3, 1942

Mountain Province, Philippines

The muscles in my lower back twinge as I stretch tall. We've spent the morning yanking weeds from one of Tio's two remaining rice beds. The only ones that haven't been burned to prevent Japanese troops from stealing our crops. The hot April sun beats down on my face as I throw my head back, relaxing the muscles in my neck.

I was overjoyed when Gabriel last visited, bringing word that Father Ortiz, Clara, and the children made it safely to San Paulo. They got out just before the Japanese marched into Timbales. The town is now under occupied rule, and I can't imagine how the people are faring.

Tia glances over at me. "Cara, you're sore already?"

I groan, rubbing my back. "Rice may be important, but pasta's a lot easier to make."

Tia laughs. "Still, someone has to grow the wheat."

"And tend the fields," says Tio.

"And harvest it, grind it into flour, and make the noodles," Papa adds.

I straighten the straw hat shielding my face from the sun and pluck a rogue weed threatening to choke the life out of a tender shoot.

"And what would you have on your pasta, Cara?" Tia asks.

Papa's homemade sauce spilling over fresh linguine comes to mind. "Fresh clam sauce," I say, my mouth watering as I picture a plate full of the rich pasta. I can almost taste the savory sauce, and my stomach grumbles. I force myself to think of something else.

"Your father's pasta is *delizioso*," Tia says.

I'm battling a particularly stubborn weed. Its roots must have grown deeper than most, tentacles gripping the bottom of the rice paddy. It simply won't budge. I lift my hands in frustration.

"Let me." Tia walks over, grasps the weed and jerks it hard. It gives way, sending her teetering. "*Aray!*" she cries as she falls backward into the muddy water. "Ahh." She groans, then sweeps her hair out of her eyes. "Spiteful impostor!" Standing, she throws the weed into the basket at her side.

I try to stifle my laughter, but Enzo's giggling makes it impossible. My aunt is usually so composed. Tia looks from Enzo to me and back again, then breaks out in a loud cackle. Tio and Isabella peek up to see the commotion. Tia bows dramatically, giving an enormous mud-speckled grin.

Tio smiles. "*Magandá!* Beautiful!"

I'm still laughing as I move on to the next weed, and I don't notice the two men walking toward us until I hear Papa's voice. "Gabriel!"

Gabriel is at the edge of the field with a man I don't recognize. He isn't Filipino.

"Arturo, this is Lieutenant Commander Jack Borda." Hearing Gabriel use Papa's first name is a surprise. He always addresses him as Signor Grassi.

The man steps forward to shake Papa's hand. "Sir, it's a pleasure to meet you."

Papa wipes his palm on his trousers and shakes the commander's hand. "I wasn't aware there were any Navy men this far north."

"Officially, there aren't. After joining up with the 4th Marines, I got separated, and, well, I'm all that's left of my unit." The commander's voice cracks slightly. The somber look on his face tells me all I need to know. He clears his throat. "Please, call me Jack."

"Nice to meet you, Jack." Papa looks around, realizing everyone has stopped working to listen. "Why don't we head to the house to talk?"

"Actually, Arturo, this is a social visit," Gabriel says, sensing Papa's concern. "Jack has word from your daughter, Rosa, in Italy." The lines on Papa's face instantly soften and everyone clusters together to hear the news.

"Rosa? How is she? Is Nonna okay?" I ask.

All eyes are on the commander. When Isabella steps out from behind Tio, Jack stands speechless at the sight of her. Isa's cheeks tinge pink and redden under his gaze. She glances away. Then she wipes her forehead with the back of her hand, adding mud to her already dirt-flecked face. Clearly flustered, she breaks the silence. "Well?"

Jack smiles, his eyes still on her. "They're doing fine, miss. Experiencing some food shortages in Florence but nothing like here."

A sigh of relief sounds all around.

"We've been very concerned, not having any word. I'm sure you can understand." Papa wipes his brow. "Let me introduce my family."

Tio and Tia shake Jack's hand eagerly. Papa continues the introductions. "My daughters, Isabella and Caramina, and my youngest son, Enzo."

I can't help but be amused watching Isabella squirm under the commander's gaze. Even in her mud-stained state, my sister is beautiful. The blush on her cheeks sets off her amber eyes.

Jack is a handsome man. His dark wavy hair gives him a boyish look. He has a funny accent. I've met other Americans, but none that sound like him.

"Forgive me, Jack. But how did you get word from Rosa?" Papa asks.

"My team is one of several—was one of several sent here for surveillance and reconnaissance. I've a good friend in Italy. Thomas got word to me. He knows your daughter and asked me to find you. She's been worried for you all, understandably. Not an easy thing to do, finding a family hiding in the jungle."

Only a few people know we've sought refuge at the farm, which was Papa's intention. Papa nods, then looks at everyone gathered around. "Why don't we go to the house? We can talk more after we get cleaned up."

Bathed and in clean clothes, I help Tia prepare a meal. At the news that Rosa and Nonna are okay, Tio declared, "This calls for a celebration," and he insisted Jack and Gabriel join us.

Food has been scarce. But Tia has been stockpiling anything that will keep. She manages to put together a few small cakes from two jars of preserved mango and a small amount of rice flour. The heavenly aroma wafts through the kitchen. A reminder of more normal days before the war.

I can hear Jack talking to Papa and Tio in the living room. He, apparently, trained with the U.S. Navy in electronics and radio communications. His group was absorbed into a Marine battalion brought to Luzon. After his unit was destroyed, Jack was alone, working to support the guerrillas and relaying information back to the Americans.

"Thomas is a good man. If he says he's watching out for your Rosa, he is," says Jack.

There is a moment of quiet, then Papa breaks the silence. "Let's have some music, shall we?"

Bing Crosby's voice floats into the kitchen crooning "Only Forever." The song is followed by a man's voice I don't recognize. It takes me a moment to realize it's coming from the radio. All shortwave radios are banned. Anyone found with one can be tortured or executed. When I first realized Tio kept his radio, his boldness surprised me. But it is oddly comforting to listen to the newsman from KGEI, the

American station we listened to every day back home. How voices can travel so far, across the wave-crested ocean, is a mystery.

Tia peeks into the living room. "Well, he's a handsome one," she whispers as she passes between me and Isabella.

"Tia!" says Isabella.

"What? He is! Don't tell me you haven't noticed? And he seems to have an eye for you." Tia bumps Isabella with her hip.

"Tia!" Isa snaps, a fuchsia flush on her cheeks.

"He does have beautiful eyes," I say.

Isa scowls. "You're not helping!"

"What? They're like the sea on a stormy day. Greenish-blue, almost gray."

The corner of Isa's lip turns up slightly.

I can tell she's fighting a smile. "I knew you noticed. I saw you peeking when you came down the stairs."

"Peeking? I don't peek. I wanted to hear what he had to say about Rosa."

I look up from the gabi root I'm chopping. The voices in the next room have grown silent. Then there is laughter. It's Papa. His rich baritone flows into the kitchen singing,

> "*La donna è mobile*
> *Qual piuma al vento*
> *Muta d'accento*
> *E di pensiero.*"

Isabella and I are quite familiar with this verse from *Rigoletto*. "Woman is flighty, like a feather in the wind, always changing her mind." Papa often sings it upon witnessing our most quizzical behavior. Just the one verse—no more. But it is always followed by his deep, bellowing laughter that now booms through the house. Isabella shakes her head in frustration, and Tia chuckles at my sister's predicament.

"Why don't we take a walk, boys?" Papa says. The sound of footsteps is followed by the thud of the front door. Papa's laughter can still be heard from the front porch.

"Ugh!" Isabella shrugs.

I smile, and Tia laughs as she places the steaming cakes on a plate.

We all sit down to a feast of rice and leftover roasted pork. Even the gabi root tastes good as Tia used more salt than usual.

Then we move into the living room to devour the cakes. I sit on the couch next to Isabella, and Gabriel settles in next to me. The cushions sag beneath us, and I let myself fall against him slightly, our legs just touching. I'm just glad he's here.

Lately, I find myself thinking about him more and more. Questions about what he's really doing in Timbales and with Captain Torres surface. I don't know if I should be concerned for his safety or not. I push away the worry and instead focus on a memory of the two of us like when we played Tio's game of Dama. We shared a mango as we moved the pieces across the chess board, laughing as we slurped to stop the tangy nectar from dripping all over. Gabriel had wiped a drop of juice from the side of my mouth tenderly, and butterflies flittered in my stomach. Sitting next to him now, I breathe deeply, contented.

Tio brings out a bottle of grappa. "Arturo, you gave me this years ago. I've been saving it for a special occasion." He pours the golden liquid, then hands around glasses.

"*Salute!*" Papa raises his glass high, and we savor the drink.

Jack regales us with tales of his New England hometown. He came from a family of Portuguese fishermen in Massachusetts. His stories of bringing in the catch as a boy are filled with humor. He practically grew up on a boat. Enzo, Tio, and Gabriel ask numerous questions and conversation flows easily. I wonder if he's homesick, having been gone so long from his loved ones.

"Caramina, won't you sing for us?" Papa asks.

"Oh no. Not tonight."

Surprised, he motions to the gramophone. "We can put on *La Cenerentola*?"

I shake my head. A feeling of desperation rises within me, and I swallow hard. "Please, Papa. No."

His eyes brim with concern. "Well, it is getting late, isn't it?" He glances out the window.

I exhale, relieved he doesn't insist. I can feel Gabriel's gaze on me, but I don't look up. I focus on the dwindling sunlight outside.

Tio stands. "Yes, it is getting late."

Though Tio's generator easily powers small items like the gramophone, fuel is now scarce and carefully rationed. Using the gramophone is an exception, a luxury. At night, we use candles to light our way.

Tia hands me a box of matches to light the candles scattered throughout the room, then heads into the dining room to clear the table. "Why don't we all help?" Papa says, following Tia. Enzo goes with him, along with Gabriel.

When Gabriel steps out, the tension in my shoulders relaxes. He's been watching me closely, and I know he's concerned. The last thing I want is to have to explain why I refused to sing. I'm so glad to see him, especially since his visits are so sporadic. I miss talking and laughing with him, especially when he's been gone for longer than usual. Sometimes, a week or two passes between his visits. Even so, expressing my feelings about music, putting into words how it has lost its hold on me, would make it real. And I'm not ready to admit that. Not to anyone.

I light the last of the four candles, set two of them on the tables flanking the couch, then carry the other two into the dining room.

Jack stays back to help Isabella with a temperamental curtain. The thick panel is stuck on the rod. Isabella yanks at the stubborn fabric to loosen it, but it won't budge.

"Here, let me." Jack reaches up, towering over her, and jerks the panel.

"No! You can't pull it so hard. It will fall!"

"Well, we either pull it or leave it be." Jack yanks the curtain again, reaching high over Isabella's head. "I've almost got it," he says, giving it a forceful tug.

"Stop! It's going to"—there is a crack, a loud whooshing sound, then a clatter as the curtain and rod come crashing down—"fall," Isabella says in muffled tones.

At the sound of the crash, I peek in to make sure she is okay.

Isa and Jack are buried beneath the curtain. Jack's hand is the only thing visible from under the mess of fabric. Somehow, he caught the rod before it fell onto their heads.

"Well, that's a predicament," he says.

I wait for a snappy retort from Isa, but it never comes. Instead, my sister erupts into laughter, joined immediately by Jack's bellowing laugh. Jack pulls at the fabric, slowly unearthing them. The two stand gazing at each other, chuckling.

Jack immediately goes to work fixing the hooks in the wall. He pulls out a knife from his pocket and tightens the screws holding the brackets. He works so fast there is nothing for Isabella to do but watch.

"One down. Two to go." Jack looks at me and Isa as he closes the curtain. "Maybe I shouldn't say 'one down.'" He grins, chuckling, and heads to the next curtain.

I smirk at Isa, who stands back watching Jack wrestle the curtains shut. Isabella says nothing, just observes, her dark amber eyes smiling. I gently pat her on the shoulder, then head into the kitchen.

"We'll need more water for the morning," says Tio.

Tia promptly sets the bowl she's scrubbing on the counter and dries her hands. "I'll ask Isabella." She rushes into the living room.

Tio shakes his head, "Ah, woman!" Even I know my aunt's intentions.

"Isabella, we need some water. Would you go to the stream and fill two buckets?" Tia asks sweetly.

"I'll go with you." Jack's offer can be heard clearly in the kitchen. I can almost feel my aunt grinning ear to ear, reveling in her matchmaking skills.

"All right," Isabella says.

I can't tell if she is frustrated with Tia. But Tia marches back into the kitchen, smiling victoriously. She grabs the bowl she'd been cleaning and resumes scrubbing. I watch Tia and Tio work side by side. Now and then, Tio glances at Tia, shaking his head and chuckling. Tia sighs. "Ah, young love," she says. Tio smiles warmly and kisses Tia on the cheek.

A half hour later, I'm sitting alone on the back porch staring into the moonlit yard. Tia and Tio have retired upstairs, along with Enzo and Papa. Gabriel has gone to the shed to repair a shelf that holds Tio's equipment. The thud of hammering keeps time, a drumbeat for the buzzing insects in the jungle night. The faint sound of Isabella's laughter floats into the backyard.

"Please tell your aunt and uncle thank you for me," I hear Jack say. A squeak sounds as the kitchen door opens, followed by the clunk of two buckets set on the floor. "I enjoyed meeting your family. It was kind of them to invite me for dinner."

"I will." Isabella speaks softly. "Is it really safe for you and Gabriel to head back this late?"

"Nah, we'll be all right." Jack speaks quiet and slow, as if he doesn't want to rush. A few moments of silence pass. "Well, I'd better get Gabriel," he says. The kitchen door creaks, and their two sets of footsteps descend the stairs, one heavier, one softer.

They stand in the yard, just within view. I hope they can't see me perched on the wicker sofa. I don't want to spoil the moment.

"I'll see you again?" Jack sounds hopeful. Isabella nods.

Jack smiles, then leans down. He's almost a foot taller than my sister. In the moonlight, I see him kiss Isa tenderly. Then he raises his hand in a quick wave and heads to the shed.

Only hours before, Jack was a stranger. How funny life can be. Is it possible to fall so quickly? Maybe it is. Regardless, I'm happy for Isa. She stands, silhouetted by moonlight, gazing up at the night sky. Silver light illuminates her smile.

26

Rosa

The ancient chestnut doors of Nonna's villa creak shut behind me. Several inches thick, they tower over the entry as if guarding a castle, and I wonder what Titan installed them long ago. I walk to a bicycle resting in the shade of a rosebush overflowing with apricot blossoms. We've just arrived, and I'm relishing the opportunity to cycle in the warm sunshine as I head into town for supplies.

I won't learn of my festival placement until days before the event. Maestro has been fiercely advocating for me to be billed in the evening despite my grade being lowered due to Armento's scoring of my quarterlies. It will be such a disappointment if I don't receive the billing I know my performance deserved. But it's out of my hands. I've thrown myself into rehearsals. One benefit to the constant busyness before La Maggio is that I haven't had time to think. When I do, my thoughts run to my family and Tommaso. He's still away. I'm not sure when he'll return.

The only break I've allowed myself is this visit to Nonna's villa for Easter. As I pedal, I take in the springtime hues of green. The hills overlooking Florence are resplendent. Cypress trees stand majestic. Sentries along the road. Everything is awash in buttery April sunlight, and cottony clouds dot the blue sky. Wildflowers bloom scattered among bright red poppies. Magnolia trees flush with pink blossoms. Drops of purple cascade from wisteria.

A gentle breeze flitters through my hair as I make my way along the road leading into the small town. At the grocer's, I wait in line along with several townswomen. No one seems to mind queuing for food in the sunshine.

Waiting in line for what little is available is commonplace now, even more so in the city. You may need milk, flour, and meat. But you take whatever is available. Twenty minutes pass, and it's my turn. The grocer gestures apologetically to his nearly empty shelves. I give him my list, and he shuffles back and forth retrieving what goods he has.

As he sets three jars of tomatoes next to the few items on the counter, I'm thrilled with my luck. But before I can place it all in my bag, I'm shoved to the side and stumble as a man with a black shirt grabs up my prized tomatoes.

"*Grazie!*" he sneers, and the grocer stands stock still.

Stunned, I watch the man spin on his heel and walk out the door with my tomatoes. I want to yell for him to stop. But it's no use. It would only bring his wrath.

I swallow my frustration and turn to leave.

"Wait," the grocer says. He unearths a box from behind the counter and pulls out a jar. Tomatoes! I can hardly believe it. He gives me a wink, and I leave after stuffing it into the bottom of my bag.

I return to the villa with my single jar of tomatoes, two suspicious-looking onions, no flour, and one egg.

"*Mi dispiace.*" Setting my meager bounty on the cucina's colossal walnut table, I apologize to Beatrice. "I'd have had more, but one of Duce's men came in."

"Bah, they think they own everything. One day, they'll get what they deserve," she says, waving away my apology.

Rushing around the kitchen, she works a miracle with such little food. Nonna brings up a few jars from the cellar. She sets them next to a small ham that she has somehow managed to procure for our Easter dinner tomorrow. I suspect from the black market in the city—which is extraordinarily expensive, but it keeps us going. Not many can afford the exorbitant rates. Nonna does so sparingly.

Everyone is doing whatever they can to sustain themselves. A few of Florence's public gardens have been torn up and replanted with vegetables. Last week, I whisked past Viale Belfiore and found a corner garden transformed into a vegetable plot. With the warmth of summer approaching, I've no doubt tomatoes and other vegetables will be spilling over pots on balconies.

Over the last month, I've done what I can to save food to bring to Betta without Nonna or Maestro's knowledge. Knowing Maestro's schedule at conservatory has made things easier. Finding food has been a challenge. But I've managed to save extras here and there, and I have brought them a few bags since finding the partisan newspaper at the café. Meager provisions for their family. But food, nonetheless.

All of Mussolini's promises to restore Italy to its former glory have fallen flat. The economy, industry, the military, agriculture. None of his promises have come to pass. Food is scarcer, industry stalled, and people are living in constant terror because of Il Duce's inflated ego and that of his henchmen. The whole country is hungry, and its sons are dying.

Mussolini's plan for expansion is a disaster. Young soldiers are without the necessary arms and supplies with which to fight, much less survive, in a battle most didn't choose. How many mothers have lost their sons already? It's sickening. Why must men be so ravenous for power?

Thank God Tommaso and Ciro don't have to fight! Only university students or those with essential positions are exempt. It pains Ciro to be the target of nasty looks from those who think he's shirking his duty. Why he cares so much what others think is beyond me. Tommaso doesn't seem bothered.

After our small meal together, Beatrice leaves and Nonna retires to her room. I spend the evening reading by the fire before going to my bedroom to write in my journal. When I finally go to bed, I lie listening to the gentle spring rain for over an hour, then get up to make myself a cup of tea. On my way, I pass the door to the attic. In all the times I've visited the villa, I've never seen the space. Curious, I go up.

Boxes line the walls. Christmas decorations spill out of one. Another box is filled with old costumes, I presume from Nonna's earliest performances. Her most cherished gowns hang in her villa armoire.

I meander through the room and come upon a box of old letters and papers, as well as a book of photographs. Inside are photos of my papa and Lorenzo, when they were young. Papa with his blond curls and Lorenzo with his dark, straight hair. In some, there is another boy. Younger than both my father and uncle. I've no idea who he might be. Family friend? Cousin? In one, Nonna is holding him with my father and Lorenzo standing alongside.

In the same box is a handkerchief. Wrapped inside and tied in a sky-blue satin ribbon is a curly lock of tawny blond hair. A cherished memento. I refold it carefully. When I turn the handkerchief over, I spot a lipstick kiss pressed upon it. Whose treasured curl is this? My father's? The boy in the photos has curly blond hair.

Though I shouldn't, I read the letters. Most are from Nonno Vittorio to Nonna when he was in Milan for work. In one dated May 1898, he wrote: "They bring the infantry, cavalry, and artillery to fight their own brothers. Sixty-thousand hungry Milanese on strike gathered at Piazza del Duomo expressing discontent at the failed policies and corruption of this government. Officials line their pockets with financial bribes while stealing bread from the mouths of their countrymen. It's no wonder people are angry. And now, hundreds have been killed and so many more wounded at the hands of these incompetent, greedy men. There must be justice."

Along with Nonno's letters, there are newspapers from 1898 filled with articles vehemently decrying the horrid treatment of workers in Milan, the food shortages, and the resulting starvation of many in the south of Italy. I had no idea there was such turmoil. Neither Nonna nor my father ever said a word.

At the bottom of the stack are copies of a much more recent newspaper article condemning Mussolini and his regime. The paper was published by a partisan group. A chill creeps up my spine as Ciro's words about Nonna helping the Resistance come to mind.

Possession of these papers is dangerous. How could Nonna have such things? Fear sweeps over me, and I stuff them away, hiding them as best I can. The one partisan paper alone warrants severe punishment or execution. Is Ciro right? Are Nonna and Maestro in *la Resistenza*?

My mind circles around the possible implications, and then I spot a photograph on the floor. It must have fallen from the photo book. It's my papa in military uniform with glittering medals. I stare at the photo, stunned. When was my father in the military? And why didn't he tell us? How do I not know this part of his life? I put the photo back in the book and head to bed.

At breakfast, I say nothing to Nonna about what I've found. One day I'll ask her my questions. But not now. Ciro was right. Playing a role is part of opera, and Nonna is an excellent performer. But it saddens me to think she's living a double life.

Why does she feel the need to keep secrets from me? I'm sure she's worried for my safety, but I'm not a child. If what she does helps stop Duce, I'm glad—though it terrifies me she seems to be putting herself in danger.

Easter passes quietly. We attend church in the morning. When we return to the villa, Beatrice is back, hard at work in the cucina preparing our meal. Nonna and I join her to help.

"Buona Pasqua!" Ciro's voice rings through the villa hours later. His face pops around the corner into the kitchen where the three of us are working.

He goes to Nonna and gives her a quick kiss on her cheek. "What can I do?"

"I'm so glad you came, Ciro." Nonna pats his shoulder gently.

I feel his gaze on me and glance at him. "*Ciao,*" I say.

"We need more firewood." Beatrice chimes in from the stove where she stands stirring an intensely aromatic sauce that is making my mouth water.

"*Sì! Non temete,* Signora! Do not fear, ladies! I have arrived to help you," Ciro declares. Comically, he puffs out his chest, then rolls up his sleeves, and heads to the door. The three of us chuckle at his antics and go back to finishing up our preparations.

Later, he returns, balancing a large stack of wood. He sets about stacking logs in the mammoth fireplace. He moves swiftly with his lithe and lean muscular limbs.

Famished, the three of us sit down to a late meal as Beatrice goes home to be with her husband. The food is heavenly. Afterward, Nonna retires to her room.

Ciro places a few more logs on the fire, and we sit before Nonno Vittorio's old rosewood chessboard. We've never played before, and I quickly realize he's quite good, moving his pawns with the strategy and intensity of a conquering general. I relish the game even though he wins.

"Where did you learn?" I ask.

"To play? My father taught me. He loved the game. 'A game of strategy,' he would say. 'Good to master, son.'" Ciro deepens his voice to what I assume is an imitation of his father's.

"You must miss him. I know I miss my mother."

He nods but says nothing. The two of us sit contentedly listening to the crackle and hiss of the fire. The last time we sat here like this was at Christmas. We've never spoken of our kiss. I catch him sneaking glances at me. Feel his gaze lingering.

I sense he's about to speak, and not wanting to discuss our kiss, I stand. "I'm exhausted, Ciro. I'm going to sleep."

He smiles warmly, then leans down to stoke the fire. "*Buona notte,* Rosa."

"It's good to have you with us."

A log splits and falls, shooting sparks above the embers. "*Sì*, I'm glad I was able to come."

"*Buona notte*," I say, and make my way up the stairs for the night.

He is a desirable man. Warm, caring, helpful, charming. And those eyes! But my heart belongs to Tommaso. I only wish he wasn't gone so often. He travels so much it seems he's gone more often than he's home.

Not only is my heart spoken for, but just a week ago, I spotted Ciro in a café with the blond violinist. Only a day later, I strolled past the university and when I came around the corner, there was Ciro. Speaking in hushed tones to a petite brunette. I wonder if the violinist knows. I can't fault the women for falling for him. His charm is magnetic, and he certainly relishes the attention. It's no surprise as he prides himself as *il maschio alfa*. The alpha male. Brutish machismo is such foolishness.

The next morning, we drive back to the city, and I head to conservatory. I'm grateful to get back to rehearsing. It's a balm to my restless mind as it keeps spinning over the contents of Nonna's attic. A futile attempt to make sense of it all.

Maestro asks about my time away. "It was restful," I say. He tells me he wishes he could've joined us but was too busy to leave with festival just a few weeks away.

Easter was a short but needed break. Though I am physically refreshed, questions swirl in my mind. Is everyone hiding secrets now?

27
=

Caramina

Not able to sleep, I creep downstairs to the sitting room. I set the recording of *La Cenerentola* on the gramophone's turntable but can't bring myself to listen. Instead, I sit staring at the disc in silence by the dim light of a candle.

Papa had stopped me on my way upstairs last night, voicing his obvious concern over my melancholy. "When times are most difficult, that's when we need to hold on to the good things, Little Bird," he'd said. "Simple things that bring joy. Laughter, a dripping mango, the sun blazing golden peach and magenta, and music. These are blessings to hold dear." I forced a smile and nodded, hoping to ease his mind.

As I contemplate his words now, voices outside startle me, breaking me from my thoughts. Men are approaching the house. I freeze, my muscles stiff with fear.

Papa rushes in. "Go in the kitchen, Caramina!"

I hurry away, dreading the next sounds I might hear. I peek around the corner to see Papa rush to a window and crack open the curtain. He exhales and opens the door.

"Arturo." It's the unmistakable voice of Jack Borda.

"We're sorry for coming so early." It's Gabriel. At the sound of his voice, pinched and grave, my stomach clenches. I glance at the clock. Something must be horribly wrong for them to arrive before six in the morning.

"I wanted you to know as soon as I found out," Captain Torres says. "We got word Matteo, along with two of my men, was taken."

Papa stands perfectly still.

"Two days ago, Matteo was on a team that attacked a Japanese troop holding a number of young women. When they got there, there were only a handful of Japs. They were able to take them and free the women. Matteo brought one of the girls, Anna, to her aunt and uncle's home. Now we know Matteo was spotted by an informer, Masao Miyoshi."

"The shoe shop owner? He's been here for years!" Papa gives a disgusted sigh.

"We suspected he was working as an informer. The Japanese have placed many expats in positions of authority. Miyoshi's been working with Captain Okamoto."

I picture the small man with dark eyes who scowled at me when Enzo and I fled the orphanage.

"We know where they're being held, Arturo," says Torres.

"Where?" The fierceness in Papa's voice is alarming. "I'm going with you."

"I knew you would."

I sway, dizzy with fear, and reach for the wall. They have Matteo. What are they doing to him? My thoughts swirl and land on the men I saw with their hands nailed to the tree. My stomach roils, and I think I might be sick. I press my hand to the wall to steady myself.

"We're ready to go." Torres motions to the men in the room. "I have men waiting. The commander will accompany us. It was his communication that led us to where Matteo and the others are being held."

Papa looks at Jack. "Thank you," he says, his voice somber.

Jack gives a nod. Torres unfolds a map and sets it on the table.

The men circle round. "We'll come in from the south. They're holed up in a small valley just over this ridge." He points to a spot on the map. "From our last reports, we know the Japanese have at least ten men standing guard."

Papa nods.

"We move in from here and here." Torres points out two places. "There's a stream here. We'll have to make sure it's clear before moving in."

"Those Japs keep a good watch. We need a diversion," Alfonso interrupts.

"These are the high points." Papa points to the map. "We need a man here and here for overwatch." I can't believe my ears. Papa sounds just like Captain Torres.

"I have two men, exceptional shots," says Torres. Papa nods, and Torres continues, "They'll take the high ground for cover. Alfonso, you and Cesar clear the stream before we head in."

"Will do." Alfonso puffs a cloud of smoke from the cigarette dangling at his lips.

"Let me get what I need," Papa says.

"I thought you could use this." Torres hands him a rifle. Papa takes the gun, along with a belt of bullets, which he slings over his shoulder. He's moving like a hardened soldier, so unlike the Papa I know.

"Thank you. I'll just be a moment." He hurries away.

Torres and the men walk outside. Papa comes down the stairs carrying a worn bag I've never seen, its brown canvas faded. He throws it over his shoulder and starts for the door.

"Papa!" I grab him, clutching him tight.

"It will be all right, Caramina. Tio will stay here. We'll be back— don't worry." He speaks tenderly, but there is no hiding the rawness in his voice. He pulls away and heads out the door.

This can't be happening. I look around the room. Papa's break- fast, a single mango, lies partially sliced on a plate, spilling golden juice onto the counter. The silence in the kitchen pulses in my ears, and my mind races. Images of Anna and the women held captive flash through my mind, along with the boy shot in front of his mother so long ago. Terror races through me. I know what they're capable of. Surely it's better to stay. What if they come here? Who will help Enzo?

But they need a distraction. What if Alfonso's right? What if not having a diversion puts Papa in danger? What if it means they can't rescue Matteo or that Papa will be taken, too? My heart beats faster. There's no time. I must do something.

I clench my fists, fingernails digging deep into my palms. Tio is here to protect Enzo. He'll keep him and the others safe. I know what I have to do. I will be the distraction. Papa would never let me go, but he can't stop me if he doesn't know.

I race out the door, careful not to make a sound. Then I run across the meadow. I can just make out the light of Alfonso's cigarette. I follow the men from a distance, stepping quietly. If they hear me, Papa will send me back.

Darkness magnifies the jungle sounds. Noises float from deep in the trees. I don't want to think about which wild animals are lurking. Walking through the jungle in daytime is one thing. Traipsing through it in the dark simply isn't done.

The men walk quietly, but their whispers drift back to me and mix with the sounds of the jungle. They turn off the main path onto a narrow trail, and my stomach grips in panic. I'm not close enough to follow on such a sketchy path. I step through the tree line, and I am relieved when my foot lands on a worn trail. It's narrow, but at least I don't have to worry about getting lost. The light from Alfonso's cigarette fades, but I can hear their quiet footsteps on the rocky path.

We hike downhill for some time, when all of a sudden a loud noise sounds, startling me. A shriek of sorts. I shudder, forcing myself to keep going. I have to focus on the men in front of me. Finally, the screeching dissipates, but it's followed by an eerie silence. It takes a moment to realize the men have stopped. Have they turned off the trail and I didn't hear them because of the awful shrieking? My heart lurches.

There is nothing but silence. Panic grips me, and my eyes sting. Then I hear Captain Torres whispering commands, followed by the shuffling of feet. The sound is dispersed. My eyes focus, and I see someone standing not far in front of me.

Carefully, I tug back a branch. Papa and Torres are only about ten feet away. There is just enough light in the early dawn to make out their faces. They're focused on two huts in the middle of a small, grassy field. I follow their gaze and see a man hunched against a tree. His head hangs low, and he sits slumped over his knees. He gives a low groan, then lifts his head slightly, and I know.

It is Matteo. I gulp and bite my cheek to keep from crying out. His face is swollen and red, his eyes black and blue. Cuts pepper his forehead and cheek. I want to run to him but force myself to be still. I'm supposed to be a distraction, but how?

I remember Papa and Torres talking about having two men on higher ground, something about providing cover. I dig my heels in the dirt and peer around. A number of Japanese soldiers are in the clearing, one right next to Matteo. Another man is tied to a tree in the back of the camp.

The soldier next to Matteo leans down till they are face-to-face. He yells something I don't understand. Matteo doesn't move. A rifle dangles from the soldier's shoulder. Then he grabs it, bringing the handle down hard on the back of Matteo's head. Matteo lurches forward. I stumble back as if I'm the one hit.

The soldier yells the word over and over, lifting the rifle high. Matteo doesn't respond. Then slowly, he raises his head. His eyes crack open for a moment, before his head lops down again.

I want to scream. Why aren't Torres's men doing anything? And where is Papa? I rack my brain to think of how to help.

Just then, a man steps out of the hut closest to me. He turns his face up to the fading light of the moon. My hands begin to tremble. It's the officer who shot the young man, the same one I saw at the building who'd thrown the girl down like a ragdoll and attacked her.

I take a slow step back, and my foot hits a root. I stumble, twisting, and fall against a rock. I lean against the large stone, face down, breathing fast. I clutch at the boulder, desperately hoping no one heard me. I hear nothing but my heartbeat pounding in my ears. I stay motionless until I'm sure it's safe.

I push myself up, crouching low. The soldier is still standing over Matteo with his rifle held high. I turn my head, searching for Papa, and I find myself staring right into the face of the officer that had come out of the hut. I gasp. He stands inches away, glaring at me with eyes black as the soil beneath me.

He bends down, leaning in close. I can feel his hot breath on my face. "You must be lost." His near-perfect English is startling. "A girl can get in trouble wandering into places she shouldn't be." He speaks slowly and stares at me, not blinking once. I swallow hard, not sure what to do.

"Get up," he says. I try to stand but am shaking so badly I nearly stumble again. "Please," he sneers, then motions for me to walk to the clearing. I drag myself up and into the camp. He stands in front of me. "I am Captain Okamoto. How fortunate for you to join us." His mouth forms a crooked arch. My skin bristles, and a bead of sweat drips between my shoulder blades.

Okamoto moves slowly toward me. He lifts one hand and brushes a strand of hair from my forehead. My stomach twists in revolt as his fingers graze my cheek. Then he stands back and looks me up and down. I want to run. I only wanted to help Matteo and Papa. But I failed.

Then a loud explosion blasts. Okamoto scrambles backward and throws himself to the ground like a wildcat.

It takes me a moment to realize the explosion is a gunshot. Instantly, blasts sound in all directions, but I can't move. I stand rigid in the center of the camp.

"Get her out of here!" Papa yells. Someone grabs me around the waist from behind and pulls me toward the trees.

"No!" I scream. I fight to go back and see Papa rush to Matteo. My legs come to life, and I kick as hard as I can.

"Stop, Caramina! Stop!" Gabriel is holding me.

"No!" I scream again. Gabriel drags me from the camp. Farther from Papa and Matteo.

Gunshots explode everywhere, momentary flashes in the dark. A soldier lunges at Captain Torres, bayonet thrust out. Torres throws himself on the man, overpowering him. A shot rings out. Both men drop to the ground. After a moment, Torres pushes the man off him. The man's lifeless body falls to the ground. Torres stands, scanning the camp.

Alfonso races past Torres, firing as he runs toward Okamoto's hut. I can see the silhouette of the Japanese captain crouching in the dark, just out of sight. Okamoto scans the area, glaring at the men who attacked. Then, he springs into the trees behind the hut, running without making any noise.

Another gunshot sounds. Papa lunges forward, his body falling onto Matteo. I shriek, fighting to free myself. Gabriel grips me by the arm, pulling me deeper into the jungle. He doesn't stop until we're far from the camp.

I give up trying to break free. All of my energy seeped out watching Papa's body slump onto Matteo. Gabriel drags me along, before stopping and telling me we have to run. He grabs me by the hand and doesn't let go until we reach a grove of ancient trees. I don't say anything, just set one foot in front of the other. We run for what seems like hours, until the familiar sounds of the jungle surround us as if nothing has happened. But my whole world has changed.

"Papa . . ." I whisper, my lips dry.

Gabriel finally stops, and I drop down against a tree. He kneels beside me and pulls out a canteen and hands it to me. "Your father knows what he's doing, Cara." There's a fierce tenderness in his gaze.

"He fell. I think he was . . ." I can't bring myself to utter the word. I have no tears. I'm numb and oddly cold. I feel myself begin to tremble.

Gabriel takes my hand in his. "He'll be okay, Caramina."

I stare at him blankly.

"What were you doing?" His eyes are pleading. "You could have been . . ." Gabriel chokes on the words. A feverish look flares in his eyes. "Those men, they could have . . ." He shakes his head, then falls silent and leans closer to me.

We rest a short while longer before continuing our trek. Once at the farm, Gabriel stays just long enough to speak with Tio before heading back to Torres's camp.

I watch him disappear through the trees. Will he be taken from me, too? An ache pulses in the hollow of my heart. I beg God for Papa and Matteo to be okay and for Gabriel's safety. And wonder if anyone is listening.

28

Caramina

APRIL 20, 1942

Mountain Province, Philippines

The night of the rescue, Torres sent a runner to let us know Papa was fine and Matteo was recovering under Doc's care. At the news, relief swelled through me. But nothing has eased my heart's numbing ache.

That was three days ago. Now, Isabella and I watch as Papa, Jack, and Gabriel drag Matteo on a makeshift stretcher through the meadow. When they finally reach the house, the sight of him is frightening. His skin is a mosaic of black, blue, and reddish brown. Even his arms and legs are badly bruised. One leg is wrapped in strips of cloth—Doc had stitched up a deep gash. We'll need to clean it and change the bandages. Any infection, he warned, could prove fatal since medicine is scarce. Fortunately, Jack was able to procure some sulfa tablets.

The house is abnormally quiet. We all want to speed Matteo's recovery. Tia, Isabella, and I take turns tending his wounds and sitting at his bedside. Tia even slaughtered one of the remaining chickens and made *arroz caldo*, trying to eke out all the possible nutrients to nurse him back to health. Doc said healing would be a long process, but he was confident Matteo would recover fully under the watchful eyes of our family.

Even so, seeing him in such a state is almost more than I can bear. "You need to drink, Matteo. Here," I whisper, trying not to startle him. His swollen eyelids flutter. I raise the glass to his lips, carefully holding it as he takes a few meager sips. Then he lies still.

I set the glass on the small table next to the bed and watch his chest rise and fall almost imperceptibly. I'm about to shut the door when he groans, stretching his hand out toward me.

"Sit, please." His words are a raspy whisper.

I pull a chair up to the bed. The creases on his brow relax, and he looks almost peaceful. I'm glad to stay with him if it eases his pain. I listen to his breathing quiet to a slow rhythm.

The door cracks, and Tia peeks in. "Why don't you go to the kitchen, Cara?" Cloth strips are draped over her arm, and she holds a basin with water.

Sleepy with the warmth of the room, I rub my eyes and stand slowly. I head outside to the tree line behind the house. Here the jungle grows wild and fast. Vibrant. I wish my spirit was the same. But it's been dulled. Strangled by war like a vine choking life from a sapling.

The weeks pass without much noise from the war. Matteo and I are on the veranda. Tio dragged the wicker sofa from the back porch out front. He was adamant Matteo get fresh air. "It'll speed his recovery," he said.

He was right. Matteo had already made great strides, literally. He could walk down the stairs from his room, slowly, but without help.

Now he is reclining on the sofa, eyes shut. I assume he's asleep, and I sit quietly on the step, eyes focused on the blurred green of the trees beyond the meadow. Tio's elixir of fresh air is not so fresh today. The air hangs heavy, steeped in humidity. I wipe dots of perspiration from my brow. Fortunately, the porch is shaded. I lean back against a column and rest.

"I haven't heard you sing in so long." Matteo's voice startles me. "Sing something. Please?"

He's right. I haven't sung in forever. Now and then, I hear Tia singing a folk song or Isabella and Enzo singing along when a song comes on the radio. But when I listen, it's as if a vault within me has been locked. And music is no longer welcome.

Matteo cracks open one eye. What remains of his black-and-blue bruising has melded into an odd yellowish hue. He stares at me, waiting.

"Caramina?"

"I can't. I haven't sung in so long."

"I know. Please?"

It isn't an odd request. Any other time in my life, I'd gladly have sung. His concern is obvious. Since his return to the farm, I've caught him gazing at me with a quizzical look whenever music drifts through the house. To Matteo, my lack of interest means something is drastically wrong. But I don't know how to fix it. Or if I even want to.

I exhale, staring down. Matteo has risked his life for me so many times. But how can a song be any help to him? Yet how can I say no after all he's done and has been through? I close my eyes, wishing and waiting for a melody to take shape. There is nothing but silence.

In the distance, a bird begins to sing. Its song niggles inside me. The fringes of a memory spark. I can hear it now, faintly. A song I learned years ago. A sad song. But the bird's notes play along with the scant melody in my head.

I straighten myself, breathe deeply, and sing the "Vissi d'arte." My first notes whisper in the air. Words slowly take shape and one by one fall from my lips. I feel a prickle in my heart that needles a dot-sized wound. The wound splits open, letting in sunlight and warmth. Words tumble out. The warmth is life-giving, oxygen to the music within me.

> *"I lived for my art, I lived for love,*
> *I never did harm to a living soul!*
> *With a secret hand*
> *I relieved as many misfortunes as I knew of."*

Overcome by emotion, I take a breath before continuing.

> *"In the hour of grief,*
> *why, why, O Lord,*
> *why do you reward me thus?"*

Music streams forth, desperate, like a sunflower reaching for light. I sing the words in Italian. They pour out, an offering and a question. I finish the last strain, and my voice quiets. I open my eyes. Hot tears stream down my cheeks.

Matteo is sitting upright on the sofa, rapt. He stares at me, then lifts his hand and wipes a tear from his eye. Visibly shaken, he says, "Thank you."

Without saying a word, I rush down the stairs. I run toward the bird, following its song like a trail of crumbs. Something has shifted inside me. Something has come to life. I can feel it—all of it—the pain, the agony of the war, the fear, and the loss. But there is something else. I dredge the depths of my heart with each step. Music is still with me, alive inside me. As I stride toward the bird, I recognize it, this new reality. It is hope.

29

Rosa

APRIL 23, 1942

Florence, Italy

Crackling through static, the announcer's voice emerges clearly. At the mention of Bataan, I freeze. He details the savage, relentless march to Camp O'Donnell that the Japanese military have forced on captive Filipinos and Allied troops. Many have been beaten. Shot. Bayoneted. Beheaded. The words are an assault on my mind and body, and I drop the cup I'm clutching, sending shards of porcelain shooting across the parquet floor of Nonna's sitting room.

The route they've taken from Mariveles north to San Fernando skirts to the east of my family's home. But Floridablanca isn't far. My chest squeezes in panic. I don't know when Nonna comes to my side. But I feel her arm around me, holding me upright. We stand listening. Helpless.

"Leave it," Nonna says, as I crumble to the floor to gather the shattered pieces. "Leave it, Rosa. *Andiamo,* let's go to Antonino's."

The mention of Maestro's first name is a surprise. I've not heard her use it before. When I look up, tears are in my grandmother's eyes. She is the strongest woman I know. But this news of such unspeakable horror so close to her beloved family has found the chink in her defensive armor.

She helps me stand, and I realize we are both shaking. I know she wants to create a distraction for me by visiting Maestro's and seeing him will be a comfort to us both. "Come," she says again.

Together, we make our way to Maestro's. He pulls open the door before we even knock, having spotted us from the window.

"Serafina." He draws Nonna into an embrace. He knows. "Rosa." He places his hand on my arm gently.

Nonna moves away from him slowly. "We must believe they are okay."

"Yes," Maestro says, solemnly.

There are no other words. I have to believe my family has sought refuge elsewhere. That they've been nowhere near these atrocities. But the reality that the Japanese would be so inhumane is stunning. Shocking.

I try to breathe deeply but find myself taking in shallow gulps.

"Rosa?" Ciro appears around the corner. He grasps my hand and holds it firmly for a moment before releasing it. "Let's sit."

Nonna follows Maestro onto the terrace, and I trail after Ciro to Maestro's dark-paneled den.

From behind the sofa, Eliana jumps up. "Rosa!" Her excitement belies her childlike innocence. Ciro's expression seems to ask if it's all right she is here.

Seeing her, Enzo comes to mind. Tears well up, but I force them back. "You must have beaten Ciro," I say, spotting the jacks on the floor.

He shoots a boyish grin at Eliana. "A little minx, this one."

She drops to the floor. "Let's play again!"

He glances at me, eyes brimming with concern.

"Yes, I'd love to watch the neighborhood champion victorious over Ciro," I say.

He chuckles, then sits cross-legged on the floor, mirroring Eliana. She giggles, and the two begin their game.

Ciro plays with a degree of patience I've not seen him demonstrate before. I don't know why that should surprise me. He's a good man. Clearly, he's quite taken with Eliana. Who wouldn't be? She's a breath of fresh air. Her sweetness, a light in the darkness engulfing my world.

The two continue to play, Eliana winning each time. Ciro pretends to be frustrated, but even Eliana knows he's joking. "You're a valiant opponent, Eliana," he says.

"I am!" she says matter-of-factly. At her unwavering confidence, both Ciro and I laugh.

Afterward, Nonna and I walk home, both lost in our thoughts. Two Blackshirts pass us, one of them leering at me. Nonna gives him a sharp look. When they round the corner, I say, "They're barbaric!"

Nonna nods but says nothing.

My frustration grows, and I want to challenge her into telling me the truth. "I know the partisans are working to stop them," I say quietly.

"Rosa, don't," she warns.

"Why? If no one does anything, how will they be stopped?"

Peering around to ensure there are no listening ears, Nonna stops. "It's dangerous to talk of such things. I promised your father I would keep you safe. I could never forgive myself if something happened to you! You must be more careful."

We walk on quietly. When we reach the Duomo, I tell Nonna to go on ahead. I stop into the church, begging God to keep my family safe. Surely He hears my prayers over the silence cramming the vast space. Kneeling, I watch my tears dot the marble floor as I consider the multitudes who've done the same over the centuries.

Afterward, I make my way to the apartment, thinking of my father. Surely he would've taken my family to my tia and tio's. The photo I found in Nonna's villa comes to mind. My father—a decorated war hero? It occurs to me he could be fighting alongside the guerrillas. My heart thuds in my chest at the thought of him in danger. I've never imagined him as a soldier before. But now? I still don't understand why he didn't tell us. What about Tia and Tio? Do they know? And did my mother?

I think of Tommaso, wishing he were here. He's gone so often. He says it's for work. But he won't share much when I ask about his trips.

Everyone is keeping secrets now, it seems. Nonna, my father, Maestro, Tommaso? Is this just how it is in a time of war?

30

Caramina

JUNE 2, 1942

Mountain Province, Philippines

The rains have begun. Here in the mountainous jungle, the rainy season lasts longer than back home. But it doesn't stop the grueling work in the fields. Tio is adamant we keep at it. It's normal practice, he says. Now and then, the wind and rain grow so strong it's impossible to work. But the occasional downpour—on a day like today—is no deterrent.

Tia asks me to run to the house and grab the small basket of food she prepared. It's barely enough to share but will have to do. We started working just before dawn, hoping to beat the worst of the heat and any impending storm. In the few hours since, we finished the water we brought and have grown hungry.

I'm grateful for the reprieve even if it's only a few minutes. I snatch a small piece of mango from the cutting board and savor its sweet tanginess. Juice drips down the corner of my mouth. I grab a rag. Singing to myself, I wipe away the pooled circles of orange on the counter.

My heart brims full, and I can't help but smile. Still singing, I stride out the door but stop when I hear voices coming from the front porch.

Matteo is still recovering. He's able to do some light work now but tires quickly. Tio and Papa won't let him help in the fields, so he stays around the house doing odd jobs. It's obvious he can't wait to get back to Torres to fight alongside his brothers. That's what he calls them.

Gabriel's voice floats into the house. "I'll leave you two to talk." As he enters, he spots me in the kitchen. "Caramina!"

Usually clean-shaven, he now has stubble on his face. He seems older. An awkward silence passes as I realize we're staring at each other. I blush, lifting my hand to my cheek. My fingers slide across the tiny moon-shaped mark. I cup my hand to hide it. More and more, the ugliness of the scar bothers me whenever Gabriel and I spend time together. I know I'm fortunate. The cut from that first explosion in our Floridablanca kitchen has healed well, and the scar is small. But still, it's there.

"I thought I heard a woman's voice," I say, hoping he'll lift his gaze.

"Anna's here."

"Anna? Is she okay?" Before he can answer, I rush toward the porch. I'm about to throw open the screen door but stop.

Crouched on one knee, Matteo is holding Anna's hand tenderly. I can't hear their words, but it is clear he's proposing! Anna's eyes glisten as he slowly stands and embraces her. Then he leans in and kisses her, pulling her toward him with one hand resting at the small of her back, and the other caught in the tangle of her ebony waves. The two move even closer as they kiss.

I've never seen such a kiss, and I am struck by the intensity. The two are clearly in love. I don't know whether to proceed to the porch or tiptoe back to the kitchen. I lean back, right into Gabriel. He catches me, steadying me. A flush moves through me as I feel the warmth radiating from him.

"Sorry," I whisper, as we continue to spy.

An enormous grin splits across Matteo's face, his arms wrapped around Anna. He takes a step back, eyes gazing into hers, and lands his foot in a basket. Both he and Anna break out in laughter as he shakes his foot to free it. I can't help but laugh, too.

Anna spies me in the doorway. "Caramina!"

Thrilled to see her safe and well, I grab her, hugging her tight. A whirl of emotion flows through me as I picture her crouching on that step months ago.

"We're going to be sisters," Anna says, glowing with happiness.

I smile, so grateful she's okay. But I can't help but notice the swollen belly beneath her white blouse. Anna blushes, but her eyes brim with joy.

"We're going to be married!" Matteo swoops Anna into his arms. Their happiness is infectious.

31

Rosa

The day of my senior finale at festival has finally arrived! La Maggio Musicale. After this performance, my time at conservatory will be complete. Nerves shoot through me like sparks from a live wire as I pace backstage.

Maestro steps away to get me a glass of water, and I spot him—it's Professor Armento. The moment he sees me, a grimace darkens his face. Of all the times to be confronted with this vile man, does it have to be now? Thankfully, he turns on his heel and slinks back into the shadows.

Days ago, I learned of my placement at festival. Second tier. Devastated doesn't begin to describe how I felt. Second tier performs in the late afternoon, and it includes mostly junior vocalists and musicians. Despite all of my efforts throughout my years of schooling, my finale performance will not garner the attention of men like Signor Gastani who are looking for new talent for their theaters. They, along with the rest of the music elite, flock to evening performances. I'm certain Signor Gastani is now at Teatro Fiorentino.

"Armento is a hateful man. And what he did is absolutely wrong, Rosa. But do not let his actions stop you. You sing! You are gifted. Men like Armento exist, but not everyone feels as he does. You rise above it and sing," Nonna told me.

His bias has cost me severely. But the sight of him today lights a fury within me. I'm even more determined he won't derail my years of hard work. I bolster myself to sing as if everything depends on this performance. It does.

And then, I stumble. Falling, I catch myself on a nearby table. Maestro rushes toward me, water sloshing over the edges of the glass in his hand. Pulling a chair to me, he commands, "Sit, Rosa."

I sit and lift my foot to see that the heel on my right shoe is broken. I sigh, thinking of how intent Signora Conti was on matching the satin on my shoes to my dress. Maestro wastes no time. Spotting a younger singer nearby, he nods curtly and points to her shoes. Immediately, she removes her simple black pumps and hands them over. Fortunately, they fit. I almost laugh with relief.

Maestro's prodding was unnecessary. The girl gave them willingly. That's one benefit to being billed with the younger performers. My peers would never be so accommodating.

"*Grazie*," I say to the young woman.

"Rosa Grassi." I hear my name called. It is time, and I walk out onto the stage. The first notes drift up from the orchestra pit. I sing with everything in me Violetta's aria from *La Traviata*. After my last note, there is complete silence. Then the crowd stands and erupts in feverish applause. A standing ovation! The overwhelming response warms my heart.

These people are my neighbors. Everyday Florentines who have come to enjoy music. That they would be so moved fills me with enormous gratitude. It's so powerful, for a moment, I forget the war. On one side of the theater, I spy Maestro and Nonna with beaming smiles.

As I walk off stage, I spot Signor Gastani. He is here! Standing alongside the others offering a rousing ovation, he catches my eye, nods his approval. I nearly burst with excitement and gratitude. His attending my performance means the world to me. I can't quite believe he is here.

Backstage, Professor Armento lurks, glowering. The man won't even look me in the eye. I pass by him. Nothing will spoil this moment.

Nonna approaches and kisses my cheek. *"Bravissimo,* Rosa!"

"Sì! Well done!" Maestro hands me a glass of wine, and the three of us toast my performance.

Maestro spots Armento, and a look of disgust falls across his face. "If he'd scored your quarterly justly, you'd have had top billing."

"Sì, but pay him no heed," Nonna says. "Not now. Not after your performance."

I know his actions have cost me opportunities. "I'm determined to continue. I'll audition for roles if I have to." His narrow-mindedness won't stand in my way.

Nonna smiles. "That's the Rosa I know."

Maestro and Nonna walk away to speak with an elderly gentleman and his wife as Ciro spins me around to congratulate me. He gallantly presents me with a garnet rose, kissing my cheek affectionately. *"Bravo,* Rosa. *Bravo!"*

"Grazie!" I tell him, enormously grateful for his friendship, kindness, and support.

The only thing to have made this moment more special would be if Tommaso were here. Unfortunately, he's still away for work. Though we've spent much time together, he's never heard me perform. Singing a little, here and there, yes. But never a full aria. One day, he will. I'll relish telling him about today when we're together again.

32

Rosa

JUNE 6, 1942

Fiesole, Italy

Nonna and I are visiting the villa. With my finale performance at festival finished and my time at conservatory complete, I intend to relax and savor the stirrings of summer infusing the hills of Fiesole. The fragrance of rosemary, the olive groves, apricot and lemon trees. And the sunflowers! Velvet, golden-petaled faces raised to the sun.

It's an immense relief to be away from the city. The heaviness of living under the watchful eye of the Florentine police chief and his thugs is exhausting. Uniformed in black from head to toe, they patrol the streets. Panthers hunting prey. They have eyes and ears everywhere. Anyone wishing payback for a slight or simply desiring another loaf of bread can fabricate lies and inform. Just a hint of displeasure with Il Duce puts you in a dangerous position.

A piano student at conservatory was arrested. It's rumored he commented that Mussolini was a short man. An insult, apparently, worthy of being jailed and beaten. Weeks later, I saw him limping and terribly bruised. One hand was so badly broken, he couldn't play for months. He's never been the same.

But being here at the villa is a much-needed reprieve. Nonna is more relaxed than I've seen her in ages. Twice before we left the apartment, I spied her sneaking out at night. The last time it happened, I asked her the next morning where she had gone. "Maestro wanted me to look over a score," she answered without pause. At night? He'd never put her at such risk. Later, I asked Maestro about the score. He wouldn't answer me, and my concern for her has only grown.

Now, after plucking peas from the untamed vines in the garden, I sit in the cucina freeing the green orbs from their pods. My thoughts turn again to what I found in the box in the attic. I still need to ask Nonna for answers.

"This will do nicely, don't you think? A Vernaccia di San Gimignano," Nonna says as she enters bearing a bottle of white wine from the cellar. She sets the wine on the table, sits next to me, and together we finish shelling the peas.

"Nonna, I have something to ask you."

"*Sì?*"

Not wanting to offend, I hesitate. She looks up at me. "What is it, Rosa?"

"When we were here last, I . . . One night, I couldn't sleep. I went up to the attic, and I found a box with papers and photos. I know I shouldn't have looked, but I was curious."

Nonna shifts on her chair. "It's time I tell you," she responds. I expected she'd be livid. But instead, she sounds relieved. "There is so much you don't know, Rosa."

I sit on the edge of my seat, impatient to hear what she has to say.

"The papers you found? They were articles written by your Nonno Vittorio. Your grandfather was a man of great integrity. His strength was what drew me to him, and his eyes—pools of cool water you could dive into. I was lost in them the first time we met. He was a handsome man." A wistful look comes over her face, and she pauses before continuing.

"I told you before how he died but not everything. He witnessed, as did I, the consequences of a corrupt government. He'd be shocked to see his beloved Italy in the hands of a man even more vile than his predecessors. 'Power corrupts, Serafina,' he would say to me. He did what he could to try to make things better. Writing articles to bolster people and hold those in power accountable. It was dangerous work. Eventually, we began traveling to get away from it all, especially after Lorenzo was born. The timing fell in line with opportunities for me to perform abroad. We returned to Italy when we thought it safe. But Vittorio was arrested and beaten for his writings. Not long after, he lost his life. I lost my love. Now, I do what I can to bring change. It is what I must do for Vittorio. For Italy."

"Nonna, I'm so sorry."

"I should have told you ages ago. You don't need to apologize."

"I can't imagine how hard it must have been to lose Nonno like that."

She peers down at the bowl filled with a mound of peas. "*Sì*, he was my love. He will always be my love." When she looks up at me and smiles, her eyes glisten.

"There is more you need to know."

What else could she possibly share? I want to stop her. This truth telling brings nothing but pain. But she continues.

"I've been doing what I can to help the partisans."

My mouth gapes at her admission.

"Maestro, too, and Ciro."

"What do you do?"

"You don't need to know specifics. It's too dangerous."

I groan.

"I do small things, Rosa. Handing off information when necessary. And I don't want you involved."

"There was a photo of my father in military uniform?"

Then she takes a deep breath and says, "Your papa . . . He fought in the Great War. A valiant, decorated soldier."

"Why wouldn't he tell me? I know the others are younger, but why not tell me and Matteo?" The idea that he fought is so foreign. My father has always been the strength of our family. But he is a gentle man. Fighting weeds with fervor but never people.

"He wanted to leave this all behind him. Protect you all," she says.

Finally, she tells me about the blond-haired little boy in the photo. Silvio. My father's baby brother. "Silvio fought in the Great War, too. He lost his life. He never came home." Her eyes darken with grief the moment she speaks his name.

I wish for the floor to swallow me whole—I've brought her such pain. I won't ask anything else. I walk to where she sits, place my arms around her shoulders, and hug her tight. She lifts one hand and grasps my arm in a backward embrace. Afterward, we sit quietly, shelling peas and listening to the birdsong drifting through the windows.

The next morning, I lie in bed mulling over Nonna's revelations. I'm grateful she has entrusted me with the knowledge that she, Maestro, and Ciro are in *la Resistenza*. Grateful there are no more secrets. But the spinning uncertainty in my mind has turned into unease and even more concern for her safety. I go downstairs, weighed down with dread. But when Nonna greets me with a smile and hug, my mood lifts.

Just before noon, Beatrice joins us, helping to prepare and share our midday meal. She makes sure we have a full supply of chicory coffee since real coffee is difficult to find.

Later, after Beatrice leaves, Nonna is setting the ceramic canister filled with the "coffee" back on the shelf when she turns to me. "Important things can be hidden in the most curious places, Rosa," she says nonchalantly, then saunters from the room.

Does she mean my diary? She knows I've been hiding it for our safety. Perhaps she's warning me to be careful. I need a better hiding place at the villa as I only set the diary in the back of the armoire in my room. Immediately, I go in search of one. I must do whatever I can to keep us safe.

Days later, we return to Florence. Tommaso is outside the apartment. The moment I see him, my heart leaps right out of my chest. Finally, I can introduce him to Nonna.

As I do, she is cool but polite. A true Italian grandmother. She once told me she believes it's her responsibility to see I'm not taken in by any nefarious characters. But Tommaso, nefarious? I chuckle at the thought. I've no doubt she'll fall in love with him in time.

Without our asking, he grabs our bags from the trunk and carries them up the stairs, winning Nonna's approval. She smiles and, after unlocking the door, says, "You must join us for a drink."

"That would be wonderful. *Grazie!*" he says, and we follow Nonna into the apartment, which is cool and inviting. In the kitchen, Nonna fills three glasses with *limonata* that we enjoy on the terrace.

Nonna asks about Tommaso's work, and he shares he is an architect. "My position requires me to travel quite a bit, unfortunately. I'd prefer to not be away so often." He squeezes my hand, smiling warmly at me. His dimples give him a boyish look. I'm so happy to see him I have to stop myself from grinning.

"Well, it's nice to meet a friend of Rosa's," Nonna says. "I think I'll go put my things away."

Tommaso gets to his feet as my grandmother stands. "Wonderful to meet you, Signora Grassi."

Nonna smiles and nods before disappearing down the hall.

We finish our drinks, and then Tommaso and I walk to the Cascine Gardens. After strolling hand in hand along the Arno, we sit together on a blanket in the shade of a copse of plane trees.

Tommaso asks about my finale performance. When I tell him about my placement in the second tier, he's so infuriated his hands fly up in the air, moving back and forth as he says, "That is a crime! How dare they treat you so poorly!"

I tell him of the audience's overwhelming ovation, and that of Signor Gastani.

"Of course they loved your singing, Rosa. You have the most beautiful voice! I wish I could have been there for you." He pulls something from his pocket. Sunlight illuminates it . . . a glass heart pendant in the most beautiful shade of turquoise.

"I was thinking of you when I was gone," he says. "It's a graduation present."

"Tommaso, it's beautiful! *Grazie!*"

"Something small. But when I saw it, it reminded me of you and how you described your home."

The color is stunning and reminds me of the waters in Boracay. I love it. He ties the gold silk ribbon around my neck. We share a kiss. It's as if no time has passed.

I lean against him as we sit. Being together is the most natural thing in the world. "Tell me about your trip," I say.

He tells me of his time in Venice and of the building in great need of repair that his firm is restoring. This trip was about reinforcing the structure. Tommaso was entrusted with ensuring the work is done in a way that retains the building's Renaissance beauty. The building must be useful to Duce in some way.

Our time together is lovely. Whatever tension is in my body seeps away. We have no secrets between us. With him, I feel lighter and hopeful.

33

Caramina

"*Magandá!* Beautiful, Anna! You're stunning!" I say, arranging Anna's hair in a braid that crowns her head. Loose ringlets spill down her shoulders.

Isabella and I are helping Anna prepare for her big day. There was no time for elaborate wedding planning. Even if there had been, supplies couldn't be found. Fortunately, Tia had saved her wedding dress. After Isabella's alterations, the simple, bias-cut, A-line gown of cream Chantilly lace hugs Anna's figure. The delicate material drapes elegantly to the floor. Isabella updated it into a surprisingly chic bridal gown, adding capped sleeves and a stylish V-shaped back.

"You and Isabella are the sisters I never had." Anna gazes at herself in the full-length mirror in Tio and Tia's bedroom.

I can't hold it in any longer and finally my words rush out. "I'm so sorry. I should have done something. I saw you there . . . on the steps at the camp."

Anna places her hand on my shoulder. "There was nothing . . ."

"If only I'd done something. Anything! Maybe . . ." My gaze falls to her belly. "I'm so sorry." I wipe my tears away.

Anna takes a deep breath and touches my arm gently. "You did do something. If you hadn't gotten away and told Matteo, I'd still be there or worse." My gaze again falls to her belly. "You helped save my life and the life of my baby." Anna's voice cracks.

How can she be so grateful—and for the little baby? The baby is innocent, but it came from such a horrible ordeal. As if sensing my thoughts, Anna's gaze drops to her swollen stomach. Her voice falls to a whisper. "I wanted to take my life, Caramina. If it wasn't for this baby . . ." She rests her hands on her belly. "My baby saved my life."

She pulls me into an embrace, hugging me tight. "And now, I have a family again. And you for a sister." When she pulls away, her eyes are glistening, and she's smiling.

Relief sweeps over me and, for a moment, I'm light as air. "I've made you cry on your wedding day."

Anna only laughs in response. The door creaks open, and Tia and Isabella enter, carrying the crowns of orchids Isabella wove for the nuptials. Anna's is made of creamy white blooms. Isabella and I will wear delicate blush-pink orchids.

"It's time!" Tia says, excited for the festivities to begin. After securing our crowns, we escort Anna outside for the ceremony.

When Anna first arrived at the farm, we learned her aunt and uncle disowned her after realizing she was pregnant. Such a thing makes my stomach turn. Especially after learning her father had sent her to her aunt and uncle's thinking she'd be safer there. He'd arranged for her to make the journey with a trusted neighbor. They were overtaken by a small contingent of Japanese soldiers and separated. Anna was taken to the camp where Enzo and I saw her, and she never knew what became of the neighbor and his family. She'd had no word of her parents. Yet, I know Anna isn't the only young woman to face cold indifference after such a horrifying ordeal. There will be others, if there aren't already.

"Reprehensible!" Papa had declared. He kept shaking his head, his eyes filled with disgust when Matteo explained Anna's predicament. "I love her," Matteo said. "I want her to be my wife."

Papa had grabbed Matteo by the shoulders and hugged him. "We're lucky to have her as part of our family." The next morning Papa greeted Anna with a grin the size of the sun. "I'd better get working on a crib for my first grandchild. *Un bambino!*" he said, grabbing his tool belt and heading to the shed. Though Anna seemed surprised at Papa's words, a smile bloomed across her face.

Now, a single orchid falls from my hair and somersaults down my skirt as Father Bautista introduces Mr. and Mrs. Matteo Grassi. My brother leans in and kisses his bride. As the two kiss, I hear Isabella sigh. I'm sure she's wishing Jack were here and not fighting in a ditch somewhere in the jungle. I glance over at Gabriel, so glad he is able to be with us.

Papa embraces Matteo and Anna. *"Congratulazioni! Bravo!"*

We're lucky. The sky is oddly clear, so the small wedding took place in the sunshine. A table is set next to the stream under the strong limbs of a tree, its branches spilling over with emerald leaves. We eat a simple meal of rice and roasted fish, but it feels like the finest wedding feast at the Manila Hotel. In place of wedding cake, we savor every morsel of Tia's steamed coconut cakes with fresh papaya and mango. The food isn't plentiful, but just having the cakes is a luxury.

"They're doing well, you know."

I look up to find Father Bautista next to me.

"Clara, Rae, all the kids from the orphanage. They're doing well. Clara's been asking about you, I understand," he says.

"I'm so relieved they're all right! Can you tell her I said hello?"

"Of course, I'll let her know the next time I send word to San

Paulo. I knew you two would become fast friends." His smile warms my heart.

"They're short on space but making do. But that's better than the alternative."

I nod. "What about Mae?"

"She stayed in town with her family."

At the look of horror on my face, he tells me Sister Faye has been helping him assist Timbales residents the best they can under the watchful eyes of the Japanese.

"I can't imagine living in town right now."

"It's better you're here, Caramina. I'm glad you and Enzo made it safely. But that was a huge risk you took leaving."

"I'm sorry," I say, not having considered his concern over our fleeing. "I was afraid I'd never see my family again."

"I know. I'm just glad you're okay." His eyes are filled with compassion. "I'd better get going before anyone realizes I'm gone."

"Thank you, Father," I say as Tia hands him a sack of food to eat on his way.

After Father's departure, Anna and Matteo ask me to sing. It's the only wedding present I can offer. I sing "When You Wish upon a Star" *a cappella,* and the newlyweds dance under the boughs of the tree. Droplets of rain sparkle, weightless diamonds drifting down upon them. When I finish, I walk to the stream and listen to the water rippling over the rocks.

"This one's falling, too." Gabriel gently reattaches a wayward orchid to the crown resting on my head. He smiles. "There."

"It was lovely."

"The wedding? It was . . ." He tilts his head slightly. "You're awfully quiet."

I take a deep breath, watching Matteo and Anna dance. Matteo sweeps Anna into his arms. He buries his face in the curve of her neck and kisses her gently. They both laugh at some shared secret.

"I just wonder how it will be for them."

Gabriel kicks at a small rock, sending it splashing into the

stream, forming tiny eddies. "I suppose it'll be better for them together than if they were apart. They love each other. Your brother's
loved Anna for a long time."

The longing in Matteo's eyes when he saw Anna walking down
the makeshift aisle reminded me of the moment Charles Boyer and
Irene Dunne finally come together in *Love Affair,* the most roman-
tic movie I've ever seen. They radiate happiness. But Matteo is set
to leave in the morning to fight alongside Torres and his men.

34

Rosa

"G*razie*, Rosa," Betta says as she takes the bag from my hand.

"I'm sorry. I wish there was more."

"No, no. You are too kind. It is a great help."

"I should go. Maestro's waiting for me at conservatory."

"*Sì*, be safe, Rosa. *Grazie!*" Betta closes her door, and I turn to go down the stairs when Maestro's door swings open.

"Rosa." The look on his face tells me he's not pleased.

"I . . . I thought you were at conservatory."

"I can see that. Come inside. We must talk." He opens the door wide for me to enter, then closes it behind me.

"Rosa, you cannot be doing this. It's much too dangerous! And not just for you but for them. It brings attention to them and possibly your grandmother."

"I don't know what you're talking about."

Brows arched, he flashes me a side-eye. "You are bringing food to Betta and Giuseppe."

I can't deny it. "How did you know?"

"I know a lot of things. You must stop, and—"

"They need food! You know how badly they're in need. I have to do something! How can you say this? You of all people." I close my mouth, not wanting to let on that I know he's helping the partisans.

He puts his hand up to silence me as if we're in rehearsal. "Rosa, you didn't let me finish. If you are going to continue to help them, do it by bringing the supplies to me. There can be no question then. You're simply bringing your old professor some sustenance. I'll make sure they get what you bring." He pauses. "I know your Nonna does not know."

"You can't tell her!" Despite Nonna's admitting to helping the Resistance, I refuse to put her at more risk by my actions.

He nods but stays silent. "So, you'll bring *me* the supplies? *Sì?*"

"*Sì,*" I tell him, frustrated at being caught but grateful I can continue.

"Now, we have a rehearsal, don't we?" He opens the door, ushering me through, and follows me out. The silence on our walk to conservatory is only broken when we enter the practice room and I begin singing.

35

Caramina

A scream pierces the night, and I shoot upright. Across the room, Anna is writhing in pain. "Anna?" I rush toward the small figure rocking back and forth.

Anna twists on her bed, clutching her belly. "It's gotten worse."

"Tia!"

Tia rushes in, tying her tattered robe shut.

"Something's wrong!" I try to sound calm, but from Anna's cries clearly something isn't right.

Tia calmly places her hands on my shoulders. "The baby is coming. Go and wake Isabella. Tell her to boil some water. And bring the clean linens I left in the kitchen."

Why isn't she as alarmed as I am? I race down the stairs to find Isa already awake, folding her sheet into a neat square. She's been sleeping on the couch since Anna arrived six months ago. Isa says she doesn't mind since she has the whole room to herself. It's a half-truth. I know she wanted to give Anna the comfort of a bed because of her pregnancy.

I watch my sister light the stove and place a pot to boil. She moves so gracefully. I wonder at her confidence, wishing I could be more like her.

"I'll take those up," she says. "Why don't you bring up the water after it boils?"

I don't need any convincing to stay in the kitchen longer.

"It'll be okay, Cara." Isa disappears through the doorway.

Water in the pot finally gurgles, splattering my wrist. I rub the burn. For a moment, I stand watching the bubbling mass, but then I grab a dishrag to protect my hands as I carry the pot upstairs.

Tia has lit a lantern in the small bedroom, and I can see Anna clearly now. She's gripping the sheet around her, moaning. I pause, afraid for her.

Tia points to a small table. "Set that down, Caramina."

Tio pops in the doorway, and Tia pulls him into the hall. "We need her now," I hear my aunt say. The sound of Tio's footsteps racing down the stairs is followed by the front door slamming shut.

Tia walks back into the room calmly. "Midge will be here soon," she says, propping herself on a stool next to the bed. Midge, the wife of Eduardo, one of Tio's former farmhands, is a midwife.

"What can we do?" I ask.

Tia shifts on the stool. "Nothing but try to make Anna comfortable—and wait. The baby will come when it's ready."

The sound of shuffling footsteps drifts into the room from the hall. Papa walks by. Enzo is slumped over his shoulder deep in sleep. Papa's bringing him downstairs, where the only noise is the clamor of the wind.

I want to run down the stairs after them. Anna's pain is terrifying. But this is where I'm expected to be, and I want to do whatever I can to help. Anna doesn't have Matteo here for support. But even if he were here, he'd be downstairs with the men.

Soon, Midge appears in the doorway. A tiny woman with gray-flecked hair pulled into a neat bun. Not nearly as old as I'd expected. She wears a simple brown dress and carries a graying canvas sack that she sets next to the bed. Tia pulls her into the hallway, whispering things I can't hear.

After a few moments, Midge returns. "Anna, I'm Midge. I'm going to help you. You do what I say and soon you have a beautiful baby to hold." Midge smiles at Anna, who opens her eyes and whispers a nearly inaudible hello, before gasping again and grasping her belly.

"It's a contraction. Her muscles contract to push the baby out," Isa whispers, and I wince.

Anna is in misery. "Can't we help her? She's in so much pain!" I turn to Midge, who just grins, and I sink back on the bed.

Sunlight is peeking through the curtains when Anna's baby finally greets the world six hours later. "A beautiful baby girl!" Midge hands her to Tia, who gently wipes the squirming newborn clean with a soft rag. She then wraps the baby in clean cloth and hands the fragile bundle to Anna, who props herself up, her back against the wall.

Anna gazes at her daughter's face and begins to cry, and I grimace. This is awful. Please don't let her see something that reminds her of her attacker, I wish silently. It seems we're all holding our breath to see her response.

"She's beautiful!" Anna whispers, hugging her baby close, then glancing around the room at each of us. "Thank you. I only wish Matteo were here."

Relieved, I exhale. Birth is a terrifying ordeal. I have no idea how Anna made it through the pain. And she's already endured so much. Anna holds the baby close, cooing at her for some time before her eyes flit from her daughter to Isabella.

"Would you like to hold her?" Anna asks. Isabella doesn't hesitate. She snuggles with the baby as Anna drifts off to sleep. I must have fallen asleep, too, because I'm awoken by Isabella's gentle voice.

"Cara, I want to go downstairs to help Tia clean up. Will you hold her?"

I prop myself up and take the infant in my arms. I held Enzo when he was a baby. But it's hard to believe he was once this fragile. This baby is so small, so vulnerable. My niece looks like a delicate porcelain doll.

Her tiny pink face is capped with downy black hair. And her rosebud lips, she purses gently. I notice the shape of her eyes, which reveal a subtle difference from most Filipina babies. She's *mestiza,* too. I hope she won't experience taunts and bullying like my siblings and me. But I know, it's likely she will. My heart clutches at the thought.

"Happy birthday, little one," I whisper.

My own birthday had come and gone with meager fanfare. It's hard to believe a year has passed since the war began. We've been living this way for so long.

"You can let her rest if you want. I just want her to know she's loved." Anna shifts on her bed and motions to the crib Papa built.

There is no question this baby is loved. I hold my niece closer. As I lean my back against my pillow, I wonder at her tiny wiggling fingers and toes.

I glance at Anna, whose eyes are now shut. Softly, I sing a lullaby, welcoming my new little niece to the world. Her eyes pop open. She peeks up at me, and her pink lips curl into a delicate smile. I sigh with contentment. I'm in love.

A week passes before Matteo meets his daughter. Gabriel comes with him. Both men stand in the living room, clothes tattered and dirty. Matteo grabs Anna and kisses her. Then he peeks inside the small basket resting on the floor. His daughter. He tries to pick her up, hands fumbling and seeming uncertain what to do with the squirming bundle. Anna reaches down and hands her to him. He snuggles the baby against his chest.

"I haven't named her. I wanted to wait for you," Anna says. "I thought, maybe, Lucia, for light. It was a starry night, the night she was born."

Gabriel stands next to me, leaning into me slightly. Together, we watch the new parents hover over their daughter.

"Lucia," Matteo whispers. "Hello, sweet Lucia. I'm your daddy, your *tatay*." He moves his hands like a puppy whose paws are too big. I've never seen my brother so unsure.

"She's so tiny." Matteo shakes his head. "She's beautiful!" He kisses her on the crown of her head, and the small family sits together on the couch.

I sense Gabriel's gaze on me and look up to meet it. His eyes pulse with emotion as if he wants to say something. But instead, he turns and walks to the kitchen. I watch as he grabs a glass and pours himself some water.

The last few times I've seen him, he's been quieter. Pensive. More than once, he'd seemed on the verge of saying something important but then seemed to think better of it. Now I wonder, after watching Matteo and Anna, if he's contemplating his own future.

The future. I'm ready for this war to be over. We all are. But am I ready to face what comes after? And what does the future hold? Music? Maybe. Is it even a possibility now? Marriage? Isabella is certainly thinking about it. She's of age, after all, and she loves Jack. It's clear with each visit from Jack that they are now each other's world.

I'm nowhere near ready for that. Yet, Gabriel's seriousness is bewildering. I glance at Lucia, not sure I'm ready to hear whatever it is he has to say.

36

Rosa

"*Grazie*, Signor Gastani." I take the music he holds out to me and place it in my bag.

"*Prego!* Of course!" he says before heading back into his office at Teatro Fiorentino.

I bundle myself into my coat and scarf and venture out into the cold, heading to Maestro's apartment. A blast of icy air hits me so I pick up my pace.

Winter has blown in and frozen the city to its core, and me along with it. I long for the warmth of summer. We've had some snow, but it is always damp and cold. Oh, how I miss the warm breeze blowing through the frangipani in Floridablanca.

Excitement over being at the Fiorentino still bubbles inside me as I prepare for my debut. Working with Gastani is a dream. Days after my senior performance, I came downstairs to find the kindest letter of congratulations with an offer to debut at his theater. I signed the paperwork soon after and am now under contract to sing at Teatro Fiorentino.

Ever since, I've been rehearsing to prepare. Signor Gastani has a heart of gold. It's been a long road with mountains of hard work to become a professional soprano. But it is worth every arduous step.

Maestro kindly agreed to help me prepare. Though my debut is planned for May, it will take place before the festival. I'm so grateful for his continued assistance. The man is a wealth of knowledge and inspiration. His experience as a renowned baritone informs his teaching. I once asked if he missed performing. He told me shaping the voices of the future gives him great satisfaction. I'm truly fortunate he sees in me talent worthy of fostering.

What opportunities lie ahead after my debut, I don't know. There are those who, like Professor Armento, wish to see me silenced. My mixed heritage is an affront to them. So many artists and musicians have fled Italy, their beloved country, and I understand why. Maestro told me there was a mass exodus over ten years ago. I had no idea Jewish musicians and composers began losing their positions then. They've suffered for so long. After Mussolini's racial laws, it's only gotten worse.

Maestro said Toscanini, the renowned conductor, did everything he could while at La Scala to counter Duce's edicts on the music world. It put him at great risk. He was physically attacked for refusing to play the "Giovenezza," Duce's fascist hymn, and he and his family fled. That was in 1931. Since then, he's had a swell of international support and he has conducted in numerous countries.

Wealthy music-loving Italians, including Princess Marie-José, have traveled across the border to see him conduct. Duce, infuriated, had their vehicles stopped upon their return, their licenses recorded, and names printed in the newspapers. It's rumored that as conductor of the New York Philharmonic, Toscanini raised money to support the partisans' efforts to end the regime. And that he, apparently, continues his efforts today. I applaud the man.

In having me perform, Signor Gastani is also taking a risk. The very idea race would have any impact on musical ability or creativity is preposterous and wrong. But here, everything is held in Duce's tight grip. Everything must support his ideas. Music as propaganda. But that's not what music is. It is an expression of the soul. If he knew anything at all, he would know this to be true.

Last week, I told Maestro I didn't want to put Gastani in danger, and he shushed my concerns. "Signor Gastani is a man of integrity, principle, and strength. He is not intimidated by men with brains the size of ants. Your job, Rosa, isn't to focus on Gastani but on giving a brilliant performance, which I've no doubt you will." His belief in me drives me to work even harder.

I think of my family and how for years I dreamed they could be with me for my debut. But it isn't to be. Tommaso is intent on attending. But his work keeps him moving. We spend a great deal of time together when he's in town. Often, he'll join Nonna and me for meals. She's warmed to him as I knew she would. The three of us talk well into the night before she retires for the evening. Then Tommaso and I have a little time alone in the sitting room. I savor this time with him as these moments are fleeting.

When I arrive at Maestro's, he opens the door and waves me inside. A clunk sounds from deep in the apartment, and I hear Ciro. "Ah, here is the problem. Stubborn hinge!" When I round the corner, he's crouched at the kitchen door.

"Can you fix it?" Maestro asks.

Ciro grapples with the mechanism, tightening a screw. "Does a tiger have stripes?"

Maestro hurries over and holds the wayward door in place as it is wrestled into submission. Finally, Ciro stands. He moves the door back and forth on its newly tightened hinges with a satisfied grin.

Maestro tests the door. "Well done! *Andiamo!* Come." He leads us into the cucina where he brings out a bottle of Vin Santo and a plate of biscotti.

The three of us sit companionably. Old friends reminiscing over our time together at conservatory. Good memories from the last few years.

Maestro tilts his glass to Ciro. "I remember your piano lessons."

A chuckle escapes me at the memory of Maestro's attempts to teach Ciro piano. It was hopeless. "This is C," Maestro had said at their first lesson. "And here . . . is F. Now, play C," Maestro had instructed Ciro in his professorial tone. Ciro promptly played an F. Maestro grimaced, chiding him, "No, this one," then commanded, "Again!" Again, Ciro played an F. I can still see his smirk.

How he tried to get under Maestro's skin! I'd had to turn away to stop laughing. The two of them had continued, Maestro's face growing redder and redder like a ripening tomato. When Ciro finally played a C, Maestro sighed heavily, shook his head, and ended the lesson by waving his hand in the air and declaring, "No more! That's enough for today." It still makes me laugh to think of the two of them.

"You did not practice," Maestro says to Ciro as we finish the last of the biscotti.

Ciro gives me a wink, then says wistfully, "It wasn't in me."

Maestro takes a slow sip from his glass. "Music is like a fine wine. To be savored. Enjoyed. But you must give it the respect it deserves."

"As you do so well, Maestro." Ciro raises his glass to us, a mischievous twinkle lighting his green eyes. "I've never seen your face so red . . . like a fine marinara," he says, chuckling.

Maestro waves his hand as if swatting away a pesky fly. "Bah!"

I laugh and lift my glass high. "To music and friendship!"

The three of us toast that which has brought us great enjoyment.

37

Caramina

APRIL 7, 1943

Mountain Province, Philippines

Rocks jut from the path and I stumble as my foot twists. Gabriel catches me by the waist, steadying me. "It's just up here," he says, leading me on a winding maze through the trees.

"What do you miss most?" he asks.

"Going to market, all the colors and scents." Esther and Stefano come to mind, and I wonder how they're faring. We've had no word of them since we arrived at the farm. "And there were always free samples. And fruit ripened on a vine, plucked at its juiciest. I wish I could go into Timbales to shop."

"Nothing much there these days. Nothing to sell." Gabriel shakes his head. "Most of the food's been confiscated. It's a good thing Father Bautista evacuated the orphanage. They're better off in San Paulo. Father has his hands full trying to stretch what's available throughout town. They're getting by, but everyone's hungry."

"The Japanese take whatever they want, don't they? It's not right! Don't they have any compassion?" I swallow my frustration, stepping carefully to avoid a root.

A resigned look passes across Gabriel's face. We walk on quietly for a while. "I remember going to market with my mother when I was little. She'd find the juiciest mango for me and let me eat it as we walked from vendor to vendor. What a mess I was, juice dripping all over," he says, smiling. "She didn't mind, though."

I glance at him tenderly. Nostalgia is a good thing. We move slowly under the thick canopy of leaves and emerge in sunlight.

Four months have passed since Lucia's birth, and food at the farm has grown even scarcer. Now and then, someone ambles across the bridge, peddling a basket of odds and ends. The wares vary. Often, there is a bit of fruit or dried fish. Once, a young man brought a chicken. Tia immediately struck a deal, bartering fabric from old sheets that could be used for clothing. The boy leaped at the offer and threw in a few overripe mangoes from the bottom of his basket.

The small amount of rice we harvested is nearly gone. But our work continues tirelessly in the fields in the hopes of bringing forth another harvest this season. Occasionally, we catch small fish from the stream or some tiny shellfish. But it doesn't seem to matter. It is never enough.

Earlier this morning, Enzo was in tears, his belly aching from hunger. My heart clutched hearing his cries. I gave him the slice of mango that was supposed to be my breakfast.

Gabriel stopped by before dawn to speak with Tio and Papa. Afterward, he asked me to go for a walk. It was perfect timing, as if he knew I was desperate to get away.

Now, he points to a large ebony boulder. "Here, let's sit."

As I rest against the rock, my dress tightens around my chest. I fight the urge to tug at it. Though I've lost weight, my bust has grown. The dress didn't bother me until now. I straighten my back and again the dress pulls uncomfortably around my breasts.

It's embarrassing to even think of such things in Gabriel's presence. Things like this are meant for talks with mothers—or sisters—in private. That he might notice my dress clinging tight is mortifying. Just thinking about it makes me blush. I draw my knees up and hug them close. I'll have to talk with Isa later about my predicament.

Gabriel moves from where he was standing in front of me.

When he sits, the view opens and I take in the scene before us. The rock we're leaning against is part of an overhang on a ridge. Before us lies a valley covered in white. It's as if snow has fallen and gently blanketed the landscape. But it's tiny blooms that carpet the valley floor. I draw in a deep breath and am immediately consumed by the sweet, citrusy fragrance. It's like nothing I've ever experienced, a place of such beauty.

Gabriel leans closer. He gazes at me tenderly, and my face warms. Instinctively, I draw my hand to my cheek, covering my scar. Try as I may, I can't stop blushing. This is silly. It's just Gabriel. Why am I so embarrassed? Finally, he looks away, staring out over the valley. I exhale.

"When I was a young boy, my grandfather would bring me here. We'd sit right at this very spot, and he'd tell me a story about them." He points to the flowers.

"There was a rich man who came to this place from far away. And seeing the beauty of the valley, decided he had to have it for himself. He searched for its owner and after some time came upon a poor farmer. The farmer refused to sell, telling the man the land had been in his family for generations. It was all he had. The rich man offered a high price. Again and again, he tried to convince the farmer to sell, but the farmer graciously told him no.

"The rich man left in a rage, determined to do whatever he could to possess such beauty. Two nights later he returned with two friends, and they cut down all the flowers in the valley. Those that fell to the ground, they trampled. Till all that could be seen was dirt.

"The farmer was devastated, but there was nothing he could do. Every morning for many months, he looked out over the empty fields. One night as he slept, he dreamt he breathed in the scent of the beautiful white blooms. He awoke in the morning saddened— his loss, a fresh wound.

"The farmer dressed and walked out of his hut as the sun was rising over the valley. He stood in disbelief. It was as if snow had fallen overnight, covering the valley floor in white. The delicate

flowers had returned. Overcome by the sight and filled with gratitude, the farmer fell to his knees. Then he rose and woke his wife to
share the beauty of the blooms."

Gabriel turns to face me. "My lolo would say, 'The beauty was
always there.' He'd tell me, 'People can try to take everything from
you, but true goodness and beauty come from deep within. It was
so with the flowers. Their beauty never left. Deep within the soil,
their roots were growing strong.'"

Gabriel tips his head toward the path we'd taken. "They can
try to steal everything from us. But they can't. They can't take our
hope. And they can't take your beauty." He gazes at me and gently
caresses the scar on my cheek. "It comes from within you, Caramina." Then he turns away, looking back over the valley. I stare at
him, speechless, then lift my hand and wipe away a tear.

As I do, Gabriel turns back around and leans in close. Then he
kisses me. I taste a hint of sweet mango on his lips. He doesn't put
his arms around me like I'd seen Jack do with Isa. I'd imagined this
moment and close my eyes, letting myself be kissed. The fragrance
of the wild blooms floats on the warm breeze. Inside me, a butterfly
flutters, its gossamer wings drifting pleasant circles.

38

Rosa

MAY 11, 1943

Florence, Italy

A knock sounds at the door. The stagehand appears, telling me it is time. I breathe deeply and follow him into the belly of the theater. My name is announced, and I take my place as the plush, ruby curtains of Teatro Fiorentino part. When I see a full house, energy surges through my veins. I still myself, listening to the first notes of "Musetta's Waltz" from *La Bohème* float up from the orchestra.

And then, I sing.

Nonna once described the feeling of performing as transcendent. Transcendent it is! I sing the last note, spent from bearing the emotion of the piece. There is a moment of silence followed by thunderous applause. The stage floor vibrates from the cacophony, and warmth rushes through my body.

Afterward, Nonna embraces me backstage, tears in her eyes. *"Bravissima, carissima,"* she says. My spirits soar. No greater compliment could I receive than from a woman who has graced some of the world's best stages. The conductor congratulates me, then leads me to the reception. Maestro hands me a flute of champagne and toasts me with bubbling gold before he is pulled away into a lively conversation with two elderly men and their wives.

I hear a deep voice behind me, as I stand, sipping. "Signorina Grassi, the beauty of a sampaguita bloom and a voice like the most beautiful of nightingales."

At his words, I shudder. *Sampaguita?* Jasmine? The flower of the Philippines. Who is this man, and how does he know? I'm not ashamed of my mixed heritage. But the fewer that know the better, given it could prove to be dangerous.

I turn and face the man. Dressed head to toe in black, he is one of Mussolini's henchmen. These men think they're entitled to whatever they want. I know to be cautious.

"Join me for a drink," he says, leaning toward me. It isn't a question.

I inhale to steady myself and nearly gag at the rank odor of alcohol on his breath. He catches the disgust that flashes across my face and moves closer.

The smell of his aftershave is overpowering. I step back. Anger flares in his eyes. "To hear such an exotic beauty sing, what a treat. *Bellissima! Brava!*"

His emphasis on *exotic* is unmistakable. He leers at me, and my stomach turns. I fight the urge to dig my heel into his black boot or slap him. Instead, I walk away, leaving him standing alone. I search the room for Nonna or Maestro to no avail, so I head to my dressing room.

The quiet of the backstage hallway is a reprieve. As I enter the room, I hear footsteps. I hope it's Nonna as she'd said she'd find me. But then I smell his rancid breath.

Before I realize what's happening, I see the black of his shirt as he shoves me against the dressing table. I fall with such force, my hand scrapes along a sharp edge. I feel him grope to reach under my gown, and I'm stunned. When I realize what's happening, I fight with all my strength to get out from under him as he pushes all of his weight against me. I want to scream, but my voice is silenced. Panicked, I flail, grasping for anything to help. The bristles of my brush graze my fingers. I grab it and rake it hard across his face.

I attempt to free myself. But now, he's enraged. He balls his hand into a tight fist, and swings, hitting the side of my head. I topple to one side, my ears ringing and head pounding. Again, he pushes against me, pinning me to the table.

Suddenly, I see Ciro. He grabs the man by the shoulders, throwing him to the floor. When the Blackshirt tries to stand, Ciro wallops him with a punch. A thwack sounds as Ciro's fist hits the man's jaw again. "*Bastardo!* Stay away from her!" Ciro's face is hardened, granitelike as he glares at the man. With a sneer, the man leaves, slamming the door behind him.

I'm shaking uncontrollably. Ciro lifts me gently and leads me to the settee. The intensity in his eyes is tempered by tenderness as he wipes my hand and wraps it with his handkerchief. "Are you all right?"

My voice sounds choked and foreign to me when I answer, "Yes."

We sit together like this for a while. I don't know how much time passes. I tell myself I am all right. But *unharmed* is too strong of a word. Ciro arrived just in time.

He'd told me he wouldn't miss my debut, but I hadn't seen him in the throng of people. If he'd come only a few moments later . . .

He stands and pours me a glass of grappa. I drink it slowly. When my trembling finally subsides, I glimpse my gown. Rumpled with a thin, ruby streak on the skirt. Blood from the cut on my hand.

"Signora Conti will be so disappointed," I say.

"It's nothing Beatrice can't fix. Don't worry about that."

When he's certain I'm okay, we leave through a back entrance. He escorts me to the apartment. Once there, he sits with me. "*Ti proteggerò sempre.* I'll always protect you, Rosa," he says, looking exactly like a fierce, overprotective brother. Perhaps that's how he thinks of me now, as a sister.

He lights the fire, then goes to the kitchen. Minutes later, he returns bearing a china cup with piping hot tea. "I'll let Nonna know you weren't feeling well, so I escorted you home." Gently, he places his hand on my shoulder. I nod in agreement, and he leaves.

I'm so grateful to him. If he hadn't been there . . . I don't want to think about what would have happened. Now I understand Nonno Vittorio's rage against men like this Blackshirt. Nonna's passion to help fight to end their reign of terror makes perfect sense.

I carry the tea to my room. My thoughts fall on Tommaso, and I feel the familiar ache of missing him greatly. He's still out of town for work. If he'd been here that man might not have left standing. I'm sure of it. I'm almost glad he wasn't. It would only put him at risk. I don't know if I'll tell him. Slowly, I drift off to a fitful sleep.

The next morning Nonna comes into my room, concerned. I tell her I tripped and cut my hand. Doubt flickers in her eyes, and I don't think she believes me. If she ever found out what really happened, I'd be horrified. I know I have no reason to feel it, but I can't shake the shame that haunts me.

Soon after, she brings me a bouquet of flowers. Somehow, Tommaso arranged to have white roses delivered. Apparently, they arrived yesterday at the theater.

A miniature ivory card is hidden in the velvety, fragrant petals. "*Ti amo, mia bella,* Rosa." His words of love grip my raw heart, and I'm unable to stop tears from spilling over. Nonna assumes they are from missing him, and I do. But a heaviness presses upon me like a dark cloud.

Days pass in a blur, and I try to put that awful man out of my mind. But my thoughts continue to spin over what happened. The shock of it all. I'm unable to sleep. When I close my eyes, I see him, his face flushed with anger.

I fought with everything I have. Yet I still felt helpless against his brute force. It infuriates me. I cycle through numbness, rage, and feeling ashamed, then start over. I've done nothing to be ashamed of and then am angry with myself for feeling this way. How didn't I hear him following me? Now any sound is cause for panic. I long for peace, and for my mind and heart to settle.

But this morning, I feel a slight sense of calm return. Perhaps, I am healing. In an effort to be a help, I tell Nonna I'll go to the grocer's. Then on my way, I spot him across the street—the man who attacked me. I can't breathe. When he sees me, he glares. My skin bristles under his cold, reptilian gaze. I freeze, terrified.

Then, I'm enraged. How dare he? How dare he try to intimidate me? I won't give him the satisfaction of thinking I'm afraid. I open the door to the *panetteria*. Surely he won't bother me here. As I enter, I hear a man's voice yell, "Nico!"

From the window, I spy another Blackshirt motioning to him, calling him away. Seeing him leave, I'm dizzy with relief, my moments of rage giving way to terror again.

I'm still shaking when the owner hands me a loaf of bread. I exit the *panetteria*, slowly. Cautiously. When I return to the apartment, I rush inside. After setting the bread on the counter, I spot it. Shimmering in the sunlight slanting through the window is one of Nonna's letter openers. Small. Knifelike. I reach for it, hesitate, then take it in hand, feeling its weight. Quickly, I place it in my pocket. I'll hide it in the lining of my purse. I will protect myself. I'm taking a huge risk since any type of weapon is banned. But I don't care. I vow never to be so vulnerable again.

Later I go to Maestro's, and Eliana is there. We play jacks, which calms me, and it's late afternoon when I return home. When I see Nonna, I still don't tell her about what happened. The last thing I want is for her to worry. Or worse, to do something that might put her at risk. There's no telling what Nico could do. Hopefully, he'll disappear down the dark hole from which he crawled.

39

Caramina

"*Bravissima!*" Papa claps his hands as the last notes of Schubert's "Ave Maria" flow from my lips. "Beautiful, Caramina! Beautiful!" He motions for me to sit. "I love listening to you sing."

I lift the needle on the gramophone, set it to the beginning, and lower the volume. "*Grazie,* Papa." I sink into the sofa. He puts his arm around me, and the two of us listen to the sacred aria. Nestled against him, I feel his heartbeat.

Today was another long day working the fields in the hot sun. Thankfully, we returned to the house earlier than usual. Papa suggested I run through Rossini's "Una Voce Poco Fa" after getting cleaned up.

It's been over a year since Matteo asked me to sing. Since that day, I haven't stopped. I find myself singing as I work—in the fields or when I help Tia in the kitchen. Even when I'm watching Enzo or helping Anna with Lucia. But it's all been in bits and pieces. A melody here and there. I still haven't given up on my dream to one day study under Maestro in Italy.

As the last strains of the song fade, the needle reaches the end of the record and skips. Papa stands to shut off the gramophone, then sits back down next to me.

"Your mother would have loved listening to you. She'd have loved to see you now, how you come alive when you sing. Oh, how she would have smiled."

I often wonder what life would be like if Mama were still with us. But I'm relieved she doesn't have to experience this war.

"I know it's your dream to sing, Cara. This war won't last forever. When it ends—and it will end—I want you to pursue your dream. You may not be able to go to Italy with Nonna. But Italy isn't the only place with good music training."

I stare at him, dumbfounded. Surely the war will end, and things will go on as they're supposed to. My heart sinks. I'm glad he wants me to sing. But my stomach clenches at the thought of not doing so with Nonna and Rosa.

"You have a gift, Cara. Not many do. It makes you who you are, and it brings others joy. Don't give that up so easily, even if it's different than you imagined."

I shift my weight and the sofa creaks. What will happen after the war? I push the muddled thoughts from my mind and lean against his shoulder, grateful he cares so much. "You used to sing more, Papa. I miss that."

He chuckles. "I don't sing like you, Little Bird."

"You have a lovely voice. I love to hear you sing."

A smile stretches across his face. "All right, all right. Well, Tio should be back by now. I should go see what needs to be done." He kisses me on the forehead. He's almost disappeared into the kitchen when Tio flies through the front door gasping for breath, the door slamming shut behind him.

"They're coming! We need to go! Eduardo ran to warn me a troop was spotted between here and town. They're heading this way. We need to go now!"

"I'll get the others." Papa races up the stairs.

I perch on the edge of the sofa, unsure what to do. How could the Japanese have found us? We're hidden on the farm. I force myself to stand, my legs heavy, and go to the kitchen, grabbing up whatever we might need.

We planned for this. Days after we first arrived at the farm a year and a half ago, Papa and Tio had led us to a place deep in the jungle. A hidden cave covered by thick greenery upstream. Papa insisted we each learn the way. In the event something happened and we were separated, we were to flee to the cloistered cavern.

Hurrying through the kitchen, I fill a basket with whatever food I can find. I pour water into a small jug and set it alongside the meager provisions. The house fills with the sound of footsteps racing downstairs. Soon the entire family gathers in the small room.

Tio kisses Tia on the forehead affectionately, then runs out the front door. He and Papa agreed one of them would stay back and keep watch, while the other leads the group to the cave.

"Let's go!" Papa opens the back door, and everyone files out, except for me.

My eyes are set on a knife resting on a cutting board. I reach for it.

"Cara!" Papa yells. Startled, I draw my hand back, hesitating. Then I grab the knife, throw it in the basket, and cover it with a towel.

"I'm coming!" I race out the door and run across the yard into the darkness of the jungle. The wind picks up as the seven of us hurry through the dense vegetation. Palm fronds and leafy ferns move like frenzied dancers in a grand jungle ballet, arms outstretched, spinning wild twirls.

We arrive in no time, having sprinted the entire way. When we reach the cave, the wind falls eerily silent.

Papa makes sure we're secure in the belly of the cave before giving instructions. The plan is for him to stay at a lookout point halfway between the cave and the house. Tio will keep watch from the tree line by the farm. If the enemy comes, Tio will be the first to know and will signal Papa. Together they'll then remain near the cave, ready to guard it with their lives.

Papa places his hand gently on my shoulder before turning to leave. The gun holstered at his hip peeks out from under his shirt. I force myself to swallow back tears as he disappears through the heavy greenery.

My eyes adjust to the dark, and I can see Enzo rolling his ball on the ground. Anna is holding Lucia tight with Tia and Isabella next to her. The thick quiet of the cave is disorienting.

"Caramina, come sit." Tia motions to a spot at her side. "We may be here for some time. It's best if we settle in."

Anna starts to cry, and Isa puts her arm around her. "It'll be okay." Isa's words, though sincere, fall empty. No one knows how this will end.

"Matteo told me"—Anna's words are jumbled—"he said they'd taken babies, ripped them from their mother's arms, and . . ." She's crying so hard she can hardly speak. "Bayonets! They used bayonets on infants!" Anna rocks back and forth, clutching Lucia tighter.

"*Susmariosep!*" Tia's hand flies to her mouth, her eyes filled with horror.

Isabella hugs Anna. "We won't let them!"

Time creeps by as we sit in silence. Breaking through the hush, Tia whispers prayers.

"I'm hungry," Enzo whines.

"We're all hungry, Enzo. But we don't know how long we'll be here," I say.

"My stomach hurts. I'm hungry." He starts to cry, and Tia reaches into the basket.

"It's early. He can wait, Tia," says Isabella.

"Nonsense, we have food. He can have a little." Tia reaches to hand Enzo a piece of dried fish when a crackling noise sounds from the entrance of the cave.

I freeze. Everyone sits silently staring at the mouth of the cavern.

Lucia, who's been quiet since we arrived, fusses. Anna pulls her closer, rocking her back and forth frantically. It's no use. Lucia's whimpers grow more intense, and she begins to cry.

The crackling grows louder. Light flickers and then disappears in the thick hanging vegetation camouflaging the cave's opening.

Isabella searches the basket for anything to give to Lucia. Abruptly, she draws her hand back. I know exactly what she's found. I run to the basket and grab the knife. Tia watches, puzzled. My aunt's eyes widen when she realizes what I'm holding.

I race to the entrance, then stand still. I dare not breathe, I'm so scared. Any noise will alert whoever is on the other side of the canopy that I'm here. My muscles stiffen, and I force myself to inhale. Then a hand appears, grasping at the tendrils of hanging vines.

I lean back to steady myself, determined to remain still. The hand morphs into an arm, and then the shadow of a man's body casts on the wall of the cave. I leap forward with the knife held out to strike. The man is too far away, and I miss. He lunges and grabs me by the wrist.

"Caramina!"

I squirm in the man's grasp, confused, but still gripping the knife.

"Cara, it's me." Papa pries the knife from my hand. "It's okay," he says. He faces Tia and the others. "False alarm. Men from a guerrilla group. They knew Torres and his men were encamped nearby and wanted to speak with him about joining forces."

Tia's gasp echoes through the cavern, and Anna begins to cry.

"Thank God! *Gracias a Dios!*" says Isabella.

Papa glances around at each of us. "We can go back. It's safe."

I haven't moved from my spot at the mouth of the cave. Every inch of me is numb, and I can't stop shaking. We are safe, and Papa is okay. The reality sets in. A relief. He puts his arm around me firmly as if squeezing strength into my being.

Enzo scuffles his feet and stands. "Can we eat now?"

Isabella shakes her head. "You and your stomach!" She tousles his hair, then bends to pick up the basket. She pulls out a banana and dangles it. "Let's go, monkey." He jumps to grab the fruit.

Anna stands slowly, clutching Lucia to her chest. Tia offers to carry Lucia, and Anna acquiesces. Gently, she places Lucia in Tia's hands. I watch them push their way through the tangle of vines.

Papa stares at me. "Caramina?"

My mouth is dry, and I can't find any words. He takes me by the arm and leads me through the entrance, holding back the twisted, trailing greenery.

That night, we sit under the glow of two torches. A small fire casts shadows on the trees around Tia and Tio's yard. A full moon shines bright in the dark sky. Relief from the scare births a spirit of joviality. Confident the area has been scouted by Torres's men and is safe from immediate threat, Papa and Tio call for a celebration.

Jack and Gabriel have joined us after getting word of our ordeal. Gabriel presents Tia with three cans of potted ham that he got from an American GI. Tia cooks a bit of rice, and Tio unearths a bottle of liquor from the dusty recesses of a cabinet. There isn't much food to go around, but everyone eats happily. Then Gabriel surprises us with two chocolate bars—also gifts from the GI.

After our small meal, we sit contentedly. Jack with his back against a tree, strumming a guitar, Isabella at his side. One of the men in Torres's group bartered the instrument in exchange for a flask. Gabriel and I sit shoulder to shoulder. Papa and Tio speak in hushed tones about what needs to be done in the fields, while Enzo draws circles in the dirt with a stick.

The only one missing is Matteo. He's with a team of Torres's men far from camp. Anna cradles Lucia in her arms next to Tia. I know Anna must be thinking of him as she rocks Lucia gently to the music.

I'm glad to see Gabriel. Other than one brief visit when he dropped supplies off a month ago, I haven't seen him since our walk overlooking the valley. I've replayed the scene in my mind over and over, trying to make sense of it. He surprised me with the kiss. I hadn't kissed anyone before and am glad my first was with him. I'm closer to Gabriel than anyone else.

After our kiss, I asked Isa about her feelings for Jack. "You love him, don't you?"

A smile brightened her face. "Yes!"

"How do you know?"

"Oh, Cara. I can't stand being away from him. It's as if life pauses when he's away. I worry for him constantly. That I might not see him again. Are you asking because of Gabriel?"

Heat blushed across my cheeks. "I don't know. I don't know how I feel."

"You will."

Later, I inadvertently spied Jack kiss Isa again. His hand lingered under her blouse at her waist, and Isa melted into his arms. I turned away thinking about how I'd seen Anna in agony over Matteo, when we hadn't had any word of him. Something is different with Gabriel. Though I care for him, my feelings don't seem to match the magnetic pull between Isabella and Jack, or Anna and Matteo. Life continues when he isn't here.

Maybe Isa's right. And the feelings will come in time. All I know is I'm glad to have Gabriel as my friend, a very close friend, and I'm relieved he's safe. We haven't talked about our kiss. And for that, I'm grateful. I'm just happy to laugh with him again. He seems his old self.

He gives me a quizzical look and tosses me a piece of chocolate, laughing when I nearly drop it. I smack his shoulder playfully, and he jokes, a mock forlorn look on his face.

Perched on a log, Tio nods to the guitar resting against Jack's leg. "May I?"

"Didn't know you played, Alejandro." Jack hands the guitar to Tio, who strums a short tune. In the glow of the torchlight, Tio grins mischievously.

"I think this calls for a dance." He winks at Tia. The notes start slowly then quicken, and I recognize the tune.

Isabella pulls Jack to his feet. "Not much of a dancer," says Jack, warily. Isa laughs and leads him to the small clearing in the center of our group. He follows sheepishly, mimicking her graceful moves. Everyone chuckles at his attempt at the Kuratsa.

Gabriel holds his hand out to me and leads me into the circle opposite Isabella and Jack. Music spills out, growing in intensity and speed. Tio plays faster and faster, and the four of us spin around keeping up with the notes racing off the guitar strings. Tio strums his big finish, and we all collapse in laughter. I fall against Gabriel. He beams down at me, smiling.

Jack offers to repeat the tune so Tia and Tio can dance. Tio declines, but Tia snatches the guitar, hands it to Jack, and pulls Tio to his feet. Jack gives his best attempt at Tio's harried folk song.

I marvel at my aunt and uncle's energy and skill. Papa and Enzo join them. Then Tia scoops Lucia up and dances with the baby in her arms. Gabriel pulls Anna to her feet, whirling her around as the music plays. A flurry of notes fly off the strings as Jack gives an impassioned finale.

"You are a true Filipino," Tio declares to Jack, who grins as he bows.

Seeing my family so joyful is a wonderful sight. I reach in my collar, fishing out my necklace. In the darkness, I can just make out the sunflower. I grasp it tight. Then Jack starts up again and Papa grabs me by the hand. We dance late into the night, spinning circles in the amber light of the torches.

40

Rosa

I stroll along the Arno as the water slips by, lapping against its bank. As I near the Lungarno Acciaiuoli, a car races past. It skids as it comes to a stop. The driver scrambles from the vehicle and through a doorway.

Moments later, the unmistakable voice of the great tenor Titta Ruffo rings out. I spin on my heels and see him perched on a balcony singing "La Marseillaise" at full volume. People rush by me. Together we gather below, listening. Spellbound. Excitement, like a rampant fever, spreads all around me as a man yells, "Mussolini has been arrested!"

Cheers of *"Libertà! Libertà!"* erupt throughout the crowd. Tears stream down the faces of those around me, men and women alike. I wipe my own tears, realizing—finally, this has come to an end.

Ruffo finishes with a flourish and to cries for more. "Encore!" the crowd yells. He smiles and lifts his hand, inviting the audience to sing along. By now, hundreds of people have gathered, witnessing this historic moment and celebrating. A multitude of voices ring out this song of freedom led by Ruffo, who stands silhouetted by the garnet damask curtains of his apartment.

As I hurry home to tell Nonna, I catch snippets of conversations. "The king is fed up with him! He forced him to resign." Florence is filled with a celebratory spirit as people take to the streets. The colors of the city seem brighter. And I realize I haven't seen many Blackshirts. Are they now in hiding since their leader is no more?

As I pass by the university, groups of students have gathered outside. I peer through the crowd, hoping to spot Ciro. A man exits the building, and I stop when I realize it's Uncle Lorenzo.

Seeing his scowl, I continue on my way. Is he upset because he spotted me? Or is he actually disappointed Duce is no more? I pay him no heed. My uncle doesn't deserve my consideration.

When I reach home, I rush into the apartment, surprising Nonna. My words tumble out as I tell her what's happened and what I've seen. I leave out Uncle Lorenzo. "The king has arrested Duce. Mussolini is no more!"

Nonna grips the chair nearby she's so stunned. I help her to sit, watching tears flow down the weathered cheeks that still show her beauty. "Ah, Vittorio. Duce is gone," she whispers. I clutch her, hugging her from behind.

That night, Maestro joins us, and together we toast the end of the decades-long nightmare that is Mussolini. Good riddance, Duce.

41

Caramina

NOVEMBER 24, 1943

Mountain Province, Philippines

"How is it possible my Cara will be sixteen?" Papa's eyes brim with emotion.

I wonder how two years have passed since the war began. If the war hadn't happened, I'd be leaving soon for Italy. But it isn't to be.

Papa's aged in the time since, as the war has taken its toll on us all. Even so, he's not lost his verve for life, and I smile back at him.

"We must have a celebration. Sixteen is a momentous birthday." Tia swishes a rag across the table, mopping up crumbs from dinner. "And it means you're one year closer to being able to marry."

I groan, and Papa chuckles. "Don't marry her off so soon! She's too young, and I'm not ready for that!" He winks at me.

"What should we have for your big day?" Papa asks. "I think sixteen calls for pasta. *Sì?*"

I wonder what he's thinking since food has grown increasingly scarce.

"Don't look at me like that, Little Bird. You never know what we might find."

I've long since given up hope of enjoying Papa's pasta. "Whatever we have is fine."

"*Lechon!* We can hunt a boar and have *lechon,*" Enzo chimes in.

"For your birthday, Enzo, maybe. Now, let's go." Papa props open the door, and the two of them head to the shed.

Two weeks pass uneventfully, and I wake up to the most glorious, savory smell. Papa insisted I sleep in on my birthday, so I took advantage of the rare opportunity. After dressing, I meander downstairs to the sunlit kitchen. Tio and Isa are seated at the table.

"Happy birthday, Caramina!" Papa says.

"Is no one working today?" I ask, confused.

"Not yet. We have something to celebrate first." Papa pulls out a bowl of pasta from behind him on the counter. The heavenly scent of tomato sauce wafts through the room.

"How? How did you do this?"

"Tia made rice noodles, and I've been nurturing some seeds into tomatoes."

"His secret project behind the shed," Tio says.

"Only a small batch so far but enough for a birthday meal." Papa raises the bowl triumphantly.

"Pasta!" Enzo enters the kitchen with Anna and plops into a chair eager to dig in.

"*Grazie,* Papa, and thank you, Tia," I tell them.

We slurp up every noodle and bit of sauce. After, Tia sets a small coconut cake before me. I could almost cry from happiness at the luxury of the meal. We linger into late morning before emerging from the cocoon of heavenly food to disperse to do our chores. Before I make my way outside, Papa stops me.

"This is for you, Cara. It was your mother's. But I think she'd want you to have it."

Slowly, I unwrap the parcel from its rough brown paper. It's a book covered in worn camel-colored leather. When it falls open, the scent of orchids greets me—Mama's perfume. And I realize it's her Daily Missal. I remember her carrying it to church. A pang of missing her stabs within me. Tucked into the inside cover is a small piece of paper. I open it to see a lipstick kiss, and a prayer thanking God for Papa, for me, and each of my siblings. Then I read her words: *"I can only hope they will find spouses as loving as Arturo. That they'll find the happiness we've shared."*

Surely Papa can't part with this. That he brought it when we fled tells me just how meaningful it is.

"Papa, are you sure?"

"*Sì.* Happy birthday, Little Bird." He hugs me. "Now, I'd better get to it."

"*Grazie,* Papa."

I'm touched by my mother's words. But at sixteen, I don't need to think of such things yet. But Isa . . . and Jack. I know their love is true. I watch Papa stroll outside, then carry the book to my room for safekeeping, grateful for this remembrance of my mother's love.

42

Rosa

NOVEMBER 24, 1943

Florence, Italy

I slip through the doors of Teatro Fiorentino. Spotting me, Signor Gastani welcomes me warmly. "Rosa!" He kisses my cheek and ushers me into his office. "*Andiamo,* we have much to discuss."

Once seated, I'm about to ask his plans for the upcoming season when a thundering noise erupts outside. Together, we rush to the entrance.

Standing alongside a few theater workers, we watch as German tanks rumble down the street with paratroopers following close behind. I force down the sickening bile that rises within. From the door, we watch stunned as the city fills with the metallic thumping of Nazi jackboots on ancient stone and the harsh, clipped sounds of German yelling fill the piazzas.

Signor Gastani waves us inside. If only the walls of the old theater could protect us from the amassing army. As he shuts the door, a hand shoves through. Gastani peers out cautiously, cracks open the door, and lets Tommaso inside. I'm overcome by a swell of relief.

Gastani leads the workers into the belly of the theater until it's deemed safe for all to return home.

"I thought you were gone," I say, and Tommaso embraces me. "What's happened?"

"The Germans declared war. We must go, Rosa." The intensity in his tone shocks me.

"Go? Now?"

"Yes, it will be safer for you in the apartment. Come, let's go!"

At his insistence, I follow him out the rear door. We creep along the backstreets. He holds my hand, peering around corners to make sure it's safe, until we finally reach the apartment. Once inside, we speak freely.

"It was only a matter of time," Tommaso says, as Nonna joins us.

In September, Prime Minister Badoglio signed an armistice joining Italy with the Allies. We'd celebrated his decision to break with the Germans, along with Mussolini's arrest.

"*Sì*, to think the Germans wouldn't retaliate is naïve," Nonna says.

Tommaso shrugs off his jacket and sets it on a chair. "Hitler's enraged."

"So now the Germans have declared war on us." I'm incredulous. "It's not enough we had to deal with Duce's thugs. Now our streets are crawling with Nazis." I shudder at the thought.

Nonna places her hand on my shoulder gently. The small act comforts me.

Tommaso stays just long enough to ensure Nonna and I are okay. "Stay inside until this bedlam subsides," he says, motioning to the window.

"What about you?" I'm frantic for his safety. I didn't even know he was back from his trip until I saw him at the Fiorentino.

"I have to go, Rosa. I'll be fine. Stay here. I'll be back, I promise." He kisses my cheek, then rushes out the door and down the stairs. I watch helplessly from the window as he sneaks along the backstreet.

German troops continue to arrive. My stomach knots with worry for Tommaso, and I can't sleep all night wondering where he might be.

Then just before dawn, there is a light knock on the door. I peek out the window to see Tommaso. The nervous tension gripping me releases, and I race downstairs. I throw open the door and embrace him, holding him so tight I'm certain he can barely breathe.

"I'm okay, Rosa," he says, peering down at me. He brushes a wayward curl from my cheek and kisses me. We don't let go until we hear Nonna approaching.

"I'm going to have to leave," he tells me, apologetically.

My hands drop to my sides. "Now? In the middle of all this?"

Nonna appears around the corner. "First, you eat."

Tommaso looks dubiously at her in response. "You need to eat. *Andiamo!*" She instructs him as if speaking to a schoolboy. Obediently, he follows her into the cucina. But not before grabbing my hand and holding it gently along the way.

Nonna's calmness surprises me. She boils water and makes *caffè* for herself and Tommaso. I make myself a cup of tea, and we share dry toast in silence.

"How is it safe for you to travel?" My question tumbles out.

Tommaso wipes crumbs from his shirt. "I'll be fine, Rosa."

I look to Nonna, hoping she'll convince him to reconsider and stay. "The Germans don't want an uprising here," Nonna says. "They've been on the same side as Italy for years. I'm sure they're counting on a peaceful transition given many have had good relationships with their Italian colleagues. Most likely, they'll let people continue with their work and daily schedules."

Tommaso nods. "I agree. But they are imposing a curfew. We need to be mindful of it. My guess is they'll let daily life continue as long as no one resists."

My stomach clutches at the word as I think of Nonna, Maestro, and Ciro. Nonna doesn't respond. I'm terrified for Tommaso and wish I could shake the fear weighing on me like an anvil.

Nonna finishes her toast and stands. "Be safe, Tommaso." She hugs him, then leaves us to say our goodbye.

"*Grazie,* Serafina. I will."

Tommaso lingers after finishing the bread Nonna foisted upon him and takes my hand in his. He pulls me close, embracing me, and whispers, "I love you, Rosa. I'll be fine. I'll be back as soon as I can, *amore mio.*"

I walk him to the door where he kisses me. Once again, I watch as he disappears down the street behind the apartment. It takes everything in me not to yell for him to stop. It would be pointless. But I already miss him. Terribly. And I don't know when I'll see him again.

How do you stop a machine like the German army? Can it be done? Silently, I beg God it might be so. I know the Allies have been fighting fiercely to stop them.

Days later, I'm writing in my journal when I hear deafening booms. Nonna and I peer out the window as the floor shakes beneath us. Bombs have fallen on the outskirts of the city. Though the bombing is far from the apartment, the noise is terrifying and sounds as if the ground will split open and swallow us alive. Thankfully, the bombing subsides, and our building isn't damaged.

I, like many Florentines, have grown used to the earsplitting air raid sirens, which are now commonplace, often without any bombs falling. People have grown complacent. Most no longer bother to find shelter. But this noise is like no other I've heard. It shakes me to the core. When it finally stops, I'm still trembling from the reverberations.

When Nonna leaves my room, I continue writing in my journal. I never thought I'd be writing about such things. Florence—an occupied city. It's crazy! I think of my family. What horrors are they experiencing under the Japanese? In Italy, we lived in Mussolini's suffocating grip for so long. And now, the Germans are here, patrolling every corner.

Our rejoicing over Duce's fall seems eons ago. Even before the Germans arrived, there was still tension in the precarious peace of the interim, though Nonna's efforts with the Resistance had slowed considerably. No longer was she sneaking out for secret tasks. No longer did I have to worry for her safety.

Now, everything has changed. The Germans have freed Mussolini. They've set him up as leader of their newly created Republic of Salò, the Italian Social Republic. Alongside the Germans, all of Duce's Blackshirts are back. Strutting around, brandishing their newly restored power with even greater hatred toward anyone not in line with the regime.

There are two governments now: the German-sponsored republic under Mussolini and the official Italian government under Badoglio and the king. But Florence is occupied. The city is now living under the oppression of the German troops and Blackshirts. I had found great relief knowing that dog, Nico, was stripped of his power when Duce fell. But now, no doubt, Nico is back on the streets terrifying good people.

It's almost dusk when the phone rings. A man from the Ministry of Popular Culture is calling, asking Nonna to attend a party for high-ranking Germans and fascists. His voice bellows through the receiver so loudly, I can hear him as I stand at Nonna's side. Nonna's tone doesn't give away her obvious disgust. She is unflappable. Calmly, she tells him she'll check her schedule and let him know.

An hour afterward, Maestro stops by, and the two of them speak in hushed tones on the terrace. I bring them an *aperitivo,* and the moment I open the door they fall silent. Still, Nonna smiles and points to a chair for me to join them.

The next day, Nonna phones the man to say she'll attend. "I'll go with you," I tell her. What good will it be for her to go alone?

She purses her lips. "I don't want you anywhere near these people."

"Will Maestro accompany you?"

"He has other matters to attend to."

Now, I'm even more concerned. "You shouldn't go alone, Nonna. How is it safe for you?"

"You must know your enemy, Rosa," is all she says.

"I'll be meeting these very same people the next time I perform."

"No." She won't hear of it and shakes her head in a definite no. I glimpse my grandmother's strength and the stubbornness that has no doubt helped her craft such an illustrious career.

Later, I'm brushing my hair when Nonna knocks on my door. She tells me that she has changed her mind and I can accompany her to the party. Maestro must have convinced her it would be all right. Apparently, my presence was requested, too.

The day of the party, I'm stuffing a music score into my bag in the conservatory hallway when I hear Ciro's voice.

"Rosa! I thought that was you. You're in a rush."

I tell him that I've only a few hours before the party and must get back to prepare, so he walks with me down the hall. Our footfalls are the only ones in the corridor. I mull over whether I should tell him about Tommaso.

"Ciro, I've been meaning to tell you. I've met someone . . . His name is Tommaso."

I peer over at him as he is silent.

"Of course you have! A beautiful woman such as yourself," he says, momentary frustration in his tone.

"I think you'll like him."

"I'm sure I will." His words have an edge.

I'd hoped he'd be happy for me. Given his constant flirting with the beautiful girls at conservatory, I wouldn't think he'd care.

"How was your visit with your uncle?" I change the topic and glance at him.

"*Molto bene,*" he says. "He's doing well. Tired of all of the chaos." Anger flashes in his eyes so quickly I wonder if I'm just seeing things.

Frustrated by his childishness and not wanting to be late, I hurry to leave. "I really must go."

"Are you seeing him? Tommaso, is it? Enjoy, Rosa." A hint of sarcasm is in his voice.

"*Buona sera*, Ciro." I wave goodbye before walking out onto the street and leaving him be.

Later that night, a black Lancia sedan pulls up outside the apartment to take Nonna and me to a palazzo on the outskirts of the city. By the time we pass through the dark doors of the monstrous building, my pulse is racing. Seeing so many German officers mixing with the Florentine music elite is unsettling. Various theater heads, officials from MinCulPop and their mistresses, a few musicians, and composers are in attendance, along with the illustrious crowd of wealthy who frequent the most important performances. Most are known supporters of the regime.

Watching Nonna, it's as if she's transformed into Leonore in Beethoven's *Fidelio.* Her words to *know your enemy* stick in my mind. Any reservations she has, she hides expertly. Mingling with men rumored to have committed such barbaric acts turns my stomach. It takes effort to keep my disgust from showing.

A young German officer approaches and asks if I've sung "Liebestod" from *Tristan and Isolde.* His gaze softens. He says, "It's one of my mother's favorites."

I tell him no, I've not performed any of the German arias.

"A shame. Perhaps, in the future you will," he says before walking away.

I sip my wine to steady my nerves. As I glance around the room, I nearly drop my glass. Nico stands leering at me from the bar. His dark, lanky frame slithers toward me. How brazen, to approach me after what he's done. Surely he won't try anything in this crowd. With a flick of his wrist, he motions to the dance floor. My blood ices as he comes near. I grip my purse, mindful of the small, sharp letter opener hidden inside.

Just before Nico reaches me, someone grabs my arm and pulls me to the dance floor. It's Ciro. He draws me into a waltz. Where did he come from? Any hint of frustration at finding out about Tommaso appears gone.

Recognition flashes through Nico's eyes when he sees Ciro. He glowers at us but, thankfully, backs away into a mess of women shamelessly fawning over a German officer.

Ciro's arms are strong around me, and I feel the tension in my muscles fading away. He leads me through another German waltz and reassures me. "He won't hurt you. I won't let him."

Still shaken, I smile to hide the fear pulsing through me. Ciro is himself, and I'm relieved. If he wasn't here . . . I'd hoped Nico had forgotten about me. But now, I know that isn't the case.

"I didn't know you'd be here," I say, and Ciro smiles. His presence at the party is a surprise. He's not part of this elite music crowd.

We're weaving our way between a flock of German officers and their partners when Ciro says, "You've read *Les Misérables*? Combeferre tells Marius that there is no greater thing than to be free. How will you help in the fight for freedom, Rosa?"

What is he thinking? We're inches from a German SS captain spinning a rosy-cheeked woman across the dance floor. I'm stunned and quickly say, "Yes, I know the book." Terrified the captain overheard Ciro, I pretend we're playing a game. "Hugo also wrote, 'It is dreadful not to live.' So, let's dance!" I tug him away from the two.

A glint flashes in Ciro's eyes, and he draws me closer. Thankfully, the captain appears none the wiser. *Grazie, Dio!*

We dance in silence with him holding me a little too tightly until the music ends. "I must find Nonna," I say and pull away.

But he holds me by the hand and whispers in my ear, "Music doesn't make you immune from what's happening. Those who don't pick a side find themselves in the most danger. I don't want that for you, Rosa."

I flick my hand away as if from a flame and briskly thank him for the dance. I leave him and find Nonna, who is standing near the musicians talking to the conductor.

What an uncomfortable, strange evening. Ciro's words circle through my mind long after we return home.

The next day I wake early and head to the *panetteria*. As I stand waiting for bread, I recognize a few of the women in line from the neighborhood. I smile at one young mother. She glares back and whispers to the old woman at her side. The frigid November air isn't nearly as chilling as their icy stares.

Then, the old woman hisses at me, *"Traditrice!"*

I stumble back as if slapped. Me, a traitor! I turn away to face the storefront, Ciro's words haunting me. If only they knew. I have nothing but disgust for the Germans and the regime. Now I understand the exhaustion on Nonna's face. Know your enemy, she said. It is no easy road to walk.

43

Rosa

DECEMBER 6, 1943
Florence, Italy

The whistle of the kettle stirs me from my writing. I make my tea, then sip it slowly, willing away the morning chill. I bring my cup to the table and reopen my journal. No sooner have I lost myself in my memories than there is a knock at the door.

It's early for visitors. Cautiously, I peer out the window. I throw open the door, surprising Tommaso as he stands hand raised mid-knock.

"You're back!"

"*Buon giorno,*" he says, a hint of tiredness in his voice.

I draw him inside and close the door against the icy air. He pulls me close to kiss me, and his stubble tickles my cheek. I savor the warmth of being close as we stand locked in an embrace in the narrow hallway. When we part, the strained look on his face has disappeared.

"I've missed you. How long can you stay?"

From his expression, I know he doesn't have much time. I'm a mix of relief at seeing him safe and frustration that our time is again fleeting. He gives an apologetic look, pulling me away from the door.

"Your grandmother?"

"She went to the Duomo." I draw him into the kitchen and pour him a cup of tea.

He sits and places a bag of chestnuts on the table. As he recounts his latest project, the weariness in his voice belies his exhaustion.

"Have you slept?"

He rubs his eyes and yawns. "I got in late last night."

I bring what leftover bread we have to the table.

"*Grazie.*" He tears off a piece of the loaf.

I tell him about the party Nonna and I attended. His eyes widen, concern etched across his brow. "If I asked you not to attend another one, you wouldn't listen, would you?"

"I can't let her go alone. Besides, they asked me to attend." I sound more confident than I was at the party. "It was certainly uncomfortable."

"If you can stay away from them, do it, Rosa. Please. It's dangerous."

"I don't know that I have a choice," I respond, while thinking of Nonna's statement about knowing our enemy.

The pained look doesn't leave his eyes. We sit together quietly eating our fill of bread and roasted chestnuts. After an hour, he glances at his watch—and I already know. He's leaving again.

"Surely you can stay a little longer?" Even to my own ears, my words sound hollow. I know it isn't possible.

"I'm afraid not, *amore mio.*"

The thread connecting our hearts frays thinner. His firm's work is directed by the regime. He doesn't have a choice any more than I. No one does.

We linger in the hallway, neither of us wanting to part. He clutches me to him and embraces me tightly. I feel his warm breath on my neck, and he whispers, "*Tu sei sempre nel mio cuore.* You are always in my heart."

I sink into his arms. Warmth blooms within me as he kisses me deeply. When we separate, I know that my fears are mistaken. His love is true. It's just this war that has everyone on edge.

I watch him go, not knowing when I'll see him again. The thread pulls tighter on my heart as he disappears from view.

Days later, to my great pleasure, Tommaso returns. He accompanies me to see Maestro at the conservatory. As we head toward Maestro's office, I see Ciro.

Leaning against the wall talking to his blond violinist, he spots us. He stands up straight, making himself taller. Since I told Ciro about Tommaso weeks ago, he's not hidden his displeasure.

"Rosa!" he says as we approach. He looks at Tommaso as if he's sizing up an opponent in a street fight. "And you are?"

"Tommaso. You must be Ciro. Nice to meet you." Tommaso holds out his hand.

Slowly, Ciro lifts his hand, then shakes Tommaso's. "We were just discussing how unfortunate it is that with Duce's Republic of Salò, his men are back in business," Ciro says.

"Sì," the violinist pipes in, "if only someone would rise up to stop them for good."

The two glare at Tommaso as if they're issuing a challenge. Anyone could hear and report us. Glowering at Ciro, I grasp Tommaso's hand to tug him away. But he doesn't budge.

The uncomfortable silence is broken by the unfortunate sounds of a trumpeter playing out-of-tune scales down the hall.

"Pleasure to meet you. Rosa, we should be going. *Arrivederci,*" Tommaso says, coolly. He tips his head to the two, then squeezes my hand, and we continue down the hall.

After my meeting with Maestro, Tommaso and I sit alone on a bench in the park.

"Of course I want an end to Duce and his reign. But I'm not going to risk my life, and certainly not yours, or my livelihood in a verbal duel in public," he says quietly, putting his arm around me and drawing me close when I shiver.

"I can't believe how foolish Ciro can be," I say. His words and actions put us all in danger. "He's not usually like that," I continue, though I know it's not completely true. "He's never been so bold before. So reckless as to speak his thoughts loudly and in public."

"Times of war change many men," Tommaso sighs.

44

Rosa

I'm wondering if I'm dreaming. But the pounding only gets louder and more furious. It's the middle of the night, and someone is at the front door. *"Offen!* Open!"

I stumble from bed, disoriented at the sound of German being yelled. A sick panic runs through me as I remember my journal. I peer around the room and at my desk, remembering that I put it in its hiding place before going to sleep.

Fear sharpens my senses, and I throw a robe over my nightgown. Nonna's steady voice can be heard downstairs. Slowly, I descend the steps, fighting the urge to rush into the room for Nonna's sake.

Standing like bulwarks in the front hall are three German SS soldiers, one an officer. I hear a grunt and turn to see, leaning against Nonna's antique bureau, Nico. That monster in my home! My pulse races, and I breathe deeply to steady myself.

"There must be some mistake, Signore. My granddaughter recently finished studying at Conservatorio Luigi Cherubini."

"There is no mistake. Where are her papers?" the officer demands, taking a step toward Nonna.

"Signore, please. Surely you see she is no threat. She is just a young woman." Despite the lightness in her tone, I catch the resolute look in her eye.

"Now, Signora Grassi!"

Nonna is like the Arno on a summer morning. Calm. A strong current hidden beneath a glassy surface. She walks to the bureau, pulls open a drawer, and hands him my papers.

His brow furrows as he looks them over. Then he looks at Nonna. "We are at war, Signora. Your granddaughter is an enemy of the state."

Nonna tries to intervene again. He waves her away with one hand, turns to me, and snaps, "Rosa Grassi, you are under arrest! Get your things. You will come with us. Now!"

The room spins. My eyes dart from Nonna to the officer, and I catch the sneer on Nico's face. This is his doing. I'm sure of it. Do they know about my bringing food to Betta and Giuseppe? I don't want to think about what will happen if they know I've been helping them.

Nonna steps forward, placing herself between me and the officer. His face is tinged with twisted amusement. "Shall I arrest you, too, Signora Grassi? It can be arranged."

"It will be all right," I tell Nonna, though the floor tilts beneath me.

Seeing the officer's menacing grimace, I've no doubt he won't hesitate to take her, too. I will do everything in my power to make sure that doesn't happen. "I need to change," I say promptly.

He glares at me. "Quickly!"

I go to my room and change out of my nightgown in a flurry. When I come back downstairs, the officer shoves me out the door and brusquely into a waiting car. Nonna follows us to the street. As I right myself in the seat, I hear her. "It will be okay, Rosa," she says, as the officer slams the door shut. We drive away into the dark city.

Several minutes later, the car stops, and the door is flung open. The officer grabs my arm and pulls me from the car. I peer at the building before me. The Villa Triste. They've brought me to Mario Carità's headquarters. Carità, the head of the Florentine fascist police, is a sadistic man. This wretched place is now also the headquarters of the Gestapo, the Nazi secret police. As I'm led through the doors, I tremble as I remember the horrific stories I've heard.

The officer leads me into a dimly lit room with a thick haze of cigarette smoke. He shoves me into a chair before a monstrous old desk, then leaves. When he returns, he plies me with questions. "You are Filipina? A friend of America, yes?"

Before I can even think of how to answer, he slams my papers onto the desk.

I'm confused. "Signore, yes, I am Italian Filipina. I am Italian. I love this country. It's been my home for—"

"Quiet!" He glares at me. I wait for him to say it, but he says nothing about my helping Betta and Giuseppe. Is he just playing a sick game?

"Get up!" He clicks his heels together, then leads me down a dark, narrow passageway. Hunched against the wall is Nico, leering at me as I pass by.

I want to scream, "You will not intimidate me!" But instead, I straighten my back and walk by silently.

We continue down a set of ancient stone stairs to a small corridor, cave-like in its darkness. Two small lamps on either side of the corridor do little to light the area. When my eyes finally adjust, I see metal bars running the length of the space. A jail. Inside are several people, some standing, some slumped on a rustic bench. The metal-barred door groans as it's pulled open. The officer shoves me inside and slams the door. The sound of the old lock snapping in place riddles the silence. I rub the sting on my shoulder from where he shoved me. I peer around, a sinking feeling in my stomach, as I realize I am now caged. Like an animal.

I fight to keep the terror rising within at bay, knowing it will not serve me. I glance around. Everything is gray. A wooden bench rests to one side, now worn into a smoky pewter like thick fog. Its knotty grain blends with the jagged, ashen stone walls. I cover my nose at the rancid smell of sweat and waste. Damp permeates the space, seeping up from the stone floor. Cut high into the back wall is a single miniscule half-moon window that shows nothing but the darkness of a moonless night. I glance at my cellmates and bristle when I realize I am the only woman.

The German officer disappears up the stairs, Nico following close behind. When they're gone, one of the men on the bench stands. Unsure of his intentions, I draw back. But he simply introduces himself. One by one, they all do.

Thankfully, my cellmates are kind. Of the ten of us being held, four are American expatriates, and one British, along with four Italians and me. The Italians tell me they were arrested after someone snitched on a conversation they'd had discussing their frustration over the dwindling lack of food in the city. The expats were arrested for being enemy aliens, like me. They tell me the Germans are rounding up anyone from the Allied nations.

How did I end up here? I rack my brain to make sense of what's happened. What crime have I committed? Other than being born in one country and living in another. Good people are in jail. Am I that threatening? All five foot three of me? How absurd. I force myself to stay calm. Don't give in to desperation, I chide myself, knowing my world has just been ripped apart.

I sit hunched against the wall, not giving in to sleep the rest of the night. Knowing Nico is involved makes my skin crawl. I don't want to be taken by surprise. I need to stay alert. Nonna knows I'm being held. Tommaso has no idea. If he did, he'd blaze in to see me freed. But could he? Oh, how I miss him. Even Ciro can be no help. We are powerless against these men.

Early in the morning, footsteps stomp down the stairs, echoing into the cell. From the window above, moonlight is now pooled onto the freezing stones of the floor. The sky has cleared. A sign of hope? Surely things will clear up, and I'll be released.

A young German soldier appears, followed by two Blackshirts, Nico, and a boy who can't be more than sixteen, balancing a large pot and some bread. The soldier eyes me on the floor and asks, "You are a singer, yes?"

He approaches the cell and holds a metal cup through the bars, motioning to me in my curled position. A futile attempt to find warmth. Needles pierce my legs as I unfold and stand. I take the cup filled with watery broth.

Nico leers at me, but I ignore him. The soldier tears a piece of bread and holds it out to me. When I grasp for it, he yanks it from reach. Is he waiting for an answer? My heart thumps against my rib cage. "I'm a recent graduate of conservatory, Signore."

"No, no. You are more than that. I've heard you are quite a singer." He throws a nod in Nico's direction. "You sang 'Musetta's Waltz,' did you not? Ah, *La Bohème*. Sing, Signorina! You will sing for me."

My blood boils when Nico's lips curl into a smirk. I set down the cup, then grip my hands tight into fists at my side, nails biting into my palms.

I remember Nonna at the party. A performance. That's what this is. I steady myself and say, "Signore, you are mistaken. I'm—"

"You are here because you are an enemy of Germany! You are Filipina, yes? A friend of America! We have your papers. It is no use denying this." With his piercing eyes and long curved nose, he is hawkish, and clearly a glutton for power. "We can make things more comfortable for you, Signorina."

At the look in his eyes, I shudder.

"Sing! Wagner's *Tristan and Isolde*. I would love to hear it. Nico, here, says you have the voice of a songbird."

I want to spit in Nico's face. I am not a bird in a cage, trapped to perform for its owners. Music isn't a piece of meat to barter. It is life-giving, and neither Nico nor this soldier will make me perform. It is the one thing I can hold on to. I will not sing on command.

The German purses his lips into a tight line. He spins on his heels and marches back up the stairs carrying the pot, broth slopping onto the cold steps. Nico glares at me, huffs, then follows.

Relief sweeps through me. Then I realize no one else in the cell has been served. I've cost them their sustenance. Bitter bile rises in my throat. I had no idea they would pay for my defiance. Immediately, I offer my cup to one of the men on the bench, apologizing. "*Mi dispiace.*"

"No, Signorina. No. It's not necessary. You need this as much as we do," he says, then pauses. "Your performance of 'Musetta' was extraordinary. I play it over in my mind. It was a beautiful night."

I'm stunned. To find such kindness in a place devoid of warmth . . . I choke up with emotion that there is still good in the world.

Days pass, and I fight to not lose track of time. One day morphs into another day's gray. A blur. The British man tells me it's been two weeks since I arrived. The German soldier, with Nico by his side, continues to play his games, taunting me every day.

One morning, after my cellmates have been given their meager provisions, he turns to Nico. "What shall she sing?"

Nico sneers. "'Giovenezza.'"

"The 'Giovenezza'! For Duce. You will sing." The officer says this as if it is a fact.

I will never sing this fascist hymn. I remain silent, and again he takes what little food should be mine and turns on his heel. This continues morning after morning. Fortunately, my cellmates are as disgusted with the officer's behavior as I am. After those dogs slink back up the stairs, my fellow inmates share their food, overwhelming me with their kindness.

The cold is unbearable, and I long for the warmth of Tommaso's arms and Nonna's apartment. At night, I ball up against the jagged stone wall that presses into my back. I'm filthy, my skirt and blouse splotched with dirt. I run my fingers through my hair in a vain attempt to comb it.

Oddly, wearing my hair down brings to mind my home in Luzon.

I miss my family terribly. I close my eyes, imagining I'm in Flor-idablanca. Home. A warm breeze blowing in off the bay, the rustle of palm trees swaying. The scent of frangipani and sampaguita. At night in my dreams, the flowers bloom. Their heady scent so strong, I ache with longing for my family. For home. I've not been so home-sick since I first arrived.

I grow delirious with fever, then dream Tommaso has come to the jail. He's next to me, calling my name tenderly, "Rosa, Rosa, it's time to go." The door to my cell opens, and the German officer stands by watching, unable to stop my flight to freedom. All thanks to Tommaso. His blue eyes, shimmering turquoise like the waters in Boracay, gaze upon me with gentleness and concern. The thought warms me as I lie shivering. But when I peer around, I see nothing but the gray stone floor and the black bars of the cell. Locked. Tom-maso is not here, and the realization brings me low.

Several of the men in the cell are badly beaten. Taken in the daytime and returned late. Some now unable to walk. Their groan-ing, along with the cries and shrieks of others in the villa being "questioned," reverberates along the cold walls every night. One of my Italian cellmates is in desperate need of medical attention his injuries are so bad. When they tossed him like garbage into the cell, he was barely conscious. A gaping wound on his chest bled pro-fusely. His friend bound the wound the best he could, and the bleeding has stopped. But I don't know if he'll survive. When his friend told the officer he needed a doctor, the German scoffed, "Traitors deserve worse."

One morning, I lie still with a song playing in my head. One my mother sang when I was young. I can hear her singing to me. "Sa Ugoy ng Duyan"—"The Cradle's Sway." Her gentle voice is a sliver of hope.

But hope is elusive, and soon I'm startled by yelling. "Up! All of you! Get up!" The SS officer's voice slices through the muddiness in my head. Slowly, my bones rigid, I stand up, then stumble over to the others.

In the officer's hand is a wooden club. He runs it along the bars of the cell. The earsplitting clanging sounds are explosions in my head. What does this mean? I fight to come to my senses. To focus. Is it possible? Are we being freed? A splinter of hope pricks my heart.

"Today," he declares, "you will be taken to Serv_gliano."

Gasps echo through the cell. A camp. Rivets of pain hammer in my chest. All hope is gone. I am being taken to an internment camp.

45

Caramina

DECEMBER 29, 1943

Mountain Province, Philippines

Walking back to the house after a long day working in the sun, I tug at my blouse. A futile effort to cool myself. "I need a bath."

Tia wipes her brow smudged with dirt. "We all do, Cara."

Suddenly I see movement at the tree line, and a young man races out into the open. I recognize him. He's one of Captain Torres's runners. Since the war began, Torres's men have patrolled the jungle, keeping close watch over the area surrounding the farm. At this man's look of urgency, my stomach plummets.

The man approaches, and Papa asks, "What's happened?"

"The Japanese officer in Timbales rounded up many of the men and boys." The man takes a breath and shrugs in disgust. "A *zona* they called it."

"*Madre Mia!*" Tia gasps.

"Gabriel! Is he okay?" I ask.

The young man gives me a sympathetic look. "We've not had word."

A sick feeling twists in my stomach.

Papa puts his hand on my shoulder tenderly, but the look on his face is one of grit and frustration. "Let's not jump to conclusions. What exactly happened?"

"Yesterday, they randomly rounded up several of the men and boys. They made them stand rigid in a line all day in the sun. No water. They beat them if they moved."

Panic flashes through me. You can die from not having enough water in this blistering heat and go blind from the sun's harsh rays.

"Several of them have been . . ." He pauses, looking to me, Tia, and Isa. Papa nods for him to continue. "Bayoneted and shot."

I'm numb and want him to stop. It's too much. These men are savages. "I don't understand," I ask. "Why?"

"We got word there are *Makapili* in Timbales," he says, and Papa shakes his head, disgusted.

Matteo once told me the *Makapili* are Filipino spies working with the Japanese.

"The *Makapili* walked along the line pointing out anyone they suspected of aiding the Americans or Torres—or just for spite."

"Those swine!" Isa says.

When Matteo told me about these traitors, I couldn't believe any of my countrymen could do such a thing. Now I know.

"Maybe they receive a few extra scraps of food. They're wrong if they think they won't find themselves at the end of a Japanese bayonet," Papa says.

It doesn't matter whether these spies can prove a charge or not. Anyone suspected of working against the Japanese is taken to the *Kempeitai,* the Japanese military police, and tortured for information, according to Matteo. The fate of the Timbales men and boys rests on the fickle mood of the enemy.

Dear God, please don't let me lose Gabriel. I want to scream. I look to Tia whose face is pale, tears flowing down her cheeks.

Two hours pass, and I'm sitting on the front porch with Papa in the dim light of early evening. Neither of us have words, so we sit silently. Suddenly, the silhouette of a man emerges through the trees.

Papa stands. "Go in the house, Cara."

The man comes closer. When he waves, I recognize him instantly.

"Gabriel!" I run as fast as I can toward him and throw my arms around him, desperately relieved he's all right.

He holds me in an embrace as Papa approaches.

"I'm okay," Gabriel says.

Papa places his arm around him in a fatherly way and leads us to the house.

"I wasn't there. I had a"—Gabriel glances at me, pausing—"meeting."

"*Grazie a Dio!*" Papa says.

A grave look falls over Gabriel's face. "It's terrible . . . what's happened."

Tears flow down my cheeks. Relief at seeing him alive and safe.

The three of us stand in the dusky, twilit moonlight. "Come, we must let the others know you're safe." Papa leads us into the house.

As the door shuts against the night air, I wonder how life has come to this. And if the Japanese will ever be stopped.

46

Rosa

Servigliano. Internment camp. At the officer's words, the stone floor beneath me pitches and pinpricks of light dot my vision. Any hope I've had of rescue is shattered. My mind races. Will I ever see my family again? And Tommaso—is he lost to me forever?

The soldier blocks my way as my cellmates are marched up the stairs. He leans close, pressing his body into mine. The bars of the door dig into my back. At the pungent smell of his greasy hair thick with pomade, I stifle a gag.

Once again, he demands I sing the "Giovenezza." He raises his hand, and my head slams against the bars as he strikes my cheek. I fight to stay alert, my head throbbing. In the silence, I hear the ticktock of his watch like a metronome and focus on the flickers of sound. Another performance, I tell myself. Stand strong. I exhale slowly, forcing myself to breathe. Just breathe.

Finally, he snaps his head up and shoves me toward the stairs. "Move!"

On the street, I watch my cellmates herded onto a truck. I stand in line as if queuing for bread. The wind gusts, kicking up dust. Church bells toll in the distance. The golden ocher buildings lining the cobbled street are gray in the winter light. Cold snakes up from the stones beneath me as if I've stepped into the Arno.

I raise one foot to the step of the truck, when a voice with a harsh German accent cuts through the chill. "Halt!"

The young soldier snaps to attention as an SS officer in a well-decorated uniform struts toward us. He waves a paper that flutters in the wind, then hands it to my jailer. The soldier's face falls and shoulders drop as he reads.

Then I hear his voice, so quiet I'm not sure if I've heard correctly or if it's just my imagination. "You are free."

My mind is playing tricks, grasping at hope.

Red-faced, he glares at me, then barks, "Go!"

I'm shocked. How can this be? Then I spot Nonna. From the doorway of the jail, she steps out onto the dusty street. She stands confident and unflinching. Like John Wayne from the Western I saw years ago with my siblings. Tears well up in my eyes. Relief surges through me, leaving me lightheaded. I fumble my way to join Nonna, my legs heavy like the marble statues that graced this city before the war.

Nonna approaches the soldier, puts her hand out brazenly, and says, "Signore?"

He grunts, then hands her the paper with Italian markings. She slinks her arm through mine, and we walk down the street. "You are Italian, *mia bambina*," she says.

We round the corner and pass the villa's main entrance. Leaning against the wall, cigarette dangling from his lips, is Nico. When I see him, anger burns bright within me. But more than my rage, I feel something else. Something more powerful. Joy.

My mother's song floods into my mind, and I can't help myself. I sing. My chapped lips sting, but I don't care. *"The stars watch over me,"* I sing. Defiantly and proudly.

Nico startles when he hears me, and his eyes darken with defeat. Then he's behind me, a figure disappearing into my past. Sunlight breaks through the clouds. I am free. Even in this occupied state of war—I am free. I will never take that for granted. How Nonna obtained citizenship papers for me, I've no idea. But I, Rosa Grassi, am now a citizen of my father's beloved *Italia*.

After returning to the apartment, I bathe, change my clothes, and go straight to bed, exhausted. I fall asleep immediately.

Later when my eyes crack open, I peer around in confusion. Suddenly I remember that I'm free and at Nonna's apartment. Slowly, I rise and change. I step down the stairs gingerly, my body aching.

From the dwindling light, I can tell it's late afternoon. I hear Maestro's and Ciro's voices, and Nonna telling them I'm not ready for visitors. I round the corner, so happy to see their friendly faces.

"I'm all right," I say, hearing fatigue in my voice. Their eyes brim with concern. Maestro embraces me tenderly and leads me to a chair. The four of us sit together. Graciously, they don't ask me questions about the jail. Maybe I will speak of it when I've sorted through all that's happened.

Later, Nonna and Maestro leave for a walk. Ciro keeps me company. "I was so worried for you, Rosa." His voice cracks. I'm touched by his obvious concern. He seems himself again.

I shiver at the chill in the apartment. Gently, he drapes a blanket around me. His care touches me deeply. Together, we sit quietly listening to the crackling fire. It is enough that he is here.

It's been one week since my release. I'm writing in my journal when I hear the clipped sound of a German voice downstairs. My heart catches in my throat, and I pull myself up in a frenzied panic to throw my diary underneath the floorboard. Hastily, I cover it with the rug. I force myself to remain calm.

I open the door and hear two voices. One German, and the calming bass of Signor Gastani in conversation. Slowly I descend the stairs, catching snippets. "Thank you, Signora," the German says. "To discuss music with one so esteemed is an honor."

"The lieutenant told me how much he appreciated speaking with you at the party, Signora Grassi," Signor Gastani says. His voice is formal, as is his use of Nonna's surname.

I creep back to my room. Relieved. The German soldier is not here for me. He had requested that Signor Gastani bring him here to discuss the merits of German versus Italian opera.

Once I hear them say goodbye, I gather my things. It's my first time leaving the apartment since coming home. Though still shaken from my experience, I force myself to resume rehearsals. It's time. And I'm ready.

The silence in the hall outside Maestro's apartment is surprising. "Where is Eliana? I was hoping to see her."

Maestro doesn't offer an answer. In jail, I heard things. Horrible things about what the Nazis are doing to the Jews. It's despicable. Evil.

"She's fine," Maestro says softly, before directing our conversation to possible pieces for me to begin preparing.

"I have something for Eliana," I say, setting a book on the table by the door. He nods in response.

I'm sure he'll see she gets it. It's one of my father's books from when he was a boy. *The Blue Fairy Book*, a collection of fairy tales. She's a little young for it yet. But I know she'll love the stories as she grows.

I leave Maestro's to head to the grocer's. After finishing up, I step outside the shop and spot Maestro on the corner. When I reach him, I see anguish in his eyes and follow his gaze. A line of Jewish men, women, and children are being marched down the street. Herded along by a group of German soldiers. My stomach drops, bile rising in my throat.

"I must go," Maestro says, racing off.

I follow him, terrified of what we might find. He stops in front of a building far from Nonna's. But we're too late. Betta and Giuseppe are on the street, a German SS soldier glaring at them.

Anger rises along with my panic. Where is Eliana? Please, let her be hiding. Then Giuseppe turns. Clinging to his leg is Eliana, her stuffed bunny, Luca, dangling from one hand.

Maestro approaches and tells the soldier there must be a mistake. The soldier scoffs and shoves Maestro aside. I move to help him, as does Betta. But the German grabs her by the arm, and she cries out. Then he pushes her and Giuseppe hard toward the Santa Maria Novella train station.

"Stop!" I yell, but the German ignores me. Maestro and I follow behind. Maybe I can snatch Eliana and pull her into the crowd without notice. Just then, Betta turns. She looks at me as if she knows what I'm thinking. At the desperation and brokenness in her eyes, tears spill down my cheeks. But I can't get to Eliana.

A soldier barks orders for them to board, and they're shoved inside like cattle. The last I see of Eliana is the terrified look on her face as she leans against her papa's shoulder, Luca's ears flopping as they disappear into the crush of people in the car.

I can't move from where I stand. Maestro gently puts his hand on my shoulder, leading me away as the train jolts and rumbles along the track. His face is ashen, and his eyes glisten.

When Maestro and I part ways, I go to Basilica di Santa Croce to pray. All I can do is weep. Does God count tears as prayers? I cry till my tears are spent.

I must do something. This horrendous evil must be stopped. I head to the conservatory. I must speak with Ciro. When I find him, I pull him aside.

"I want to help the Resistance," I say. "What can I do?"

He looks at me as if I've sprouted wings. "Your nonna will not be happy."

"It's my choice."

He arches an eyebrow, a doubtful look in his eyes. This is infuriating. How many times has he tried to convince me to join the fight? And now that I've decided, he's changed his tune.

"I'll find a way with or without your help." Frustrated, I turn to walk away.

He places a hand on my arm. "Rosa, stop." His momentary frown gives way to a dimpled smile. "So, the songbird is finally ready to fly from her cage?"

"What is wrong with you?" I say, disgusted. "Don't you know? I can't sit by and do nothing when they've rounded up good people and herded them away to who knows where."

"What are you talking about?"

"Eliana. And Betta and Giuseppe. They've been arrested. The Germans forced them onto cargo cars at the station. Like cattle. With all of the other Jews the Nazis could find."

Ciro's jawline tightens, and anger flashes in his green eyes.

"You didn't know?"

"I've been here all day, working downstairs." He runs a hand through his hair, mussing his blond curls. "I had no idea."

"I have to do something. Ciro, you've been badgering me for months."

"All right," he says, then tells me about a meeting that afternoon in the back of an old tailor shop off a piazza in the Oltrarno district, not far from Boboli Gardens.

It's nearly four o'clock when I arrive, and Ciro introduces me to the leader of the group, Pietro. Pietro tells me he's happy to have me working with the group and that my skill set will prove valuable. Performing, he means. Then Ciro and I sit as Pietro calls the meeting to order. He's barely begun when he looks up and says, "Ah, *il Cigno* is with us."

I spin around to see the Swan enter. My breath catches when I see it is none other than Nonna. She spots me, and surprise flickers in her eyes. But she says nothing and takes a seat. He mentions someone called *l'Aquila,* the Eagle, who is on a reconnaissance mission.

Pietro gives assignments to a few of the people eagerly listening. Nothing for me. Yet. But the Swan—Nonna—he instructs to deliver a music score in a few days' time with a hidden message to a partisan contact in Piazza Santa Trinita near the Colonna della Giustizia. The Column of Justice.

"Nonna, I'll deliver the music in your place," I tell her once we're back at the apartment.

"Absolutely not! It's too dangerous, Rosa! You must keep up your schedule of rehearsing."

She is a force of nature. But in this, she is wrong. I will help how and when I can. She shakes her head with frustration at my stubbornness.

"If anything happens to you, Rosa, I could never forgive myself."

I place my hand gently on her arm. "We're at war. If I don't do something to help, I won't be able to forgive myself."

I try several times to persuade her to let me make the delivery. "The Piazza Santa Trinita is always filled with German soldiers. It's extremely risky, Nonna."

But she won't budge. She tells me to stay away from any future meetings. Then I tell her about Eliana and her parents, choking back tears.

The fine lines around her chestnut eyes deepen as she sighs and lowers herself to the chaise. "Your grandfather would've been horrified to see what is happening. This country is not even recognizable." After a few minutes, she shakes her head and walks away to her room in silence.

47

Rosa

Maestro's door shuts behind me, and I step out onto the street. Despite Nonna's protestations she'd be fine, I couldn't concentrate while rehearsing. Singing at a time like this seems ridiculous.

When I round the corner to our apartment, I immediately know something is terribly wrong. Nonna is hunched over on the front steps. Seeing her balled up in pain, I break into a run. "Nonna!"

"I'm all right," she says, her voice weaker than I've ever heard. I help her up. Her head is cut, and a deep scratch runs along her hand and leg. We're struggling up the stairs when Ciro comes around the corner. Thank goodness! How he always appears at the right moment, I don't know.

"*Mamma mia!*" Ciro says, seeing how badly she is hurt. He rushes forward, and we guide her up the stairs together.

"I'm fine!" Nonna says, as we get her into the apartment and into bed, where she waves us off.

"What happened?" Ciro asks after we're out of earshot of Nonna, and I shake my head.

"I found her on the stairs. You have to get Maestro. Will you?"

"*Sì!*" He rushes out the door.

Soon, he returns with Maestro, who immediately goes to Nonna's room. "*Dio mio!*"

"Antonino." She reaches for his hand, and he grasps her hand in his. "I'll be fine. You can all stop hovering. I just need to rest."

Maestro hands me the empty glass on the bedside table. "Rosa, why don't you get some water for your grandmother."

Ciro, who's been leaning against the wall quietly, follows me into the kitchen. As we exit the room, I hear Maestro, his voice flush with urgency. "What happened, Serafina?"

"I heard footsteps. And then someone shoved me as I was walking up the stairs. I didn't see them. Look at me. Such a mess!"

Maestro grunts in anger. And I can feel my fury growing.

"Who would do this?" I ask Ciro. He shakes his head, without an answer.

Nonna is a force of nature. Seeing her so weak is beyond alarming. Ciro gently places his hand on my shoulder. "She's strong, you know."

His attempt to reassure me does nothing to stop the image of her crumpled body on the steps from replaying in my mind.

"Rosa . . ." He moves toward me. "It will be all right."

Warmth radiating from him melts the chill that lingers from the frigid winter wind and my fear. Then, he stoops to kiss me. For a moment, I'm shocked he would do this. I push him away before our lips touch, and he flinches.

We've barely parted when Maestro comes through the door. "I must get to class," Ciro says brusquely and leaves.

What is he thinking? Is this a game to him? I can't deny how much he's helped me. But he knows I love Tommaso.

I wish Tommaso were here. Why must he be gone so often? Especially when I need him the most. My feelings are all muddled.

I have no one to speak with to make sense of it all. I wish my sister Isa were here. She is always so wise in matters of the heart.

Nonna assures me she'll be fine. But I know she isn't well. I never should have let her go. It should have been me. I won't make that mistake again. Next time, I'll be the one to make the drop. I fervently pray she recovers soon. May God be merciful.

48

Caramina

JANUARY 12, 1944

Mountain Province, Philippines

"Take Enzo with you." Tia's voice floats through the kitchen. I grab a basket, then stroll outside to find my brother.

I head to the stream where Enzo is cooling off. At ten years old, he's like a gangly colt. All legs and energy. He's almost my height but not quite, a fact I relish. "Tia wants us to see if there are any mangoes."

He doesn't need convincing. He skips along the stream's edge, splashing me as he steps. The droplets are cool and refreshing.

I stroll along the shoreline, focusing so intently I don't see Enzo scoop up water. He splashes me.

"Enzo!" I laugh.

He kicks the water, splashing in it. "You're no fun."

"Really?" I stoop, reach into the water, and with one flick of my wrist douse his face. He giggles and tries to retaliate, but I'm faster. We're drenched by the time we reach the grove.

I squeeze water from my hair, and Enzo immediately begins his hunt for ripe mangoes. I follow, walking tree to tree, carefully placing the fruit in the basket.

I start to sing a song that I love and watched my parents dance to long ago. *"The nightingale tells his fairy tale . . . A paradise where roses bloom,"* I sing, plucking a stubborn mango free from its branch. The words are so beautiful I lose myself in the song.

I turn to face the stream, letting my voice decrescendo. Before the last word forms on my lips, I freeze. Crouched over the water, on the far side of the grove, is a man staring at me. His sleeves are rolled up and his arms wet.

It's Captain Okamoto.

I gasp, and my hands shake as I remember how he brushed hair from my face and leered at me when I tried to help rescue Matteo. The basket falls from my grip, thudding upon the ground. Mangoes spill onto the dirt.

"Please, continue," he says.

My breath catches as fear snakes up my spine—he is moving toward me. He eyes me with the same look he had that day long ago, and my chest clenches. I take a step back.

Where is Enzo? I turn to see him standing by a far tree, eyes wide. Okamoto's gaze follows mine. He jerks his hand, commanding Enzo to come. Enzo doesn't budge.

"Come here!" Okamoto seethes. When Enzo doesn't move, he roars, "Come! Don't you hear me, boy? Come here! Now! What? You help the enemy? I know you do!" Okamoto yells, and my ears buzz. He bares his teeth as he pushes past me, rushing at Enzo with his bayonet.

"No!" I shriek.

Okamoto stops. Slowly, he turns and glares at me, eyes blazing. It is now or never. I need to distract him. I won't let him harm Enzo.

I steel myself. In one clumsy movement, I grasp the hem of my skirt. My hand shakes, sending ripples over the damp fabric. I lift it slightly. If I can just distract him long enough, Enzo can get away. Then maybe I can, too.

Okamoto stands still with his bayonet held high. A frightening fervor flares in his eyes. He leers at me again. My stomach drops, and I gag.

"Run, Enzo! Run!" I scream, willing him to move as fast as he can away from this monster.

Enzo is trembling. His eyes dart, frantically, from me to Okamoto.

"Run!" I yell and Enzo startles. I know he's desperately weighing how best to help me, to protect me. Seeing the terror in his eyes, I choke back tears. Then he sprints from the grove.

At least he'll be safe. But now I have no idea what to do. Okamoto's head spins from me to Enzo who is getting farther and farther away. Now, with his eyes squinched in anger, he marches toward me. A torrent of words explodes from his lips. He's so close now I can feel his hot breath on my forehead.

"You think someone will help you? You like American songs? Americans will help you? No! We kill them, all of them. No more Americans! Not here. Not in America. We kill them all! You understand!"

Spittle from his mouth lands on my cheek, but I dare not move. I want to scream for help, but I am sure no one will hear.

His face is red with anger. His eyes bulge so wide, I think they might pop right out of his head.

He opens his mouth, leaning closer. I brace myself for the tirade. The voice that meets my ears startles me. "You like 'Stardust'?" His voice is low and quiet.

I look up at him and see him leaning back, face oddly calm. His calmness terrifies me more than his rage.

"I like 'Stardust,'" he says. "You, sing!"

I swallow, my throat dry and pinched. I can't believe his words. I don't know if I should sing or if I can if I even try. He's glaring at me, waiting.

"I can't," I mumble, barely able to get the words out.

A crackling noise sounds in the grove. Okamoto spins around, searching for the source. I know better. I know the sounds of the animals. It's probably a monkey high up in the trees.

He turns back. "You think someone will help you?" The words spew from his lips.

My heart races, and I breathe faster and faster. I inch backward. I have to run. Now.

Then Okamoto swings at me, landing a blow on my cheek with his fist. I fall back, slamming hard on the ground, unable to breathe.

I lie stunned, staring up at the maze of sky and leafy branches overhead. I will myself to take a breath. But for a moment, my lungs are in a spasm. Gasping for air, my lungs finally fill. Just behind me is a fallen log. A few inches more, and I'd have hit my head.

Before I can fully catch my breath, he throws himself to his knees, pinching my leg underneath. He grabs my other leg, his hands rough.

I gulp at the pain, letting out a small scream. Squirming, I try to free myself. But it's no use. I'm pinned to the ground. With all my strength, I try to push myself up. But he is too strong. I thrash from side to side, shoving him away. He won't budge. Then I hear him laugh.

I see his lips pursed in a crooked line as he laughs again, and rage shoots through my body. I reach frantically for anything to help.

He seems even more amused by my effort and leans forward. At the smell of his rank breath mixed with the stench of his sweat, my stomach turns. Bile fills my mouth, and I think I might vomit.

Then my fingers hit on something rough and cool. A rock. I grab at it furiously, but it's lodged against the log. Desperately, I try to pry it loose.

Hearing the grunting noise he makes sickens me. I try to scream for help, but it's pointless. He reaches down to his belt.

Finally the rock comes loose. I grip it in my palm. Swinging it as hard as I can, I smash the side of his head.

A stunned look comes over his face as a rivulet of blood runs down his temple. A gurgling noise leaves his mouth. His body slumps forward, and he lies limp on top of me.

I glimpse my hand as I attempt to wriggle from underneath him. The rock. I throw it down next to me and try to catch my breath. Then I spot a photograph on the ground next to his shirt pocket. A woman with jet-black hair stands next to him. On his other side is a beautiful young girl about my age.

I glance at it, then at the monster before me. It's a photo of him with his wife and daughter. I'm disgusted that this man has a daughter.

I have to get free. I have to run. But as I move, he pushes himself up slightly, and his gaze clears, falls on the photograph too. Recognition and a momentary softness flicker in his eyes. I hold my breath, hoping for mercy.

Then he looks back at me. Whatever anger he'd had was a trickle compared to the avalanche of hatred that spreads across his face. He claws at my arms, trapping one against the log. The bark of the fallen tree pierces the skin on my shoulder.

Okamoto straightens himself and reaches again for his belt.

I thrash from side to side with all of my might.

But suddenly, he starts to squirm. It takes me a moment to realize he's being dragged away.

Matteo has one arm gripped around his neck. He drags him to the center of the grove and wrestles him to the ground. Okamoto's arms fling back and forth wildly.

I can tell from their faces they're making noise, but the only sound I hear is my own breathing. My heart beats faster and faster as I gasp for air.

There is no question Matteo recognizes Okamoto as the man who held both him and Anna captive. I watch them thrashing, arms splayed out. Okamoto's rifle lies between them and where I sit.

Matteo is the younger and stronger of the two. Struggling, Okamoto yanks a knife from his belt. Matteo jerks to one side as Okamoto lunges. The knife strikes Matteo's arm, and he pulls back. Okamoto leaps onto him.

I have to do something. I gape at the rifle and the two men battling on the ground.

Okamoto spies me eyeing the gun. He grabs it from the dirt before I can move. Then he swings around and smashes the butt down on Matteo's head. Matteo buckles and falls.

Okamoto raises his bayonet high. He twists it in his hand, aiming for Matteo's chest.

"No!" I yell for him to stop.

Just then, Papa bursts through the trees, speckled with dirt and breathing heavily. His eyes flash with terror when he spots me on the ground. Then he sees Okamoto.

Papa lunges, throwing him to the ground and knocking the rifle from his hand.

Okamoto is like a cat, back on his feet in a second, now spotting Papa's pistol at his belt. Papa stops him, grabbing him by the shoulders. He flips Okamoto onto his back, and the two wrestle. Papa punches, landing an uppercut to Okamoto's chin. He struggles to hold Okamoto down as they fight for the pistol.

Okamoto's rifle lies a few feet away. I scoot along the ground and stumble to my feet. If I can just get the rifle, I can stop him. I've never held a gun before, but I have to do something. I'm almost to the rifle when a loud blast explodes, shaking the trees around me.

Birds screech and a flurry of feathers flap high above the grove. Then I see Okamoto throw Papa's limp body off him.

"Papa!" I scream. I run to my father, pulling him in my arms.

Okamoto picks up his rifle. He stomps toward Matteo. He lifts it, taking aim at Matteo's head.

"No!" I shriek.

Another explosion splits the air. In confusion, I watch as Okamoto falls to the ground.

Dead.

Then I see the young Japanese officer, Hiroshi. In his hand is a rifle identical to Okamoto's, and it's still aimed at his senior officer's body. I stare at him, uncertain what he'll do.

Slowly, he lowers his gun. He walks over to Matteo and reaches out his hand. Matteo looks up at him, shocked. He takes Hiroshi's hand, groaning as he moves to get up.

I look at Papa. A dark red circle of blood on his shirt grows larger.

"You're okay? You're okay, Little Bird?" he rasps.

"I'm okay, Papa." I'm crying so hard I can barely speak. I hold him tight as he convulses.

"Papa!" Matteo drops to his knees at Papa's side.

Papa exhales, and his body shudders. He lies still.

"No!" I bury my face in his chest. My body shakes as I clutch him. Every ounce of energy I had escaped with his last breath.

I won't let him go. I can't. He can't be gone.

Matteo stares at Papa, dazed. Pain contorts my brother's face. He reaches down and shuts Papa's eyes. Slowly, he walks around Papa's body and gently lifts me off him. I don't want to let Papa go.

Matteo leads me to the edge of the grove. I hunch against a tree, sobbing. Then he walks over to Hiroshi, who has been waiting silently.

"We must bury him." Hiroshi speaks quietly, pointing to Okamoto's body. "It's better if he just disappears."

49

Rosa

"The cough is worrisome. Keep doing what you are doing. Make sure she rests, and I'll check back tomorrow," the doctor says after examining Nonna.

A week has passed since the attack, and now Nonna has a cough. A bad cough. And her color is bad. I've been cleaning her wounds with warm water and applying aloe and calendula.

Yesterday morning, Maestro brought a chicken for me to make soup. It must have cost a month's wages. I've been feeding Nonna cupfuls of *zuppa di pastina* since. It's mostly broth, but I'm hoping it brings the nourishment she needs to heal.

Now, I enter her room and begin opening the curtains to the winter morning light. "*Buon giorno,* Nonna."

"Rosa, this is for you," she says, holding out some papers.

"What is it?" I ask absentmindedly, finishing with the curtains.

"Identification papers."

"I have my papers."

"You may need these one day." Her voice is grave.

Looking them over, I realize these are the papers she used to free me from jail.

"Nonna, you need to focus on healing. Don't worry about me." I shush her worries. "I'll get your breakfast. You need to eat and get your strength back."

What is she thinking? Clearly, she isn't herself. Immediately, I go to my room and put away the papers before making her morning meal.

When I return with toast and tea, questions I've had come to mind.

"Nonna, I've been wondering since Villa Triste. How did you obtain the Italian papers for me?" Getting citizenship papers is extremely difficult.

"I have a friend who helped."

"It wasn't Uncle Lorenzo?" He's never liked me, but I know he has influence.

Sadness floods into her eyes, and I'm sorry I asked.

"No. Lorenzo did not help me." Her disappointment breaks my heart. She bites into the toast and offers nothing else. I know she won't tell me who helped.

In the afternoon, Maestro visits. He's greatly concerned for Nonna. I know she should be resting, but she seems better after his visits. And often, he'll sit quietly with her while she sleeps.

"You need to get out of the apartment, Rosa. Fresh air will do you good," he tells me.

"I don't want to leave her."

"I'll stay. You're no good to her if you are sick from exhaustion."

He's right, and I appreciate his kindness. Reluctantly, I venture outside. The cold air is bracing but a welcome change to the warm apartment. I wander the city aimlessly and find myself by the University of Florence. Perhaps I can talk to Ciro and set things right. He should be here since he has a class that gets out about this time.

I've not seen him since the day of Nonna's fall. It's unusual for him not to check on Nonna.

Ciro is nowhere in sight, but near the entrance to the main building, a man is climbing into a black car parked on the street. For a moment, I think it might be Uncle Lorenzo. The car speeds away before I can tell. I've not slept well in days. My eyes are surely playing tricks. I can't imagine he'd come to Florence and not see his own mother. It must not have been him.

50

Caramina

Dark soil caked on my cheeks mixes with my tears, leaving a muddy smudge on my worn cotton pillowcase. I weep, face pressed into the pillow despite the pain of my swollen cheek. I cry until my eyes burn, and I feel myself slipping away. When sleep finally comes, it's a welcome reprieve.

Upon awakening, I'm greeted by the sweltering heat of the afternoon sun. I must have slept well into the next day. The moment I open my eyes, I see Isabella and remember. Papa is gone.

Isabella helps me to the washroom, where she prepares a bath. I step into the tub, my body aching as I move. I sit in the still water. I stare at my arms and legs. Bruises and scratches run along them haphazardly. They seem oddly unattached to the rest of my body, as if they belong to someone else. But the memory of Okamoto's hands gripping me sickens me.

"I'll be right back," Isa says, quietly leaving the room.

In the tepid water, I rub soap onto a washcloth and scrub at my skin. I scrub and scrub, desperate to scour off any reminder of what has happened.

Isabella opens the door, towel in hand. Spotting my reddened arms, she rushes to my side, her voice aching with concern. "Oh, Cara!"

Slowly, I follow her gaze to my raw skin. I peer down at the washcloth, and Isa pulls it away gently.

After I rinse myself, Isa wraps me in a towel, careful not to aggravate my cuts and bruises. She helps me dress. Then we walk down the stairs to the back porch where I sit for the rest of the day, staring at the trees from the wicker sofa. Papa slept here only two nights ago. I lean into one of the pillows gracing the couch, meeting the faint scent of his aftershave.

I'm in a haze. Tia says I'm in shock. I've been shaken—body and soul—like a palm tree after a hurricane. Trunk stripped of bark and fronds, warped and limp. Dulled to everything around me. I try to push the image of Okamoto's face from my mind to no avail. The repulsive smell of his sweat and the heaviness of his legs against mine. I want to rip him to pieces. He will never hurt me or anyone I love again. But he murdered Papa.

I realize if no one had come to help, things would have ended very differently. Papa would still be here. Would I? I was no match for Okamoto's strength, and that is maddening. My mind spins thinking over what happened. And the heaviness weighing on me is crushing. And how can I face a tomorrow without my father who was ripped away from me so brutally?

Tia and Isabella take turns sitting with me, their faces lined in grief and concern. I've not spoken of what happened to me. Not even to Isabella. I don't have the words. Doing so would let loose a torrent of emotion that might swallow me whole.

Anna is the only one who understands. I see it in the raw compassion in her eyes when she joins me on the porch. She knows. We sit without speaking, Lucia playing quietly at our feet.

We sit for what seems like hours, when Anna stands. "I'll be right back," she says. She gently places her hand on my shoulder, before walking away to get a drink for Lucia.

Lucia peeks up at me, her eyes wide with concern. Does she know? Does she know her grandfather has died?

She smiles at me tenderly, her bright eyes brimming with compassion. Even at just over a year old, my niece seems to sense something is terribly wrong. Lucia shimmies close, and I lift her on to my lap. "Nonno?" She gazes up at me, wondering where her grandfather is. I have no answer. Fortunately, Lucia doesn't demand one. Instead, she snuggles against me, and I fold her into a tender embrace.

Then she raises one tiny, plump hand. As gently as a wisp of wind, she touches the tears on my cheek. For the first time since Papa was killed, the tiniest spark of life flickers inside me.

Hours later, I sit in the kitchen as Tio and Tia work on preparations for the small meal to follow the funeral the next day. Neither Tia nor Tio asks me to help. They move about quietly, offering a space of solace.

Matteo walks into the room, hair disheveled and cheeks red.

"Matteo?" Tia's voice is calm and full of compassion. Tio puts down the knife in his hand and focuses his attention on my brother.

"He didn't want to fight. I did! He said I was too young. I told him he was a coward." Matteo chokes out the word, a tortured look in his eyes. "He told me his job was to protect our family. I couldn't help him. He's dead!" Matteo's voice pierces the stillness. He scrapes his fingers through his mess of dark hair, shaking his head.

My heart clenches seeing him in pain.

Tio places his hand on Matteo's shoulder. "Matteo, your father chose to put you children first. He knew firsthand what war was like and wanted to keep you—all of you—as far from it as he could."

Matteo's head shoots up. "Firsthand?"

"Son, he was a soldier. Captain Arturo Grassi. He fought in the Great War. Even received a medal of valor. The things your father saw . . ." Tio shrugs. "I think, when he first came here with your

Nonna, he thought he'd finally outrun war. He couldn't. No one can. He never wanted you children to know. He thought he was shielding you by not saying anything. He was so proud of you, Matteo. Stubborn, he called you. But he knew, like father, like son. Fighting to protect the ones they love. He wanted to protect you. This wasn't your fault."

Matteo's eyes grow red and wet. I've rarely seen my brother cry. But some tears, like these, are the healing kind. It never occurred to me he might feel responsible for Papa's death. It isn't his fault. Though I know it isn't mine, I blame myself. If only I had been more alert. Cautious. Perhaps Papa would still be with us.

Afterward, I follow Matteo out the door and we walk in silence. "How did you know? I thought you were at Torres's camp," I say.

"I was headed back to the farm. Torres wanted me to give Papa news about a guerrilla troop he'd been in contact with. I was following the stream and heard noises. I was worried it was a Japanese scouting party. Then, I saw you . . ." His voice drops off, and his gaze falls to the ground. "Oh, I almost forgot," he says, pulling something from his pocket.

It's my necklace. I didn't even realize it was gone until this moment.

"The soldier, Hiroshi, found it on the ground."

Emotion surges within me. It must have come loose in my struggle with Okamoto. I'm still shocked by Hiroshi's behavior. That an enemy would help us and put himself at such risk is nearly unbelievable. Yet, he did. And I will be forever grateful.

Matteo fastens the necklace around my neck, and I reach up to hold the locket. I wince as my fingers graze a large scratch and a bruise on my collarbone. Matteo grimaces, and I see my pain reflected in his eyes.

"There is so much we didn't know about Papa," I say.

He nods. "I wish he would have told me. There's so much I want to ask him." His voice rasps with grief.

"It wasn't your fault, Matteo."

He stands silent before speaking. "And it wasn't yours." At this, he looks at me intently as if to make sure I understand.

"He was a war hero."

"It makes sense now. His attitude and his behavior since the war began . . . It all makes sense," he says.

I draw the locket toward me and open it. A surge of warmth meets me when I see Mama's gentle eyes. Seeing her picture, Matteo smiles. I shut the locket, letting it fall against me, and the two of us walk to the stream, the sound of bubbling water filling the aching silence.

51

Rosa

JANUARY 14, 1944

Florence, Italy

As I balance the gray-flecked mound that passes for bread from the *panetteria* along with my market bag, one of my navy kid-leather gloves drops to the ground.

"Too cold to lose one of those."

When I hear the voice, relief pulses through me as the tension I've held over the last few weeks breaks. "Tommaso!"

He stoops to retrieve my abandoned glove and offers it to me. "*Amore mio.*"

"*Grazie,*" I say.

I am at a loss for words, and I see his brows furrow. But having him returned to me, my heart is lifted. He is safe. *Grazie, Dio!* He takes my market bag, offers his arm, and together we stroll to Nonna's. Once inside, I nearly knock him over with my embrace.

"I was so worried for you, Rosa."

"Worried?"

"Maestro just told me you were arrested and jailed. You are okay?" He pulls back and looks me in the eyes, his gaze intense.

"Yes, I'm okay. But . . ."

"But?" Pain flickers in his eyes, and he leads me to the sofa.

As I tell him of my time at Villa Triste, he strains to remain calm—but the more I share, the angrier he becomes. I've never seen him so furious. The veins on his neck protrude. He reminds me of Papa. A fierce protector of those he loves. He doesn't have words when I finish. But his outrage and concern over what I endured are palpable.

"I should've been here, Rosa." His voice is low and cracks. "I am so sorry."

"There's nothing you could have done. Nothing anyone could have done," I say, aware of the weariness in my own voice.

He draws me close and holds me tightly. The strain of these past weeks slowly melts away. It's heaven to be in his arms again.

I tell him what happened to Nonna, and again anger flares in his eyes. "Is she up to having visitors?"

"She'll be thrilled to see you."

Together, we go to her room. Nonna is happy to see him returned safely and relishes our company. We sit with her until her eyes are drooping, then leave so she can rest.

"She reminds me so much of my grandmother," Tommaso says.

He's grown quite fond of Nonna, as she has him. I know he's homesick. He's not seen his family in so long. His last trip to Brindisi was before the Germans arrived. Though he's spoken with his mother, he, understandably, is concerned.

It's late when he leaves. "I'll be back in the morning, *amore mio*," he reassures me. I'm reluctant to let him go since he's only just returned. But morning is only a few hours away.

I wake to the sound of Nonna's hacking in the bare predawn light. Her cough has worsened significantly. I call for the doctor, who examines her and insists she needs treatment that can only be provided at the hospital. He makes arrangements for her admittance.

Tommaso arrives soon after the doctor leaves, and he accompanies me to see that Nonna is settled comfortably at the Ospedale di Santa Maria Nuova. The sterile white of the room adds a coldness to the January morning though the room is warm. Seeing Nonna lying helpless in the hospital bed breaks my heart.

"We'll do everything we can to speed her recovery," the nurse assures me.

Two hours pass before the doctor arrives. He examines Nonna and prescribes medication, which the nurse administers. Then the doctor insists we leave to give Nonna her rest.

Tommaso kisses my cheek softly. "I'll give you some time alone. I'll be in the lobby." He glances at Nonna, his gaze gentle.

Exhaustion is scrawled across Nonna's face from the dark shadows under her eyes to the sallow color of her skin. I don't want to overtire her and am about to say my goodbye when she opens her eyes. "Rosa." She puts out her hand for me to hold. I take her hand in mine. "Beatrice got more chicory coffee. For you. She knows how much you love it," she says just before her eyes fall shut again.

Clearly, the medication is affecting her memory. Nonna and Beatrice know I detest chicory, and Beatrice never comes to the apartment. I kiss her on the cheek. "You need to rest, Nonna."

Reluctantly, I leave her with the hospital staff for the night. They seem competent and caring. She is in good hands. I pray she has swift healing.

A week passes before Tommaso is called to leave Florence. His firm wants an assessment of the current damage in several cities. Though it pains me to see him go, I'm grateful for the time we had. Being with him has given me newfound energy. Remembering his love and passionate kiss goodbye gives me strength.

As I'm rushing into the conservatory to pick up music from the library, I run into Ciro.

"Nonna's been hospitalized."

He shifts on his feet. "I'll stop by to visit her this afternoon," he says.

He cares for her as if she were his own nonna. Seeing his concern, I'm overcome with emotion. He reaches for my hand. No doubt, to comfort me. When his hand lingers, a haze of awkwardness settles between us and I pull away.

"And Tommaso? Has he returned?"

"He was here but had to leave again."

"He's certainly busy. A man with lots of priorities."

There's an edge to his tone, and my blood simmers at whatever insinuation he's making. And I'm upset that he's not even checked on my grandmother. "And what about your priorities? You haven't been to visit Nonna for over a week—or you would've already known she's in the hospital. Or have you been too busy flirting with your girlfriends?"

Mischievousness glints in his eyes. "*Ragazze?* Girlfriends? Rosa, my only companion is the fight for *la Resistenza.*"

We walk to the library in silence until I can stand it no more. "You don't like Tommaso. Why, Ciro? I'd hoped the two of you could be friends."

"Friends?" He smirks. "Well, we do have similar priorities."

I swallow a sigh of exasperation.

"I must go," he says abruptly. "But tomorrow, there's another meeting with Pietro's group. At the tailor shop."

"I'll be there," I tell him, watching him walk away.

52

Caramina

Elephantine milky white blooms blanket the ground, having fallen respectfully from the Katmon tree for such a solemn occasion. The mosaic of white petals against the freshly dug black dirt contrasts the light and the dark. Life and death. The tree's boughs hang heavy, adorned with the fragrant flowers. I inhale their scent, wondering if it will forever be linked in my memory to this day.

"'Death is swallowed up in victory.' We know He will change our lowly bodies to conform to His glory. Thus, we shall always be with the Lord. We know if we have died with Him we shall also live with Him." Father Bautista pauses and takes a deep breath. "But those of us left here mourn. Our hearts are heavy with grief. Blessed are those who mourn, for they will be comforted. We ask for Your comfort, Father. Amen."

Matteo, Jack, and Captain Torres lower Papa's body wrapped in strips of cloth. They move slowly, reverentially. Shadows fall over Papa's shroud, the sunlight blocked by the deep walls of the pit. All of my tears have been spent. My eyes sting, now dry and raw.

Father Bautista turns to me, motioning he is done. I've barely spoken a word since returning to the farm days ago. But now I'm supposed to sing. I look at my family standing in a somber circle around Papa's grave. Matteo glances at me, his kind eyes weary. Isabella's gaze doesn't leave the mound that is our father, while Enzo shuffles from one foot to the other next to her, his cheeks red from crying.

Peering into the dark soil, I can't seem to pull my eyes from the grave. Dirt falls in shovelfuls over Papa's body. Father Bautista inches closer and places his hand gently on my shoulder.

I tear my gaze away from Papa and close my eyes, gathering my frenzied thoughts. I exhale, then breathe deeply and sing.

"*Ave Maria . . . Gratia plena . . .*"

The words ebb and flow on waves of grief. With each note, I struggle. The pain that has filled me since Papa's death mixes with the life in the song, and I lose myself in the music. I open my eyes after the last strain.

Gabriel stares at me from across the grave. My family looks stunned, their hearts quivering between grief and relief from the song. Their tears fall, an offering of love upon Papa's grave. Even Tio rubs rogue tears from his weathered cheeks.

Tia breaks the silence, asking everyone to follow her to the house. I stand staring at the fresh mound of dirt. A bamboo cross marks where Papa now lies. Gabriel walks to my side and stands quietly.

"I'll be there," I say. "You can go. I just want a moment alone."

But Gabriel doesn't move. "It was beautiful . . . your song." He has heard me sing a little but never one of the sacred arias. "Are you sure?" he asks.

I nod. He hesitates a moment longer before walking away reluctantly.

I drop down next to the grave. I want to be close to Papa. I rest my hand loosely on the mound. During the service, I'd been clutching an orchid. Now, I lay the ivory bloom next to the cross.

Then I hear footsteps. Father Bautista approaches the foot of the grave. I want to cover my face, to shield myself. I just want to be alone.

"I'm so sorry for your loss, Caramina." His voice is full of compassion, but I can't bring myself to look up. "Your song honored your father. He'd have been proud . . . We served together. He, Torres, and I. He didn't tell you, did he? Torres and I attended university in the United States. When the Great War broke out, we enlisted in the army. We served with the American Expeditionary Forces in 1918. The Italian Alps. The Battle of Vittorio Veneto. When we met your father, he was leading a group of soldiers on that mountain, us included.

"He risked his life saving Torres, pulling him to safety when Torres was hit, despite the fact that we were under constant mortar fire. Your father was one of the bravest men I know. He always treated us with respect, unlike most of the officers, who acted like we were all peasants.

"Sadly, your father carried around a lot of misplaced guilt over his youngest brother's death. Silvio, I believe. Silvio died serving alongside him at the Battle of Caporetto. Your father desperately tried to save him but couldn't. He'd promised your grandmother he'd keep Silvio safe. But that's not a promise we can make.

"His anger at the mismanagement of the forces at Caporetto by those who led so many young men to their deaths, compounded by his grief, made him walk away from the military and the accolades he received after the Veneto victory. He was a distinguished officer. A hero with a promising military career. But he walked away from it all and, soon after, came here to stay.

"I don't know if you're feeling responsible like your father, Caramina. But you shouldn't. What happened to him was not your fault. He would have wanted you to know that."

Something inside me breaks, loosening the dam full of regret and grief and the feeling of being responsible for Papa's death. Tears flow down my cheeks.

Father Bautista hands me a handkerchief and sits silently until my tears subside. "God's given you a gift, Cara. You honor Him and your father when you use it. Don't stop." He gets to his feet. "Okay?"

"Yes." I nod, and Father offers his hand to help me stand. Together, we walk to the house in the dwindling afternoon sun.

53

Rosa

FEBRUARY 1, 1944

Florence, Italy

Perched on a worn folding chair, I listen to Pietro update our group on urgent tasks. He assigns two young women with observing how many Germans are patrolling the Arno. A common assignment to female members since no German soldier would think them up to anything but going about their daily errands.

They're called *staffettas.* They're often tasked with making deliveries as well. Supplies hidden under food in bicycle baskets. Messages on paper rolled up and stuffed into handlebars. All brave women.

Pietro dismisses the meeting quickly. Once again, I've been overlooked. Disappointed, I'm about to approach him when he turns and catches my eye. "Stay," he mouths, motioning for me to meet him in the corner of the room.

"I need you to sing for a concert at Palazzo di Fiori," Pietro says. "If you're willing, Maestro will help you develop hand movements. Gestures to convey a message to a contact who'll be in attendance."

"I'll do it!"

"I thought you might." He smiles. "You'll also need to hand off your score in this." He grabs a leather portfolio from the table and hands it to me. "After the concert, go to the bar. A man with an emerald-green handkerchief in his pocket will sit down. Leave your portfolio on the counter, swapping it for his identical one."

Maestro joins us with a pained look on his face. "Your nonna would not approve."

"I must do this. You know no one else can do this job, Maestro."

"You'll help with the hand gestures?" Pietro asks him.

"*Sì,*" Maestro says begrudgingly.

"I'll leave you two to discuss the particulars. Good luck, Rosa." Pietro walks away to join the small group of partisans gathered by the door.

The following day, I meet Maestro at his apartment where we add the needed gestures to the improvisational section of the "Una Voce Poco Fa." I've sung the piece from *Il Barbieri di Siviglia* many times in rehearsals, so I'm comfortable performing it.

"What do they mean?" I ask.

"Rosa, you cannot know! It's extremely important you don't know what message these convey. Your safety and that of others depends on it." Maestro is adamant.

"I don't need to know." I place my hand gently on his arm to calm his concern. "And I'll be fine."

He gives me the side-eye, shaking his head. "Oh *mio!*"

When the day of the concert arrives, I'm ready. The number of German officers mingling with Blackshirts at the palazzo makes my skin crawl. I try to focus on the glamorous gowns of the bejeweled women on their arms to steel myself against the images that constantly flash in my mind—the cold, gray cell at Villa Triste and the battered bodies of my cellmates.

As it's almost time to start, I peer out at the audience to search for my contact. Not a single man wears a green handkerchief. But then I spot Tommaso! My spirits soar, bolstering me against a twinge of nerves.

Then I see a little girl enter with her father; she twirls at the back of the room. Eliana's sweet face comes to mind. Hot rage pumps through my veins, and I'm again reminded why I'm risking everything.

Then it's time. I sing, using the gestures I rehearsed. No one appears the wiser, not even the SS officer in the front row. A wistful look of reverie flits through his eyes, and he stands in ovation after the last note fades.

After the applause, I step away, intent on delivering the score. As I walk toward the bar, Tommaso approaches, stopping me. A pang of panic stabs as I realize I must lie to him. If he knew about my assignment, it would only put him in danger.

"Rosa!" he says and kisses my cheek. "Your voice. So beautiful! I had no idea."

My face flushes at the depth of emotion in his eyes.

"How did you know I was singing here tonight?"

"I just got back. Maestro said you were performing."

Several people pass by, breaking the tenderness of the moment. I realize I must get to the bar quickly or I'll miss my opportunity for the handoff. With the portfolio under one arm, I clasp his hands in mine and tell him, "I'll be right back."

His gaze is full of love. And trust. Guilt churns in my gut. "I'll be here," he says.

I force myself to not break into a run as I hurry to the meeting place. The bar is set up in an indoor courtyard dotted with marble statues and lemon trees under an ornate glass-paned ceiling. I approach, portfolio in hand, and set it on the walnut counter. The bartender places a flute of champagne before me, and I sip it. Moments later, a man steps up to the bar and orders a Campari. In the pocket of his suit is an emerald-green handkerchief.

I feel a twinge of nervous energy as I realize this is my contact. The bartender splashes vermouth and gin over ice and tops it off with Campari. Ice tinkles against glass as he hands it to the man, who sips the cocktail slowly.

"Lovely night," he says nonchalantly, picking up my portfolio and walking away without even a glance my way.

I take his portfolio, identical to the one I brought, and peer around. No one appears to have noticed. It worked! Nonna was right—it was a performance like any other. I head back to the gallery in search of Tommaso.

Spotting me, he grabs two flutes of champagne from a waiter's tray and leads me out to the terrace where we can be alone. As we exit, I spot Ciro. I'd not realized he attended. His face falls into a frown when he sees Tommaso take my hand, but Ciro's brooding won't spoil my night.

Once alone, Tommaso turns to me, his brow furrowed, and my stomach turns.

"Rosa, you need to be careful," he says soberly. The blue in his eyes darkens like the storm-tossed sea, his concern palpable.

Before I can say a word, the conductor appears, wanting to whisk me away to greet some interested dignitaries. I give Tommaso an apologetic look, and he nods his understanding.

"I'll wait, and walk you home," he says.

An hour passes before the Ministry of Popular Culture officials and their wives tire of conversation, and I'm free to leave.

Tommaso escorts me home. Our walk is filled with small talk, neither of us ready to discuss his concerns. It's late when we get to the apartment. "I'm so glad you're back," I say.

He kisses me goodnight, and we linger in our embrace, neither of us wanting to part.

"You're exhausted. I'll see you tomorrow, and we'll talk," he says.

"Buona notte, amore mio," I say as I ascend the stairs. Once in the darkness of the apartment, I head to my bedroom, spent from the night.

I leave early the next morning to meet with Pietro's group and deliver the exchanged portfolio before heading to Maestro's. When I arrive, I hand the portfolio to Pietro and then quietly take a seat in the back. Quickly, Pietro begins, reporting the mission at the palazzo was a success.

My heart swells knowing I've helped in the fight to overcome the Nazis and the regime. It's a small task, but I'm enormously proud. There are congratulatory glances and nods from the others before Pietro continues.

"Today, we're fortunate to have *l'Aquila* with us." The Eagle. The elusive partisan who has been working to establish a network of resistance groups and foster communication with the Allies. A man emerges from the dark shadows of a side room. My heart stops.

It's Tommaso.

He glances at me, taking in my bewildered, pained look. To think I felt awful about not being truthful with him. And all this time he was the one living a lie. I grip my seat, fighting the urge to bolt from the room as he gives a rundown of the partisan groups in the north and the Allies fighting in the south.

The moment Pietro dismisses us, I jump up and leave. I intend to go to Maestro's but, instead, pace the empty sidewalk in front of the building.

"Rosa, wait!" Tommaso calls out, catching up with me.

I whirl around to face him. "Did you know what I was doing?"

He pulls me just inside the doorway, glancing up and down the street to make sure we're alone.

"Is this why you're always away on business trips? Why you approached me at the café when we first met? So I could help the group? Have you been lying to me all this time? To all of us?"

He flinches at my words. "Rosa, I realized only last night you were helping Pietro. My contact in Florence up till now has been with Pietro alone. I didn't know about your nonna, Maestro, or Ciro. I suspected Ciro, but I didn't know for sure. Yes, I've lied to you. But not because I wanted to."

I turn away. He pulls me to face him. "My feelings for you are real. What I do is extremely dangerous. Any knowledge of it puts you at great risk. I love you! And that has nothing to do with what you're doing for the group." His face softens as he continues. "Last night, when I heard you sing—I've never heard anything so beautiful. You have a gift. But even if you didn't, being with you makes me happier than I've ever been. And, frankly, that's a miracle if there ever was one—finding happiness in the middle of this wretched war."

At his sheepish desperation, the sting in my heart fades.

"Doesn't hurt you're a beauty, too."

I laugh. How can I be angry with a man sacrificing his own life for me, for those I love, for everything I care about in this country?

The furrows in his brow relax, and he draws me into a kiss. Is it possible to fall even deeper in love? I kiss him back with an intensity I didn't know I had.

Then he walks with me to Maestro's and we stop on the doorstep. He brushes a curl behind my ear and kisses me again, this time tenderly. *"Ti amo così tanto.* I love you so much, Rosa Grassi," he whispers in my ear. "I'll see you later, *amore mio."*

I watch him go, then float up the stairs. My papa would always say, *"Fatti, non parole."* Deeds not words.

54

Caramina

JUNE 5, 1944

Mountain Province, Philippines

With the blackout curtains shut and candles lit, Gabriel sits next to me on the couch. Everyone is gathered in the living room, waiting as Tio fiddles with the radio. Across from us, Jack slings his arm around Isa. The radio crackles and the announcer's voice emerges clearly.

"Now from the U.S. Office of War Information. The Allied Fifth Army swept forward on the road to Rome yesterday. Swift staggering blows. General Mark Clark's forces, within less than four weeks, closed in on the very outskirts of the city. Europe's first capital to fall to the Allied Armies, Rome is now liberated from German troops."

At the news, Isa inhales sharply, and we all lean in to listen closely, except for Enzo, who is stacking blocks on the floor for Lucia, who is happily knocking them down.

"Italian civilian fighters in action behind Nazi lines for months seized German prisoners and turned them over to Allied Fifth

Army forces. The Fifth Army is now in pursuit of the enemy.
But in Rome, the Eternal City, the Vatican bells of St. Peter's
rang in peace as two hundred and fifty thousand citizens filled
the square for a joyful celebration."

The news continues about the war in Europe. Nothing about Florence. And all I can think about is Rosa and Nonna. When the newscast is over, Tio shuts off the radio.

"If the Allies have reached Rome, it won't be long before they reach Florence, will it?" I ask.

"War is never straightforward. But we can be hopeful. This is great news," Jack says.

"I just wish we knew how Rosa and Nonna were doing." I've been worried for them even more since Papa died.

"I wish it were easier to get word from them. Getting and sending transmissions is difficult and dangerous," Jack says. "But I keep an eye out for opportunities to do so. You have my word."

I know Jack is doing what he can. Every transmission he sends for the war effort puts his life at risk. The Japanese monitor the airwaves to close in on radio operators. It's extremely dangerous work and the reason why Isa is on edge when he's gone. Making contact with someone here who can then send word to Rosa is next to impossible. Word of her from her friend, Thomas, was a fluke or a miracle.

"We have to believe they're all right, Cara." Isa flashes me a sympathetic look.

"Time for bed, little one." Anna scoops up Lucia, and everyone disperses except for Gabriel, Enzo, and me.

"She's right, you know. It doesn't do any good to think the worst," Gabriel says.

I lower my eyes to hide my sadness. "I know. But I can't stop worrying."

Gabriel inches closer. He lifts his arm, draping it around me and pulling me toward him like Jack did with Isa. Though uncertain how I feel, I lean against him, grateful he cares. We sit together for a few minutes like this.

"I should go find Tio before it gets too late. Goodnight, Caramina. Night, Enzo." Gabriel stands. I watch as he disappears down the hallway and force myself to believe the best for Rosa and Nonna.

"Ew!" Enzo says, stirring me from my thoughts.

I look up to see Jack kissing Isa in the kitchen, and Enzo grimacing.

"They're in love, Enzo. One day, you'll have a girlfriend and you won't think it's so awful."

"A girlfriend! Yuck!" He looks at me like I've lost my mind. "Well, maybe Rae."

"Rae?"

"She sure could kick the ball."

"Ah."

"She kicked it so hard it almost knocked Enrico over. I was sure he'd be mad."

"Was he?"

"No. He laughed and said she could always be on his team. And I guess she's kind of . . . pretty." Redness blooms across his cheeks.

"Pretty?"

"Well, she's not ugly!"

I stand, smiling, and tousle his hair. "Time for bed, Enzo."

As we head toward the stairs, Jack stoops down to kiss Isa once more.

"Ugh!" Enzo groans, and I stifle a laugh.

55

Rosa

JUNE 30, 1944

Florence, Italy

"We're hopeful," the doctor tells me as Tommaso and I stand in the hallway peering into Nonna's room. "She is strong. Her healing is taking some time, yes. But she's elderly. We'll keep monitoring her and prescribe more medicine as needed."

"*Grazie, dottore,*" I tell him before he leaves, and we enter Nonna's room.

"Ah, Rosa! And—" Her words are interrupted by the cough that started up again three weeks ago. I pour a glass of water, hand it to her. She drinks, and the coughing subsides. "Tommaso," she finishes.

"I think I saw some bread on the cart in the hall. Would you get some for Nonna?" I ask Tommaso.

"Of course. Good to see you, Serafina. I'll be back."

"Nonna, are you resting as they've instructed?"

"Of course. What else is there to do here?" She looks around the room, sterile and colorless.

Her recovery has taken many months. She'd improved so much

she was transferred to convalesce in a wing for more stable patients. Then the coughing started again, and she was moved back to her original room. Since her cough worsened, she's been running a fever. The doctor told me they were now giving her sulfathiazole, which helped immensely with her cough when she was first admitted.

"Rosa, I'll be fine," she tells me. "Now, tell me, how are you doing? Are you still rehearsing?"

"I am, a bit."

"I know Maestro won't let you stop. You must keep going, Rosa. Don't let this . . ." She points with disgust at the two flags hanging in the hall, one Nazi and one for Mussolini's Republic of Salò. "Don't let all of this stop you."

"I won't, Nonna."

"Your papa was so proud of you and Cara. 'My Rosa and Cara. One day they'll sing like you, Mama,' he told me. He was like a peacock, his chest puffed out in pride." She laughs, and her laughter is broken by another fit of coughing.

"Here." I hand her the glass again.

"I'm so glad you came to Florence, Rosa. Having you with me— I've felt young again. I love you, *carissima*. Don't forget that."

"Nonna, why are you talking like this? You must stop! You're getting better." I lean down and hug her. "But I love you, too."

"I have felt stronger today."

"You're the strongest nonna I know."

Tommaso appears in the doorway, smiling and bearing a gray lump masquerading as a roll. He sets down the small plate next to Nonna's bed. The three of us eye it suspiciously.

"*Grazie,* Tommaso. What I wouldn't give for one of Beatrice's freshly baked *cornetto alla crema,*" Nonna says.

"*Sì!* If only," I say.

"I'll just have to pretend." Nonna lifts the roll to her lips. At the smell, she grimaces, and the three of us laugh.

The doctor appears in the doorway. "I'm sorry. Visiting hours are over." He waits to usher us from the room.

I stoop to hug Nonna one more time and kiss her warm cheek. "I'll see you tomorrow," I tell her, and we leave.

The next morning, I swing open the door to Nonna's room to find it, oddly, empty. Perhaps she's been moved again.

I'm about to leave the room to find the staff that flitters back and forth throughout the hall, when a nurse appears in the doorway. Gently, she sets her hand on my shoulder. "I'm so sorry," she says. "She passed away in the middle of the night."

The floor drops from under me. Her voice echoes as if I'm under water. I can't breathe. I can't speak. My legs are wobbly. The nurse pulls out a chair, and I crumble into it.

Sneering at us from the corridor is a Nazi officer who stands alongside a Blackshirt. There must be some mistake. Surely Nonna is on another floor and has just been moved. I look into the nurse's eyes and find nothing but desperate compassion.

"But the medicine?" My voice is a raspy whisper.

She moves her hand, almost imperceptibly, gesturing to the chart hanging at the foot of the bed. Nonna's name is written at the top. On the line for medication, there is nothing. Has been nothing for days. It's blank. I look at the nurse, and she shakes her head, her eyes flitting momentarily to the men in the hall.

Her strained look tells me everything I need to know. I peer over at the men and realize what has happened. They saw that Nonna wasn't given the medication she needed. And I had no idea. The agony of my grief and failed responsibility sweeps over me, pinning me to the chair.

The nurse hands me Nonna's things, and I stumble from the hospital onto the street. I don't remember the walk home.

None of this seems real. I find myself thinking Nonna has simply gone to the *panetteria,* and at any moment she'll waltz through the door, calling for me to join her on the terrace for *merenda.* The aroma of orange blossoms wafts through the apartment, and I turn, certain she's strolled past. But I find it's not Nonna with her fragrant perfume, only the scent of blossoms drifting through the open windows.

When Tommaso arrives, I'm huddled in Nonna's bedroom. Did I leave the door unlocked when I fumbled up the stairs?

"Rosa," he whispers as if approaching a wounded animal. I feel his gaze upon me as I sit by the window. The moment I look up at him, he knows.

"She's gone," I say.

He sweeps me into his arms, embracing me. I haven't cried until this moment. A dam bursts, and I weep. We walk from Nonna's room to mine. He holds me close, caressing my back as we sit upon my bed. The light fades as the sun sets, the day giving way to evening. The soft sound of his breathing steadies me as I lie against his chest.

I fall asleep in his arms and don't wake till birdsong floats in the window in early morning. "You are not alone, Rosa. I'm here, always," he tells me, as we linger till late morning.

But then he tells me he must leave again. For how long, he can't say. Every time he goes, I worry it will be the last time I see him. He puts himself in great danger working to obtain information on the Germans. He refuses to give me specifics. I've no idea where he will go. I know it's to fight the very men responsible for Nonna's death. It's the only reason I can bear parting. I hope he burns them all to the ground. But must I find my love only to worry constantly that he, too, will be taken?

We stand in the doorway. He kisses the curve of my neck tenderly, then leaves a trail of kisses up to my lips. Warmth flushes through me as we linger in our embrace. "I'll be back, my love," he says.

The thread binding our hearts is strong. I'm torn at the thought of what might happen. Yet grateful for the time we've shared. Life and love are precarious in war.

As Tommaso walks reluctantly down the steps, Ciro appears

around the corner. He pauses, then turns away. I don't know if he saw us or not. Perhaps Ciro thought he was being watched. Blackshirts are everywhere. A couple in love is hardly reason for suspicion but a group is another matter entirely.

Ciro doesn't know about Nonna. Later in the day, I stop by the university, hoping to give him the news on my way to Maestro's. I spot him in deep conversation with an older man on the steps. They part moments later, and Ciro rushes into the building. No doubt he's late for class. I'll tell him later, I decide.

From behind, the man resembles Uncle Lorenzo. Before I reach him, he ducks into his waiting car and drives away. Earlier I tried, unsuccessfully, to reach Lorenzo by phone. Despite their differences, surely he would want to know his mother has died.

As I wander the streets, I think of my father and siblings. I pray they are safe and well. One day we will be together again, and we can remember Nonna as she was with our family. Singing, always. Her voice—a celebration of life and love. Her stories were a testament to her strength, will, humor, and beauty. And her unwavering belief that goodness can be found despite one's circumstances.

News is the Allies have liberated Rome and are now moving north. I hope their journey will be speedy and Florence will soon be liberated. May there be a swift end to this. I miss my family terribly, and I pray they've been spared the pain of this war. I imagine them at Tia and Tio's splashing in the stream and feasting on dripping mango with Tia's sweet rice cakes. I will hold them in my heart until I see them again, along with Nonna, and my love, Tommaso.

56

Rosa

I awaken from a night of little sleep to the realization again—Nonna is gone. It was just Maestro and me, and a few onlookers strolling the small cemetery, who attended Nonna's funeral. It's not the burial Nonna deserved. But given the war, it was the only option. Ciro would never have missed the service, but I've not seen him since Nonna's death. He doesn't even know she's passed away.

It's late morning when a knock sounds at the front door. Hovering in the doorway is Ciro. With a portfolio tucked under one arm, he holds out a paper-wrapped bundle.

"A steak," he says. He's also brought a loaf of bread, far better than the bitter mounds at the *panetteria*. How he afforded such luxuries, I've no idea. The grocer hasn't had meat for months.

Though I have no appetite, we cook the meat and share a meal as I tell him about Nonna.

He nods, pensively. "Maestro told me this morning." He studies a spot on the floor before looking up. "I'm devastated, Rosa. I'd hoped this"—he motions to the food—"could serve as a distraction from your loss . . . our loss." He reaches across the table and places his hand gently on mine. "I'm here for you."

I'm touched by his gesture.

Abruptly, he stands and brings his dish to the counter. "Pietro has another assignment for you," he says, a momentary edge to his tone.

"Now?" I say, still reeling from grief and lamenting Ciro's timing.

"The handoff must happen this afternoon. Without Nonna here, you are the only one who . . ."

"I'll do it," I tell him, drawing upon what little strength I have. If I can do anything to stop this war machine that has crushed so much of what I love, I'll do it. It will only bring Tommaso back to me sooner.

Ciro hands me a portfolio, similar to the one I handed off at the palazzo concert. I'm to go to Piazza San Marco and sit on a bench to meet a man with an aubergine tie and a cane. The swap is to be just like at the palazzo bar. Approach, sit, leave my portfolio, and pick up an identical one left by my contact.

"Why didn't Pietro ask me?"

"No time. This just came up, and it's urgent."

I nod my understanding, and he leaves.

Later that afternoon, when I step into the piazza from Via Cavour, several people are milling about. I pause, shielding my eyes from the sun, and pretend to admire the seventeenth-century facade on the Basilica di San Marco. The bench where I'm to meet my contact is empty. I take a step forward. Then I spot a man lurking in the corner of the piazza, directly across from me, and I gasp. It's Nico.

Thankfully, he hasn't noticed me. I follow his gaze to the opposite corner where two German soldiers stand, one looking right at Nico, the other peering out over the crowd, eyes searching. Then Nico nods in my direction.

My heart stops. The portfolio in my grip is a two-ton anvil. If caught with it, I'll be thrown into the clutches of Carità's men. Beads of perspiration trickle down my spine.

This is no handoff. They knew I was coming. I back away, trembling, and quickly join a group of teenagers exiting the piazza. Then I race to the apartment.

I quickly gather my thoughts. What should I do? They are most likely on their way to arrest me. Then I remember Nonna's words about hiding important items in the coffee jar. I run to the kitchen, then tear open the jar, praying there is something of help hidden inside. Buried under the grinds is a packet wrapped in linen. I pull it out, open it, and inside find papers and a journal. Ration coupons. Money. And false identity papers. For me—Francesca Russo from Naples.

I race to my room and grab my bag, filling it with a few necessary items. I pull up the floorboard and grab my diary, replacing it with the portfolio. Thankfully both my diary and the journal from the jar are small and fit through the torn seam of my jacket, which I hold folded across one arm. Taking them is a huge risk. But I can't leave them behind.

I force myself to focus. If I go to Maestro's, I'll endanger him. Then I remember how he often spoke affectionately of his sister in his hometown of Castellammare di Stabia. It's my only hope. I race from my room, down the stairs, into the living room. In the corner chair sits Ciro.

He looks at me, tears in his eyes. "You must leave," he says.

"Why? What have you done?"

"Rosa, you know I love you. You know there's never been anyone else but y—"

"What did you do?" I ask, seething with anger.

He looks away, eyes downcast. "I told them about Pietro and the group. He's already been taken."

"How could you?" I fight to keep from screaming. "And Nonna?" I want to strike him. "She was like a mother to you. She loved you. You betrayed her!"

He stands up and tells me he's been working with Nico Casale.

"Nico? You're working with that monster!"

Guilt flashes in his eyes. He tells me that after being brought before the Germans at Villa Triste, he started working with Nico and Uncle Lorenzo. They'd long suspected him of being in the Resistance. He'd practically advertised his involvement. They picked him up months ago, offering his life, as well as food and money, in exchange for names and information. Arrogant coward! It was Lorenzo I saw meeting Ciro at the university. He tells me it was Lorenzo's job to weed out any partisans at the schools, and they believed there was a group inside the conservatory.

"I've been hungry for so long. You don't know what that's like, Rosa! You with everything you need because of Nonna and your family," he pleads. "And they killed my father!"

"What? Who?" I ask, confused. "The regime did."

"No, the Resistance! People like Pietro. My uncle finally told me when I visited him. The bomb that killed my father was set by a partisan!"

I fall back, stunned. "How many people have died at the hands of Mussolini? And what about the bombs you, yourself, set for our group?" I want to tear him to pieces.

Desperation flares in his eyes. "They pointed a gun at me, Rosa, and gave me a choice. Help them or be executed. But first, they'd torture me. What choice did I have?"

"You sacrificed everyone to save yourself? Only a coward would do such a thing!"

My words hit him square in the chest. He hunches forward, a broken look in his eyes. "It's why I had to warn you. You must go, Rosa. Now."

Panic strikes as Maestro comes to mind. "I have to tell Maestro." I start toward the door.

"It's too late. He's gone. Carità's men picked him up late last night."

My stomach twists, and I think I might vomit. Then, it occurs to me. I nearly scream, "Tommaso?"

At the mention of his name, anger flickers in Ciro's eyes, and his cheeks redden. "No one has seen him. I don't know where he is."

"You betrayed me and everyone who cared about you," I storm, rushing out the door, leaving him to rot.

At the train station, a young German guard scrutinizes my papers. He looks up at me, and my stomach clenches. I feel the edge of the letter opener in the seam of my coat and force myself to soften my gaze. Smile warmly. Just another performance. His lips curl into a smile, dimpling his cheeks. He hands me my papers. "Perhaps, Fräulein, I'll see you when you return." I nod coyly, dizzy with relief as he waves me on.

I board the train for the long journey. As it speeds forward, I stare at the blur of landscape with no thought but Tommaso. How will he know where I am? It occurs to me he might never find me. Leaving Florence, I may never see him again. Staying, I may never see him again. My very presence puts him in danger. My heart splits as the train shrieks through a tunnel. I wipe my tears, grateful for the darkness, and beg God to keep him safe.

When I arrive in Castellammare di Stabia, I find a small town perched on the striking teal waters of the Mediterranean. Across from the harbor is an osteria, the only restaurant on the town's main piazza. It's empty but for the owner.

"Do you know the Silvieri family?"

"No," he says, and I stumble out into the blinding sunlight with no clue of what to do next.

I sit on a crumbling stone step facing the water. Moments pass, then I feel someone gently place their hand on my shoulder.

"Rosa?" a woman asks in a hushed tone.

I turn to see a beautiful woman with long white hair swept into a loose chignon. Her warm gaze oozes kindness, and I nod. "Yes . . . I am Francesca," I say.

She nods and smiles. "Antonino told me you might be coming."

Unfazed by the puzzled look on my face, she pulls me into an embrace. "Come, give your Zia Teresa a hug. You've arrived just in time for *merenda*."

I hug her, inhaling the scent of lemons and lavender in her hair. Over her shoulder, I spot a German soldier who has just walked up from the harbor.

"*Andiamo*," she says. "Let's get you settled." Any concern she has over the German doesn't show. She links arms with me and leads me up numerous antiquated stone steps to a whitewashed home high on a hill overlooking the water sparkling in the sun.

57

Caramina

The radio crackles, and then the announcer's voice comes in clearly:

"General MacArthur has made good on his promise and has returned to the Philippines. Yesterday, he and his troops landed in Leyte. After landing, the general gave word to the people of the Philippines."

"He's done it! He's returned! *Salamat sa Diyos!*" Tia grabs Tio by the shoulders, hugging him tight as we crowd closer, eager to hear MacArthur's announcement.

"People of the Philippines: I have returned. By the grace of Almighty God our forces stand again on Philippine soil—soil consecrated in the blood of our two peoples. We have come, dedicated and committed to the task of destroying every vestige of enemy control over your daily lives, and of restoring, upon a

foundation of indestructible strength, the liberties of your peo-
ple."

The announcer finishes the broadcast with well wishes for my country, and I'm heartened by MacArthur's rallying speech. We all feel a sense of hopefulness for the first time in so long.

"He'll do it. He'll finish this," Tio says.

"Oh, that he might bring an end to this war," says Isabella.

It's a momentous announcement, and though we'd all like nothing more than to revel in it, everyone disperses to finish the work stalled so we could listen.

At the table, I pick up the curtain I've been mending. Normally, Isa would do this. But I promised her I'd finish it. As I move needle and thread back and forth through the black fabric, my mind wanders once again to Papa.

The night of his funeral, I shared with my family what Father Bautista told me about Papa and his younger brother, Silvio. Everyone was stunned. Even Tia and Tio. Papa never spoke of Silvio. His determination to keep us all safe makes even more sense knowing the immense loss he experienced while blaming himself for Silvio's death. There is so much I wish I could speak with Papa about, including his past. This last year has been painful. Often I'll be contemplating something and, for a moment, think, *I'll just ask Papa.* Then I remember, I can't. Those moments are the worst.

I have kept up my singing. Listening on the gramophone to *La Cenerentola* or the other pieces Papa brought was, at first, difficult, as if the music mourned his death as well. But slowly, the pieces have come to life, and my voice has grown stronger.

The ebb and flow of grief is like the crescendo and decrescendo in music. Without the depths, there is no true appreciation for the crests of joy. And so, I've allowed myself to grieve.

I set the fabric down and place a record on the gramophone, setting the volume low to listen as I work. Music has been a natural part of healing,

I've realized it's no longer a means to prove myself. I've never needed to. I'm enough regardless of whether I receive praise from others or if it changes some narrow-minded person's opinion of me. The knowledge my singing impacts a listener deeply is a welcome reward. But I've never needed to prove myself—to anyone.

I've decided I'll sing for myself. And enjoy all the richness music brings into my life. After Papa's death and what happened with Okamoto, I'd thought it impossible to survive but, somehow, have. Singing is a large part of that. It's taken some time, but I've found I can sing again. With all my heart and soul. And that is something to be grateful for.

58

Caramina

MAY 31, 1945

Mountain Province, Philippines

"Hand me that, dear." Tia points to the empty wooden bowl. We've spent the last hour sorting mung beans, pulling tiny green spheres from their pods. It's monotonous work. As I unearth the little beans, I find myself moving to the rhythm of a song in my head.

Mung beans are now a staple. Our small meals consist of gabi root, mung bean stew, and a bit of rice. It's been months since Tia cooked the last of the chickens. Occasionally, we catch tiny shellfish from the stream, and Tia adds them to the rice or mung-bean mixture. With barely any salt available, our diet is bland. Yet, it is enough to keep us going.

Lately, I find myself thinking about Rosa. We've only received word about her and Nonna from Jack's friend, Thomas, twice in the last few years. Over a year has passed since Thomas's last contact.

The war in Italy is over. I still worry for Rosa and Nonna and hope they are doing well. They do not know of Papa's passing. Can they sense it? Can you feel such a significant loss so far away? It's already been nearly a year and a half since we stood under the Katmon tree to say our goodbyes to Papa.

I once heard Esther say, "Losing one's child is worse than death." Maybe it's better they don't know. Maybe they are gone, too. A shiver creeps down my spine. Please God, don't let it be so.

In February, Gabriel brought word that Allied forces had landed on Luzon and were fighting near the Lingayen Gulf and moving south toward Manila. I wondered how much longer it would go on. Tio was confident the Allies would be successful. But it's now the end of May, and they are still fighting.

Ever since Papa's passing, both Jack and Gabriel have made an effort to visit more frequently. Gabriel has brought a sense of lightness to the ongoing drudgery. His presence is a steadying one, as he's patiently waited for my heart to heal. It's taken some time. But I've found myself smiling again.

Now, I watch Tia rinse a pile of mung beans, swishing them in a bowl. The front door swings open. Jack and Isabella's laughter rings through the house. Moments later, they appear in the kitchen doorway, holding hands, grinning ear to ear. Isabella's face gleams.

"Well, we're goin' to be married. Issie's agreed to marry this old chap." Jack slaps his thigh, and his laughter booms through the kitchen. He picks up Isabella and spins her around.

"It's about time!" Tia sets down the bowl, slopping water and beans everywhere. She embraces Isa and her soon-to-be nephew-in-law. Her face is almost as rosy as Isabella's. I can't help but smile at my aunt's excitement.

"Well, miss, what say you? A new brother? I'm not much of a singer, but I can hold my own with a guitar." Jack struts toward me.

"I think I can give my permission," I say in mock seriousness, and Jack salutes me. Laughing at his antics, I embrace them both.

"What's this I hear?" Tio peeks his head into the kitchen, feigning ignorance. We all know Jack asked Tio's permission to marry Isabella days ago.

"This calls for a celebration!" says Tio. "What do we have, Mama?"

"Mung beans." Tia pinches her lips, sounding deflated.

"Mung beans it is!" Tio slaps Jack on the shoulder, and Jack's laughter bellows through the house.

59

Caramina

Snowy white flakes drift into the growing pile in the bowl at my feet as I shred coconut for Tia to use. As I scrape the white flesh on the blade, I see Isabella walk outside into the backyard, a pensive look on her face.

The excitement of Jack and Isabella's engagement has continued long after Jack's proposal. Unfortunately, war has no respect for love. They've been forced to put their wedding on hold. It's been months, and I know she's impatient to be married.

The front door swings open, and I look up to see Tio, red-faced and breathless. Startled, I nearly kick the bowl.

"It's over!" Tio says, bent over, hands on his thighs, catching his breath.

Concern in her eyes, Tia asks, "Over?"

"The war! It's over. The Japs surrendered! Emperor Hirohito announced the surrender to the Japanese. Torres sent a runner to give us the news."

My aunt drops the bowl of rice she is carrying. White kernels rain down. She falls to her knees weeping, and Tio stoops to hold her. Isabella and Anna run into the kitchen. Both wear the same look of dread.

"It's over," I whisper. There are no other words. The end of the war means the end of living in constant terror. It means life and freedom and peace.

Tio helps Tia to her feet, and everyone embraces. Enzo rushes into the kitchen, Lucia bobbing up and down on his shoulders. Both children look uncertain about what craziness has overtaken the adults. Our four hard years have come to an end.

Anna grabs Lucia and spins her around. "It's over! Daddy can come home!" Tears spill down her cheeks as she props Lucia against her swollen belly. The new baby is due any day now. Maybe Matteo can be home for the birth.

I watch Isabella's face brighten with the realization that soon she'll be married and leave with Jack to live in Massachusetts in America. She grabs me in a hug and holds me tight.

The farmhouse is filled with the unmistakable sounds of celebration.

Days later, a calm has settled upon the farm. A respite after the chaos we've lived through. Lucia rolls a ball back and forth to me as we sit on my bedroom floor. Isabella and I have been watching her to give Anna needed rest.

A racket sounds downstairs, and I hear Tia's voice rigid with concern. "Here, come here. Sit! Sit down."

Leaving Lucia with Isa, I immediately run down the stairs to find Gabriel in the living room. My stomach drops when I see blood on his sleeve. I rush toward him. "Gabriel!"

"I'm fine! Really. It's nothing."

Gabriel tells us that despite the Japanese military officially surrendering, they're still fighting.

"But they surrendered!" I say.

"Do we need to leave?" At the urgency in Tio's voice, I cringe. Over the last year, we've made several runs to the cave. I wait breathlessly for Gabriel's answer.

"No, you should be fine here." A sickened look passes over Gabriel's face. "The Japs have fled. They burned several homes and tried to burn the church. Father Bautista and several of the townspeople did their best to put out the fires before all of Timbales was destroyed. The church is okay, but many of the residences are gone. They're using the center as a shelter for those who've lost their homes. The Japs joined up with those MacArthur chased out of Manila months ago. With the Americans closing in from the south, they've been making their way north ever since."

Tia looks stricken. The farm is a few miles north of Timbales.

"They're heading northeast toward Cagayan Valley. Torres and his men and the other troops are chasing them. You should be safe here." Gabriel rubs his temples.

"You're certain?" Tio's voice is strained.

"We've had men on the outskirts of town. Not one Jap's gotten by this way. They all ran northeast over the mountain toward Cagayan." Gabriel's voice is weak.

Tia rushes to the kitchen and returns with a glass of water. Gabriel drains it in a few quick gulps. He winces, and I notice the ruby circle of blood on his sleeve growing. I can't stand seeing him in pain.

Lately, I've found myself thinking about him more and more. In the middle of helping Tia or watching Enzo, my thoughts fall on Gabriel. The sound of his voice, the way his hair flops onto his forehead, or the way he looks at me as if no one else is in the room. No, I cannot lose him.

"Sit, son." Tio drags a chair over. "We need to clean that before it gets infected."

Gabriel drops into the chair. Tia brings some rags and supplies, and Tio sets about cleaning and suturing Gabriel's small wound. As Tio stitches Gabriel back together, I turn away.

"There," Tio says, finishing. "Now, you rest."

Gabriel stands slowly, swaying. "I have to get back."

"You won't get far if you don't rest." Tio walks him to the sofa, and Gabriel sinks into the cushions.

Moments later, he's sleeping soundly. I settle into the couch next to him, watching the gentle rise and fall of his chest. Not even Lucia's cries wake him. I spend the remainder of the day alternately sitting with him and helping in the kitchen. He looks so peaceful as he sleeps, and I wonder what he was like as a boy.

It's dusk before he stirs. When he finally cracks open his eyes, he shifts and groans. Slowly, he sits up and, running his fingers through his hair, yawns.

"What time is it?" Then his lips arch into a wide grin. "Have you been sitting here the whole time?"

My cheeks warm. "It's almost six."

"I have to go!" He shoots to his feet, a new man. Rest has reinvigorated him.

I inhale deeply, grateful his exhaustion had more to do with fighting and a lack of water than his wound. I'd hoped he would stay longer. "Are you sure you're okay?"

"I feel worlds better now." He smiles warmly. "Thank you."

"Ah, the boy rises!" Tio slaps Gabriel gently on the back. "Surely you can stay and eat first."

"I told Torres I'd get back as soon as I gave you news of town."

A thought strikes me. "If the Japanese are heading northeast over the mountains, maybe it's safe to go home?" I speak in a hush as if saying it aloud might frighten away the possibility.

"No!" Gabriel snaps, his voice harsh. I flinch. Immediately, there is regret in his eyes. "I'm sorry," he says. "It's not safe to travel yet."

I know he's sorry. But my heart stings as my dream of home fades. Gabriel looks helplessly at Tio, who puts his arm around me.

Tia runs in with a small parcel of food. "Here, take this." Gabriel takes the parcel obediently. "It's not much, but it should help." Tia embraces him.

Not for the first time, I see how great my aunt's affections are for Gabriel. He is the son she never had. "Be safe," she says.

Tio looks Gabriel in the eye and nods in agreement. Then he follows Tia into the kitchen.

Gabriel's eyes dart to the rucksack on the floor and the dull metal bottle propped against it. "I need to fill my canteen."

"I filled it for you."

"*Salamat.* Thank you."

"Be careful."

"Always am."

I tilt my head, eyeing his bandaged arm.

He smiles sheepishly. "Well, I try to be." He grabs his bag from the floor, straps on his canteen, and slings the bag over his shoulder. "Bye, Caramina." Pausing in the doorway, he gives a hopeful smile. "I'll see you again soon."

I smile, and he shuts the door behind him.

60

Rosa

The faint crackle of the radio floats out the kitchen window as I set clothes to dry in the sun. Thankfully Teresa, like Nonna, kept a wireless through the war despite the ban. The Radio Londra announcer's voice emerges clear and strong. *"Today, onboard the USS Missouri in Tokyo Bay, Japan signed the Instrument of Surrender. Japan has surrendered."*

I drop the blouse in my hand and race to find Teresa. We nearly collide as she rushes out the kitchen door to find me. Tears of joy spill down my cheeks. The war in the Philippines is truly over.

At the end of April, we'd listened to the news report that Mussolini had been shot and killed. His body was hanged alongside his mistress and cronies in Piazzale Loreto in Milan. A fitting place given that is where, months before, he and the Nazis executed fifteen presumed partisans. Then in May, the Germans surrendered. What rejoicing there was even in a tiny hamlet like Castellammare di Stabia.

Every night I write in the journal Nonna gave me, despite strug-

gling to find the words. In my recent entry, I wrote about my un-
ending gratitude toward Teresa. She insists I call her aunt, my Zia
Teresa. Maestro has been like family to me. Pictures of him as a boy
dot this space, and I can see the fire in his eyes even then. It's a
balm to my soul to be welcomed so warmly into their family home.

"Having you here has been a joy, Rosa," Teresa tells me while
peeling a potato.

"You've been so kind."

"This war . . . It has stolen so much."

I place my hand on her arm gently. She's lost her brother and is
now the last of her family.

She looks at me knowingly. "And you, you've lost greatly."

"I will always miss Nonna. But every time I think of Tommaso,
it hurts." I place my hand on my heart. "Memories of him pop up in
the most unexpected ways. The sunlight on his hair when we shared
a meal in the park. His blue eyes shimmering like the Mediterranean. Or when we danced . . ."

"You will always feel his loss. But, perhaps, in time the pain will
lessen and lose its sharpness." She grasps my hand tenderly, then
stands and walks to the cucina counter.

I know she's right. But I can't escape my memories, and I'm not
sure I want to. They come as I prepare meals, stroll to the *panetteria* for what little bread is available, or wander the ancient streets of
town. Always, I end up at the water's edge, gazing out over the vibrant endless blue wondering if, by chance, he's alive. It's wishful
thinking, I know. On the other side of the great moving expanse of
water, my family is out there. At least, I pray they are, and that one
day I'll see them and Tommaso again.

One afternoon not too long after, I'm plucking lemons from the
trees sagging under their weight in Teresa's garden and savoring
the fragrance of sun-warmed lavender and rosemary. A low, rugged
stone wall surrounds the vibrant space bursting with life and I

stand, my back to the gate. A song flitters through my mind, and I hum the melody. I haven't sung a note since rehearsing with Maestro so long ago. The music lifts my spirits. Then I sense it—a presence.

The crunch of footsteps on the gravelly path beyond the garden blends with the birdsong. Before I spin around to see who is here, I hear my name.

"Rosa."

I gasp, not wanting to turn only to be disappointed. Surely it's my imagination. My breath hitches in my throat. The snap of the gate latch breaks the silence. Slowly, I turn. Standing before me is Tommaso. My basket drops to the ground. Lemons spill everywhere, a blur of yellow through my tears, and I run into his arms.

"How?" I whisper, so overcome I'm shaking.

He doesn't answer. He embraces me, then kisses me deeply. After, he leads me to a shaded bench under an orange tree. "*Mia amata,* my love, let's sit."

"How did you find me?" Tears dot my skirt. I've imagined this moment countless times. Knowing that likely it was just wishful thinking. And now, he's here. So close I can feel the warmth of his body against mine.

"When I returned to Florence, I immediately went to your apartment and found it deserted. I knew Maestro would know where you were and went to see him. His building was empty. His apartment, torn apart. I knew then he'd been arrested. I rummaged through the rooms hoping to find anything that might lead me to you. My worst fears were realized, Rosa, believing they'd taken you.

"Strewn across the floor I found broken picture frames with photos of the only family I remember Maestro mentioning. His sister, who lived down south on the coast. In one, the two of them stood in the entrance of a restaurant. Osteria Castellammare. I grabbed the photo, begging God that I would find you here."

"I was sure you were . . ." I can't bring myself to finish the sentence. He pulls me close and holds me. After a quiet moment, he continues.

"I must tell you. After I left Maestro's, I headed to the train station. Walking through Piazza della Repubblica, I spotted Ciro approaching Caffè Gilli. Gilli's was spilling over with Germans and a few Blackshirts. He saw me, and I knew when I saw the remorse in his eyes. I knew he was responsible. He turned away, stopping just in front of the café, and yelled, "Nico!" One of the Blackshirts looked up. Ciro raised his gun and shot him. Point blank. Within seconds, every Blackshirt and Nazi had their weapon in hand. They opened fire, and Ciro was dead before he hit the ground."

My heart clutches hearing Tommaso's words. Ciro protected me from Nico more than once. He was my friend. But he betrayed me and everyone I loved. I tell Tommaso about Ciro's confession. How he worked with Uncle Lorenzo to take down our group. His eyes darken, hearing how Ciro betrayed us. He cost Nonna her life.

Tommaso has no news of Maestro, other than that he's been taken to a camp. I grip the bench as he speaks, holding on to a sliver of hope that he has survived and knowing we must tell Teresa.

Tommaso then tells me Lorenzo was killed by an angry mob. Shot, soon after the war ended. Someone recognized him as one of the Blackshirt leaders. I don't know how he could have been a son of Nonna's or my father's brother. He was nothing like Papa.

Tommaso takes my hand tenderly. "Rosa, I don't want to waste any more time." He drops down on his knee. "I've been wanting to do this since the day we danced in that empty apartment." He lifts his other hand from his pocket. In his palm, a glimmer of gold sparkles. "Will you do me the honor of being my wife?"

"Yes!" I throw my arms around him and kiss my fiancé for the first time.

We sit, breathing in the sweet scent of orange blossoms, holding each other lest we be parted again.

The sun slips low, a golden apricot flush over the Mediterranean when Teresa comes out to introduce herself to Tommaso. She's prepared a meal. We tell her of Maestro. Then the three of us eat. We sit for hours talking under the pinpricks of starlight that speckle the midnight blue sky.

Days later, Tommaso and I marry in the tiny church in town and stay in the small cottage on the edge of Teresa's property. It was once used by Maestro for rehearsing. Teresa prepared it for our wedding night. The whitewashed walls and white and blue linens are lovely. We've now spent many happy days and nights in this cozy home.

I am now Mrs. Thomas Donati Ridgefield, wife of an Italian American officer who worked covertly to help the Allies!

I can't get used to calling him Thomas. He prefers me to call him Tommaso, anyway. I'm happier than I've ever been. War has not stolen everything good. Our love has transcended the devastation, and I'll never take it for granted. I won't waste a moment of precious time with Tommaso.

61

Rosa

The rumble of the train fades as I lose myself in Nonna's words in the small journal I discovered hidden in her coffee jar. I'd forgotten it, but in packing to return to Florence, I found it again.

Tommaso is asleep, so I read quietly. Nonna never mentioned keeping a diary. Though the entries ended many years ago, reading them still feels like an intrusion.

Folded carefully inside is a letter from my papa. From the Great War: *I'm so sorry, Mama. I have failed Silvio. I have failed you. Silvio is gone.* The ink is smudged with water marks. Nonna's tears? My father's? *Silvio was hit. I tried to get to him, to pull him to safety. But I couldn't. Mortars continued to fall. One of the men that serves under me held me back. I desperately tried to save him, Mama. I promised I would bring him home. Now, he is dead, and I am to blame. Please forgive me.* My own tears blur the words.

Then, I read Nonna's first journal entry. *My beloved, Arturo. Not once have I blamed you for Silvio's death. It was never your fault. War took him, not you. Do not blame yourself, my son. I am*

*only grateful you were spared and that God brought you back
to me.*

This must be why my father never spoke of his time in the army.
All these years, he blamed himself for his brother's death. Knowing
Nonna, she spoke these words to him in person. She loved him
greatly. Her beloved Arturo. I pray he's found peace. It's what
Nonna wanted and what I wish for him, as well.

Teresa accompanied us to the train station to see us off. Leaving
her was bittersweet. "My home is yours," she said, tears in her eyes.
I promised to visit.

It's been almost two months since Tommaso found me in Castellammare di Stabia. And now, we're returning to the city of so
many memories. The train pulls into the station, and I remember
watching Eliana and her parents shoved onto a car, most likely to
their deaths. The memory pricks my heart.

As we make our way to Nonna's apartment, we approach the
Arno, and I gasp. Florence's beautiful bridges are gone. Piles of
rubble remain where they once stood for centuries. Tommaso tells
me the Germans destroyed all but the Ponte Vecchio.

When we step into the apartment, I feel a fresh ache of grief.
Not seeing Nonna in these rooms is difficult, but I know she'd be
thrilled Tommaso and I are married. I can almost see her smiling
face.

Days later, Tommaso surprises me. "Let's take a stroll," he says. So
we walk to the Boboli Gardens. As it comes into sight, I almost leap
with joy.

"Rosa!" It's Maestro! I nearly topple him with my embrace.

I feel a tug on my skirt, and I look down to see Eliana. Betta
stands behind her.

"Oh! Hello!" I swoop Eliana up and hold her close until she
wiggles to be free. I look to Betta, realizing Giuseppe is not with
them. From the look in her eyes, I know. I hug her tight.

Betta leads us to a blanket warmed by the bright sun. For November, it's an oddly warm day and we sit reveling in each other's company. Eliana circles a nearby tree, enthralled by the ruby leaves dotting the ground.

"Ciro," Maestro says, shaking his head in disbelief, "he turned on us . . ."

I nod. "What happened to you?"

"They came for me. Arrested me and took me to Villa Triste. Then they sent me to Fossoli. And that's where I found these two." He looks to Eliana and Betta.

"He helped us survive the camp." Betta wipes tears from her eyes.

"Bah, we helped each other. *Sì?*"

My eyes glisten as I hesitate to ask about Giuseppe.

Betta nods, understanding. "He almost made it," she says.

Maestro places his hand on her shoulder. "Giuseppe was very ill. He passed away a few days before the Germans surrendered."

I can't believe the injustice, and I can't stop my tears. "I'm so sorry, Betta."

"*Grazie,*" she tells me. "At least, we were together."

I can't imagine what they went through, and we sit in silence.

Eliana approaches and takes my hand, pulling me up. As I stand, Tommaso, Maestro, and Betta begin discussing the state of Florence.

"I lost Luca," she says.

"Your bunny?"

"*Sì,* in camp."

The loss of a father is unspeakable. Must it be magnified by the loss of this small creature comfort? I will find her another stuffed bunny. It won't be Luca, but I hope it will bring her some enjoyment.

"Come see the leaves, Rosa!" She leads me to the pile she's stacked.

Afterward, I tell Maestro of Teresa's kindness and help. He smiles knowingly when we tell him about our wedding. "This one, he's a good man! Your nonna would be so happy for you both." His happiness fills me with joy.

"You are Nonno to me," I say.

His face reddens with emotion, and he pulls me into a grandfatherly embrace. "*Sì, sì.*"

Before we part ways as we leave the park, he stops. "Rosa, Signor Gastani is still here in Florence."

I've nothing but the utmost respect for him. "He was so kind to me. I'm relieved to hear that! *Grazie!*"

Later that night, we all share a meal at Nonna's apartment. Despite the loss of the last many years, we celebrate our loved ones, toasting life, goodness, and love. It is good to be with family, which is who they've become.

The next day a telegram arrives from Tommaso's friend, Jack, in the Philippines. It says my family is doing well. But then I read *"Papa has died,"* and I drop to my knees. I knew it was a possibility, but the news is crushing. I'm not ready to say goodbye to my father. Tommaso, once again, tends my broken heart with gentleness. He's like the shorelines of the Arno, holding me steady, helping me move forward through the swirling currents of grief.

A week later, Maestro, Betta, and Eliana see Tommaso and me off when we leave Florence to start our life together in America. Tears spill down my cheeks as I say goodbye to Maestro. Leaving him now is especially difficult.

His eyes glisten when I mention Nonna. "I miss her so much," I tell him.

"*Sì, sì,*" he says, choking back emotion. He loved her, I know. And she loved him. "She would want you to continue, Rosa. You must sing."

"I will try," I assure him before waving one last time and boarding the plane.

When we arrive in Boston, Tommaso's family is enormously welcoming. Their kindness warms my heart. Our apartment is near the New England Conservatory. A few days after we've settled in, I meet with the dean about my sister Caramina. He assures me that he'd be thrilled to have her as a student. I've also contacted a friend of Maestro's to see about possible performing opportunities for myself.

I'm not in any hurry. Rather, I'm content to simply be here with Tommaso. Life has a way of turning upside down. The things that are essential—love and hope—I already have. In spades.

62

Caramina

NOVEMBER 20, 1945

Mountain Province, Philippines

My gaze flits around the backyard and lands on the bamboo arbor, dripping with velvety white blooms. Tio built the structure for the wedding, finishing just hours before the ceremony. The flowers seem to blossom directly from the bamboo, and more spill over from nearby trees. Only an hour ago, Isabella and Jack were pronounced husband and wife under that arch.

Now I watch as Isa gazes up at Jack, her face beaming with joy. Jack's fierce affection shows as he gazes back. Their love reminds me of Papa and Mama's.

The November ceremony was simple but elegant. Isabella is lovely in Tia's gown. She made alterations again to the dress, this time to fit her own tiny frame. Her brunette hair shines with highlights from the sun and is pulled into a loose chignon. She reminds me of the models in her *Harper's Bazaar* magazines from long before the war.

Lucia was the flower girl and took her responsibility with all the seriousness an almost three-year-old can muster. Isa had sewn her a dress from eyelet curtains Tia used before the war. A buttery yellow dress with a bow around the waist and a tiny rosette adorning the collar. Lucia twirled around and around like a miniature ballerina.

The wedding is the first real celebration my family has hosted since the war's end. General Yamashita officially surrendered in September and is now on trial for war crimes. We'd all crowded around Tio's radio to listen to General MacArthur after the surrender ceremony:

> *"Today the guns are silent. A great tragedy has ended. A great victory has been won. The skies no longer rain death—the seas bear only commerce, men everywhere walk upright in the sunlight. The entire world is quietly at peace."*

At his words, tears fell freely. Even Tio was overcome with the realization the war was truly over. After MacArthur finished, the announcer reported General Yamashita and his staff would be heading to Manila, along with more than ten thousand Japanese prisoners of war. An additional forty thousand are to be involved in the surrender, and it could take months before they are all rounded up.

It's hard to believe the war that has consumed our lives for so many years is at an end. I'd hoped we'd be able to return home immediately. But Matteo and Tio are still adamant we wait, given how many enemy troops are evading capture. Despite the situation, Torres and several of his men attended the wedding, including Alfonso, Cesar, and Ray.

Music is flowing into the yard from Papa's gramophone that Tio set up in the kitchen window. Everyone is jovial as we enjoy the meal Tia, Isabella, Anna, and I prepared. For the first time in a long time, there is no shortage of food. Guests have offered up whatever they could bring, eager to celebrate. Tio and Matteo have even prepared Enzo's favorite, *lechon*.

Soon it's time for the bride and groom's first dance. Jack and Isabella waltz graceful circles around the yard. I brim with joy seeing Isabella so happy.

After they finish, Tio holds his hand out to Isabella for the father-daughter dance. My eyes glisten, and I'm not alone. A glimmer of sadness flickers in Isa's eyes. Papa's absence is deeply felt. He'd have been thrilled to be a part of this day.

Later, Matteo turns on Tio's radio again to give Ray and Cesar a break from playing guitar. Static buzzes through the air till the sound of horns emerges, pumping out "Sing, Sing, Sing." The song is a bolt of energy, lifting all the guests to their feet.

Gabriel grabs me by the hand and pulls me into the group. He's intent on swing dancing, though neither of us have any idea how. By the time the brass sounds the final notes, I'm gasping for breath, and the two of us collapse in a heap of laughter.

"I'm so thirsty," I say as we make our way to a table set with drinks. Gabriel pours us guava punch, and we walk to a far table set up near the crystal waters of the stream.

I drink the last of my punch and set down my glass. Another song comes on the radio, the unmistakable opening notes of "Stardust." My heart grips as I'm brought back to the day I last sang it. The day Okamoto attacked me. The day Papa died.

I bite my lip, furious that joy has been stolen from such a lovely song, corrupted by awful memories. It was one of Papa and Mama's favorites. I step forward, bringing my foot down as if bringing down a gavel, making my decision. Okamoto will not steal anything else. The war has taken enough. I will remember the song for what it is. A testament to my parents' love.

Gabriel places his arms around me gently and pulls me close to dance. The shimmering water is mesmerizing. Rays of sunlight dance on ripples that appear and disappear in a game of hide-and-seek. We sway to the music. I rest my head against his chest, listening to his heart beat in step with the melody. It feels good to be held by Gabriel. I trust him. I let myself sink into his arms.

Shifting his body, he pulls me closer. He stands a head taller than me, and I raise my head to look up at him. He meets my gaze. Then, he kisses me softly. His lips are warm and familiar. I kiss him back, breathing in the fragrant scent of the blooms, losing myself in the kiss. Where his hand rests at the small of my back, my skin tingles.

The song ends, and we pull away. He gazes at me with a contented smile. We both stand still, not knowing quite what to say. This kiss, unlike our first, I anticipated. Maybe even hoped for in some small way.

Gabriel breaks the silence. "I was going to tell you, I've had some good news. I've been asked to stay in Timbales to help with rebuilding. Many of the buildings are in good shape, but several have been destroyed. I know it will be a lot of work, but I'm up for it. Since the mayor's gone, a few of the men want me to stay and help in his place. They've given me a house, Caramina! Imagine, helping run the town. It's more than I'd ever hoped for." He looks at me like it's a dream I share.

"Gabriel, that's wonderful! You'll do a great job." I smile, genuinely proud of him. I'm not surprised. I've known for some time his activities during the war helped both the guerrilla troops and the people of Timbales. Matteo explained Gabriel's role after I begged him relentlessly when the Japanese surrendered. Gabriel had been bringing information on the Japanese in town to Captain Torres, including their plans, schedules, any knowledge of troop movements, changes in leadership. Anything that might help stop them. All of it was used by the guerrillas and passed on to the U.S. troops.

A dark curl flops onto his forehead, covering his brow. His lips curl slightly, leaving a tiny dimple on his cheek. An awkward silence passes, and I shuffle nervously.

Gabriel takes my hand. Then he kneels on one knee. But instead of excitement, panic runs through me. I inhale to calm myself. This can't be happening. It's too soon.

"Caramina, I've known for some time you're the one for me. I wanted to wait until I had things set up, and now I do. I love you, Cara. I'd be honored if you would be my wife. Will you marry me?"

I stare at him, stunned. I don't know what to say. I can't believe he's proposing.

Before I can say a word, Tio calls to me. Jack and Isabella are about to cut the wedding cake. Spotting Gabriel, Tio nearly drops the knife in his hand. Then everything falls silent. People are beginning to watch.

"I . . . I . . ." I mumble.

A whoop sounds behind Tio. "Ah! *Salamat sa Diyos!* Thank God!" Seeing Gabriel on one knee, Tia is nearly bouncing with joy. Guests rush toward us, peppering us with well wishes.

"Congratulations! Welcome to the family, son!" Tio chuckles as he shakes Gabriel's hand.

I stand still and smile. There is nothing else to do. The glow of happiness on Gabriel's face lights a warm smile across his lips. He looks at me, his gaze tender.

Isabella pulls me into a hug. "Caramina, I'm so happy for you!"

"Please, let's cut the cake. We have even more to celebrate now!" Tia's face is beaming as she directs everyone to the cake table. Gabriel and I are swept away to watch the newlyweds cut the cake, which is adorned with a mountain of ivory blooms.

I glance at Gabriel as he watches Jack and Isabella. He is genuinely happy. He takes my hand and holds it gently. A feeling of contentment buds inside me. Perhaps this is how love feels. I care for Gabriel. He loves me. He'll take care of me, I have no doubt. He's a good man. A kind man.

But a thought twists in my mind. What will every day be like for the rest of my life?

Later, with the last guests gone, I'm grateful to finally have a chance to talk with Isabella alone. We sit in the living room, feet up after an exhilarating but tiring day.

"Isa?"

Isabella tilts her head toward me.

"How did you know Jack was the one? I mean, were you ever not sure?"

"I can't imagine living without him, Cara. I don't know how. The feeling— No, the certainty is, I don't want to spend the rest of my life without him. I can't."

A pained look falls over my face.

"Cara?"

"I never said yes," I whisper.

"It did happen quickly."

"I didn't know what to do. I still don't. I care about him. I *think* I love him."

Now Isabella has a pained look. "You need to be certain. This is the rest of your life, Caramina. It's not fair to you or to Gabriel. I want you to be happy. And if this is how, then I'm thrilled for you. But if not, I want you to find happiness."

I nod. "I just need time."

"It'll be okay," she reassures me.

The house is quiet and still. Isabella leans back into the couch, and I notice a letter resting on the table. Someone must have left it during the festivities. Isabella turns it over. When she sees the handwriting, she gasps. I know immediately. It's from Rosa.

"Read it!" I say.

We're both giddy, my predicament momentarily forgotten. Isabella carefully pries open the envelope. Inside are two sheets of blush pink stationery covered on both sides with Rosa's beautiful script, along with a form. Isa sets the form on the table and reads Rosa's words aloud.

We both exhale upon hearing Rosa is safe. She writes she is still in Italy. But soon she'll be leaving for the United States with her husband, Thomas Ridgefield. Jack's friend!

"What else does she say?"

Isabella reads on quietly for a moment. Her eyes darken.

"What is it?"

Isabella places her hands in her lap. Clutching the letter, she tells me in a hushed voice what I've already feared. "Nonna's gone."

I nod, taking in the news as my eyes brim with tears.

"Rosa says she passed in her sleep, peacefully." Isabella chokes the words out, placing her arm around me. The two of us lean close, absorbing the news.

"There's more." She wipes a tear splotched on the letter, careful not to smudge the ink. "Florence has been devastated. Much of Italy has. It's no place for Caramina," she reads.

My spirits sink even deeper at Rosa's words. Isabella glances at me, patting my hand as if to offer comfort. Then she reads on quietly.

"She's contacted a music school in the United States, the New England Conservatory of Music. It's not far from where she and Thomas will live in Boston. They have an exceptional vocal music program. She's already spoken with them about you, and they're interested in having you attend. She wants you to apply, Caramina."

It's a lot to digest. Nonna is gone. Italy doesn't make sense anymore, not without Nonna and Rosa. I've never considered going anywhere else. But music is part of me, one of my loves. My great love. Maybe Rosa is right and I should apply. Or maybe, this is a sign that marrying Gabriel is the right thing to do.

"She's included an application." Isabella unfolds the heavy paper. "I think you should do it, Caramina. It's been your dream your whole life. You can come with us to the United States. Now Rosa will be there, and so will I. We can help you."

Papa's words skim through my mind. "The war won't last. When it ends, and it will end . . . I want you to pursue your dream." Though I may not be able to go to Italy, Italy isn't the only place for good vocal training. That's what Papa said.

Isabella hands me the form, and I stare at it. "This is for another day. I'll read it later. Today is your wedding day! Where is that husband of yours? Let's go find him."

Isabella puts her hand on my arm gently. "Cara, you know you always have a home with me." She pulls me into an embrace, and we're interrupted by a familiar voice bellowing into the kitchen.

"There's my wife! I thought I lost you before we'd been married one full day!"

Isabella and I both laugh. Jack is so good-natured—he reminds me so much of Papa. As he approaches, he spots the letter in Isabella's hand and concern falls across his face. "News from Italy?"

Isabella nods. "We need to tell the others."

"I'll get them," he says.

It seems news of Nonna's passing was expected. Both Matteo and Enzo are saddened, but they take it in stride. They understand loss is an inevitable part of war. The news of Rosa's marriage to Thomas Ridgefield is uplifting for the whole family. Tia and Tio are relieved to hear their oldest niece is safe and happy. Tia, especially, is thrilled all three of her nieces will soon be married and settled.

Isabella begins to explain, "Rosa also sent word of a sch—"

"Where did she say they'd be living?" I interrupt. I need time to think before telling anyone about the school or my thoughts about marrying Gabriel. I need to decide on my own.

I make my way to my bedroom and yawn as I close the door. After crawling onto the bed, I pull my legs up under me. A bird sings its evening song in the distance. Light from the lantern on the bedside table glints gold on the paper resting on my lap. Slowly, I unfold the form. Though I'm torn about what to do, this is like unwrapping a long-hoped-for present. I skim the words, drinking them in like notes on a music score. This could be my future.

I close my eyes, breathing in the warm air. There is an excitement, a nervous energy bubbling inside me. I go to my dresser drawer to unearth the bundle of letters hidden beneath my blouses. Reading Nonna's words is like sitting with her, close enough to feel her warmth and smell the orange-blossom fragrance of her perfume. Nonna always knew what to do. I wish I could speak with her now.

After propping myself on the bed, I untie the ribbon. I open letter after letter, searching for Nonna. An ache stabs within me. Grief.

As I read Nonna's words, the ache slowly melts away. I've read them many times before. But it's as if Nonna is speaking to me for this very moment. Somehow, she'd known this day would come. Nonna was clear she didn't want me to lose myself in loss or fear.

A tear sketches a crescent down my cheek. I swipe it away before it falls. Then I pull a pencil from the small table and write out my answers on the form. After reading it over, I fold it carefully. Tomorrow, I'll have Jack mail it.

I blow out the lantern, watching a spiral of smoke rise to the ceiling. As I sink into my pillow, my locket shifts around my neck. Its presence is a comfort. A little piece of Nonna, still with me.

My eyes adjust as darkness falls over the room, and the glow of candlelight from the shed flushes softly upon the bedroom wall. A warm breeze blows through the window. The candlelight flickers to darkness, and I drift to sleep by the silvery light of the moon.

63

December 21, 1945

Dear Ms. Caramina Grassi,

I am pleased to be writing on behalf of the New England Conservatory of Music. Your sister, Rosa, contacted us with a recommendation for you from Maestro Antonino Silvieri. It is my understanding you were to begin your voice training studies in Florence with the Maestro, but the war disrupted those plans.

The Maestro and I studied together when we were young, and I have many fond memories of that time. His endorsement is one not easily given.

This war has upended many things. After hearing of your passion and talent as a soprano, I would love to invite you to attend our conservatory for your vocal studies. We would be honored to have you as a student.

I understand timing may be of issue for you to begin at the start of the semester. However, in light of the circumstances, we would love for you to attend when you are able.

We have your completed application and will keep it on file. I realize this is unconventional. However, these are unconventional times. I sincerely hope you will choose to study with us. I look forward to meeting you and hearing your beautiful voice.

Most sincerely,
Dr. Randolph Edwins
Assistant Dean of Opera Studies

64

Caramina

The letter took weeks to arrive. I sit poring over the words before me. I've read it five times already. From the bedroom next to mine, I hear my baby nephew, Crisanto, crying. It seems he's been crying since the day he was born.

If I marry Gabriel, I, too, could soon be a mother. The very thought makes me a bit queasy. I'm not ready for that yet. Since Gabriel proposed, I've only seen him once; he's been so busy in town. The one visit he made to the farm was to give Tio news of Timbales. I was working in the rice fields and barely had the chance to say hello before he rushed off.

I'm conflicted. I care for him without question. But do I love him enough to give up my dreams? Rebuilding the town is his dream. Not mine. It's important to him. And I want it for him. Dreams are something no one should take from you.

I scan the letter resting in my lap again. "We would be honored to have you as a student." The assistant dean had scrawled his signature in black ink at the bottom of the letter. Isabella had been confident the school would want me. I had reined in my hopes in the event I wasn't accepted. But now, if I want, I can join Rosa and Isabella in the United States to study voice at one of the finest conservatories in America. A school picked out by my sister. A school that wants me.

I jump to my feet. Spin around. A bird's song drifts through the window. Rays of sun ripple waves of light on the floor, filling the room with a golden patina. I can't remember being this happy. I wish I could run and tell Isabella she was right—that the school wants me. But I'll have to wait. Not long after their wedding, Jack and Isabella left for the States.

I haven't told anyone else about applying. And Jack and Isabella kept quiet at my request. Now, I'm ready to tell my family. Letter flopping wildly in hand, I race down the stairs two at a time to find Tia and Tio. When I reach the last step, I'm about to turn into the kitchen. But then I see them in the living room. And Gabriel.

"Gabriel!"

He smiles at me. I'd hoped to tell Tia and Tio the news before anyone else and have the chance to talk with them.

"Caramina, Gabriel has something for you," Tio says.

I look from Tio to Gabriel. The tone of Tio's voice gives me pause. The paper shuffles in my hand as I look at Gabriel. Tia and Tio step back, and Gabriel walks toward me awkwardly. A lump forms in my throat.

"Caramina, I'm so happy you've agreed to be my wife. I've wanted to give you this for some time, but I had trouble finding it. Now that I have it, I couldn't wait." On his palm is a tiny gold ring. He reaches for my hand.

My heart sinks. I have to tell him. My hand rests at my side, motionless, and a puzzled look falls across his face. The letter in my hand begins to shake.

Tia steps forward. "Caramina?"

"I'm so sorry. I just . . . don't know," I stammer.

Hurt flashes in Gabriel's eyes. "It's okay. I understand. This is a big decision. I thought it was what you wanted . . . I'll give you some time." With pain etched across his face, he draws my hand to his lips and kisses it gently. He smiles warmly, then slowly walks out onto the porch.

"Cara! He loves you. He always has. He proposed!" Tia stares at me, incredulous. "What more could you want? It's what all girls dream of."

My eyes brim. "I never said yes," I whisper. "I don't know if I'm ready to be married. I was going to tell him, but I haven't had a chance to speak with him. The one time he came, he left so quickly. I . . . I love Gabriel. I really do. But I wanted to talk with you about this." I lift the paper. Tio walks over and takes the letter. He reads it quietly.

"I know this is what you've always wanted, Caramina. And if it really is, you should pursue it." Tio pauses and looks down for a moment. "Gabriel is a good man. Tia's right. He's loved you from the first time he met you. He'd be a good husband to you. But if you don't love him the way he loves you . . . Well, I want you to be happy. Both of you. It's your decision. But we support you either way." Tio hugs me, then hands the letter to Tia.

The confusion on Tia's face disappears as she reads. As she hands the letter back to me, the pained look in her eyes makes my heart stab and pinch.

Tio nods toward the porch. "You need to give him an answer, Cara."

"I don't want to hurt him. I do care about him. Deeply." Panic rushes through me, and my cheeks grow warm. Gabriel is my closest friend.

"He's a good man, Cara," says Tio. He puts his arm around Tia and leads her into the kitchen, leaving me all alone.

Crisanto's cries have grown into wails. I can hear Anna's footsteps circling upstairs as she tries to calm him.

The quiet of the porch is a grateful reprieve. The screen door clanks shut behind me. Gabriel sits overlooking the meadow. I take a deep breath as I sit next to him. We've sat here, side by side, so many times over the last four years.

Slowly, he turns to face me. "The last thing I wanted was to rush you, Caramina. I've loved you since the day we met . . . and the day at the stream."

"We hunted for stones . . ."

He grins. "You weren't happy I interrupted your singing. But then . . ." His voice falls away.

"Gabriel, I'm so glad I met you. I can't imagine going through these last four years without you. I do love you. You're my best friend."

He winces. I'm not making any sense. The letter is still in my hand. He doesn't even know about the school. I hand him the letter. Lines around his eyes crease as he reads. He nods.

"It's what you want?"

This is so hard. "I'm only eighteen. I know it's old enough to be married. But I'm just not ready. And this, this is my dream." I point to the letter.

"Caramina." He takes my hand in his. "I love you. I want to spend the rest of my life with you. Rebuilding the town and helping run it—it's something I can do. Something we can do together. It's an opportunity I could only have dreamed about. Now it's real, and I can provide for you and for our family one day." He takes a deep breath. "But if you're not ready, or if you're not sure of me, I understand."

As he speaks, he caresses my hand with his thumb absentmindedly. "Whatever you decide, I'll understand." Sadness permeates his eyes. "I'll never stop loving you." He leans in and kisses me gently. "This is for you." He holds out his other hand. In his palm, the tiny gold ring glints in the sunlight. "I want you to have it. I'd hoped to give it to you on your birthday." He places the ring in my hand.

"Gabriel?" The thought of losing him makes my heart buckle, and my chin quivers. But this isn't right. The ring isn't mine.

"No, I found it especially for you. I want you to have it, regardless of what you decide. And know . . . whatever you decide, I'm here." He smiles warmly, the smile I've come to know so well. He kisses my cheek tenderly, then walks down the steps.

"I love you," I whisper, as he makes his way through the meadow, a line of khaki cutting emerald. I watch him go, wincing as my heart splits in two.

65

Caramina

I push open the door to my old bedroom. Memories flood in from childhood, and the night we fled. I peer around, taking it in. The walls are bare. I step into the room, and something catches my eye. From under the bed, I pull out a large piece of rolled-up paper.

It's the poster from Nonna's performance at the Manila Grand Opera House. My spirits lighten seeing Nonna's face. After setting it down, I put away the few clothes I have left.

Opening my bottom dresser drawer, I see a box pushed to the back. Instantly, I recognize the faded pink tissue through the cellophane window on the lid. It's my dress! The one Papa gave me for my fourteenth birthday.

"What did you find?" Esther appears, broom in hand. Having her here after so many years apart is honey to my soul. Sadly, Stefano, like Papa, didn't make it through the war. I lift the dress for her to see.

"Your dress!"

"I'm sure it won't fit."

"Nonsense! When I'm through with it, it will be like new." She insists on cleaning and altering it for me.

Two days later, Esther's completed her alterations, and I stand trying on the dress in my room. I take my time changing and can hear her dusting Enzo's room, waiting for me.

Tia's voice floats up from the kitchen as I shuffle into my gown. My aunt and uncle accompanied us to our home. Tio made arrangements for Eduardo to look after the rice fields until he returned. They'd planned to stay until we were set up in the house but haven't been able to bring themselves to leave us yet. Having them here makes me smile.

Though I'm grateful to be here with my family, Papa's absence is profound. I'm not sure I'll ever get used to him not being with us. With Papa gone, the house is now Matteo's. At thirteen, Enzo will stay with Matteo and Anna until he's ready to be on his own.

When we first entered the house, we were surprised to find it almost the same as when we left. Furniture had been thrown around, some destroyed and some moved. But on the whole, it was in good condition. We learned from a few townspeople the house had been occupied for a short time by a small group of Japanese officers. After several hours of cleanup, everything was back in order.

Other homes haven't fared so well. Anna's family home is badly damaged, but she's thrilled to be reunited with her parents. They're working to fix their house with the help of Matteo, Tio, and Enzo.

Yesterday, word came from Gabriel to Tio about the rebuilding efforts in Timbales. He also sent a note for me.

My dearest Caramina,

Though I wish things were different, I understand your decision. Sing with that beautiful voice of yours. Study hard. Write and let me know how you're doing. I can't wait to hear you perform at the Manila Opera House. One day, maybe, we'll see each other again. I will always love you, Cara.

With all my love,
Gabriel

My heart pinches, thinking of him. I miss him. But I know I made the right decision. I finish dressing, walk into the hallway, and turn a circle.

"*Magandá!*" Esther says. "Beautiful gown for a beautiful young soprano."

I smile. "*Grazie,* Esther."

Several weeks have passed since we returned home. Standing on the tarmac in Manila now, I hear the roar of engines in the distance.

Rosy pink and tangerine hues brush across the sky. The fiery sunset over Manila Bay, a watercolor canvas. Birds dot the ether. Notes on a score.

Behind me, Matteo grapples with a large wooden crate that houses all of my belongings, except what is contained in the little straw purse dangling from my arm and the turquoise luggage resting at my feet. Peals of laughter squeal from Crisanto as Enzo tickles his belly.

My family circles around me next to Papa's Packard. Memories of the long drive to Tia and Tio's at the start of the war flash in my mind. But today is about looking forward. My family has come to see me off. A man calls out, signaling they are boarding the plane. I stare at each of my loved ones. A knot forms in my belly, and my eyes well up.

Tia rushes forward and grabs me into a tight hug till I can barely breathe. "Write and let us know how you're doing, Cara." My aunt dots her eyes with a lace handkerchief, then kisses me quickly on the cheek.

I smile at her warmly. "I will, Tia."

Tio grabs me next, pulling me into a strong embrace. "You always have a home with us," he whispers.

I nod. The knot in my belly slowly untwists as everyone takes turns saying goodbye.

Enzo throws both arms around me, sweeping me into a hug. He picks me up so my feet dangle just off the ground. He's taller than me now. "I'll miss you," he says, setting me down.

I look at my little brother, remembering the many times I fought fiercely to protect him. He's a young man now. I hate to leave him. But I know he's in good hands with Matteo. I smile, choking back emotion. "I'll miss you, too. Watch out for wild boars."

He chuckles.

I hug Lucia, then pick up Crisanto and hold him tight. He reaches up, coiling a tendril of my hair around his chubby fingers. Then he plants a wet kiss on my cheek and kicks his legs to get free. I laugh and set him down, watching him crawl to Lucia.

I hug Esther and then Anna goodbye. Matteo embraces me next. "You'll do well, Caramina. I'm so happy for you. Let me know if you need anything." He looks at me with his dark eyes and, in that moment, reminds me so much of Papa.

"I love you all," I say, fighting back tears. I glance at each of them, committing their faces to memory.

Matteo walks me to the plane, and I make my way up the stairs. Then I look back at my family.

"This way, miss," a man directs me.

I settle into a window seat. My family forms a semicircle watching the plane. I wave, and they wave back.

The pilot's voice booms through the cabin announcing our take-off. The plane lurches forward. Then we pick up speed, barreling down the runway. I watch my family get smaller and smaller. As I strain to see them, the chain around my neck twists.

I grasp Nonna's locket and the ring from Gabriel, and I hold them close to my heart. Running one finger along the face of the locket, I feel the familiar sunflower. I lower my hand, palm open, and gaze at the charm. Hope for my future rushes through me, and I know I'm exactly where I'm meant to be. Sunlight streams onto the locket, and the tiny flower blushes coral in the light of the sun.

Epilogue

"I can't find my scarf." Rosa's voice floats into the room.

"On the settee," I answer, absentmindedly. Rosa snaps up the ruby silk scarf with a quick smile, then rushes back into her bedroom. Tommaso has already left for work, and the apartment is abuzz with energy as we prepare for the day.

Breathing out a sigh, I take in the room around me. I can't believe I'm here—in America. I smile contentedly, knowing that this is where I belong. Sipping my tea, I think about how I've slipped into life here since my arrival weeks ago.

It was an emotional reunion when I saw my sisters for the first time in so long. Being together again has given me newfound energy after so many years of difficulty.

I've adapted easily to my new home and schedule as the days have passed. Staying with Rosa is a comfort. Isa offered for me to stay with her and Jack. But Rosa and Tommaso's place is closer to the conservatory. Soon though, I'll start looking for a place of my own. Rosa's apartment is perfect for a couple, but not roomy enough to accommodate three adults permanently. And now, Isabella is expecting. Once I find my own place, I'll still be close enough to see my sisters every day, and soon my new little niece or nephew.

Rosa's schedule has picked up since she started performing again. Right now she's singing at a theater not far from where we live. Tommaso has taken a job at an architectural firm downtown. Seeing Rosa so happy and in love makes me smile. Tommaso, like Jack, is a good man, and I've enjoyed getting to know my new brother-in-law.

When Jack and Isa first arrived in the city, Isa found a job as a seamstress for a design house. But soon, they set out looking for a place for her fledgling business as a dressmaker. They were fortunate to get a lease on a small space that now houses her studio. After Rosa wore one of Isa's designs for a performance, word of Isa's talent got out. Now Isa's working feverishly to complete a set of dresses for two performers who sought her out. Jack, with his background in electronics, started his own business. He's beginning to enjoy the fruits of his labor as projects have started to roll in.

I glance around the small living room, and my gaze falls on the mahogany bureau. Days ago, I came upon Rosa's diary while searching for sheet music. The rose and gold swirls of the Florentine cover caught my eye. Quickly, I realized the petite book was a diary. Rosa walked in just as I was setting it back in its place.

"I've been meaning to share that with you. It was a way for me to stay connected to you all when communicating wasn't possible," she said. "I want you to read it, Cara. I want to share what happened. It was so hard being separated from you all during the war, not knowing what you were all experiencing so far away."

I didn't want to intrude on her most private thoughts. But Rosa insisted. When she left for work that day, I spent the morning reading. Her accounts were visceral. I found myself wiping tears away, realizing what she endured. I'd been naïve to assume things were easier in Italy. War is war.

We three sisters are even closer given our harrowing experiences. The loss is still real. But it is softened by the good memories we share from before the war and its toll. And now, the new ones we're creating.

With the excitement over Isa's baby, new jobs, and my schooling, there is much laughter and joy. I miss my brothers immensely. All three of us do. But I'm grateful to have the opportunity to do life with my sisters. It is a gift. I'll never take my time with them for granted. I'll never take anyone I love for granted.

We've started planning a visit to the Philippines. I plan to see Clara when I return. We've kept in touch. Clara wrote me saying when she ages out of Santa Maria's, she intends to search for her mother. After all the violence and displacement of the war, she yearns to be reunited with her only family. I hope she'll be successful.

Gabriel and I have also exchanged letters, and I hope to see him again one day. He offered to come to Floridablanca, when and if I return.

"Don't forget Isa and Jack are coming for dinner tonight," Rosa says, pulling me from my thoughts. I throw on my aubergine cardigan and grab my handbag. "I won't." I kiss her on the cheek, and she smiles affectionately, watching me head out the door.

As I walk down the street, taxis speed by. People bustle along, rushing to their jobs. The city pulses with life. This is the time I love. The morning sun peeking over the tallest buildings. Cherry blossoms, pink and full, on the trees lining the streets to the conservatory.

I arrive early to warm up alone. By the time my professor enters the auditorium and props open the door to the warm May breeze, I'm on stage and ready. "Up with the birds this morning, Miss Grassi," he says. I smile. "Please, begin." He nods to me as he sets his worn, tawny leather briefcase next to a seat in the front row.

From the open door, the faint sound of birdsong floats into the theater. I sing, joining my voice to their song.

Readers Guide

1. Both Rosa and Caramina experience profound loss. For Caramina, music was a large part of the healing process. What has played a role in your healing process after experiencing loss? How can music have a healing effect?

2. Why do you think Ciro did what he did at the very end of the story? Do you think he could have found peace after his actions had dire consequences for so many lives? Do you think Rosa could ever forgive Ciro?

3. Tommaso tells Rosa, "Times of war change many men." How is this true for all those affected by war?

4. The bonds of love and burgeoning love are strong in the story. What did you think of Caramina's decision at the end? How did witnessing her parents' love, Tia and Tio's, and Isa and Jack's impact her decision?

5. Longtime friends, Nonna and Maestro are very fond of each other. Both grieved the loss of their spouses years before this story begins. Do you believe they are in love? What makes it possible to start over in love later in life?

6. How does the setting of each sister's experiences (Caramina's in Floridablanca and then in the mountainous jungles of Luzon, and Rosa's in Florence, Italy) affect them?

7. In the beginning, Caramina is given a gift from Nonna, a tangible item to remember Nonna's advice to always look for the good. She struggles with this considerably as she experiences the horrors of the war. Yet, she is aware of the small moments of joy and beauty, and they do give her hope that good exists.

Rosa, at one point, says that Nonna had an unwavering belief that goodness can be found despite one's circumstances. How have you found, in times of difficulty, that looking for the good has been a help?

8. Caramina and Rosa are separated, initially by Rosa's plans to study in Italy, but then for many years by the war. In many ways, their family bond kept them close despite that. How have you stayed close with loved ones that you are separated from?

9. Although I grew up hearing the stories of my mother, aunts, and godmother about their time during the war, while doing research for the book I realized just how complex these two war fronts were. Did anything surprise you about the war in the Philippines or in Italy?

10. Rosa chooses to help the Resistance after witnessing the injustice and horrors of living under Mussolini and his henchmen, the Blackshirts, and later under Nazi occupation, placing herself and her loved ones at great risk of harm and death. If you were in her place, would you make the same choice? Why, or why not?

11. Unfortunately, in being considered different, both Caramina and Rosa experience discrimination. Enormously grateful for the war's end, they and their family joyfully move forward with their lives. How did their being made to feel "other" impact their thoughts, decisions, and choices, or didn't it? As in life, there are many examples of individuals being made to feel "other" in the book. What are some of the examples? Have you experienced being made to feel "other"? If so, how has it affected you and have you found a way to move forward?

12. Which character(s) resonated with you? Why?

13. What did you take away from Rosa's and Caramina's stories?

Author's Note

One of the best compliments I could receive about this book was given by my godmother, who, after reading an early draft, to my great surprise and pleasure, thanked me for writing this story, which in her words "hadn't been done," and for the "opportunity to revisit my childhood in a way that honors my memories." Treading upon the soil of wartime memories of those I love is something I do not take lightly.

As a child, I was fascinated by the stories told by my mother, aunts, and godmother of their time growing up in the Philippines, as well as the stories they parceled out about WWII. Though they were careful not to burden me with the harsh realities of war, their joyful talk of family, a loving father, the beauty of their country, faith, and the enormous role music played in their lives in bringing joy and hope shaped my understanding of how we can walk through difficulty and, with resilience, not just survive but thrive. I was also greatly moved by the stories told me by my aunt who, like Rosa, after leaving the Philippines to voice train in Italy, found herself facing a terrifying wartime separated from her family.

Like Caramina, my mother dreamed of voice training in Florence to become a professional soprano like her nonna, Syla Lanzi, who performed with the Grande Compagnia d'Opera Italiana. Some of my favorite memories are of listening to the rich tones of my mother's beautiful voice as she rehearsed arias in our home and sang in church. A woman of strength, courage, and strong faith, she gave me an example that has had, perhaps, the most profound effect of anyone upon my life. This story was born from a wish to honor her.

I learned early on that the events that took place in the Philippines during the war are not widely known. It is my desire to bring to light the war in this country of many islands, along with what it cost the Filipino people and, in particular, young Filipinas. Also, as *mestizas,* my mother and aunts experienced some discrimination.

There are myriad ways people are made to feel "other." In my own life, I've come to realize that when someone is viewed as different, people often have difficulty understanding, and sadly, grace can be lacking. It is my hope that this story aids in building empathy and love for those viewed as different.

Research for this book took place over many years. It includes firsthand accounts from my family, along with resources dealing with the war in the Philippines and in Italy, particularly about music under Mussolini and the women who played a role in *la Resistenza.* Though this is a fictional account, I've tried my best to stay as close to the factual record as possible. However, I am fallible and hope the reader will forgive any errors on my part.

Philippines

Like Caramina, my mother fled her Floridablanca home with her family to seek refuge at her aunt and uncle's house in the Luzon mountains. The account of the townspeople fleeing was based on real accounts of the many who fled in fear of the approaching Japanese.

Timbales was created to allow for a town within a day's travel from Tio's farm. San Paulo, where the orphans are evacuated to, is also fictional.

Father Bautista describes how he and Captain Torres served under Papa in World War I. In July 1917, the Philippine National Guard (PNG) was formed. Though they didn't serve directly in World War I, many of those Filipinos enlisted and served in the American Expeditionary Forces (AEF) on all fronts of the war. The 332nd U.S. Infantry Regiment was initially sent to France but was then directed to serve in the Italian campaign. In addition, some Filipinos studying in the United States enlisted in the U.S. military when the war began. The account of Bautista's, Torres's, and Papa's service is based on these disparate facts.

The comfort house Caramina is witness to is based on the true accounts of numerous young Filipinas who were taken captive and brutally forced into sexual slavery by the Japanese military. Tragically, many of these women carried their wounds, physical and emotional, throughout their lives in silence for fear of being made outcasts. Many only began recounting their experiences as elderly women in the 1990s.

The Filipino people also endured the roundups of men and boys who were forced into labor, and the arrest, torture, and execution without trial of civilians at the hands of the military and the Kempeitai (Japanese military police).

Nearing the war's end, Rear Admiral Sanji Iwabuchi ordered his approximately twenty thousand soldiers to fight to the death. They went on a drunken rampage committing barbarous atrocities upon the people of Manila. An estimated hundred thousand men, women, children, and infants were massacred. By the time Manila was liberated, the city lay in ruins as one of the most devastated cities of World War II alongside Warsaw and Berlin.

Many members of the Japanese military, including the commander of the Japanese forces in the Philippines, General To-moyuki Yamashita, were tried and executed for war crimes for their barbaric actions. Rear Admiral Iwabuchi committed suicide toward the end of the battle for Manila, thus escaping prosecution. Captain Okamoto is based on a composite of these men.

Italy

The Palazzo di Fiori where Rosa performs, signaling a message for the Resistance, is fictional. However, Rosa's efforts and the activities of the partisans were based on real accounts. By late summer 1944, there were more than thirty-five thousand women in the Italian resistance. These brave women served mostly in noncombat roles. Their activities were crucial and extremely dangerous.

With Rosa's palazzo assignment, I took liberty with the dates for how the messages might be encoded. In July 1943, the Germans became aware the partisans were using invisible ink that could be read when heated over a flame. Rosa's handoff of the score with an encoded message takes place in 1944. For the story's sake, I kept the practice in play with the Germans none the wiser.

Villa Triste is where sadistic leader of the *Banda Carità*, Mario Carità, and his men conducted bloody interrogations on those they imprisoned without trial. Many of those arrested were innocent, yet they were tortured and executed under suspicion of working with the Resistance. Rosa's imprisonment is based on the account of my aunt's arrest and imprisonment for being an enemy alien during the German occupation. Like Rosa, she wasn't released until her nonna was able to obtain her Italian citizenship papers.

The professor who unfairly marks Rosa's performance down was based on a Florentine conservatory professor who was an Aryan racial theorist known for his tome on race, *Il Razzismo*, published in 1936. Mussolini used *Il Razzismo* in implementing his racial policies.

On September 25, 1943, Allied bombs fell, targeting Campo di

Marte railway to stop the traffic of German supplies. The target wasn't hit. Bombs fell to the north of Florence's historic center. I've moved this incident to November 24, 1943, for the sake of the story.

Head over to my website for more information and to check out some of the resources used in my research.

Website: www.angelamshupe.com
Instagram: @angelamshupe
Newsletter: https://angelamshupe.substack.com

Acknowledgments

Naming every person who has touched this story to make it what it is today would make this an extremely lengthy note. I'm grateful to everyone who has spoken into this project with kindness and encouragement.

A huge thank you to my godmother, Belen Torres, for advising me on the events of Luzon before, during, and after the war, and for reading an early draft to make sure it rang true. Thank you to my aunts, Angelita, Lourdes, and Conchita, who, though I hadn't yet decided to make the story into novel form, answered my many questions about our family and their time in the Philippines and in Italy when my mother could not.

Thank you to Jamie Lapeyrolerie for her keen editorial insight and all-around kindness throughout the publishing process. I'm enormously grateful to have her as an advocate and champion for Caramina's and Rosa's stories.

Thank you to Tamela Hancock Murray for her unwavering excitement for this story and determination to see it come to fruition, and for her encouragement and support.

I'm enormously grateful to the wonderful, talented team at WaterBrook for helping bring this story to beautiful book form—and for your kindness to a debut author. Thank you to Laura Wright, Julia Wallace, Kevin Garcia, Rose Decaen, Rachael Clements, and [t/k], plus Ava Perego, Shauna Carlos, Ginia Croker, Oghosa Iyamu, Douglas Mann, Johanna Inwood, and Levi Phillips, and to book designer Jo Anne Metsch.

Special thanks to Laura Klynstra for her gorgeous cover design.

I am forever grateful to the lovely Sarah Branham for her kindness while sharing her astute and wise editorial skills, and for being a constant champion for this story.

Thank you to Laura Chasen, whose kind editorial assistance early on helped move the story forward. Thank you to Heather Webb and the late Amy Sue Nathan for their kind and thoughtful wisdom and insightful editorial eyes on the first pages of an early draft of the manuscript. Thank you to the late Meghan Masterson for her kindness and generosity in sharing her knowledge and wisdom about the publishing process.

Thank you to Camille Pagan for her generous encouragement, kind spirit, and wisdom about this publishing journey.

Thank you to S. Kirk Walsh for her keen editorial insight on my short story that ended up a portion of Rosa's story.

To my good friend, the lovely and talented Elizabeth Wafler. Thank you to the Women's Fiction Writers Association, and specifically to Lisa Montanaro and Elizabeth Parman.

Thank you to Catherine Liao for her kind help in ensuring the Filipino story rang true.

Thank you to Anna Vincenzi, PhD, and Anne L. Saunders, PhD, for their assistance in helping direct me to research regarding Florence during the war, and specifically the Florentine resistance.

To the late Janos Shoemyen (alias Lawrence Dorr) for his generosity and kindness in workshopping my writing early on, and whose encouragement spurred me on to write this novel.

To my dear friend and fellow bibliophile Suzi Phaneuf, who

decades ago gave me a notebook to "get those ideas down." The memory I carry of her joyful laughter, love, and book-filled life still encourages me every day.

To my mother, Carmen, whose love, strength, and support grew me into the woman I am today.

To my husband, who is my greatest cheerleader. Your unwavering encouragement and love make my life so much richer every day. This book would not exist without you. A huge thank you to my son and daughter for giving me the space over so many years to write this story, and for the constant love and encouragement you've shown me that has bolstered me when I faltered in this journey.

I thank God for life and breath and for the opportunity to do this work. In the words of Ralph Waldo Emerson, "All writing comes by the grace of God." His grace is what carries me each and every day.

Finally, thank you, reader, for spending your precious time in these pages. I hope you walk away inspired and bolstered with the knowledge that despite the difficulties we may face, we can find ourselves resilient and hopeful, and with hearts full of joy and gratitude.

ABOUT THE AUTHOR

In the Light of the Sun is Angela M. Shupe's debut novel. Her writing has been awarded, and her shorter work has appeared in various literary magazines, including *The Examined Life: A Journal of the University of Iowa Carver College of Medicine; Westview: A Journal of Western Oklahoma;* and *The Bitter Oleander.* Previously, she worked as an editor and as a communications coordinator for a public school district. She holds a bachelor of arts from the University of Detroit in English with a minor in political science. A member of the Historical Novel Society and the Women's Fiction Writers Association, Ms. Shupe lives in Michigan with her husband and daughter.

ABOUT THE TYPE

This book was set in Caledonia, a typeface designed in 1939 by W. A. Dwiggins (1880–1956) for the Merganthaler Linotype Company. Its name is the ancient Roman term for Scotland, because the face was intended to have a Scottish-Roman flavor. Caledonia is considered to be a well-proportioned, businesslike face with little contrast between its thick and thin lines.